The Song of

PANNE

Being Mainly About Elephants

JONATHAN DOWNES

Typeset by Jonathan Downes,
Edited by Jessica Taylor
Cover and Layout by SPiderKaT for CFZ Communications
Using Microsoft Word 2000, Microsoft Publisher 2000, Adobe Photoshop CS.

First published in Great Britain by CFZ Press

Fortean Fiction
CFZ Press
Myrtle Cottage
Woolsery
Bideford
North Devon
EX39 5QR

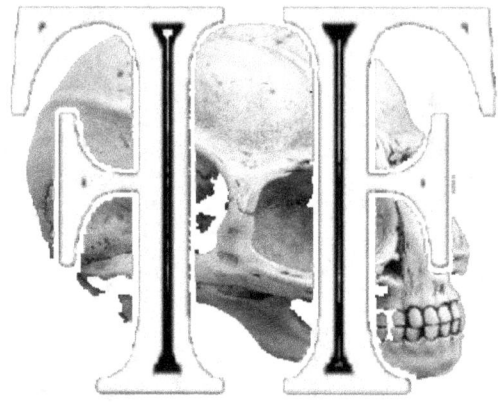

© CFZ MMXV

ISBN: 978-1-909488-36-6

To Harriet, but for whom the story would never have started,
and to Harry, but for whom it would never have continued...

with love

The globe was covered with a crisscross of energy pathways traversing the aether like a huge electronic string vest; something that one would not even have considered only a few short years ago. Those of us who have been involved in more esoteric pursuits had always suspected that when such a thing happened the knock on effects would be spectacular, but I, for one, had put those suspicions to the back of my mind, where other suspicions and certainties lay decomposing. Like any other rational human being with half a brain I knew that we were not just heading for an ecological disaster, and a Malthusian crisis, but that such things were upon us, and that - unless something terrible were to happen - the world that my Granddaughter will inherit will be nigh on unliveable in. But like everyone else, I have done my best to ignore the inconvenient reality and instead hope that something will just magickally come along.

And then it did.

But like everyone else I didn't recognise it, and - at least at first - I had no idea what was happening. And by the time I did know it was too late.

By these three was the third part of men killed, by the fire,
and by the smoke, and by the brimstone, which issued out of their mouths.

Revelation 9:18 - King James Bible
"Authorized Version", Cambridge Edition

AUTHOR'S NOTE:

Why all the footnotes? [1]

Whatever I do, but especially when locked into a quasi-Fortean morass of high strangeness, I am overwhelmed by information; some of it relevant, some of it vital, and some of it totally pointless. I just thought that you, gentle reader, should understand what it feels like to drown in information.

You must make up your own mind which bits are relevant, which bits are interesting, and which bits are neither.

---

1. Notes are most often used as an alternative to long explanatory notes that can be distracting to readers. Most literary style guidelines (including the Modern Language Association and the American Psychological Association) recommend limited use of foot and endnotes. However, publishers often encourage note references in lieu of parenthetical references. Aside from use as a bibliographic element, notes are used for additional information or explanatory notes that might be too digressive for the main text.

In particular, footnotes are the normal form of citation in historical journals. This is due, firstly, to the fact that the most important references are often to archive sources or interviews which do not readily fit standard formats, and secondly, to the fact that historians expect to see the exact nature of the evidence which is being used at each stage. The MLA (Modern Language Association) requires the superscript numbers in the main text to be placed following the punctuation in the phrase or clause the note is in reference to. The exception to this rule occurs when a sentence contains a dash, in which case the superscript would precede it

---

XTUL

Communique #1

1st May 2014

Who do you think we are?

Xtul is a little village on the Yucatan coast of Mexico. In 1966
thirty members of the Process Church of the Final Judgement settled
there for a while, and during a hurricane wrote their most profound
piece of neotheologising. Four years later, on the other side of the
world I fell in love with a book by an eccentric English aristocrat,
who based the 13 year old heroine on his eldest daughter, who ended
up in Yucatan with The Process when the book and I were both seven
years old. Forty years after I first read the book my dog bit Febru
ary Callender, and a whole sequence of events was put into progress.

Xtul is a process. Well, it would be wouldn't it? Many Gods, no
masters, to subvert a saying or two.

Xtul is a performance piece with no fixed performers, a nucleus of
vaguely evolved higher primates who influence each other's dynamic
and take the performance to places no one has dreamed.

Xtul is a cripple with the head of an elephant

Xtul is a place deep in the woods where the truth can sometimes dare
to go naked. But truth is, as Pontius Pilate knew, a highly subjective
concept. 30 4 13 7 40. The omniverse is ruled by numbers, but who
rules the numbers

Xtul is what happens when chaos rules her own brand of evolution.

Xtul is a schoolgirl dressed as a usually priapic, but unusually
gender neutral Hellenic deity, and a madman with a mission.

Xtul is a story spread across many platforms and taking many forms;
a story with rules, a beginning and an end, although no one involves
actually knows what any of them are.

Xtul is a woodland ritual writing itself, and is as unpredictable as
are all arcane steps into Holy Magick. The Green Woods Laugh? I
wouldn't go that far.

From the desk of the Minister for Information

I

It says a lot, I think, about the calibre of the young people who spend some of their leisure hours working with the animals at the CFZ, that when confronted by something unquestionably strange they don't bat an eyelid. The other afternoon [1] I was unwell (something which happens with depressing frequency these days) and I had retired to bed. One of our volunteers, a twelve year old girl, was sitting in my study trying to count the relative numbers of Endler's livebearers [2] and knife livebearers [3] in the tank on my desk, when a cacophony of canine contumely heralded the arrival of a visitor to my door.

She remarked to me afterwards that it was strange that she didn't hear the gate open, and that Mark Raines, who was working in the garden didn't notice these visitors arrive. They were two tall thin bearded men wearing long, black, hooded robes. They didn't introduce themselves, just demanded to see me. When told that I was asleep, ill in bed, they gave her an envelope containing a key drive, and without speaking, walked along the path to the gate, and left.

1, The first dozen or so of these entries were written as they happened, so this was written just after Bealtaine 2014. It is only later in this narrative when things started happening thick and fast, and I started to lag behind in chronicling them, mainly because I needed to give my own mind time to make sense of what had happened. The final entries, therefore, were written at the end of July 2015, even though they describe events that took place at the beginning of the previous winter.

2. *Poecilia wingei* is a very colorful guppy species, similar to the fancy guppy often found in pet shops. The species was first collected from Laguna de Patos in Venezuela by Franklyn F. Bond in 1937, and rediscovered by Dr. John Endler in 1975. The latter were the first examples of this fish to make it to the aquarium trade. More have been collected since then, notably by Armando Pou, to expand the captive breeding stock. The original Laguna de Patos population is threatened by runoff from a municipal garbage dump. Though it is rare in pet shops, this species is seen occasionally in the aquaria of enthusiasts. Although not yet taken up into the IUCN Red List of endangered species, they are in danger of extinction in the wild, as humans enter their natural habitat, polluting and destroying it. To me one of the most interesting things about this species is that it was not actually given a scientific name or description until 2005, nearly seventy years after it was first found.

3. *Alfaro cultratus* is an uncommon little fish from Costa Rica, Nicaragua and Panama. I think they look like miniature porbeagle sharks and am very fond of them.

When I woke up later, my volunteer had gone back to her family for tea, and I only heard the story second hand. I opened the envelope, put the key drive into the computer (which, with the benefit of hindsight was a remarkably stupid thing to do, because it could have contained any number of unimaginably horrid computer viruses) and was totally aghast at what I found.

It was a letter and a number of sound and video files. The letter was from someone called Mister Loxodonta, who identified himself as a member of a collective called *Xtul*. This grabbed my interest from the start as the name had resonances throughout my own personal mythology. [1]

It started off conventionally enough, but then it turned out that Mister Loxodonta was (or at least claimed to be) a terminally ill half naked man with the head of an elephant who sometimes wrote in conventional prose, but had the off-putting habit of launching into regular metred rhyming couplets, of the sort that my late Mother called "tum te tum te tumty tum" and the even later Rudyard Kipling was wont to indulge in.

> *My name is Mr Loxodonta*
> *And when your mind begins to wander*
> *Into places that you know*
> *You really shouldn't let it go*
> *In the gaps between your dreams*
> *Where you hear the idiots scream*
> *That's basically where I can be found*
> *Playing games with light and sound*

> *My name is Mr Loxodonta*
> *I'll find you when you don't want to*
> *Explore realms of world as myth*
> *And pantheistic multiperson*
> *Solipsism 101,* [2]
> *The games of chance have just begun*

---

1. Xtul, for example, is a small village in the state of Yucatan, Mexico. It is on the north Gulf of Mexico coast, located 24 km west of the city of Progreso inside of the Progreso municipality, about halfway along the road between Sisal and Progreso. It is noted as the location where some 30 members of The Process Church of The Final Judgment went in 1966. They set up camp in an abandoned salt factory. While there they were hit by Hurricane Inez. The resulting storm lasted for 3 days. It was during this time that the basic theology of The Process Church was formed, and later written as "The Xtul Dialogues". The Process were complete nutjobs in my humble opinion, but I'd had dealings with one of the girls from Xtul some years before, and for a number of reasons she loomed high in my personal iconography.

2. "Pantheistic solipsism is a technical term (properly "Pantheistic multiple-ego solipsism") that has been advanced for the World as Myth idea proposed by science fiction writer Robert A. Heinlein in several of his books and stories, although the concept has little in common with either pantheism (the universe is God) or solipsism (nothing exists but my mind)... The World as Myth involves the idea that a powerful author, such as Edgar Rice Burroughs, Isaac Asimov, or Heinlein himself, creates a parallel universe simply by writing about it. It incorporates the portrayal of all myths and fictional universes existing as parallel universes to our own and that persons and beings from these various "worlds" interact with one another."

I'm dying but it doesn't matter
My alter-ego just gets fatter

Apparently there are five or six of them, but only three are named:

*   Mister Loxodonta
*   Mistress Discordia
*   Panne

From the badly scrawled drawings, and fantastickal photoshop constructs that I have been sent, Discordia is a statuesque blonde lady with a skull for a head, and Panne is a schoolgirl dressed as a goatman, or perhaps a goatman who has taken on some of the characteristics of a schoolgirl.

Then, later that evening, I got an email. It was from an old acquaintance (I won't say 'friend' because although we have known each other for a third of a century so far, I don't think either of us has ever liked the other very much. His name is Danny Miles/Danny Myles/Danny Myers (choose whichever name suits you and him best at the time). I first met him in 1981, and the circumstances of our meeting are chronicled in my 1999 book *The Blackdown Mystery.*

> I first met Danny Miles at an obscure North Devon rock festival during the late summer of 1981. In those days I was an innocent and not very streetwise fellow in my early twenties, and I still believed that world peace could be achieved by the ingestion of various noxious substances whilst sitting in muddy fields listening to musical ensembles make whooshing noises on (what seem to me now) to be very primitive synthesisers.
>
> I was, I believe, watching Hawkwind playing a spectacularly inept version of Master of the Universe, and like most of the rest of the audience, who were cold, muddy and uncomfortable, pretending that I was enjoying myself whilst in reality I was in dire need of both a lavatory and a nice cup of tea and totally unwilling to avail myself of the horribly rudimentary versions of either facility that had been laid on for our "comfort" by the euphemistically named "organisers" of the event. About a hundred yards to my right were the serried ranks of the local Hells Angel fraternity who were encamped en masse like an iron clad phalanx of doom.
>
> It was only twelve years after Altamont, and even in the bucolic wastelands of rural Devon, they felt that they had something to live up to. Unfortunately, for me at least, they had decided to set up camp immediately between the area where I had set up my tiny tent and parked my car and the main exit, and several of the nastiest and meanest looking of them were patrolling the area armed with pool

cues and what I think were hollowed out pickaxe handles that had been filled with molten lead. I was therefore somewhat marooned, and feeling uncomfortable, isolated, alone and more than a little frightened.

Suddenly, in the middle of what appeared to me to be a sea of greasy black leather jackets, emerged a delicate, fey looking figure, wearing an extraordinary array of satins and silks in a variety of peacock colours. It looked for all the world as if one of the gaily coloured inhabitants of one of Arthur Rackham's fairy paintings[1] had suddenly been transported into the middle of a field of leather-clad Neanderthals. The figure tripped gaily towards me, and appeared to my addled brain to be floating like a surreal, and rainbow-hued butterfly above the sea of mud and motorbikes. As it got closer I could see that it was a youth, hardly old enough to shave with an angelic halo of light brown hair surrounding a face that was covered with intricate paintings of butterflies and lotus flowers. He came and sat next to me and my companions.

Much to my amazement everyone else who was with me seemed to take this apparition in their stride. "'Lo Danny", one of them grunted cheerfully, "'ow are y'doing?". Another friend asked him what the hell he had been doing wandering blithely through the middle of the taciturn, unfriendly and potentially dangerous crowd of bikers. "Ahhhhh they're harmless." he said, in an Irish accent that he seemed to be able to turn on and off at will, "and anyway they wouldn't hurt me...I am legion, I am many".

His name was Danny Miles, and for reasons known best to himself he had recently adopted the nom-de-guerre of 'Legion the Cosmic Dancer'. I got to know him reasonably well over the next few years, and he would occasionally drift into my life, causing chaos for a few weeks and then disappear as simply as he had arrived. During the years when fashions were led by Culture Club and the New Romantics, Danny was in his element. He paraded his omnisexuality for all to see like some magnificent, (if slightly deranged) bird of paradise and flirted outrageously with boys and girls alike. As the decade of Thatcherism

---

1. Arthur Rackham (19 September 1867 – 6 September 1939) was an English book illustrator. His first book illustrations were published in 1893 in To the Other Side by Thomas Rhodes, but his first serious commission was in 1894 for The Dolly Dialogues, the collected sketches of Anthony Hope, who later went on to write The Prisoner of Zenda. Book illustrating then became Rackham's career for the rest of his life. By the turn of the century Rackham was regularly contributing illustrations to children's periodicals such as Little Folks and Cassell's Magazine. In 1903, he married Edyth Starkie, with whom he had one daughter, Barbara, in 1908. Although acknowledged as an accomplished book illustrator for some years, it was the publication of Washington Irving's Rip Van Winkle by Heinemann in 1905 that particularly brought him into public attention, his reputation being confirmed the following year with J.M.Barrie's Peter Pan in Kensington Gardens, published by Hodder & Stoughton.

advanced and my life became more normal, and I drifted into my disastrous marriage and the twin pitfalls of a job and a mortgage I saw less of him, but he would still turn up once in a while, and we would sit up long into the night drinking wine, gazing at the stars and talking about nothing in particular as I dreamed dreams of my lost youth. Danny never seemed to either grow any older or to settle down.

My first wife disliked him intensely, and I don't think my second wife has ever met him. He has turned up in my life on various occasions over the past thirty years, but I have only heard from him occasionally (and not seen him) since the turning of the millennium when he turned up at my house unexpectedly talking nonsense about succubi and clutching a gift basket of blueberry muffins for me; a gift which he then proceeded to eat entirely himself.

But, like a bad penny, he has turned up again. According to his peculiar email, which he dubbed "A Communiqué from the *Xtul* Underground", he (dubbing himself *Xtul*'s 'Minister for Information'[1] was letting me in upon "The Summer of the Great Secret"[2] and had decided that it was my "Holy Mission" to help propagate the "Message of the Neo-Godz[3] in the Vineyards of Madness", which seems to mean helping him with a Facebook page for (what

1. This is where it all gets a little bit difficult to unravel. Danny had obviously taken bits and bobs from all sorts of late sixties/early seventies countercultural sources. John Sinclair, for example was the 'Minister for Information' for the White Panther Party. The White Panthers were a far-left, anti-racist, white American political collective founded in 1968 by Pun Plamondon, Leni Sinclair, and John Sinclair. It was started in response to an interview where Huey P. Newton, co-founder of the Black Panther Party, was asked what white people could do to support the Black Panthers. Newton replied that they could form a White Panther Party. The counterculture era group took the name and dedicated its energies to "cultural revolution." Sinclair made every effort to ensure that the White Panthers were not mistaken for a white supremacist group, responding to such claims with "quite the contrary." The party worked with many ethnic minority rights groups in the Rainbow Coalition.

The concept of brief, terse 'communiques was probably taken from the Angry Brigade, a British anarchist group responsible for a series of bomb attacks in Britain between 1970 and 1972. The Angry Brigade decided to launch a bombing campaign with small bombs - in order to maximise media exposure to their demands while keeping collateral damage to a minimum. The campaign started in August 1970 and continued for a year until arrests took place the following summer. Targets included banks, embassies, the Miss World event in 1970 (or rather a BBC Outside Broadcast vehicle earmarked for use in the BBC's coverage) and the homes of Conservative MPs. In total, police attributed 25 bombings to the Angry Brigade. The bombings mostly caused property damage; one person was slightly injured. The British White Panthers were run by a mate of mine, but more of that later.

2. A children's novel by Monica Edwards first published in 1948 and set in the village of Rye Harbour which was renamed Westling. The Romney Marsh towns of Rye and Winchelsea were also renamed Dunsford and Winklesea respectively. The stories feature many real-life characters (with changed names) which the author remembered from her childhood there, such as the ferryman Jim Decks and the villainous Hookey Galley

3. The Godz were a New York City based avant-noise psychedelic band that originally existed from 1966 to 1973. The Godz musicians were guitarist Jim McCarthy, bassist Larry Kessler, autoharpist Jay Dillon, and drummer Paul Thornton. They started the band after Larry Kessler met Jim McCarthy and Paul Thornton when they all took jobs in the 49th Street location of the musical instruments store Sam Goody's. According to McCarthy they came up with their musical approach on this situation: "One day Paul came over to visit them, and the three gathered in Larry's living room to smoke a joint." What happened next was purely accidental, according to Jim: "There were all these percussive instruments lying around and out of total frustration, I got up and started shaking a tambourine or something like that, and that's how it all started. We all started to get up and make noise like a bunch of maniacs, expressing our frustration." For the record I always thought that they were bloody awful.

appears to be) a rather interesting little band operating in much the same territory as the late lamented KLF.

I have cautiously agreed for a number of reasons.

- ·Firstly, I like the music
- I like the challenge – this reminds me of one of the peculiar magickal art games like THE CASE that I played with Doc Shiels [1]
- Danny knows where the bodies are buried (in my case at least) and it would be unwise for me to cross him
- My life has been getting a little dull recently, and if there is one thing I have learned over the years, it is that life with Danny is never dull

So onwards and upwards. Let us see what this summer will bring.

1, Anthony Shiels was born in Salford, UK in 1938. After attending the Heatherley School of Fine Art in London, he moved to St Ives, Cornwall where in 1961, following the resignation of Barbara Hepworth, he was made a member of the committee of the influential Penwith Society of Arts. In St Ives he ran the progressive 'Steps Gallery', where he showed artists like Brian Wall and Bob Law. He had several solo exhibitions in London before then leaving St Ives following a drunken incident, in which he threatened police with genuine guns that he had obtained from painter-friend Terry Frost.

In the late 1960s after moving to live in Ponsanooth near Falmouth, he rediscovered stage magic - something he had been taught as a boy by his father and grandfather - and wrote articles for The Linking Ring and The Budget magazines. This included interviews with Ray Harryhausen and Ray Bradbury. He also published a trio of magic books: which were sold in both the UK and the US and led to him being associated with 1970s bizarre magic. Between 1970 and 1974 he performed as 'Doc Shiels: Wizard of the West' at festivals and fayres in Cornwall, UK. This, presented with the help of friend Vernon Rose and the rest of the Shiels family, was a magic show that incorporated illusions such as the headless woman, the sub-trunk and the buzz-saw.

In 1975 he set up 'Tom Fool's Theatre of Tom Foolery', which started as a troupe of 'mummers', before worked closely with the famous Footsbarn theatre. In 1976 he was involved with a series of 'monster-raising' exploits, which brought him extensive media coverage, particularly when he started 'invoking' the monsters with the help of a coven of nude witches. His attempts to 'raise' Morgawr the Cornish sea monster, were covered by BBC TV, *Fortean Times*, local newspapers, and appeared in national newspapers such as *Reveille* and the *News of the World*. At around the same time he reported on sightings of the now legendary 'Owlman' of Mawnan. In 1977 he obtained photos of the Loch Ness Monster which appeared on the front page of *The Daily Mirror* newspaper.

This and his associated 'Monstermind Experiment' featured in numerous other media outlets including *The Daily Telegraph* and Radio One's Newsbeat. Alongside the monster-raising, Shiels continued to perform both as Doc Shiels and as a member of Tom Fools Theatre, and he wrote several plays including 'Spooks', 'The Gallavant Variations', 'Nightjars', 'Cloth Owl the Winking Curtain' and 'Dr Beak Hides his Hands'. One of his plays, 'Distant Humps', was co-produced by Ken Campbell and co-starred Christopher Fairbank. The events of the 1970s and 1980s were covered in his own book, *Monstrum*, and in my 1997 book the *Owlman and Others*.

He is also a dear friend of mine, and I love him very much indeed.

II

I HAVE KNOWN Danny Miles for nearly all my adult life, and whilst I don't like him very much (and never have, if I must tell the truth) it does seem that our destinies are somehow peculiarly linked. In many ways we are very similar; he is the part of my psyche which is unbelievably promiscuous, completely feckless and commodifies people to an insane extent. I am the part of his psyche who worries about things, drinks too much brandy, actually achieves things apart from mischief making, and has a conscience (although doesn't always pay it much attention). About the only thing that we have in common is that we both want to change the world, albeit in completely different ways and for completely different reasons.

I am never particularly surprised when he turns up in my life, and so when he re-appeared a few weeks ago in the guise of the 'Minister of Information' for a group called *Xtul* I took it in my stride., It so happened that this time I knew a bit about – if not what he was talking about – what he was pretending to talk about. I also knew from whence he had lifted his influences.

Danny has always been a magpie, stealing ideologies from all and sundry. When I first met him back in the early 1980s, he had taken bits of the philosophy of Timothy Leary [1], mixed it with large chunks of Charlie Manson [2], and a pinch of Crowley [3] and dressed it up in the then current peacock fashion styles of the New Romantics [4], and fused it all together to start a peculiar psychedelic sex cult. I was sucked in hook, line and sinker for a few months and even

1. Timothy Francis Leary (October 22, 1920 – May 31, 1996) was an American psychologist and writer known for advocating psychedelic drugs. Leary conducted experiments under the Harvard Psilocybin Project during American legality of LSD and psilocybin, resulting in the Concord Prison Experiment and the Marsh Chapel Experiment. Leary and his associate Richard Alpert were fired by Harvard University amid controversy surrounding such drugs (although some have claimed that the experiments produced useful data).

2. Charles Milles Manson (born Charles Milles Maddox, November 12, 1934) is an American criminal who led what became known as the Manson Family, a quasi-commune that arose in the California desert in the late 1960s. In 1971 he was found guilty of conspiracy to commit the murders of seven people: actress Sharon Tate and four other people at Tate's home; and the next day, a married couple, Leno and Rosemary LaBianca; all carried out by members of the group at his instruction. He was convicted of the murders through the joint-responsibility rule, which makes each member of a conspiracy guilty of crimes his fellow conspirators commit in furtherance of the conspiracy's objective. His followers also murdered several other people at other times and locations, and Manson was also convicted for two of these other murders (of Gary Hinman and Donald "Shorty" Shea). He reappears at various times during this story.

3. Aleister Crowley (born Edward Alexander Crowley; 12 October 1875 – 1 December 1947) was an English occult-ist, ceremonial magician, poet, painter, novelist, and mountaineer. He founded the religion and philosophy of Thelema, identifying himself as the prophet entrusted with guiding humanity into the Æon of Horus in the early 20th century. All these biographical notes are, by the way, taken from Wikipedia and then slightly adapted by myself. There is reasoning behind this which may eventually become apparent.

4. New Romanticism (also called Blitz kids and a variety of other names) was a pop culture movement in the United Kingdom that began as a nightclub scene around 1979 and peaked around 1981. Developing in London and Birmingham, at nightclubs such as Billy's and the Blitz, and fashion boutiques such as PX in London and Kahn and Bell in Birmingham, it spread to other major cities in the UK and was characterised by flamboyant, eccentric fashion.

now my sleep (usually fairly calm due to the enormous amounts of chemicals my Doctor prescribes me) is sometimes shattered by lightning flashes of memory as I relive nights in the middle of a thunderstorm, dancing naked together with a group of other like-minded idiots - under the full moon, off my tits on psilocybin [1]. Something that I really wouldn't recommend to anybody reading this. [2]

But now he was back, and once again stealing ideologies from anyone he cared to. All the bits about Minister for Information where from John Sinclair's White Panther Party in the 1960s who, in turn, had stolen them from Bobby Seale's Black Panther Party. The idea of sending cryptic communiqués out anonymously was stolen piecemeal from The Angry Brigade, a relatively obscure British terrorist group of the early 1970s, and even the name *Xtul* had a long and somewhat sinister provenance. It so happened that, totally by chance, I knew quite a bit about all three of these subjects. And I also knew that Danny did.. because most of his information had come from me in the first place. So after my first contact with him on the matter of *Xtul* a few weeks ago, and a couple of impressive looking Communiques which turned up in my email inbox but which, when one looked hard enough were purely sound and fury which signified nothing at all, I wasn't particularly surprised when he turned up at my front door.

Like the protagonist of *The Monster Mash* I was working in my lab late one night. Well, actually, I was. In 1800 there was a fire that burned down two very old cottages on the outskirts of Woolsery. Five years later a single, large cottage was built on the ruins, utilising bits of the ruins which were intact and at least 300 years old. In the 1950s a bit was built on the side, and in the 1970s another extension. My family have lived here since 1971, and I still do today. On the end of the house is an ancient lean-to that originally housed potatoes. It is my office, study, recording studio, editing suite, and yes…laboratory. And I was working in the potato shed late one night when my eyes did behold a terrible sight. It was Danny Miles dressed in a peculiar paramilitary uniform flanked by two tall figures wearing dark, hooded robes.

Here we go again, I thought.

He opened the door and the three of them walked in without knocking. I often sleep very badly, and so it was about 3:00am and Mother had gone to bed about three hours before. An hour or so later, Corinna (my lovely, and long suffering wife) went to bed, followed by the small gaggle of carnivores who always accompany her (two cats, a terrier and what seems at first to be a small pygmy hippo which upon closer investigation is a bulldog x boxer bitch called Prudence).

---

1. Psilocybin is a naturally occurring psychedelic compound produced by more than 200 species of mushrooms, collectively known as magic mushrooms. The most potent are members of the genus Psilocybe, such as *P. azurescens*, *P. semilanceata*, and *P. cyanescens*, but psilocybin has also been isolated from about a dozen other genera. As a prodrug, psilocybin is quickly converted by the body to psilocin, which has mind-altering effects similar, in some aspects, to those of LSD, mescaline, and DMT. In general, the effects include euphoria, visual and mental hallucinations, changes in perception, a distorted sense of time, and spiritual experiences, and can include possible adverse reactions such as nausea and panic attacks. I have not taken it since Boxing Day 1981, and would not actually recommend it to anyone reading this.

2. See the appendix

3. A 1962 novelty song and the best-known song by Bobby "Boris" Pickett. The song was released as a single on Gary S. Paxton's Garpax Records label in August 1962 along with a full-length LP called *The Original Monster Mash*.

There were various fish, and amphibians, doing their own inimitable thing in their tanks which are scattered about the building, there were Corinna's pet rats, and of course there were the various ghosts with which the house is infested, but I was the only primate still awake.

They came in to my study uninvited; the two robed figures stood implacably by the door, and – as far as I am able to remember – said nothing at all during the whole time they were with me, and Danny (unsurprisingly for anyone who has ever met him) started to talk – nineteen to the dozen – as soon as he entered.

Once again he was talking about a band called *Xtul*. He had played me a few songs by them before, and sent me a few more via Dropbox, and I thought that they were truly excellent. Danny really didn't have to blackmail me into writing about them. But approaching things in a conventional style, like asking a music journalist to write about a new band just isn't his style. He had something on me (he was privy to information about me that he thought nobody knew, although that wasn't actually the case) and was determined to use it as leverage to use me for his own nefarious ends.

I couldn't be bothered to argue the toss with him, (it was pointless to explain that her husband never did find out, and that she went on to marry someone else well over fifteen years ago) and so I sat him down and did my best to find out some more information about this peculiar band *Xtul*. It so happened that I knew a bit about a certain quasi-Satanist occult group who apparently took legal action against Ed Sanders [1], author of the Charlie Manson biog *The Family* saying that their inclusion in the book has brought the Satanist occult group into disrepute. They had lived in a Mexican coastal village called Xtul for a while, and I wondered whether there was any connection between this and this mysterious musical ensemble? Or whether, as was perfectly possible, Danny had just nicked the title from somewhere because it sounded good.

He told me a little bit more about them. Apparently there were three of them – Mr Loxodonta, Mistress Discordia, and Panne - and none of them were human anymore. When he started talking up a farrago of occult nonsense about how each of them had been turned into Gods and/or Daemons by events of an incalculable cosmic majesty my brain started to go to sleep. I remembered only too well how a harmless practical joke played by two Wildlife Officers upon a spectacularly inept UFO Research Group, once sucked into the vortex which is Danny Miles and spat out again, became a sinister conspiracy theory that nearly got my arrested by Special Branch, and involved an escaped murderer, several occult rituals, and the consumption of large quantities of alcohol and drugs.

If you don't believe me, check out a little thing I wrote fifteen years ago called *The Blackdown Mystery*. It is mildly amusing, and whilst I made some of it up (mostly to take the piss out of Nick Redfern [1]) it does provide a valuable object lesson in how not to take Danny Miles too seriously.

---

1. Edward Sanders (born August 17, 1939) is an American poet, singer, social activist, environmentalist, author, publisher and longtime member of the band The Fugs. He has been called a bridge between the Beat and Hippie generations. Sanders is considered to have been active and "present at the counterculture's creation."

I have taken what he said *cum grano salis* ever since. Three Gods, with a coterie of hooded followers who happen to play guitars, piano and bass? Three malevolent Gods with no reason to perceive humanity with anything but contempt and anger? Three Gods (one male, one female, and one gender neutral) who happen to form a progressive hip hop band? I didn't believe a word of it!

III

This is the busiest time of my year. In mid August each year I promote the CFZ Weird Weekend, and a motley mix of scientists, academics and oddball researchers descend upon North Devon. I have had quite a lot of problems with this year's event due to some intransigence and internal politics on the behalf of the local community centre where we have held the event for the past eight years. On top of that, I have been having some serious problems with some of my associates who have been running me ragged and robbing me blind, and so as a result of the stress and my ridiculous work levels, I have been keeping very strange hours. Often I am awake all night and only get too bed for fitful sleep at round about dawn, and so it was on the night that I had my latest strange visitors.

Corinna and Mother had gone to bed, and I was sitting in my study working on an article about yellow legged tortoiseshells. It is possibly symbolic of the strange times in which we are living that at the time that I write this we are undergoing an interesting invasion from Eastern Europe.

In 1953 a single specimen of an eastern European butterfly called the Scarce or Yellow Legged Tortoiseshell (*Nymphalis xanthomelas*) was caught in Kent. Another specimen was found dead in the Shetlands in November last year. But now, following a huge invasion of western Europe, they have turned up in some numbers in eastern England. There is now speculation that they might breed here. [2]

I said to Corinna that as my stepdaughter Olivia lives in Norfolk she should give the forthcoming baby the middle name of Xanthomelas in honour of this extraordinary invasion, and she just looked at me with barely disguised disdain.

1. Nicholas "Nick" Redfern, born 1964 in Pelsall, Walsall, Staffordshire, is a British best-selling author, Ufologist and Cryptozoologist now living in Dallas, Texas, United States. Redfern is an active advocate of official government disclosure of UFO information, and has worked to uncover thousands of pages of previously classified Royal Air Force, Air Ministry and Ministry of Defence files on unidentified flying objects (UFOs) dating from the Second World War from the Public Record Office. His 2005 book, Body Snatchers in the Desert: The Horrible Truth at the Heart of the Roswell Story, purports to show that the Roswell crash may have been military aircraft tests using Japanese POWs, suffering from progeria or radiation effects. He is also an old and dear friend of mine, and we have written a series of non fiction books and novels in which we libel each other outrageously.

2. It appears that they did, because they have been seen in small numbers in the Spring of 2015.

I am a fairly heavy drinker, and I was sitting typing with Archie the Jack Russell asleep on my lap, and a bottle of cheap bourbon by my side. I was also listening to the first solo album by Damon Albarn, which is my favourite record of the year so far and I was fairly deeply engrossed in what I was doing, so I didn't hear the door open. I just looked up and there was Danny Miles grinning at me knowingly. He was accompanied by a slight figure in a long black hooded robe, with the hood pulled down so I couldn't see its face.

"'Lo Jon" he said. I grunted in reply. I was not in the mood for dealing with any more of his bullshit. I was enjoying the music and the whisky and was engrossed in my task, and didn't want to hear any more of his nonsense about demi-Gods performing hiphop. "What do you want?" I grunted rudely.

"There's someone I want you to meet", he said. "Say hello to Panne", and the robed figure spoke to me shyly in the voice of a young teenage girl, "Hello Jon".

I was still unimpressed. "Look man" I said to him, rudely ignoring his companion. "I don't wanna be rude to either of you, but I am not in the mood for this. I have got lots of work to do, and I don't want to be distracted... by anyone".

Danny looked at me smugly. "I know that you found the story that I told you hard to believe, so I thought that I should try and convince you". He gestured to his companion. "Take your robe off Panne".

She did as he asked, and with horror I saw that she was wearing nothing underneath it.

I am nearly 40 years too old to be having naked teenage girls in my rooms, and I reacted with horror! I have told you before how I have never liked or trusted Danny Miles, and how he was already attempting to blackmail me into helping him with his insane schemes. Back in the late 1990s, after my divorce from Alison, I was having an affair with a married woman who was not only notorious in her own right, but was then married to a well known and very influential businessman in the computer games industry. Danny had already intimated that he would make this affair public, if I did not help him with his project. What he didn't know was that not only did Corinna - my second wife - know all about it, but that the lady in question was now divorced from her influential husband and married to someone else. We still send each other Christmas greetings on Facebook and occasionally swap Leonard Cohen bootlegs, but that is the extent of our relationship these days.

They say that when you are close to death your entire life passes before your eyes in slow motion, and as Corinna and I nearly died in a car crash on the M25 about seven years ago, I can confirm that this is actually true. As I stared at the naked figure before me, exactly the same thing happened. I immediately jumped to the conclusion that Danny had decided to take advantage of the current socio-political situation following the revelations about the late Jimmy Savile [1] and the conviction a few weeks back of Rolf Harris [2]; he had brought a naked girl into my study in order to attempt to blackmail me further. It is exactly the sort of thing that the bastard would have done. Then I realised something: the person before me was indeed unclothed, and had the slight figure of a thirteen or fourteen year old girl. But she was covered in silky brown fur, she had two cloven hooves where she should have had feet, and two – rather cute, I have to admit – tiny horns peeking out from the curly hair on her forehead. Then my inner zoologist kicked in, and I noted – clinically – that she (I still thought of her as female) had no external secondary sexual characteristics, and that the shape of her face, shoulders and forearms were such that whatever she was….she was certainly not human.

"Fuck!" I said, and took a deep swig from my whisky and coke.

IV

O h how times have changed. I am not talking about the Scottish independence vote [3], or the events in the Middle East, but - for once - for me personally. As regular readers of my blog will know I have done something unpleasant to my neck and because this unpleasant something is exceedingly painful, I am now on a complex cocktail of muscle relaxants and narcotic pain-killers, which is pretty much the cocktail of chemicals that I used to use for recreational purposes about a quarter of a century ago. The results are fairly similar (except that I am not dancing around the office to the *On U Sound* system [4]) and I am what I used to describe as "out of my gourd".

1. Sir James Wilson Vincent "Jimmy" Savile, OBE, KCSG (31 October 1926 – 29 October 2011) was an English DJ, television and radio personality, dance hall manager, and charity fundraiser. He hosted the BBC television show Jim'll Fix It, was the first and last presenter of the long-running BBC music chart show Top of the Pops, and raised an estimated £40 million for charities. At the time of his death he was widely praised for his personal qualities and as a fundraiser. After his death, hundreds of allegations of sexual abuse were made against him, leading the police to believe that Savile was a predatory sex offender, and that he may have been one of Britain's most prolific sexual offenders. There had been allegations during his lifetime, but they were dismissed and accusers ignored or disbelieved.

2. Rolf Harris (born 30 March 1930) is an Australian entertainer whose career encompassed work as a musician, singer-songwriter, composer, comedian, actor, painter and television personality. Harris's career as a popular entertainer was ended by his conviction and imprisonment for sexual offences in the summer of 2014.

3. A national referendum was held in Scotland on 18 September 2014. Voters were asked to answer either "Yes" or "No" to the question: "Should Scotland be an independent country?" During the week prior to the election, there were heated debates about the consequences of a "yes" vote for Scotland's economy, military, finances, currency, government pensions, its share of UK debt, question of passports/citizenship, whether the Queen would be retained as Head of State, and its relations with NATO, The Commonwealth of Nations, the United Nations, and the European Union. The "No" option won, achieving 55.3% of votes, compared to the "Yes" proportion of 44.7%, from a voter participation rate of 84.5%

4. Adrian Maxwell Sherwood (born 1958, London, England) is an English record producer specializing in the genres of dub music and EDM. Sherwood has created a distinctive production style based on the application of dub effects and dub mixing techniques to EDM tracks as well as mainstream songs. Sherwood has worked extensively with a variety of reggae artists as well as the musicians Keith LeBlanc, Doug Wimbish and Skip McDonald. Within his role as a record producer, he has worked with a variety of record labels, however his most well-known label is On-U Sound Records, which he founded in 1979.

The weird thing is that now, instead of finding it a pleasant sensation, I am feeling mildly nauseous, very drowsy and wondering why I ever paid good money to feel like this.

I wonder if I put *The Happy Mondays* [1] on, whether it will make the sensation any better. It always worked for me back in 1990. (I tried. Sadly, it didn't)

But as a result of this new chemical regimen, I am keeping peculiar hours, and last night, after everyone else was fast asleep in bed, I was downstairs with the smaller of my two dogs listening to music on my iPad, and reading *Brandy of the Damned* by John Higgs [2], which is an extraordinary book about which I shall be writing in some depth at another juncture. But my mind is as ephemeral as a newly hatched mayfly, and if I go off at a tangent and talk about Higgs' book, I will never finish telling you what I want to talk about. So I won't.

I was sitting with Archie the Jack Russell in my favourite armchair, lost to the world, when he began to whimper and cower in submission. I looked up, and Panne was standing there looking down at me.

*****

My father was a strange man. He suffered from the dichotomy of being a devout Christian of the old-fashioned Anglican variety, and also having leanings towards Paganism. His mother had been a witch and had introduced several of my cousins to the craft, and whilst my father knew this and occasionally alluded to it in his conversation whilst the old lady (and, believe me, she was very much a lady) was alive, I don't think he ever completely accepted it.

However, despite being a Churchwarden and a Lay Preacher, he could also divine water (as can I) and charm warts (which I can't) and I will always remember one day when I was about nine. We had left my beloved Hong Kong for six weeks, and were on a family holiday on Dartmoor. My little brother (now in his early 50s and a high ranking Army Chaplain, who – I suspect – doesn't really approve of the path that my life has taken) was unwell, and my mother and grandmother were back at the B&B looking after him. My father was saddled with the job of taking the 10 year old Jonathan for a long and brisk walk.

---

1. Happy Mondays are an English alternative rock band from Salford, Greater Manchester. Formed in 1980, the band's original line-up was Shaun Ryder on lead vocals, his brother Paul Ryder on bass, lead guitarist Mark Day, keyboardist Paul Davis, and drummer Gary Whelan. Mark "Bez" Berry later joined the band onstage during a live performance after befriending Shaun Ryder and served as a dancer/percussionist. Rowetta Satchell joined the band to provide backing vocals in the early 1990s.By the late 1980s, the Happy Mondays were an important part of the Manchester music scene and personified rave culture, and were THE band for aspiring hipsters to take drugs to.

2. A Gloriously Surrealchemical novel, the Amazon blurb of which reads@ "Russell, Penny and Will have not seen each other for twenty years. Why, then, do they spend a month driving around the coast of Britain in a van refusing to listen to music? Why do they find little blue bottles washing up on the shore containing pages from a future Bible? And why is Penny carrying such a huge spade? Funny, surprising and good-hearted, The Brandy of the Damned is a dream-like short novel which reveals different things each time it is read. It is the literary equivalent of stepping off the path and heading out into the woods, knowing that if you can't see what's ahead you will never be bored."

My father was a Dartmoor man born and bred, and he knew far more about the place than he ever let on. On this occasion we parked the little Mini Clubman that he had hired for the duration of the holiday in the carpark next to Hound Tor, where these days there is usually parked a mobile café with the greatest title of all time – 'Hound of the Basket Meals' and walked up the narrow incline towards the tor itself. For those of you who do not know such things, the tors of Dartmoor are great formations of granite – fossilised volcanic cores – that stick out of the top of moorland hills on Dartmoor and Bodmin Moor. I have always thought that they look like enormous stone cowpats, and they dominate the landscape making it look unearthly and more like something from the cover of a 1970s progressive rock album [1] than something that one expects to find in a National Park in southern England.

My father and I walked up the hill in silence. We had always had a difficult relationship, and for some reason I had the Biblical story of Abraham and Isaac in my head [2] as it began to drizzle and we trudged on. The tor itself was seething with holiday makers and so rather and climb to the top, we walked on past it, and down the hill on the other side in a vaguely easterly direction to find somewhere where we could have our lunch.

Eventually we found ourselves in a patch of ancient woodland that I have never been able to find since. Much of the woodland that you can see if you examine the area on Google Earth is relatively modern, coniferous forest, either planted by the Forestry Commission, or by private landowners, who – in the years following WW2 – had done their best to jump on the bandwagon and turn unproductive wilderness into the location for a lucrative timber industry which usually failed to materialise, but scattered amongst these dark green and regimented fir forests were small pockets of native deciduous woodland, not as gnarled and overtly witchy as places like Wistman's Wood, but still with their own ancient magickal vibe.

We sat down, resting against huge boulders and ate out sandwiches and crisps, and it was whilst masticating on our desert of individual Walls fruit pies (I always particularly liked the blackcurrant ones) when we heard a noise.

It was an eerie, low, pulsating sound unlike anything I had ever heard before. It was the wildest and most exciting noise that I had ever heard; it was recognisably music. But it didn't sound like any other music that I had ever heard before.

"W-w-what's that Daddy?" I asked, hesitantly, not sure that anyone but I could hear it. Even at such a young age I was aware that I could sometimes here things and see things that no-one else could, and I was always afraid to admit such a fact (although if I had done, my psychosis would probably have been treated decades before it actually was).

But I needn't have worried. Just one look at my father showed that he was as enraptured as I, but it seemed to be more familiar to him. Unlike me, he didn't seem scared.

---

1.   Yes Tor, just down the road is on the cover of a 1978 album by *Yes*
2.   Oh God said to Abraham, "Kill me a son". Abe says, "Man, you must be puttin' me on"
      God say, "No." Abe say, "What?" God say, "You can do what you want Abe, but
      The next time you see me comin' you better run" Well Abe says, "Where do you want this killin' done?"
      God says, "Out on Highway 61" Genesis:22

The music filled me with strange, exciting longings. The nearest that I have ever come to being able to describe it was in the lyrics to a *Pet Shop Boys* song I heard a third of a century later: *"I feel like taking all my clothes off, and dancing to the Rite of Spring, but I wouldn't normally do that kind of thing".* [1]

I wanted to rip my clothes off and dance naked amongst the ancient woodlands, but my father was there, and of course I wouldn't do such a thing in front of him.

So I asked for the third time, and this time he answered, in a strange, soft voice.

"It's Pan, boy. The God of the Woods. Those are his pipes, and what you are feeling is Panic".

I had, of course, read *Wind in the Willows* [2] and my favourite chapter of it had been 'Piper at the Gates of Dawn' in which Portly the lost baby otter is discovered in the care of the hornéd God of the ancient woodlands, so I knew exactly what he was talking about. I started chattering excitedly and this broke the spell, and my father's eyes filled with an immense sadness, and I realised that I had just done something else to him that he could add to the long list of things for which he would never be able to forgive me.

In the ensuing years I have heard snippets of what I thought could have been those pipes again. But never as clearly, and I have never again felt that full-blown rush of feral joy course through my veins. I have heard it in the wilder parts of England. Once I heard it in the hills of Hong Kong, and most recently, during July 2004 in the El Yunque Forest of Puerto Rico. When I was younger I tried to invoke it by dancing naked in the woods and screaming out Crowley's Hymn to Pan but to no avail.

But, like the protagonist of the *Waterboys* song *The Return of Pan* [3] I know one thing beyond doubt. I know that the "Great God Pan is alive".

But what was the relationship between Pan and Panne?

---

1. From the 1993 album *Very*

2. The Wind in the Willows is a children's novel by Kenneth Grahame, first published in 1908. Alternately slow moving and fast paced, it focuses on four anthropomorphised animals in a pastoral version of England. The novel is notable for its mixture of mysticism, adventure, morality, and camaraderie and celebrated for its evocation of the nature of the Thames valley. "The Piper at the Gates of Dawn" tells how Mole and Rat search for Otter's missing son Portly, whom they find in the care of the god Pan. (Pan removes their memories of this meeting "lest the awful remembrance should remain and grow, and overshadow mirth and pleasure".)

3. From the 1993 album *Dream Harder*. "The Return of Pan" was also released as a single, with the songs "Karma" (also the name of one of Scott's earlier musical projects), "Mister Powers" and an untitled track. "The Return of Pan"'s lyrics recount an episode from Plutarch's "The Obsolescence of Oracles". Plutarch writes that, during the reign of Tiberius, a sailor named Thamus heard the following shouted to him from land; "Thamus, are you there? When you reach Palodes, take care to proclaim that the great god Pan is dead." After retelling the story, the singer of "The Return of Pan" insists that "The Great God Pan is alive!". The single charted at position twenty-four on the UK singles chart May 1993.

Even before I had heard these verses, I had always tried to follow the moral compass given:

At sea on a ship in a thunderstorm
On the very night that Christ was born
A sailor heard from overhead
A mighty voice cry, "Pan is dead!"
So follow Christ as best you can
Pan is dead, long live Pan!
From the olden days and up through all the years
From Arcadia to the stone fields of Inisheer
Some say the Gods are just a myth
But guess who I've been dancing with
The great god Pan is alive

And now I had this little goat-footed soul standing before me for the third time.

This time (s)he was alone. Archie treated Panne with a respectful deference that I had never seen him do to anyone or anything before. I had already figured out that (s)he was neither human nor animal, and I didn't feel like I was in the presence of a God. As I have tried to describe before, Panne had the slight, boyish figure of a young teenaged girl, but was covered with short, wiry, chestnut brown hair which simmered in the reflexion of the light from the fishtanks in the corner of my room. I got the overwhelming impression that (s)he was not male, and not female, but whether Panne was neither – or both – was something that I have not yet been able to work out.

Back in a previous life, when I was the acting Night Nursing Officer at the long defunct St Mary's Hospital in Axminster, I had looked after a middle aged person with a hermaphroditic disorder. This person had been raised as a woman, and I always thought of her as such, but between her legs, as well as a vagina she had a small, but – apparently – fully functioning penis and testicles. She was not only severely clinically subnormal but was dying of cancer, and was bedridden. I had to bed bath her often, and her dual physical gender both repelled and fascinated me. The fact that she sprung an erection every time she was bathed and powdered for bedsores was particularly disturbing. But this patient of mine was a freak. The psychic vibes that she gave out were of a wrongness that even surgery could never expunge. Both her her body and her soul were deformed due to a teratological anomaly and she had been doomed to a long, horrible and unproductive life in hospital, and I was relieved and happy for her when she died.

But Panne is not like this. Whatever (s)he is (and I still have no idea) (s)he is perfect and healthy and exactly the way (s)he is meant to be. And, peculiarly, I am not in the slightest bit scared of her. And the fact that (s)he had suddenly turned up in my sitting room in the middle of the night without warning, didn't seem in the slightest bit disturbing.
I looked up at her.

"Hello Panne" I said.

(S)he looked back in silence.

"What can I do for you?" I asked, feeling slightly embarrassed at asking such a banal question under such extraordinary circumstances.

Panne stared back at me with her unblinking yellow eyes with their vertical caprine pupils.

"Have you any chocolate?" (s)he asked shyly.

V

I got another one of Danny Miles' stupid bloody "communiqués" in my e-post this morning, and it irritated me so much that I decided that I really had to break silence.

There is a well-known syndrome in both fact and fiction that someone to whom strange and inexplicable things happens refuses to tell anyone because they didn't want to appear to be losing their sanity. This doesn't apply to me. No-one has ever considered me to be sane, nor have I ever pretended that I was. All sorts of strange things have happened to me throughout my life, and I have usually written about them. The only reason that I have not been doing so over the events of the past few weeks, is that I don't care. I have far more important things going on in my life at the moment than Danny Miles and his damn fool attempts at being a Black Panther, and even the fact that a strange Halfling from the depths of the forest has taken to visiting me in the middle of the night in search of chocolate pales into insignificance in comparison with my main concern of the moment. A few weeks ago I became a Grandfather for the first time [1], and the doings of the rest of the omniverse really do not matter a damn in comparison with that.

So I have been doing my best to emulate a proverbial ostrich; I have been sticking my head in the sand and ignoring everything else while I try to grok the biggest and most momentous thing ever to have happened to me.

I have never made any secret of the fact that I am bipolar. I am also not that far away from being a Paranoid Schizophrenic, and I also have a fair parcel of neuroses and personality disorders sprinkled here and there as well. Physically I am a fairly uncontrolled diabetic, I have a heart condition, arthritis and a number of other things wrong with me. I am also overweight, drink heavily, smoke more cigarettes than I admit to my doctor and occasionally partake in more exotic diversions, so both my physical and mental condition is pretty ropey. [2]

I have tried to kill myself, twice. The last time was fifteen years ago and I don't think I shall try and do it again. Russell Hoban described it best in *Turtle Diary*:

1, Evelyn Lilah Smithson was born in September 2014

2. Actually I quit both cigarettes and narcotics after nearly unintentionally overdosing at Bealtaine 2015 and making myself very ill indeed.

XTUL

From the desk of the Minister for Information

Communique #2
September 11th 2014
Who do you think Xtul are?
Why should you care?

We are living in strange and disturbing times. But they are about to
get worse. All across the universe the forces of chaos are rising. The
black flags are rising. "Before the beginning of great brilliance,
there must be chaos. Before a brilliant person begins something great,
they must look foolish in the crowd". You have to destroy in order to
create, and the time for great destruction is at hand.

Art is the window through which we see the universe. Xtul are the
insane children with half bricks I their hand intent on smashing the
window, and as a result one shall be able to perceive the Universe in
its fractured whole.

Who are Xtul?

All will be revealed eventually, come will be revealed soon. The
story of the Elephant Man and the tiny Goddess who both achieved
their own Nirvana will be revealed first.

Why?

Why Not?

Something will be done before the end of the world. Terrorism is a
matter of perspective, Art Terrorism even more so. May the world
beware, the day of Xtul is at hand.

"It was absolutely uncanny, gave me the creeps. That woman actually thought I'd been thinking of suicide. I had been thinking of it right enough, often do, always have the idea of it huddled like a sick ape in the back of my mind. But I'd never do it. Well, that's not true either. I can imagine the state of mind, I've been in it often enough. no place for the self to sit down and catch its breath. Just being hurried, hurried out of existence. When I feel like that even such a thing as posting a letter or going to the laundrette wears me out. The mind moves ahead of every action making me tired in advance of what I do. Even a thing as simple as changing trains in the Underground becomes terribly heavy..."

Over the last decade and a half I have acquired an ever expanding extended family, and the main reason that I don't think that I will try and kill myself again is because of them, and especially because of my wife whom I love very much indeed. But the thought of it is always huddled like Hoban's sick ape at the back of my consciousness, and I have never much cared whether I lived or died, as long as my departure from this world is not as unpleasant, painful; and undignified as most people's seems to be. That is why I still drink, smoke and do other things potentially injurious to my health. Because my particular sick ape tells me that it won't really make much difference whether I do or I don't. But now things have changed. I have a reason to live. I want to see my granddaughter Evelyn grow up.

This is the biggest change in my mindset for decades, and I am trying to get my head around it, which is why Danny Miles' damn fool nonsense has not really made much of an impact on me over the past few weeks. However, now I begin to think of it, the events of the past few weeks really do need to be written down whilst they are still fresh in my head.

The night that Panne turned up in my sitting room was the beginning of it all. (S)he had come through two locked doors without disturbing either of my dogs. Archie, the smallest and most volatile of them had been sitting on my lap as I vaguely scratched his tummy whist reading, listening to music and vaguely worrying about the journey to Norfolk which we would be undertaking a week or so later to be there for when Olivia gave birth.

The fact that even when (s)he appeared before us, Archie didn't rush about excitedly, barking like a mad thing, but lay respectfully at her feet and silent as the grave was weird enough, but it was his/ her completely banal request for chocolate that floored me. I smiled at him/her and went into the Dining Room which doubles as my wife's office and broke about six squares of Cadbury's Fruit and Nut off a big bar that I knew that she had secreted next to her scanner. I went to the Court Cupboard that Lady Christine Hamlyn had given to my Grandmother as a Christening present back in 1898 [1], and grabbed a bottle of brandy, the cheapest that Asda could provide, that I had bought at the supermarket the previous day, and went back into the Sitting Room.

Panne was still there; motionless and silent, with Archie supine at his/her feet. I passed her the

---

1. Constance Hamlyn-Fane, was the wife of John Manners-Sutton, 3rd Baron Manners (1852–1927). Lady Manner's childless sister Christine Hamlyn had inherited Clovelly, and had intended to bequeath it to her eldest niece Mary Christine Manners, who unexpectedly died at the age of 17. According to family legend she asked to adopt my Grandmother Lilian Gladys, whose father was the coastguard at Clovelly. My family refused, but she became her Godmother.

chunk that I had pinched from my wife's chocolate bar, and poured myself an enormous brandy and coke, lit myself a cigarette and wondered what I was going to do next.

I was still trying to come to terms with the fact that there was what appeared to be a naked Godling covered with hair standing in front of me eating my wife's chocolate. I remembered Mr Beaver's advice from *The Lion, The Witch and the Wardrobe*:

> "But in general, take my advice, when you meet anything that's going to be human and isn't yet, or used to be human once and isn't now, or ought to be human and isn't, you keep your eyes on it and feel for your hatchet." [1]

But I didn't have a hatchet. Or rather I did – it was in the fireplace awaiting its task of cutting up kindling if the winter of 2014-5 is cold enough to warrant more log fires than we needed last winter. But Panne was between me and the fireplace, and my mobility is so severely impaired these days, that even had I wanted to I wouldn't have been able to outfox her and get to the fireplace in time and grab it. And even if I had wanted to I wouldn't have done it. I instinctively knew that Panne was good, or at the least morally neutral, and – even if I had been in possession of my hatchet – I was never going to use it to attack a creature that appeared to be a very sweet, slim fifteen year-old girl, albeit one covered in hair, with cloven hooves on her feet, and cute horns curling out of her forehead.

So I took a drag on my cigarette, gulped down a huge mouthful of brandy and diet coke, took a deep breath, and – for the first time – summoned enough courage up, and spoke to her.

"You know who I am, Panne. But who are you?"

Time seemed to stand still. She looked straight at me, and I gazed into his/her deep yellow eyes with the caprine vertical pupil, as she stared back at me in silence.

Then she slowly stepped towards me and – even more slowly – bent down towards me. For a few moments I stared back in horror, thinking that she was going to kiss me. I was still very aware that she may have been covered in hair, and may have had hooves and horns and the amber coloured eyes of a wild goat, but still in part appeared to be a naked teenage girl, and furthermore one who was (in some arcane way) allied to Danny Miles, who I have known for well over thirty years, and wouldn't trust further than I could throw him.

I started to protest, but she put one finger over her lips in the internationally recognised symbol for silence, bent nearer and rested his/her two horns on my forehead.

Then everything changed forever.

---

1. *The Lion, the Witch and the Wardrobe* is a high fantasy novel for children by C. S. Lewis, published by Geoffrey Bles in 1950. It was the first published of seven novels in The Chronicles of Narnia (1950–1956) and the best known; among all the author's books it is the most widely held in libraries. Although it was written as well as published first in the series, it is volume two in recent editions, which are sequenced according to Narnia history (the first being The Magician's Nephew). Like the others, it was illustrated by Pauline Baynes, and her work has been retained in many later editions.

VI

Anyone who has ever been in truly excruciating pain without the benefit of analgesics will know what I mean when I say that for a few seconds after Panne's horns rested upon my forehead I felt a brief lightning flash of electric blue pain, and then momentarily lost consciousness, but then – a few moments later – I woke up, and I was in the last place that I could ever have expected.

I was standing outside the main ward block of Hawkmoor Hospital, just outside Bovey Tracey, and it appeared to be sometime in the mid 1970s.

Now, this is where it gets weird. I like to pride myself on being a reasonably good writer, but here – quite literally – words fail me. I have always been mildly irritated when I read a novel in which a passage like this appears, but quite truly I cannot find words in the English language for what happened to me next.

As anyone who has read my inky fingered scribblings here and elsewhere will be aware, that over the years my central nervous system has not been a stranger to chemical stimulation. I am not one of these people who struts around the place figuratively wearing a T Shirt saying "I take Drugs, Me" any more than I go around proclaiming my taste for sex, curry, alcohol, or the books of Robert Heinlein, but I have – at various times in my life – indulged in various psychoactive chemicals. Those days are largely over, but I remember the experiences vividly, and none of them were anything like this. I took psychedelic drugs (LSD and magic mushrooms) for a few months over thirty years ago, and have not touched them since, but even in the depths of my most profound excursions through the doors of perception I always knew what I was experiencing were hallucinations. What I experienced the other night was completely real!

The nearest analogy that I can give is what happened to me about seven years ago when Corinna and I were involved in a serious car crash when I was driving our new Jaguar on the M25 and a car jack-knifed into us after being hit by a lorry and we spiraled out of control. For a few moments, as I desperately remembered what my father had taught me when I was learning to drive, I tried to right the car, but we hurtled into the crash barriers in the middle of the motorway and I truly thought that we were both about to die. During those moments I felt remarkably calm, but my life actually *did* flash before my eyes, or at least selected scenes from it did. And this was what was happening now, Except that it wasn't my life. It was someone else's.

Peculiarly, however, bits of my own experience were interspersed within the narrative, which was more like a cross between a particularly lucid dream and watching a film in 3D except without those stupid cardboard glasses that always make my nose itch. Initially I panicked, but unlike when I thought that my wife and I were about to die in a tangled maelstrom of flesh and bone on the M25, I knew that there was nothing I could do about it, and so I decided to treat the experience as if I was watching a film. So, with the slight figure of a woodland godling bending over me with his/her horns pushed against my forehead, I sat back in my chair, reached for my brandy, and decided to see what happened. As I did so, Archie jumped onto my lap, burrowed his way under my blanket and went to sleep.

Hawkmoor Hospital was opened in 1913 as part of a national programme to build hospitals and sanatoriums for the treatment of tuberculosis. It became part of the NHS in 1948, but within a few years was well on its way to being redundant as new antibiotic treatments made TB as a widespread disease in Britain largely a thing of the past. It then slowly became used as a unit for residential care of long term Mentally Handicapped adults, which is what it was when I went there a few times during the summer of 1984. Its days were already numbered; the Thatcherite programme of 'Care in the Community' which was doomed to failure because – on the whole – the community not only didn't care, but didn't give a fuck, and the hospital was already scheduled for closure.

At the time I was a Student Nurse working towards my RHMH qualification, and I was doing a placement with the Torbay Mental Health Community Team, who were pivotally involved with the management of the hospital during its final years. According to the Internet, by 1984 there were over a hundred patients living there, but I don't think I ever saw more than a couple of dozen – severely mentally and physically disabled, sat in a row of wheelchairs in a room reeking of pine disinfectant positioned in front of a TV with the volume off for hours on end.

I found the whole place really upsetting and said so, which did not make me popular with the Community Charge Nurse in charge of my education at the time, so I was dismissed peremptorily, and told to make myself scarce. This I did, and I spent the next hour or so exploring what had once been a charming period sanatorium straight out of the pages of Agatha Christie. One could easily imagine Hercule Poirot and Captain Hastings furtively sneaking about the place, avoiding the *Mycobacterium tuberculosis* bacilli and searching for clues.

At the top of the hill was a handsome, but horridly run down, building which had once been some kind of pavilion. Much to my surprise, whilst pootling around on the internet while I was supposed to be working on something else, I found a photograph of the building in an article on Hawkmoor Hospital in one of the pdf magazines published by the Devon Historical Society. I remember it as being bigger, longer and more magnificent, both from my memories of my visits there thirty tears ago when it was used as a storeroom for broken and unserviceable hospital equipment and my experience of the other night, but it is certainly the same building, and mildly reminiscent of the Cricket Pavilion back at my rather shabby provincial *alma mater*. And just like the aforementioned Cricket Pavilion, when I went snooping around it back in 1984 it was showed every evidence of being used regularly by the locals as a place to indulge in sexual fumblings and smoke cigarettes.

The other night, however, in my mind's eye, I saw it restored to full function, with patients in wheelchairs enjoying themselves in the sun, and nurses in crisp blue uniforms

... Act, ... ust tho...
... at compre...
o this should be made by ... ties.

... ity lay with the County Council, and with Devonport, Exeter
... h Councils. It was under this scheme that Devon and Exeter
... ide the new
... moor. On the first
... five patients, housed
... elters, but plans were
... ved for 80 beds in three

... popular site for
... e of the importance
... quality fresh air as part
... nt. Plymouth's response to the
... policy was to fund a wing, the King

Open Air Tuberculosis Shelter, Boulton and Paul
catalogue, 1912

... ward VII Memorial Pavilion, at the Didworthy Sanatorium, near South Brent, run
... 03 by the local branch of the Association for the Prevention of Tuberculosis.

... m treatment, Devon County Council planned long-term care b...
... wton Abbot and at Tiverton, for example. Schemes already...
... roups, such as the open-air shelters in Crediton and Ti...
... ital in Torquay, were adopted. 'Dispensaries', cleari...
... l were also estab... Those initia...
... Exeter a... ... tle S...

bustling around with busy looks on their faces. Various people in mufti were also to be seen doing their own inimitable thing, and from the haircuts and footwear I would hazard a guess that the year was sometime post Ziggy and pre-*Sex Pistols*; approximately 1975.

Although I assumed that I was seeing the spectacle through Panne's eyes, I saw a small girl on a tricycle with a teddy bear riding pillion. She was pootling up and down the path outside the front of the pavilion and as none of the other people who were obviously either resident or working there were paying her any attention it appeared as if this personable little girl with the bright pink dress and the teddy bear was an accepted part of the landscape.

This intrigued me. Even in the early 1980s when I first started working for the NHS, the once proud beacon of democracy, and – arguably – the only good thing to result from the Second World War, was crumbling beneath the weight of bureaucracy and administration, and although it was many years before the Health and Safety Executive started to make this country impossible to live in, small children were not allowed to play unsupervised in the grounds of psychiatric institutions.

This intrigued me. I had to be seeing this little girl for some reason. What could it be?

By an effort of will I discovered that I could change my vantage point and 'follow' her along the path as she happily rode her tricycle, and carried out a long) and presumably one sided) chuntering conversation with her teddy bear. So I followed her as best I could trying to find out who she was and what she was doing there. I had by suspicions about the former, but the latter was a complete enigma.

Strangely the fact that I was sitting in my armchair, underneath a blanket, cuddling a very cowed Jack Russell and swilling brandy like it was going out of fashion, with the horns of a naked and hairy half goat/half androgynous human pressed to my forehead, didn't phase me anything like as much as the fact that there was a small child playing happily forty years in the past in the middle of a residential hospital.

I zoomed in on the child and realised, not really to my surprise, that the little girl was Panne. Or rather she was part of what would eventually become Panne at some time in the future. I opened my mouth to speak but although brandy was perfectly able to go in, words seemed unable to come out. It was like one of those dreams when you try so hard to speak or shout, but find yourself unexpectedly and inexplicably mute.

So I tried to "think" the question. Maybe I could communicate with Panne in another way. And suddenly the scene changed again. Changed completely. And this time it was another devastating surprise. Because although I was still at Hawkmoor, but this time I was looking at a 24-year-old version of myself. And I was completely alone.

I was reliving the events of the summer of 1984 when I was exploring the semi-deserted grounds of the hospital after having annoyed my supervisor so much that I had been cut loose to fend for myself for an afternoon rather than spending it attending a series of dull, but informative meetings to gain brownie points towards my nursing qualification.

However, here I have to say that I only have the vaguest memory of actually going to Hawkmoor Hospital at the time. Nothing important happened during my visit and it did not therefore impinge on my memory at all. So I am not sure whether what happened next actually happened at the time in 1984, or only happened to be in ur-space the other night, or whether these events had any objective reality at all.

The law forbidding staff in NHS institutions from smoking on the premises had yet to be brought in, but I was aware that I had already blotted my copybook more than I should have done, and as I wanted nothing more than to sit down, have a cigarette and read my dog-eared copy of *The Number of the Beast* by Robert Heinlein [1], I found myself furtively exploring the rear of what I had begun to think of as The Pavilion.

The ground was littered with cigarette ends and as I approached, two surprisingly able-bodied looking patients each wearing the shameful stigmata of prefrontal leucotomy [2] shuffled away embarrassedly, adjusting their clothing as they did so.

This was not a very wholesome place to be, but I continued my walk. I came to a pair of big French Windows, and looked in to see a pile of battered hospital beds, some Bristol Maid medication trolleys that had passed their best, and – in a corner – a battered red child's tricycle and a dusty teddy bear.

I gasped. Panne pulled away from me with a start, and Archie started to bark. I was back in the present day, and sat alone in my armchair, there was no sign of Panne, and only a chocolate wrapper on the carpet gave any hint that (s)he had ever been there at all.

---

1. The book is a series of diary entries by each of the four main characters: Zebadiah John Carter, programmer Dejah Thoris "Deety" Burroughs Carter, her mathematics professor father Jacob Burroughs, and an off-campus socialite Hilda Corners. The names "Dejah Thoris", "Burroughs", and "Carter" are overt references to John Carter and Dejah Thoris, the protagonists of theBarsoom novels of Edgar Rice Burroughs.

The four travel in Zebadiah's modified air car Gay Deceiver, which is equipped with the professor's "continua" device and armed by the Australian Defence Force. The continua device was built by Professor Burroughs while he was formulating his theories on n-dimensional non-euclidean geometry. The geometry of the novel's universe contains six dimensions; the three spatial dimensions known to the real world, and three time dimensions - t, the real world's temporal dimension, τ (tau), and τ (teh). In the novel, the biblical number of the beast turns out to be not 666 but $(6^6)^6$ or 10,314,424,798,490,535,546,171,949,056, the initial number of parallel universes accessible through the continua device. It is later theorized by the character Jacob that the number may be merely the instantly accessible universes from a given location, and that there is a larger structure that implies an infinite number of universes.

2. Lobotomy (Greek: λοβός *lobos* "lobe (of brain)"; τομή *tomē* "cut, slice") is a neurosurgical procedure, a form of psychosurgery, also known as a leukotomy or leucotomy (from the Greek λευκός *leukos* "clear, white" and *tome*). It consists of cutting or scraping away most of the connections to and from the prefrontal cortex, the anterior part of the frontal lobes of the brain.

VII

Whatever I did after that it would be an anti-climax, so I polished off the brandy and Archie and I trotted off to bed to join Corinna and Prudence (Corinna being my wife and Prudence being a large, ungainly animal whose antecedents included bulldog and boxer, and who looks more than a little like a pygmy hippo). The excitement and the brandy proved too much for me and I was asleep within minutes, dreaming of a normal world, where normal things happened and I was not privy to the complex emotional history of a strange half human Godling who had ventured out of the deep woods in search of chocolate.

The next day I awoke with a mild hangover and got on with my daily business. The events of the evening before had been so strange, that I really didn't feel able to talk about them with anyone, not even my wife, so when Danny Miles burst into my office in a state of what I believe the authoresses of historical 'bodice ripping' dramas would call 'High Dudgeon' I was not best pleased. As anyone who has read these memoirs so far will probably realise, I am not best pleased when Danny Miles turns up in my life at the best of times, but when he burst in through the door, yammering at the top of his voice and waving his arms about, before I had even finished my breakfast, and when my second cup of coffee had not yet dispelled the faint fronds of a hangover, it was really beyond the pale.

"What the fuck do you want?" I asked grumpily.

"What have you done with Panne?" he screamed at me with panic in his eyes.

I have learned quite a few lessons in diplomacy over the years, and I decided that it would be best if I adopted a position of what I believe the security services call 'plausible deniability'.

"I haven't done anything with her. What the hell are you talking about?"

"She has disappeared" he said, ashen faced, "and all hell has broken loose".

Much against my better judgement I sat him down, entreated my darling Mother-in-law who was carrying out her own arcane morning activities with a dustpan and brush, to make me another cup of coffee and give Danny one as well, and as I blithely ignored my vague resolution not to smoke in the mornings, I lit a cigarette and did my best to try and find out what on earth this was all about.

Danny was not the most articulate of people at the best of times. His strengths lay in getting people to do stuff for him whilst he took a load of drugs and played the part of some metaphysical Mr Fixit. In all the years that I have known him I have never before seen him in a state of panic, but when one considers the derivation of the word, somehow this seemed quite appropriate.

"The word panic derives from the Greek πανικός, "pertaining to shepherd god Pan", who took amusement from frightening herds of goats and sheep into sudden bursts of uncontrollable fear. The ancient Greeks credited the battle of Marathon's victory to Pan, using his name for the frenzied, frantic fear exhibited by the fleeing enemy soldiers."

From Wikipedia, the free encyclopedia

Slowly I got the story out of him. Although he has been portraying himself as *Xtul*'s Minister for Information, he is basically nothing of the sort. This didn't surprise me overmuch. It has been many years since I was actually impressed by anything that Danny Miles said or did.

He was actually a fairly lowly go-between who had no real idea of who the three members of *Xtul* actually were, let alone their true nature, where they actually came from, or what they were doing.

He had got involved with them by accident, and – following his usual *modus operandi* – was just exploiting the situation as best he could in an entirely opportunist manner.

He was even cagier than usual about how he had got involved with them, but from what I could gather, at some point at the end of last year he had been driving up from Cornwall to visit his old friend and sometime lover Basil at his home which was in a hut deep in the Somerset Levels.

He picked up two girls who were hitchhiking along the A39 in torrential rain. Knowing him as well as I unfortunately do, I am sure that his motivation was purely venal, but whether his intentions we consummated or not he did not reveal, and I really didn't care. He was quite prepared to go off on some pulchritudinous tangent, describing how the two girls were "soaked to the skin, leaving little to the imagination" but I did my best to shut him up, and return him to the matter at hand.

It turns out that the unlikely trio stopped off at the *Westcountry Inn* for lunch, and according to his description, they were all over him "like a rash", considering him as "their hero" for having rescued them from the torrential downpour. I hate to admit, however, that I doubted it. It is an indisputable fact that when he was younger, Danny had some indefinable magic which seemed to appeal across the board to young women who fell for his peacock prettiness, his silks and satins, and his air of debauched elegance. But he was a third of a century older, and whilst time has not been particularly kind to me, I have no pretensions as to being any kind of Love Machine, being quite happy in my self-imposed exile as some kind of middle aged hippy academic, with a wife, a mother-in-law, two stepdaughters, an infant granddaughter, a gaggle of adopted nieflings, two houses, mortgage and a couple of dogs.

Danny, however, was about five years younger than me, and had attained his half century unencumbered by responsibility, and still seemed to be trying to attain some personal Nirvana via the medium of casual sex and substance abuse. Now, I will admit that this was exactly what I was doing about seventeen years ago, but this phase only lasted a few years with me, in the aftemath of my particularly unpleasant divorce, and was over by the time I was about a decade younger than Danny is now. With the benefit of hindsight (good old hindsight) I can see that this was not a particularly dignified way for me to spend my time, but in my defence, I was only in my late thirties, and my life had just - very spectacularly – fallen apart. Danny (by now in his early fifties) sported a 'smart casual' haircut of the sort which looked tacky back in the late 1980s and merely looked ridiculous now. His rapidly greying hair was far thinner than he was prepared to accept, and his clothes were whatever the male equivalent of 'mutton dressed as lamb' is.

Although Danny had only one - mildly unsavoury - motive in mind, he did his best to worm himself into the confidence if these two hapless young women, so he attempted to feign some sort of interest in their lives. And so when they told him that they were hitch-hiking across the country in order to meet up with the rest of their so-called 'Spiritual Family' who lived in a community where clothes and guns were optional, somewhere deep in the woods somewhere in North Devon, he suddenly started to show interest.

I have known Danny for a long time, but have always been ware of the unfortunate fact that he has had somewhat of a Charles Manson fixation ever since I have known him. This is something that I can understand, because back when I was about eighteen I had one too. It was the summer of 1978 and due to a concatenation of unfortunate incidents I found myself living with my cousin Pené and her first husband, in a house owned by the Devon and Cornwall Police in Plymouth.

That summer the Manson biopic *Helter Skelter* [1] was shown for the first (only?) time on British TV and I was completely blown away. I was eighteen, unemployable, sexually confused, and completely lost, and I suddenly found something that appealed to me. Despite the fact that Manson and all of his main followers were (and still are) incarcerated or dead didn't put me off. The idea of an unruly tribe of social malcontents living a life of dune buggies, drugs and nudity in the sunshine of California's Death Valley, was completely irresistible to me.

Amusingly, the very next day after watching the second part of the film on BBC2, I was in Plymouth City Centre looking for a job. Well, I was supposed to be looking for a job. After

---

1. *Helter Skelter* is a 1976 TV film based on the 1974 book by prosecutor Vincent Bugliosi and Curt Gentry. In the United States, it aired over two nights. In some countries it was shown in theaters with additional footage (nudity, language and more violence).

The movie is based upon the murders committed by the Charles Manson Family. The best-known victim was actress Sharon Tate. The title was taken from the Beatles' song of the same name. According to the theory put forward by the prosecution, Manson used the term for an anticipated race war, and "healter skelter" [sic] was scrawled in blood on the refrigerator door at the house of one of the victims. It recounts the murders Manson committed, the investigation, and the 1970-71 trial where prosecuting D.A. Bugliosi attempted to draw connections between the Manson family and his violent convictions.

The 1976 film, directed by Tom Gries, stars Steve Railsback as Manson and George DiCenzo as Bugliosi. Writer JP Miller received a 1977 Edgar Award from the Mystery Writers of America for Best TV Feature or MiniSeries Teleplay.

having dutifully paid a visit to the Job Centre, to find there was neither anything there that I wanted to do, or - if I am gonna be completely honest about it - nothing available that I was *able* to do, I was wandering about the City Centre with £1.50 in my pocket, trying to decide whether I was going to go to the pub, or have something to eat, when a smartly dressed young man approached me. "Do you want to turn your life around?" he asked.

Irritated, and assuming that he was trying to sell me some sort of religious experience, I turned round to him, and was just about to tell him to "fuck off" when I saw that he was accompanied by a girl who looked just like Sadie Mae Glutz [1]. She was massively beautiful, and underneath her semi transparent blouse she was not wearing a bra.

"Do you want to eat?" He asked. I was insanely hungry, and hoping that he was not speaking metaphorically, I nodded in the affirmative, whilst doing my best not to ogle the Susan Atkins lookalike.

The two peculiar young people took me for a long walk into the suburbs where they ushered me into an unimpressive suburban house where I found about fifteen young people, all attractive(ish) and all eating lentil stew. "This is Brother Jonathan" my new friend announced and the assembled company rose to greet me.

My introduction to the world of living in a cult was not a success. I cant remember whether they were The Moonies or The Scientologists, or somebody else entirely, but they were very earnest and talked a lot about meditation and abstinence, when all I wanted to know was where the guns were. After the meal I started to drop heavy hints about drug fuelled orgies, and was peremptorily shown the door

All this was a long time ago. I was young and psychotic at the time, and was so well balanced that I had a chip on both shoulders. I felt that I had been treated appallingly badly by 'straight' society, and that there must be something better out there. To a horny, unbalanced, and socially challenged teenager the idea of a love and terror cult had certain irresistible qualities, although I doubt whether I would have enjoyed it much if I had actually joined one. More probable e is that I would have irritated the leadership of the cult as much as I did those 'straights' that I despised so much, and would probably have ended up in an unmarked shallow grave somewhere on Dartmoor. But even thirty six years later I could understand why Danny had found the stories that his two nubile hitchhikers had told him so irresistible.

---

1. "Susan Denise Atkins (May 7, 1948 – September 24, 2009) was a convicted American murderer who was a member of the "Manson family", led by Charles Manson. Manson and his followers committed a series of nine murders at four locations in California, over a period of five weeks in the summer of 1969.

Known within the Manson family as Sadie Mae Glutz or Sexy Sadie, Atkins was convicted for her participation in eight of these killings, including the most notorious, the "Tate/LaBianca" murders. She was sentenced to death, which was subsequently commuted to life in prison. Incarcerated from October 1, 1969 until her death – a period exactly one week short of 40 years – Atkins was the longest incarcerated female inmate in the California penal system, having been denied parole 18 times"

"So what happened then?" I asked with interest, momentarily forgetting that Danny was a near psychopathic nuisance who had committed the unforgiveable sin of bursting into my study before I had finished my breakfast, read my post, and perused my daily dose of *Bad Machinery*[1] which, as my family knows, is an almost capital crime in my eyes. From what Danny told me, the amusing irony about how the events of that rainy late autumn lunchtime transpired was that he had taken them into *The Westcountry Inn* planning to spend as little money as possible and seduce one or both of them. What actually happened was that he ended up maxing out his credit card on an exceedingly expensive lunch for three, and being seduced - both intellectually and emotionally - by his two young companions.

They told him how the three leaders of the group ("although we don't really have leaders y'know man, but they are Gods so we have to do what they tell us, especially Mr Loxodonta") had bought a piece of woodland in the middle of the deep woods. I knew from my own experience that there are quite a few online agencies which sell land like this which cannot be built on, and - indeed - I have often toyed with the idea of buying a plot myself in order to manage it as a nature reserve, and have a little bit of England to which I could retreat whenever the real world got too irritating.

The three leaders then, apparently, brought their divine powers into play and did something that would be difficult for a mere mortal, but not impossible, as Danny pointed out especially if one was an experienced computer hacker. Apparently they had paid a visit to the London offices of the Land Registry, and done something to their computer records, so as to all intents and purposes their ten acre parcel of trees no longer existed, and as it was surrounded by deep and tangled fir plantations, which had been planted in the early years of the 20th Century, just before, and during the early part of WW1, before Lord Lovat had become the first Chairman of the nascent Forestry Commission, and the owner had been killed at Passchendaele where he drowned in a sea of mud, nobody actually knew who it was that owned the forest, so the trees could never be cut down. So this unruly band of raggle taggle gypsies lived safely impregnable on a remote slice of land that was untraceable by any normal, and most abnormal processes. Here the three gods lived in seclusion with their ever growing band of neo flower children. They spent their days making music and lying around doing nothing very much. The two girls suspected that the three gods had some mysterious purpose in mind, but they didn't know what it was. And they certainly made music. They had some on a MP3 player…

"It was really good" said Danny.

"And when I heard about the cult family, and listened to the music some more, and looked at the two girls, I thought, 'I want a bit of that'"

And he leered at me in a most unsavoury manner and winked at me conspiratorially. I looked at Danny aghast, and not for the first time in the thirty three years that I have known, and been infuriated by the bloody man, I realised quite how shallow he has always been. the motivating factors in his life have always been sex, money and power over people weaker than himself. I don't think that I have ever disliked him quite s much as I did then. I gulped at some more coffee, lit

1. A webcomic by John Allison which can be found at www.scarygoround.com

another cigarette and asked him to continue.

Of course he started to talk about the two nubile young hitchhikers again, but I managed to head him off that subject with some difficulty, and tried to find out some more about these peculiar people who wee living as a family out in the deep woods. "Of course I didn't believe that these three people were Gods, they had to be just ordinary people who were better at social manipulation than the people who followed them. Its amazing what a few conjuring tricks and some masks will do to impress a bunch of stoned homeless hippies" he blustered, and for a moment I actually believed him.

"At least that is what I thought at first" he admitted, looking surprisingly shamefaced. "I found out a bit more later and was forced to change my mind, but at that stage I just wanted to get closer to the girls, if y'know what I mean", and once again he winked at me in a horrid manner and became the sleazy cocksman that I have learned to despise for all those years.

Realising that Danny's thoughts were once again verging towards the carnal, and wanting to find out what the hell this was all about, whilst still being only too aware that I had a long and difficult day ahead of me, and Danny's tomfoolery was just going to compound the problems I had to face. So I did my best to bring him back on track without actually grabbing him by the scruff of the neck and banging his head repeatedly against the wall. I am not a violent man, but I am afraid that Danny Miles brings out the worst in me.

Back at *The Westcountry Inn*, Danny had apparently told the two girls, whose names - he informed me - were Sable and Araminta, that he wanted to meet the other members of what they described as 'The Children of The Three' and asked whether this could be arranged. Araminta, slightly nervously made a phone call on her mobile, and spoke to someone called 'Skullfuck' who she later described as the Sergeant at Arms.

I pricked up my ears at this; back in my mis-spent youth, soon after I Had met Danny for the first time, I knew a biker in the South Devon village of Kenton with just this unlovely soubriquet. Surely there couldn't be that many people called 'Skullfuck' living in the Westcountry. Realising that if this was indeed someone that I used to know then I had an ace up my sleeve that Danny might not know about. Many years of dealing with the bloody man has taught me that when dealing with Danny Miles one needs as many cards in one's deck as possible, so I filed the information away for future reference, took another drag on Messrs Benson and Hedges' finest, and asked Danny to continue.

About half an hour later, Araminta's phone rang, and she muttered a conversation whilst making the odd furtive sideways glances at Danny, and giggling nervously. then, when the call was over, she lent over to Sable and whispered in her ear. The two girls squealed delightedly, and dragged Danny to his feet. They danced around him, showering him with kisses as they did so, and then delightedly pulled him out into the car park to his car.

Danny asked me whether I knew the area at all. Of course I did.

Back in 1978 my Father taught me to drive along these very lanes, and long the main rod which led from Clovelly down to Bude. In more recent years I had explored quite a few of these back lanes at night with Corinna and one of our students, who was doing a project about the nocturnal fauna of this part of Devon, but although we were dutifully logging the badgers and foxes that we saw, we were really hoping that we would have an encounter with one if the big cats that are more and more commonly reported in the region.

I explained this to Danny, and he told me how the two girls, by now twitching with almost palpable excitement had instructed him to drive back in the direction of Kilkhampton for a few miles, until they came across a blind turning on the left. They drove down this little lane, and were now surrounded by the tall grey green pine trees of the Forestry Commission. Showing admirable restraint and far more common sense than I was used to from him, Danny was only driving at about twenty five miles per hour down what my Father used to describe as a 'Devon Dual Carriageway', an unkempt road with grass growing down the centre leaving a separate 'carriageway' for each wheel. This was a good thing, because suddenly two dark figures stepped out of the undergrowth about twenty feet in front of the car, the two girls screamed "Stop!!!" In unison, and Danny slammed his foot on the brake, and they screeched to a halt, and Sable, who was in the back seat behind him, giggled manically, produced a hunting knife from up her sleeve, and held it to his throat.

The two figures who had stepped out of the bushes in front of them approached the car, and Danny saw to his horror that they were wearing grubby black dungarees, their faces were covered by realistic rubber pig masks, and they were carrying what looked suspiciously like semi automatic rifles which seemed far too big for them. It was only then that Danny realised that by their stature they could not have been more than ten or eleven years old.

Danny was frogmarched out of the car, a black bin bag was put over his head, one of the pig children took the keys from the ignition, opened the boot of the car and his four captors unceremoniously bundled Danny into it, slamming it shut a few centimetres above his head.

"Bloody Hell" I said, whilst - for the first time in about thirty years - actually feeling mildly sorry for Danny Miles.

XVIII

I don't know how many of you have ever been kidnapped at knifepoint by a beautiful girl over thirty years younger than you, whom you had been hoping to seduce, had a bin bag unceremoniously plonked on your head, been bundled at gunpoint into the boot of your own car by pre-teen terrorists wearing pig masks, and driven lickety-split down a bumpy country road. I certainly haven't, so any comments that I make upon the subject have to be purely conjectural. However, this is exactly what Danny Miles claimed had happened to him, one morning in late autumn when he sat in my office looking scared to death. Although he tried to make light of it, the experience had obviously terrified him, and even the process of reliving this all was difficult and cathartic for him.

I have never been particularly good at writing speech down, and in this particular case Danny, who is usually self-assuredly voluble, was nothing of the sort. He muttered and stuttered, slurred his words and kept on stopping in the middle of sentences and even in the middle of words, upon which I had to gently prompt him into continuing. The only time in my life that I have ever found myself interviewing somebody who was as neurotically reticent as this before was way back in the autumn of 1995 when my first wife and I interviewed a young man to whom I later gave the *nom de guerre* of 'Gavin' who had (five or six years before) had an encounter with the "thing" (as Ivan T Sanderson [1] would have called it) that is generally

1. Ivan Terence Sanderson (January 30, 1911 – February 19, 1973) was a biologist and writer born in Edinburgh, Scotland, who became a naturalized citizen of the United States. Sanderson is remembered for his nature writing and his interest in cryptozoology and paranormal subjects. He also wrote fiction under the name Terence Roberts. In "Things" and "More Things", two books originally published in the late 1960s, Sanderson recounts fantastic phenomena which remain scientifically inexplicable to this day, from telepathic ants to mechanical dowsing, flying saucers and UFO nests, water monsters, giant skulls, the Toonijuk, and much more. Divided into chapters on "Live Things", "Dead Things", "Man Things", "Funny Things", and "Nasty Things", "Things" and More "Things" is a singularly fascinating delve into matters weird and mysterious, enthusiastically recommended for metaphysical studies collections.

referred to as The Owlman of Mawnan [1]. He had been suffering from a sort of short term Post Traumatic Stress Disorder brought on - or so I surmised - by the trauma of having to re-live, under questioning, one of the nastiest and most emotionally horrific experiences of his young life. I recognised the same, or at least very similar, symptoms in Danny, and - whilst his story was so bizarre, as to be bordering on the unbelievable - I was sure that Danny, at least, believed the absolute truth of what he was telling me.

The car trundled on down the bumpy road, and eventually turned off into something even more bumpy which Danny surmised was some kind of cart track, and after about twenty minutes (or so he estimated) the car shuddered to a halt. The doors opened, and Danny could hear the sound of muffled voices and laughter, but remained locked in the boot for what seemed like an eternity. "Then I fell asleep" he muttered shamefacedly. "Under the circumstances I know that it seems insane, but I was very tired and whatever reserves of strength I had, just ran out!" [2]

His sleep was rudely awakened minutes or hours later, when the boot of his Astra opened suddenly and, still with the bin bag over his head, he was pulled out of the car to his feet. His captors roughly jerked the bin bag off his head, and - although the sudden influx of bright daylight was almost too much to bear - he did his best to take in as much of his surroundings as he could, and found (not altogether to his surprise) that his car was parked on a rough cart track which was entering a small woodland clearing. Around the sides of the clearing, half-hidden by trees, were some large khaki tents of the sort that are usually advertised in Army Surplus stores as 6-8 berth, and a number of young people were wandering around. They were all wearing pig masks, and some were clutching guns.

Over to his left was an open fronted marquee, again khaki canvas, and shrouded in camouflage netting. Inside was a long trestle table, and sat at the table were more young people, all wearing rubber pig masks tapping away industriously at laptops. Danny opened his mouth to speak but Sable kicked him hard in the shin and told him to shut up. They led him a little way into the deep wood, where there was a canvas chair. Roughly they sat him down, and Sable and Araminta turned and left. Without a backwards glance they were gone.

Danny was left alone with the two children, still silent as the grave, still wearing rubber pig masks and still carrying what appeared to be AK47s which were far too big for them.

---

1. The Owlman of Mawnan has been described as a grey/dark brown feathered, 5 -6 feet tall creature, its feet clawed with hybrid owl/humanlike features. With a wingspan of approximately 10 feet, a loud hissing / screeching noise accompanies the spectre, its large eyes glow a fiery crimson. The first sighting of the Owlman took place on April 17, 1976, June and Vicky Melling (aged 9 & 12) and their family were on their Easter break in Mawnan Smith, they saw a "bird man" hovering over the tower of Mawnan Old Church. Running to the police station the girls were taken into different rooms and independently drew a similar image of what they saw. So frightened by their encounter the family cut short their holiday.

2. Kipling described something similar when two bullies received their well deserved comeuppance: "The head did not lift. Sefton was deeply asleep. "That's rummy," said McTurk, as a snore mixed with a sob. "'Cheek, I think; or else he's shammin'."

"No, 'tisn't," said Beetle. "'When 'Molly' Fairburn had attended to me for an hour or so I used to go bung off to sleep on a form sometimes. Poor devil! But he called me a beastly poet, though." Rudyard Kipling: *Stalky and Co* (1903)

You could almost feel sorry for Danny at this point. With more than the usual human capacity for self-delusion, he had managed to convince himself that the two girls he had picked up hitchhiking along the A39 were going to take him to a paradise full of bare-breasted flower children living in squalor. What he actually found was something akin to a neat and tidy military encampment full of fully clothed children brandishing guns, and engaged on some complex computer-related activity. He had hoped for free love and drugs, and had blundered into a nightmare full of paramilitary pig children armed to the teeth.

A tall dark figure strode through the wood towards him. Long haired, leather-jacketed and booted, he was well over six foot tall, and - according to Danny - had the musculature, gait and bearing of a gorilla. Now, gorillas are peaceful, gentle, knuckle walkers and mostly vegetarian, but rather than remonstrate with Danny about his pitiful lack of knowledge of the physiology of the higher primates, I let this one be, and assumed that the person who was swaggering towards them up the woodland path towards them was completely human. Anyway, I had my suspicions about whom he might turn out to be.

As he got closer, Danny could see that he was an enormous biker, bare-chested under his leather jacket, and with a distinctive tattoo of a skull with a wreath of roses across its cranium on his barrel chest. My suspicions were confirmed. I didn't think that there could be many people in the Westcountry with the unlovely soubriquet of 'Skullfuck', and this bloke only had the name because I had given it to him.

Thirty plus years ago, when I was a Student Nurse at the Royal Westcountry Hospital in South Devon, and living at the nurses' home at an old, tumbledown, and rather beautiful art deco house called Staplake, in Starcross [1], I used to drink at a pub called *The Dolphin Inn* in the neighbouring village of Kenton. It was a nice little pub, and I used to drink there because I could happily chat away to the landlord about tropical fish, politics and all sorts of other things that have always amused and interested me. For some reason that I have never understood, Kenton had always been home to a sizeable biker community, and - over the years - I became friends with some of them.

A bloke called Pete, mildly hippyish and a bit of a Jack the Lad also drunk there, and one night he invited me and a bevy of the local bikers back to his flat for 'a drink and a smoke' which invariably meant cider and Afghan black.

We all tumbled into my car, and I drove unsteadily (because I had ingested five or six pints already, and had originally planned to spend the night in my car in the pub car park). We drove up a windy lane, and we could see the way before us illuminated in the moonlight.

Driving across a little humpbacked bridge which crossed a silvery stream, which babbled in the moonlight, we headed up a hill, and at the peak of the hill was an enormous Gothic mansion

---

1. Both the hospital and Staplake House were knocked down in the late 1980s. The former as a result of the late unlamented Margaret Thatcher's Care in the Community programme which incidentally meant that a load of valuable real estate suddenly became saleable, and the latter as a result of a fire which may or may not have been arson, and which gutted the building.

which appeared out of the darkness like something out of the 1963 film of *The Haunting*.[1] "This is it," said Pete cheerfully, and directed us to a small car park by a side entrance.

It turned out that the mansion was owned by his grandfather, and that Pete was in charge of having it converted to luxury flats. However, the process was scheduled to take at least another three years, and in the meantime, Pete was quite happy to play at being Lord of the Manor. He led us in through the side entrance where we found the sort of hippy crash pad that I have seen on innumerable occasions over the years. If you can imagine a spacious but grubby area containing (in no particular order) a poster of Che Guevara [2], another of Jimi Hendrix as painted by Martin Sharp [3], several cardboard boxes containing (in total) several thousand LPs in dog eared covers, makeshift bookshelves made from planks and bricks and containing a selection of the de rigueur hippy tomes like *The Lord of the Rings*,[4] *Jonathan Livingstone Seagull* [5] and *Zen and the Art of Motorcycle Maintenance* [6], some joss sticks

1. The Haunting is a 1963 British psychological horror film directed and produced by Robert Wise and adapted by Nelson Gidding from the 1959 novel The Haunting of Hill House by Shirley Jackson. It stars Julie Harris, Claire Bloom, Richard Johnson, and Russ Tamblyn. The film, about a small group of people invited by a paranormal investigator to stay at a haunted house that comes to life, is often cited as one of the most frightening films ever made.

2. Ernesto "Che" Guevara (1928 – 1967), commonly known as el Che or simply Che, was an Argentine Marxist revolutionary, physician, author, guerrilla leader, diplomat, and military theorist. *Guerrillero Heroico* (English: "Heroic Guerrilla Fighter") is an iconic photograph of Marxist revolutionary Che Guevara taken by Alberto Korda. It was captured on March 5, 1960, in Havana, Cuba, at a memorial service for victims of the La Coubre explosion. By the end of the 1960s, the image especially printed in red and black by Big O posters, in conjunction with Guevara's subsequent actions and eventual execution, helped solidify the charismatic and controversial leader as a cultural icon.

3. James Marshall "Jimi" Hendrix (born Johnny Allen Hendrix; November 27, 1942 – September 18, 1970) was an American guitarist, singer, and songwriter. He is widely regarded as one of the most influential electric guitarists in the history of popular music, and one of the most celebrated musicians of the 20th century. The Rock and Roll Hall of Fame describes him as "arguably the greatest instrumentalist in the history of rock music". Martin Ritchie Sharp (21 January 1942 – 1 December 2013) was an Australian artist, underground cartoonist, songwriter and film-maker. Sharp was Australia's foremost pop artist. His psychedelic posters of Hendrix, Bob Dylan, Donovan and others, rank as classics of the genre, and his covers, cartoons and illustrations were a central feature of Oz magazine.

4. The Lord of the Rings is an epic high-fantasy novel written by English author J. R. R. Tolkien. The story began as a sequel to Tolkien's 1937 fantasy novel The Hobbit, but eventually developed into a much larger work. Written in stages between 1937 and 1949, The Lord of the Rings is one of the best-selling novels ever written, with over 150 million copies sold.

5. Jonathan Livingston Seagull, written by Richard Bach, is a fable in novella form about a seagull learning about life and flight, and a homily about self-perfection. It was first published in 1970 as "Jonathan Livingston Seagull — a story." By the end of 1972, over a million copies were in print, Reader's Digest had published a condensed version, and the book had reached the top of the New York Times Best Seller list, where it remained for 38 weeks. In 1972 and 1973, the book topped the Publishers Weekly list of bestselling novels in the United States. In 2014 the book was reissued as Jonathan Livingston Seagull: The Complete Edition, which added a 17-page fourth part to the story.

6. Zen and the Art of Motorcycle Maintenance: An Inquiry into Values (ZAMM), first published in 1974, is a work of philosophical non-fiction, the first of Robert M. Pirsig's texts in which he explores his Metaphysics of Quality. The book sold 5 million copies worldwide. It was originally rejected by 121 publishers, more than any other bestselling book, according to the Guinness Book of Records. The title is an apparent play on the title of the book Zen in the Art of Archery by Eugen Herrigel. In its introduction, Pirsig explains that, despite its title, "it should in no way be associated with that great body of factual information relating to orthodox Zen Buddhist practice. It's not very factual on motorcycles, either." The book is generally regarded as an American cultural icon in literature. I found it unreadable.

burning in plant pots, two well fed and indignant looking tabby cats, and dozens of unwashed mugs and plates. The atmosphere smelt mildly of cat pee, masked partially by the smell of incense and stale hashish, and I immediately felt at home.

The two bikers turned out to be working with Pete, whilst simultaneously signing on. They were brothers, and the youngest was contemplating getting his first tattoo. At the time both Pete and I were very much into *The Grateful Dead* [1], and he rummaged through his grubby LP collection and got out a copy of the band's self named album from 1971. The cover is iconic.

> "The skull and roses design was composed by Alton Kelley and Stanley Mouse, who added lettering and color, respectively, to a black and white drawing by Edmund Joseph Sullivan. Sullivan's drawing was an illustration for a 1913 edition of the Rubaiyat of Omar Khayyam. Earlier antecedents include the custom of exhibiting the relic skulls of Christian martyrs decorated with roses on their feast days. The rose is an attribute of Saint Valentine who according to one legend was martyred by decapitation. Accordingly, in Rome, at the church dedicated to him, the observance of his feast day included the display of his skull surrounded by roses. This was discontinued in the late 1960s when Valentine was removed from the Roman Catholic canon along with other legendary saints whose lives and deeds could not be confirmed. Kelley and Mouse's design originally appeared on a poster for the September 16 and 17, 1966 Dead shows at the Avalon Ballroom. Later it was used as the cover for the album Grateful Dead. The album is sometimes referred to as Skull and Roses (or Bertha)."

Another name for the album is 'Skullfuck' (a vulgar term for oral sex), and it is a matter of record that the band wanted this unlovely moniker for the album, but that their record company put their foot down and (quite sensibly) refused. "Why don't you have this for your tattoo?" Pete suggested. having ingested far more alcohol and hashish than was wise, I was slurring my words massively when I muttered, "If he does, he is gonna have to change his name to 'Skullfuck'!" He did get the tattoo, and the nickname that I gave him whilst trying to be clever and showing off my exemplary knowledge of Bay Area psychedelic rock music stuck. With this new revelation from Danny it seemed that, thirty something years later it was still sticking.

Now, when I was living at Staplake, during the time immediately before I got engaged to Alison who I married in 1985 and stayed with for the next eleven years, Skullfuck and Pete were reasonably regular visitors, as was Danny, but it seemed that they had never met, or if

---

1. The *Grateful Dead* were an American rock band formed in 1965 in Palo Alto, California. Ranging from quintet to septet, the band was known for its unique and eclectic style, which fused elements of country, folk, bluegrass, blues, reggae, rock, improvisational jazz, psychedelia, space rock, for live performances of lengthy instrumental jams, and for their devoted fan base, known as "Deadheads". "Their music," writes Lenny Kaye, "touches on ground that most other groups don't even know exists." These various influences were distilled into a diverse and psychedelic whole that made the *Grateful Dead* "the pioneering Godfathers of the jam band world". The band was ranked 57th in the issue The Greatest Artists of all Time by *Rolling Stone* magazine. The band was inducted into the Rock and Roll Hall of Fame in 1994 and their Barton Hall Concert at Cornell University (May 8, 1977) was added to the Library of Congress's National Recording Registry. *The Grateful Dead* have sold more than 35 million albums worldwide.

they had, Danny was (as usual) been so wrapped up in his own self-importance that he had no memory of anyone who didn't actually impinge into his own peculiarly insular little world.

I decided that on this occasion that discretion would prove to be the better part of valour. I had no idea where this peculiar journey was going to end up taking us.

But I didn't trust Danny further than I could throw him, and Skullfuck and I had shared quite a bit of history for a few years following our first meeting, and I would like to think that if our paths crossed again, that he would be kindly disposed towards me.

So I kept my own council, and asked Danny what happened next.

"Well, he didn't seem very clever," said Danny sneeringly at me. I knew Skullfuck's sad history and said nothing. "He kept on asking me who I was, and what I was doing there. And as I thought that it wouldn't be a very good idea to admit that I had only been interested in the two chicks, I told him that it was because of the music. And it seemed as if that was exactly the right thing to say," he said.

One of the big buzz words of our early 21st Century social economy is 'Identity Theft', and Danny didn't bat an eyelid as he brazenly explained how and why he had proceeded to steal MY identity.

He wasn't even slightly apologetic as he explained how he told Skullfuck how impressed he had been with the music that the girls had played him in the pub. How he, himself had worked in the music business for many years, and could tell a hit record when he heard one, and how he wanted to help make these people stars!

The trouble is, that none of this was true. Apart from a few years as a male escort in the early 1980s around the time that I first met him, he had never worked as anything. He had never been employed in any industry, having led a charmed life drifting from one disaster to another, and leaving debts wherever he trod. I, however, much against my better judgment had never actually turned him away in the third of a century that I had known him, and had worked intermittently on the fringes of the music industry for many years. Currently I am editing a weekly online music magazine and doing the odd bit of contract work for my old mate Rob Ayling at Gonzo Multimedia, and am in the process of starting up my own community orientated record company together with a mate called Martin Eve.

Although we hadn't seen each other for years, Danny had kept vague tabs on how my life had been progressing, and as he got more enthusiastic talking to Skullfuck, he stole more and more of my personal back story and made it his own. He explained how he had got unique powers and skills as a polemicist, a publicist and a student of rock and roll history, and if anyone could manipulate the 21st Century media into making this unique band of musicians into stars, it was him.

"What were they called, by the way?"

"*Xtul*," grunted Skullfuck.

I gulped; my past was really coming back to haunt me this time.

I believe that in the current vernacular, what Danny was doing is known as 'Social Engineering', - the psychological manipulation of people into performing actions or divulging confidential information. A type of confidence trick for the purpose of information gathering, fraud, or system access, it differs from a traditional "con" in that it is often one of many steps in a more complex fraud scheme. He soon engineered the situation to one where he was asking the questions and the poor hapless biker before him was not only giving Danny the answers, but was treating him like an honoured guest rather than a prisoner, and Danny was soon manipulating the poor fool into doing exactly what he wanted.

Skullfuck told Danny much the same as the two girls had some hours early. This woodland was the home for a group of people who were trying to save the earth, and who lived together as 'The Children of the Three'. He confirmed that 'The Three' were Gods who had come to change the world forever. But he added two other pieces to the jigsaw. The two girls had been sent out specifically to find someone with a car, use their womanly whiles to fascinate the driver, and bring him back to the wood. They were then supposed to kill him and steal the car, but things hadn't quite worked out that way.

Danny was so shocked, not only by his recent brush with death but at quite how badly he had misjudged the situation, that he didn't really take the second bit of information on board. The three members of *Xtul*, the people responsible for some of the most amazing music he had ever heard, were the Gods themselves.

"I didn't believe for one moment that these people were Gods. They were just people who were better at social engineering than me, and had better computer skills than I had," he blustered, going on to tell me that for the first time he not only thought that he was going to get out of there alive, but that he felt he could "make a few quid" out of the situation. So he struck while his figurative iron was hot. By rights he should have been buried in a shallow grave deep in the woods with a bullet in the back of his head. But he had turned the tables on his captors through his own extreme cleverness, and it was Danny that was now calling the shots.

"I want to meet one of the Gods," Danny demanded, and by this time poor Skullfuck was so confused that he was regarding Danny as a cross between Brian Epstein and that irritating bloke with the smug smile on *Pop Idol*, and nodded his consent. Motioning to the two pig headed children with guns that they were no longer needed, he escorted Danny deep into the woods where a small log cabin had been built. "Come In!" thundered a voice from inside, and Danny went in.

"And you are not going to fucking believe this, man," he said. "In that cabin deep in the woods was a man in a wheelchair. He was wearing a neat and obviously expensive dark grey suit. And wait for this......he had the head of a fucking elephant on his shoulders!"

IX

An Elephant???"

I looked at him feigning shock and awe (if I can borrow a term). In fact I was nowhere near as overawed as I had pretended, because I had already got quite emotionally involved with a strange lost little goat person from (presumably) those very same woods, and if those woods could produce Panne, the idea of a half man, half elephant in a wheelchair was no real paradigm shift.

I have never been a very convincing liar, and I am a terrible actor, so instead of carrying on pretending to be shocked and awed, I lit yet another cigarette, made a mental note to light a candle to St Bernardino of Siena [1] who is not only the Patron Saint of lung problems, but looks - in a painting by Jacopo Bellini [2] from about 1450 - more than a little like Andy, the current lead guitarist with *The Pink Fairies* who is a vague chum of mine, and asked:

"So what did you do then?"

"Give me one of those fucking things.." he gestured towards my rapidly depleting pack of B&H.

Now I was shocked. I have known Danny for about a third of a century. Not only have I never seen him smoke, but he has always been vehemently annoying in his opposition to the habit.

I passed him a cigarette, lit it for him, and whilst he coughed and spluttered, I made encouraging noises and tried to get him to continue with his story.

"The elephantman looked at me for what seemed like hours, but was probably less than a minute, and asked 'Give me one good reason why I should not kill you immediately?'"

---

1. Saint Bernardino of Siena, O.F.M. (also known as Bernardine; 8 September 1380 – 20 May 1444) was an Italian priest, Franciscan missionary, and is a Catholic saint. He is known in the Roman Catholic Church as "the Apostle of Italy" for his efforts to revive the country's Catholic faith during the 15th century. His preaching was frequently directed against gambling, witchcraft, sodomy and usury - particularly as practiced by Jews.

2. Jacopo Bellini (c. 1400 – c. 1470) was an Italian painter. Jacopo was one of the founders of the Renaissance style of painting in Venice and northern Italy. His sons Gentile and Giovanni Bellini, and his son-in-law Andrea Mantegna, were also famous painters.

3. Pink Fairies are an English rock band initially active in the London (Ladbroke Grove) underground and psychedelic scene of the early 1970s. They promoted free music, drug taking and anarchy and often performed impromptu gigs and other agitprop stunts, such as playing for free outside the gates at the Bath and Isle of Wight pop festivals in 1970, as well as appearing at Phun City, the first Glastonbury and many other free festivals including Windsor and Trent-ishoe.

He dragged on the cigarette, which despite everything seemed to be calming him down, and continued…

"Well, although I am sure that he knew perfectly well what I had really wanted from the two girls, I couldn't really admit that, so I told him that I was a music journalist who was incredibly impressed by the music that the two girls had played me, and wanted to know more"….

This seemed to have been the right answer. At least, the bestial elephantman had not smote him down immediately, so sensing his tactical advantage, Danny gabbled on. He was involved with a community record company which was being set up, he lied, and both with that and with his unique relationship with the editor of Britain's leading weekly music e-zine he wanted to get involved and help bring this remarkable music to a wider audience than it had at the moment.

As the audience to which he was referring was presently about thirty runaway teenage and preteen cultists living in surprisingly Spartan conditions in the middle of the woods, this quest would not be a difficult one to fulfil.

Both his "involvement with a community record company which was being set up" and his "unique relationship with the editor of Britain's leading weekly music e-zine" were of course down to the fact that he had known me, and been an on-off thorn in my side for over thirty years.

"But we are nowhere near being Britain's leading weekly music e-zine", I blustered, but for once Danny seemed sure of his facts.

"Back in February the BBC quoted: 'The NME website gets 1.4m users per week, while the digital edition of the magazine sells 1,307 copies a week, and thousands of people attend NME live events and concert tours'." He said proudly, and looked me in the eye with the face of someone who is particularly proud of his own cleverness.

"Well yeah, we do get more readers than that most weeks", I admitted, "but you are nothing at all to do with the magazine, and while I am editor you won't be…"

"Details, details" he spluttered, and continued with his story…

"For some reason the elephant man whose name was – by the way – Mr Loxodonta – seemed quite impressed by all this bullshit of mine, and I began to think that I might be able to get away with it all, and live to fight another day".

One of Danny's most annoying characteristics has always been to talk in clichés, but I let him get away with it, as he continued his story.

"So I bullshitted like I have never bullshitted before" he said proudly, "and you know how I can bullshit!" He looked at me as if this was an accomplishment of which he should be justly proud. In my opinion it probably isn't, but I smiled wanly at him and nodded for him to continue...

"So I told Mr Loxodonta that what he needed was a Business Plan, and how he needed to market his cult for all that it was worth"

This was probably true. Cult leader Charles Manson has been in prison since 1969, but his records are still remarkably popular despite the fact that they are bloody awful and that the only USP that they have is that they sound mildly disturbing only because of what and who he is.

Danny continued:

"I gave him all sorts of ideas, and promised to come up with a cogent business plan and some ideas for how to market this stuff. It helps, I think, that unlike most music made by cults and cultists, this music is really pretty damn good"

I nodded, actually truthfully being able to agree with him for once. The music truly is pretty damn good.

"He asked me if I would like to be their publicity officer. I didn't answer but thought really hard. Then I remembered your mate Mick Farren [1] who died last year. He was the head honcho of the UK White Panthers, so I decided to steal one of his ideas.

'No man", I told him. ' I want to be your Minister for Information'".

Apparently this struck some kind of chord with Mr Loxodonta who nodded as enthusiastically as a half man half elephant sat in a wheelchair can do. It seems that on the numerous occasions in the past thirty years that Danny has stayed in my spare room or wherever has doubled as my ever-growing personal library has borne fruit...for him at least. Because I am a ridiculously voracious bibliophile, some would say packrat, and despite regular pruning and weeding sessions I still have over 5000 books on a variety of subjects including Forteana, magick (of various hues), politics (also of various hues), music and animals.

It turned out that over the years Danny had read a lot of these books, and had cherrypicked

---

1. Michael Anthony 'Mick' Farren (3 September 1943 - 27 July 2013) was an English journalist, author and singer associated with counterculture and the UK Underground. Farren was the singer with the proto-punk band The Deviants between 1967 and 1969, releasing three albums. Over the next thirty years he put out a sporadic list of records and books. During the early 1970s he contributed to the UK Underground press such as the International Times, also establishing Nasty Tales which he successfully defended from an obscenity charge. Farren organised the Phun City Festival in 1970. He has long been associated with the Hells Angels (UK) who provided security at Phun City; they even awarded Farren an "approval patch" in 1970 for use on his first solo album Mona. He was a prominent activist in the White Panthers UK movement, a group that most notably organised free food and other support services for free festivals from the Windsor Free Festival onwards. I met him first about two months before he died and we were well on our way to becoming friends.

information that he was now regurgitating to Mr Loxodonta like a mother pigeon feeding her offspring.

Thinking completely off the cuff in a stream of consiousnesss way that I have to admit that I grudgingly respected, he took the idea of regular 'Communiques' delivered anonymously to various media outlets from The Angry Brigade (an anarchist group active in London during the mid-1970s), the idea of Art Terrorism from The Situationist Movement (with a hint of Banksy), more odds and ends from Mick Farren and the leader of the American White Panthers John Sinclair, and then wrapped the whole thing into a business model based on Damon Albarn and Jamie Hewlett's conceptual band *The Gorillaz*..

"Their records are fucking great man, but they are cartoon characters and everyone knows that. What if you had progressive hip hop – I'm not gonna call it fucking 'Urban' cos its not fucking 'Urban' – made by actual double A class fucking Gods! Gods that have real powers and should scare you shitless! Gods that can smite you to dust! Can you think of a better fucking incentive to buy their record?"

I have to admit, that much though I abhor his method of speech, and the way that he said 'Fuck' more and more often as he became more excited, and the fact that all the best bits of this were things that I should have come up with myself years ago, he had a point.

Then it seemed things really started to happen. Mr Loxodonta made it known that he was in favour of these plans and that he wanted Danny to go away and think about these suggestions and come back with some cogent plans. He was given a telephone number to ring next time he wanted to get in touch, the bin bag was put over his head (gently this time) and he was (also gently) put back into the trunk of his car and driven back to a layby a few hundred yards from the A39.

It was the huge and (if you didn't know that he was actually a pussy cat – I knew him back when he was called Jeremy, and I wondered whether he still collected stamps) terrifying figure of Skullfuck, who lifted him out of the boot of his car, dusted him down and helped him into the driver's seat. "You've been lucky today" he said, and strode back into the forest as Danny took a deep breath and continued his journey back up the A39 towards the link road, the M5 and his long-time boyfriend Basil in the Somerset Levels.

X

The following story was printed in the Christmas issue of _The Gonzo Weekly_ to accompany the surprise release of a seasonal EP called _Winter_. Look on iTunes for the record and on YouTube for the video.

The tired, shrivelled husk of a man sat at his computer staring blankly into the screen waiting for inspiration to arrive when the message flashed up.
If Xtul is just a story it is a very good one.
If Xtul is for real it is the end of life as we know it.

There was a clickable link, so the man clicked it. A strange dirge-like song in 5/4 time started to play through his computer speakers and an unearthly, horrible voice sang:

The only gods you seem to want AROUND
are the ones YOU THINK ARE
GONNA make your WRETCHED LIFE SEEM better
there is no room in your psyche for a
BONA FIDE Old Testament type psychotic blood letter

you didn't know YOU were doing it
but YOU still created us in your own image
and you ended up with something that
you never will be able quite to envisage

Soon he became bored and switched the music off, and resumed his search for internet pornography.

Meanwhile in a small village in North Devon a musician who calls himself *4th Eden* was preparing to go to bed. Much to his surprise there was a knock at the door. He answered it and two young female children wearing dungarees and pig masks and brandishing knives burst into his front room.

Behind them was a tall, voluptuous woman wearing a silver catsuit. She appeared to have a grinning rictus skull instead of a head.

While the two children grabbed him, the tall woman approached him and thrust a key drive into his hand. "Make a Master Recording of this!" she ordered. *4th Eden* whose real name is Martin told me afterwards that despite the undoubted horror of the situation, it all made a strange kind of sense to him, so he fired up his laptop and spent the next four hours tweaking, and polishing the eldritch music that he found on it.

As the first rays of dawn lit up the winter sky, he finished his task, gave the wav file back to the tall woman who nodded her thanks and then, together with the two young girls left the room. Martin was completely dazed, and spent the next few hours sat in his favourite armchair afraid to go to sleep.

Later that day I was sitting in my study working on the latest issue of *The Gonzo Weekly* when Danny Miles sheepishly walked in. He handed me a key drive and explained that - at last - *Xtul* were ready to release their first proper single.

Earlier in the year they had released a two track single - *The Song of Pan* backed with a hastily cobbled together remix called *A Cry in the Darkness* which I had cobbled together in my home studio. Later in the early summer another song called *Mr Loxodonta* was leaked onto YouTube, but now it seems that the three Woodland Deities and their frightening coterie of genius level runaway schoolkids had decided that it was time to put out a proper single.

The key drive contained master copies and videos for two songs. Danny explained to me how Discordia, the self-proclaimed Goddess of Chaos had paid a visit to my mate Martin in what Frank Sinatra called 'The Wee Small Hours' and forced him at knifepoint to master the single.

I was furious. Martin is a mate of mine and I said as much to Danny.

"Yes, we know" he said. "That's why they went to him".

I found this whole concept monumentally chilling. Were none of my friends and family safe any more from these bloody lunatics? Apparently not. Even Danny was beginning to have a hunted feral look about him. It seemed that mere humans did not benefit from prolonged exposure to these psychopathic creatures, whatever, or whoever they would eventually turn out to be.

Danny told me that *Xtul* wanted me to put together "a zip file of goodies" that could be downloaded from the *Xtul* website during the week leading up to the Winter Solstice.

I agreed to put it together on the proviso that none of my other friends or loved ones would ever again have nocturnal visitations from knife wielding psychotics.

I put together a pdf of all the stories that I had written about the *Xtul* story to date, and also added the three tracks that had previously been released by the band as extras, and - basically because I felt that we owed the poor bastard something to give some little recompense for his ordeal of the previous evening - I also included a *4th Eden* track called *A Winter's Dance* which seemed to fit the sonic mood, if not the apocalyptic sentiments of the two new songs from *Xtul*.

I then uploaded them to the *Xtul* website, and sat back to see what would happen. Would anyone bother to listen to them? Would anyone watch the videos on YouTube? But above all a far more important question troubled my dreams that night.

Would there prove to be any substance in these vague apocalyptic threats that these people, or rather these "Things" as the late Ivan T Sanderson would have no doubt described them, had made, and continue to make.

What was going to happen in 2015? Would the whole thing fizzle out, or - in the words of Danny Miles' uncharacteristically slick prose - would this truly be the end of life as we know it?

XI

Oh the universe is a strange place. But you don't need me to tell you that I am sure. I have been telling you the story of my totally unexpected relationship with a band called *Xtul*, and their Minister for Information, Danny Miles, whom I have known for over thirty years and have done my best to ignore for most of that time. However, because my time is limited, and my space within the various places that I have been telling this story is even more so, I had only got as far as the second week in September when we got close to the end of the year, and the band broke silence and released a particularly scabrous slice of undanceable sound collage, and labelled it their Christmas single. So I had to write about that, and then we came to the big Christmas double issue, and so I had no time to write any more, and we are still stuck back in mid-September, with a story to tell that I had planned to get done and dusted before Christmas.

But that's the way the world is, and so I am left here, as the rest of the Kingdom is dealing with a surfeit of mince pies, trying to pick up the pieces of the narrative. I am not going to backpedal and tell the story again, because the previous episodes are all readable on the band's website, and I am just going to try and pick up where I left off....

Apparently Danny returned to the forest about a week later. As he drove along the A39 towards the Cornish border he telephoned the number he had been given. Skullfuck answered, and Danny explained who he was and what he wanted. "It was all so bloody normal" he complained. "It was like telephoning your bank manager to make an appointment, back in the days when you actually *had* a bank manager, and not a load of energetic young people in bright yellow T Shirts bouncing all over the place, trying to sell you mortgages and life insurance". But nothing could make it that normal, because nothing could take away the fact that he was on the telephone to a feral biker with an obscene name, and the person with whom he was trying to make an appointment was a wheelchair bound half-man half-elephant chimera surrounded by psychotic children with machine guns and pig masks. Even Nat West [1] hasn't changed to that degree.

He drove down the little lane that led off the main road towards the hamlet of Meddon [2], and once again he was stopped by armed girls wearing pig masks. But this time he was expecting them, and got into the boot of his own car voluntarily, and made no attempt to struggle against his captors.

Again, after a relatively short journey, they arrived at their destination. Skullfuck was there to help him out of his confinement, and he ushered him along the path through the forest to the army surplus pavilion where Mr Loxodonta (for that is the name given by the elephant-headed cripple) seemed to spend his time. This time around Danny managed to take in more of his surroundings. The green canvas walls were draped with a mixture of cheap looking oriental and Indian tat which Danny described as the sort of stuff that you could pick up "for a couple of bob" on market stalls. Loxodonta didn't invite him further into the tent, which appeared from the outside to be the size of a marquee, and with a number of other rooms, that Danny couldn't see.

Mr Loxodonta was obviously waiting for him, and with a politely old-fashioned gesture he motioned to Danny to sit down in a canvas backed director's chair facing him.

By the way, just in case you don't already know what Loxodonta means, African elephants are elephants of the genus Loxodonta (from the Greek words loxo (oblique sided) and donta (tooth). The genus consists of two extant species: the African bush elephant and the smaller

---

1. National Westminster Bank Plc, commonly known as NatWest, is the largest retail and commercial bank in the United Kingdom. Since 2000 it has been part of The Royal Bank of Scotland Group, ranked among the top 10 largest banks in the world by assets. NatWest was established in 1968 by the merger of National Provincial Bank (established 1833 as National Provincial Bank of England) and Westminster Bank (established 1834 as London County and Westminster Bank). Traditionally considered one of the Big Four clearing banks, it has a large network of 1,600 branches and 3,400 cash machines across Great Britain and offers 24-hour Actionline telephone and online banking services. Today it has more than 7.5 million personal customers and 850,000 small business accounts. In Ireland it operates through its Ulster Bank subsidiary.

2. The village of Meddon is located about 1 mile from the border between Devon and Cornwall, and is 1 mile inland off the A39 Atlantic Highway, at Welcombe Cross, between Bideford and Bude. The Village Hall is a converted school house, originally constructed in 1906. The original conversion to a village hall took place soon after the school closed in 1946 and it was upgraded, with additions to the main structure in 2001. The structure is of stone under slate roof with wooden beams and timber-framed windows. The building is single-storey and has a licenced capacity of 100 for dancing (utilising seating at tables) and 60 for close-seated audience.

African forest elephant. Loxodonta is one of two existing genera of the family, Elephantidae. Fossil remains of Loxodonta have been found only in Africa, in strata as old as the middle Pliocene. Mr Loxodonta has been known to claim the Given Name of Eliphas, and as the other genus of elephants is Elephas, that seems to make some sort of twisted sense, but - of course - there is a long tradition of the use of that name within magical circles, including Eliphas Levi, and at least one major character in the Harry Potter universe [1].

"What have you got for me?" Asked Mr Loxodonta gravely, and Danny gave what he described as a totally "fuck off presentation with graphs, and projections and all that shit" which appeared to please the probiscodean cripple, who asked a number of questions, before telling Danny that not only was he now the Minister for Information, but that he was on the payroll, and that he wasn't going to kill him "just yet".

I asked what he meant about a payroll, and Danny explained that as he was leaving with his first bundle of objectives (which mostly seemed to be about convincing me that *Xtul* were viable musicians, and to get them regular mentions in the magazine which I edit, something that we all know that he achieved without too much difficulty) Skullfuck gave him an ATM card which seemed to have access to potentially unlimited funds. "but how much can I take out?" He asked. Skullfuck shrugged back. "As much as you need".

Danny was confused. "Who decides how much I need?" He questioned. "You do," came the answer.

"But what if I take too much?" He stuttered, and was not truly surprised by the answer that if he did, his new elephantine master would send his girls after him, and that they would kill him.

"Oh dear," said Danny.

All this had taken place in the late spring and through the long and surprisingly warm summer of 2014 Danny had gone back to the woodland camp every few weeks, whilst simultaneously setting up, with the help of two of Mr Loxodonta's hacker girls, a sophisticated online presence that he refused to describe to me in any more detail. "It's more than either your or my life is worth, man.... And anyway you don't need to know".

Despite having been to the woods over half a dozen times, the people the Children of the Three still treated him with a certain amount of suspicion. The way he described it, Skullfuck

---

1. Elphias Doge (born c. 1881) was a wizard, a Ministry of Magic jurist, a member of the Order of the Phoenix in both the First and Second Wizarding Wars, and also a close friend of Albus Dumbledore. In the summer of 1995, Doge was part of the Advance Guard, in which he met Harry Potter. After Dumbledore's death in June, 1997, Mr. Doge wrote him an obituary for the Daily Prophet. Later that same summer, he attended the wedding of Fleur and Bill Weasley at The Burrow, and managed to Disapparate from there seconds before the Attack at the Burrow that ensued when Death Eaters arrived after the fall of the Ministry.

was firmly in charge of the humans there, and was the only male human that he had met. The rest were all girls, and apart from the two that he had met whilst hitchhiking, they all wore pig masks. He was now aware that the first two had been just a sophisticated honey trap, although he had no idea how they could possibly have known that he was going to be driving along the A39 that spring day when it was a last minute decision on his part, and he didn't know himself until he did it.

"But you keep on calling them 'The Children of the Three"....who are the three?" I asked. I was pretty sure I knew who two of them were, but I wanted to hear it from the horse's mouth, with Danny being the horse.

He confirmed my suspicions.

"I've told you all that I know about Mr Loxdonta...." (Actually, he hadn't, but I didn't know that at that point) "....and you met Panne the first night I came to see you.

But the third one is a mystery. I occasionally caught glimpses of a tall woman in a silver suit, but always out of the corner of my eye, and only for a split second. And it was always terrifying. As Skullfuck was the only person who would talk to me I asked him, but he just shrugged and told me that it was none of my business and that I would know soon enough.

Panne let it out by mistake once that all three of them had once been human, although they weren't anything like human anymore, and that brings me to what I wanted to talk to you about. Panne has disappeared!"

And he looked at me accusingly. I stared back guiltily, and summoned up the reserves of skill that I had learned back during the 1970s when I became quite good at lying to my headmaster at Bideford Grammar School. "How the hell should I know?" I lied through my teeth, not for a moment thinking that a consummate con man like Danny could be fooled by a mere amateur like me. Amazingly he was....

"Well, according to Skullfuck the only time she had ever left the compound was the time that she came here with me..." But I could see that he was beginning to doubt himself. Danny has always had such a high opinion of his own importance - after all, he had been personally chosen by deities to do their dirty work for them - that he couldn't imagine that any of this Unholy Trinity would ever want to visit someone as ordinary as me for any reason imaginable. The idea that the little forest Godling came to see me for chocolate, and maybe a little affection, was completely beyond his comprehension.

They say that it is impossible to cheat an honest man, and so as Danny is one of the least honest men that I have ever met, pulling the wool over his eyes was a reasonably straightforward task.

About five minutes later, after cadging a final cigarette from me, he left after exacting a promise from me that I would contact him if Panne actually turned up at the CFZ. Completely mendaciously I agreed, determining quietly to myself that I would do no such thing.

Just as I heard the resonating clang of him tossing the gate shut behind him, I heard a rustling sound from a cupboard beneath one of my fish tanks; a cupboard far too small to hold anything apart from a couple of boxes of aquarium paraphernalia. I knew exactly what it was, and called out, "It's OK, he's gone", and the slight figure of Panne emerged from a tiny space that could not possibly have held her.

She looked at me in silence, and I passed her the last of my wife's chocolate.

XII

Corinna and I were still in bed at about 8:30 on Monday morning when the telephone rang. It was my younger stepdaughter Olivia who had just gone into labour. We leapt out of bed, rousted Mother out of the library where she has been living for the past year or so, and grabbed our bags. The news was hardly unexpected; what I believe is called her 'due date' had been on the previous day, so our bags were packed and we were literally ready to leave at a few minutes notice. Our old Vauxhall Astra which we had bought for seven hundred quid at the beginning of the year was ok for trundling around the lanes of North Devon in, but we didn't like the idea o trusting it to a journey of something in excess of 800 miles, so we had booked a hire car for the week, and were able to travel up to Norwich in relative comfort.

We shouted to Graham, telling him to look after the animals, and left the house in a rush. This was to be our first Grandchild, and I was terrified. I think that Corinna was not far off it, and I have no idea what mental state poor Olivia was in. So it was not the most pleasant drive that I have ever undertaken, and the fact that I couldn't smoke in the car, and that we were too much in a hurry to get to our destination to be able to indulge in the luxury of pitstops that weren't absolutely necessary, made it even less enjoyable.

I cannot remember who it was that said that a little knowledge is a dangerous thing, but I was a nurse about thirty years ago. I wasn't even a proper nurse, but one who specialised in the care of what were then called the Mentally Handicapped, and so the only thing that I knew about obstetrics was what happened when things went horribly wrong. Even then my knowledge was thirty years out of date and half forgotten. Being prone to paranoia I was fearing the worst, and had managed to work myself up into what my dear, late, mother would no doubt have described as a 'right tizzy'. However, knowing that Corinna was likely to be in a worse one (Olivia and her unborn baby being flesh of her flesh, after all), I kept schtum, and as always when I keep schtum I need something to distract me and stop me going stark staring mad.

I had my iPad with me. I have always been slightly scathing of the sort of people who are always accompanied by their trusty tablet computer, but since getting an iPad free with

Corinna's new phone last summer, I am embarrassed to say that I have become one of those people, and so - to keep my mind off the horrors which I had convinced myself were waiting for us - I played continual games of Tetris, and that other game when you have to match up brightly coloured jewels. But then, a considerable way up the M5, at Michael Wood services just north of Bristol, something peculiar started to happen.

I had actually forgotten all about Panne in our haste to leave. After all (s)he was just another of the shades and phantasms who inhabit my little slice of Gramarye [1], and I have lived with them on and off since I was eleven, and before that I lived in Hong Kong, which may be commonly seen as the biggest outpouring of unbridled capitalism outside Las Vegas, but when I was a child was still the land of living ghosts and fox fairies, and as far as I know still is. OK Panne is the only one of my spectral co-inhabitants to eat chocolate (as far as I am aware) but (s)he seems harmless enough, and - as far as you can trust a hairy forest Godling to do anything - I trusted Panne not to do anything untoward or destructive. However, Panne was the only member of the other-realm to ever come to me for help, even in such an abstract way as (s)he did, and I felt mildly guilty at having left her alone without saying goodbye.

I have a set of runes on my iPad. I was taught about runecraft by a very wise woman many years ago, and so, as we drove up north of Bristol on the M5 I did a little runeworking in my head to apologise to Panne for having left her in the lurch, then the overwhelming worry of the day came back to the front of my consciousness, and I quickly forgot about the little Godling.

However, when we pulled into the Michael Wood services something very peculiar happened. I have been interested in British butterflies since the mid 1960s, and I have seen most species. However, I have never seen a brown hairstreak (*Thecla betulae*) . This is one of the last of the British butterflies to emerge, being on the wing in July, August and early September. This is the largest hairstreak found in the British Isles. It is a local species that lives in self-contained colonies that breed in the same area year after year. This species can also prove elusive, since it spends much of its time resting and basking high up in tall shrubs and trees. The female is particularly beautiful, with forewings that contain large orange patches, and was once considered to be a separate species known as the "Golden Hairstreak".

This species is found in the southern half of England and Wales, and also around the Burren in Ireland. In England its strongholds are in West Sussex, Surrey, Oxfordshire, Buckinghamshire, North Devon and South Devon. Strongholds in Wales are in

---

1. It is actually the same word as grammar and grimoire, Middle English *gramarye, gramarie*, modification of Middle French *gramaire* grammar, grammar book, book of sorcery, but I use it after T.H.White who named his fictionalised Brtain thus in *The Once and Future King,* an Arthurian fantasy novel first published in 1958, and mostly a composite of earlier works written between 1938 and 1941. The central theme is an exploration of human nature regarding power and justice, as the boy Arthur becomes king and attempts to quell the prevalent "might makes right" attitude with his idea of chivalry. But in the end, even chivalry comes undone since its justice is maintained by force.

Cardiganshire and Carmarthenshire. In Ireland it is primarily found in the Burren limestones of Clare and South-east Galway. The northernmost sites are found in North Lincolnshire.

As far as I have been able to ascertain there are no known colonies in Gloucestershire. Also, for the species to still be on the wing in the middle of September would be extraordinarily unlikely, even with the deviant weather patterns which global warming has thrust upon us. But there, fluttering about a flowering bush by the edge if the car park at Michael Wood services was a pristine male specimen of *Thecla betulae.* [1] I emailed a brief account of it to Adrian at the Bug Alert website, although privately I would not have been surprised if no-one apart from Mother and I had seen it. Mother has the innocence that comes with advanced age, and I was pretty well convinced that our encounter with this pretty little forest butterfly was nothing more than a gift and a message from a pretty little Forest Godling to let me know that (s)he quite understood why I had gone away without letting him/her know, and that (s)he would keep a beneficent eye on the dogs, cats, birds and other animals who share my, Corinna's, Mother's (and now Panne's) abode.

Uplifted though I was, I could not shake off my inherent paranoia that something horrible was about to happen. And the further we got away from home the stronger these feelings became. It was almost as if we were all under Panne's protection, but that the geographical area of that protection was limited. Of course, part of this was that the further we carried on driving, the longer Olivia had been in labour, and the nearer to the moment of truth we were getting. And weird things were beginning to happen as well.

As far as I had been aware, *Xtul* consisted of three beings of indeterminate origin living with a coterie of young followers, and a retired biker in an isolated stretch of woodland on the North Devon/Cornwall border. And as far as I was aware, the only conduits that *Xtul* had with the outside world were me and that insufferable arse Danny Miles. So, how then was the band's name, and - more chillingly - slogans associated with them spraypainted on

---

1, The Latin name of this butterfly seems to have been named after an apocryphal saint. Her story reminded me of that of Panne as I slowly began to unravel it. Thecla or Tecla (Ancient Greek: Θέκλα, *Thékla*) was a saint of the early Christian Church, and a reported follower of Paul the Apostle. The earliest record of her life comes from the ancient-apocryphal *Acts of Paul and Thecla*. According to the Acts of Paul and Thecla, Thecla was a young noble virgin who listened to Paul's "discourse on virginity" and became Paul's follower and a Disciple of Paul's teachings and Ministry. Thecla's mother and her fiancé Thamyris became concerned Thecla would follow Paul's demand "one must fear only one God and live in chastity", and punished both Paul and Thecla.

Thecla was miraculously saved from burning at the stake by the onset of a storm and traveled with Paul to Antioch of Pisidia. There a nobleman named Alexander desired Thecla and attempted to take her by force. Thecla fought him off, assaulting him in the process, and was put on trial for assaulting a nobleman. She was sentenced to be eaten by wild beasts, but was again saved by a series of miracles when the female beasts protected her against her male aggressors. Thecla gained a massive "cult-like" following, and became perhaps the most prominent figure for female empowerment at the time. She listened to Paul's teachings to fear nobody but God, and live in chastity. She demonstrates these teachings on several occasions starting from the first time she heard Paul speak by leaving Thamyris, fighting off Alexander, and surviving several life threatening situations. She traveled to preach the word of God and became an icon encouraging women to also live a life of chastity and follow the word of the Lord. *Thekla* was also a boat owned by the late Viv Stanshall who had my friend the equally late Jane Bradley stay there on a number of occasions.

various of the concrete bridges traversing the M5, the M42 and the M6. Slogans like "Black Flags Rising" which I knew was the name they had chosen for their debut album (some of which I had even mixed) when it finally came out. because Mother is well into her mid eighties we had to stop off more often than we probably would have done otherwise, and every time we stopped off at a Motorway Services and I was suddenly within range of WiFi coverage again, than I began to get some disjointed and rather unpleasant IMs through on my iPad.

These were particularly disturbing because I didn't believe that they were coming from Danny Miles.

After out heart to heart about ten days before he had explained to me in fairly precise detail how he had fed Mr Loxodonta with a complex farrago of bits and bobs of Charles Manson, John Sinclair and the Process Church of the Final Judgement [1] in order to come up with a disparate mishmash of pseudopsychic psychobabble that would sound impressive, but which actually signified absolutely nothing.

---

1. All of whom have been explained in some depth in earlier footnotes, however it might make a little bit of sense at this stage if you take some time out to read John Higgs' book about the KLF and the *Illuminatus Trilogy* by Robert Anton Wilson and Robert Shea, but that is only advice. It is completely up to you.

Then the messages started to come through even when we were on the road and apparently not within range of any wifi network whatsoever. "No Sense Makes Sense" said one oft repeated message, "From the world of darkness I did loose demons and devils in the power of scorpions to torment" read another. "Pain's not bad, it's good. It teaches you things. I understand that", and over and over again "dying is easy". I knew that these were all quotes from Charlie Manson, but who was sending them to me and why.

About half way between Coventry and the end of the M6 there is a motorway services whose name I can never remember, and as soon as we pulled in, I made a mumbled excuse and disappeared in search of a telephone box. I telephoned Danny, and as soon as he answered, screamed down the phone at him: "What the fuck do you think you are doing to me you arsehole! My stepdaughter is about to have a baby, and your tomfoolery is the last thing that I need!!

Danny sounded shocked, and asked me what I was talking about in a very plausible manner. i told him about the messages that I was receiving every few minutes on my iPad, and the slogans that were appearing with ever increasing frequency on the concrete motorway bridges that we drive beneath.

There was a stunned silence on the other end of the line. "C'mon Danny. Fucking say something. What the fuck is going on?" I asked. There was a nudge in my ribs. I turned round to see a middle aged Matron in a Salvation Army uniform staring at me and prodding me below my ribcage. "Is there any need for language like that?"

I looked back at her blankly. "Yes, madam, I think that there probably is," I said.

XIII

I would like to pretend that I am some sort of iconoclastic smash the system type of dude, but - truly - I am nothing of the sort.

No matter how hard I try, how scruffy I get, or how long I grow my hair, I am still a respectable English gentleman of the old school, which is exactly why I spoke to the woman from the Salvation Army in the way I did. I like to think that my breeding and savoir faire showed through at that moment, because just as she had spoken to me, I was looking around vacantly and I saw the message "Xtul Lives, Xtul Rules, doesn't in Jon?" scrawled surprisingly neatly in violet magic marker above the telephone.

Admittedly all sorts of people knew that we were travelling to Norfolk that day; I had put it on the CFZ blog, for example. But nobody outside the three of us in the hire car knew that we were going to be stopping off at that particular Motorway Services. And nobody apart from me, and possibly my ex-wife, knew that the blurb on the back of the 1980s paperback edition of *Foundation's Edge* [1] by Isaac Asimov had always irritated me. It was an over the top screed which had no real emotional empathy with the story. It started "Foundation Lives, Foundation Rules!" After all these years even typing it out for the purposes of this narrative is mildly irritating.

However, I was not about to try and explain all this to a late middle-aged lady God Botherer [2], so I apologised again, muttered something about being stressed because my stepdaughter was in labour and went outside for a cigarette. When I came back in I had a mild diabetic moment, exacerbated by the huge amounts of Diet Coke that I always seem to imbibe during long car journeys. So I went into the disabled loo, and there written on the door was a very similar message. I was beginning to get seriously spooked.

We ate an expensive and relatively unappetising snacky thing and resumed our journey down the M6 towards East Anglia. And on nearly every bridge was spray-painted an easily recognisable four letter word beginning with X.

This is the point in the story where most authors would probably say that they were beginning to doubt their own sanity, but I have never been under the misapprehension that I am even slightly sane. I have been diagnosed bipolar for over twenty years, and about ten years ago I was told by a consultant that I had a schizoaffective disorder and was only a couple of inches away from Paranoid Schizophrenia as well, and so, although I was not going to be so stupid and vainglorious as to doubt my own sanity, I was beginning to doubt the evidence of my own eyes.

Did these messages have any objective reality? Or were they just messages from my subconscious telling me a whole slew of things about which I was only too painfully aware; that I was in over my head in a peculiar situation mostly not of my own making, and that my understanding of the affair, and about everything that had happened, was completely

1. *Foundation's Edge* (1982) is a science fiction novel by Isaac Asimov, the fourth book in the Foundation Series. It was written more than thirty years after the stories of the original Foundation trilogy, due to years of pressure by fans and editors on Asimov to write another, and, according to Asimov himself, the amount of the payment offered by the publisher.

The premise of the series is that the mathematician Hari Seldon spent his life developing a branch of mathematics known as psychohistory, a concept of mathematical sociology.

Using the laws of mass action, it can predict the future, but only on a large scale. Seldon foresees the imminent fall of the Galactic Empire, which encompasses the entire Milky Way, and a dark age lasting 30,000 years before a second great empire arises. Seldon also foresees an alternative where the interregnum will last only one thousand years. To ensure the more favorable outcome, Seldon creates a foundation of talented artisans and engineers at the extreme end of the galaxy, to preserve and expand on humanity's collective knowledge, and thus become the foundation for a new galactic empire.

It might amuse you that the English translation of *Al Quaeda* is 'The Foundation'.

2. I have always wondered whether God Botherers are people who bother the Almighty with continuous requests, or bother their peers with religious talk. Or possibly both.

overshadowed by the stress that I felt knowing that the young woman I love very much indeed was about to give birth to my first granddaughter.

I like travelogues, and I have written quite a few of them of my own over the years, but although I would love to do a *Heart of Darkness* to you at this point, it is quite beyond my skills as a wordsmith to extract Conradesque prose from an account of a journey from the end of the M6, up to Peterborough, and up to Norwich. I have always loved the English countryside and have been carrying on a love affair with it since I was a small boy, but motorways are motorways, and A roads are A roads, and although often Corinna and I enliven long journeys by making a list of bird species seen, or playing silly word games, this occasion was too solemn to be enlivened in such a manner, and so we travelled on in silence, ignoring the autumn countryside, each lost in our own thoughts.

We got the occasional text message from Olivia's elder sister Shoshannah, who lives in Staffordshire, and had therefore several hours start on us. By the time we were skirting the manifestly unattractive town of Corby, famous for being home to my ex-publisher, and hometown to King Boy D [2], she was already driving hell for leather through the outskirts of Norwich on her way to the hospital. Olivia's partner Aaron (who is, by the way not only a bloody good chap but the bass player in a band called *Azolas*, who play heavy metal with skill and gusto) was sending text messages to Shoshannah who passed the content on to us. Olivia's waters broke sometime whilst we were on the A14 and the stress levels in the car rose up another notch or two.

Then there was a tell tale pinging noise from my iPad, and I thanked the Elder Gods of technology that both my darling wife, and darling Mother-in-law didn't know enough about technology to realise that I shouldn't have been able to receive Facebook messages as we were

---

1. *Heart of Darkness* (1899) is a novella by Polish novelist Joseph Conrad, about a voyage up the Congo River into the Congo Free State, in the heart of Africa, by the story's narrator Marlow. Marlow tells his story to friends aboard a boat anchored on the River Thames, London, England. This setting provides the frame for Marlow's story of his obsession with the ivory trader Kurtz, which enables Conrad to create a parallel between London and Africa as places of darkness.

Central to Conrad's work is the idea that there is little difference between so-called civilized people and those described as savages; Heart of Darkness raises important questions about imperialism and racism.

Originally published as a three-part serial story in Blackwood's Magazine, the novella *Heart of Darkness* has been variously published and translated into many languages. In 1998, the Modern Library ranked *Heart of Darkness* as the sixty-seventh of the hundred best novels in English of the twentieth century.

The most famous adaptation is Francis Ford Coppola's 1979 motion picture *Apocalypse Now*, which moves the story from the Congo to Vietnam and Cambodia during the Vietnam War.

2. William Ernest "Bill" Drummond (born 29 April 1953) is a South African-born Scottish artist, musician, writer, and record producer. He was the co-founder of late 1980s avant-garde pop groupThe KLF and its 1990s media-manipulating successor, the K Foundation, with which he burned a million pounds in 1994. More recent art activities, carried out under Drummond's chosen banner of the Penkiln Burn, include making and distributing cakes, soup, flowers, beds and shoe-shines. More recent music projects include No Music Day, and the international tour of a choir called The17. Drummond is the author of several books about art and music.

speeding along a trunk road deep into the heart of East Anglia. Feigning a nonchalance that I didn't feel, I picked up the tablet, pushed in the button thingy at the bottom, and opened Facebook. The message was from someone called Lynette, and it was simple. "Look out of the window" it read. I did so, and then saw, stencilled in spraypaint on the side of a wooden barn, the *Xtul* logo in perfect Abbadon ttf font.

Then the came another message from the same source:

"...this time Helter Skelter truly is coming down fast", and I knew exactly what it meant. It was a bowdlerised line in a song by *The Beatles* [1,2], and - depending on who you believe - it was either a complex conspiracy scenario invented by a man called Vincent Bugliosi [3] with the sole intention of framing an innocent hippie called Charlie for a series of crimes that he didn't commit, or it was something much more intense and frightening.

According to this scenario in later years Charles Manson became inspired by a belief in "Helter Skelter," a term taken from *The Beatles*' song of the same name, which signified an apocalyptic race war he believed would arise between blacks and whites. As well as the music of *The Beatles*, Manson's scenario was also inspired by the New Testament's Book of Revelation. His first known use of the term was at a campfire gathering of the Family on New Year's Eve 1968, at their base at Myers Ranch near California's Death Valley. By February 1969, Helter Skelter had developed into a scenario in which Manson and the Family would

1. "Helter Skelter" is a song written by Paul McCartney, credited to Lennon–McCartney, and recorded by the Beatles on their eponymous LP *The Beatles*, better known as The White Album. A product of McCartney's deliberate effort to create a sound as loud and dirty as possible, the song has been noted for both its "proto-metal roar" and "unique textures" and is considered by music historians as a key influence in the early development of heavy metal. In a special stand-alone issue, *Rolling Stone* ranked "Helter Skelter" fifty-second on its "100 Greatest Beatles songs" list.

2 . Helter skelter
Helter skelter
Helter skelter

Do you, don't you want me to make you?
I'm **coming down fast** but don't let me break you
Tell me, tell me, tell me the answer
You may be a lover but you ain't no dancer

3. Vincent T. Bugliosi, Jr. (August 18, 1934 – June 6, 2015) was an American attorney and New York Times best-selling author. During his eight years in the Los Angeles County district attorney's office, he successfully prosecuted 105 out of 106 felony jury trials, which included 21 murder convictions without a single loss. He was best known for prosecuting Charles Manson and other defendants accused of the seven Tate–LaBianca murders of August 9–10, 1969. Although Manson did not physically participate in the murders at Sharon Tate's home, Bugliosi used circumstantial evidence to show that he had orchestrated the killings.

4. The Book of Revelation, often known simply as Revelation or The Apocalypse, is a book of the New Testament that occupies a central place in Christian eschatology. Its title is derived from the first word of the text, written in Koine Greek: apokalypsis, meaning "unveiling" or "revelation". The Book of Revelation is the only apocalyptic document in the New Testament canon (although there are short apocalyptic passages in various places in the Gospels and the Epistles).

The author names himself in the text as "John", but his precise identity remains a point of academic debate.

create an album which they believed would trigger the conflict and inspire America's white youths to join the Family. He believed that black men, deprived of white women, would commit violent crimes in frustration, resulting in murderous rampages and a swiftly-escalating conflict between racial groups.

According to the scenario which Vincent Bugliosi, who turned 80 a month before we drove to Norfolk, and died as I was beginning to typeset this book, used to convict Manson of a series of crimes led by the Tate/LaBianca murders, these killings were intended by Manson to spearhead a race war that would destroy the vast majority of the human race and leave Charlie and his Family of the Infinite Soul Inc in control of the destiny of humankind.

The political situation in the Middle East had been deteriorating for some years, and by the middle of 2014 vast swathes of the area were under the control of homicidal madmen. The insanity had started to spread to the UK, the US and even Australia, with beheadings, bombings and shootings beginning to happen apparently at random.

The words 'Race War' were beginning to be used by serious political analysts, rather than just angry nutjobs on the fringes of society. I have no idea whether these claims of an imminent conflict between races on the streets of my own country are true or not, but I am afraid. No, I am terrified, that if the culture of fundamentalism, which is currently holding sway across much of the Middle East, does spread in earnest to the UK, and the US (and remember that this was some months before the horrific events in Paris in January 2015) that Helter Skelter would indeed be coming down fast.

Then I realised, with horror, who Lynette was, or at least whom she pretended to be. But what the hell had this got to do with *Xtul*? What the hell did this have to do with the little goatfooted Godling presently residing in the cupboard where I keep my tropical fish equipment, and what the hell did it have to do with me?

I don't think I have ever felt quite so alone in my life. I love my wife and usually I can discuss anything that I want with her, but what sort of bastard would I be to add to the unbelievable amount of tension that I knew was coursing through her veins, with her youngest daughter in the most physically and emotionally vulnerable position that she had ever been since Corinna herself had been in the same position and had given birth to her twenty seven years before?

How could I add to that by telling her that I was beginning to worry that I had become tangentially involved with a death cult who were working to manipulate people's interpretation of events on the world stage to bring about the end of the world as we knew it, oh yes and, "by the way honey, there is a hairy Godling, half girl and half goat, living in my office, and she has been eating your chocolate!"

So I kept my own counsel, prayed quietly for the safe delivery of Olivia's baby, and as the late afternoon sun lazily pierced the branches of the trees on either side of the road, we drove in silence towards Norfolk.

XIV

I was horrified.

By this time every few minutes my iPad would make a bleeping noise and either a piece of vaguely disturbing text, or - worse - a collage consisting of a photograph of one of the latest atrocities in the Middle East with a quote from Charlie Manson plastered on it. This was not very high tech stuff, each collage would only have taken a couple of minutes with Photoshop, but it was undeniably disturbing. And these were the last things that I wanted to look at when I was trying to commune with my maker, and the little hire car sped across the flat lands of East Anglia towards Norwich where my youngest stepdaughter was about to make me a Grandfather.

Like any other person with any knowledge of the world stage, I had been following the events in the Middle East with a feeling of mounting distress. each day in the news we were confronted with stories of the sort of atrocities which one thought had been left behind centuries ago, and that - I for one - never thought that I would see again. Burnings, floggings, mutilations and crucifixions - how on earth could things like this happen in the 21st Century. On top of that how could SOMEONE, (and although all the available evidence pointed towards this being the *Xtul* 'Ministry of Information', I wasn't too sure) defy all the laws of physics, the internet and - let's face it - everything else in order to beam disturbing messages straight to my iPad from across the aether.

And who was going to take quotes from a long incarcerated serial killer, fiddle about with them, and try to tie them in with the current socio-political events in the Middle East? Again, the available evidence pointed to Danny Miles, but why would he? The week before he had spent several hours with me in my study, bumming my cigarettes and drinking my coffee, and I truly believed that what he had told me had basically been the truth. I know that he had a distressing obsession with the life and works of the aforementioned serial killer, and some of this stuff had his metaphorical fingerprints all over it. But why bother? He had already told me of his involvement with this group (whoever or whatever they were), and surely he could not have thought that this stuff was going to impress me.

And surely even for Danny, trying to tie in a semi-mythical progressive hiphop band with the appalling predations of ISIL[1] in the Middle East was beyond the bounds of good taste. Here, however, it should be pointed out that this is probably the first time that anyone has ever used the words Danny Miles and Good Taste in the same sentence. I couldn't believe that even Danny would have bothered to try and pull the psychohistoric[2] wool over my eyes only a week or so after

1. The Islamic State of Iraq and the Levant - abbreviated ISIL or ISIS; Arabic: الدولة الإسلامية في العراق والشام also known as the Islamic State of Iraq and Syria or the Islamic State of Iraq and ash-Sham, or simply Islamic State (IS) - is a Salafi jihadi extremist militant group and self-proclaimed caliphate and Islamic state which is led by Sunni Arabs from Iraq and Syria. As of March 2015, it has control over territory occupied by ten million people in Iraq and Syria, as well as limited territorial control in Libya and Nigeria. The group also operates or has affiliates in other parts of the world including southeast Asia.

2. Psychohistory is the discipline founded by Hari Seldon in the *Foundation* series by Arthur C Clarke,

telling me all that he knew about the cult and their activities.

All the instant messages were signed 'Lynette' and although I had no idea who this 'Lynette' actually was, I had a pretty good idea who she was pretending to be. Over to Wikipedia:

> "Lynette Alice "Squeaky" Fromme (born October 22, 1948) is an American would-be assassin best known for attempting to assassinate U.S. President Gerald Ford in 1975. A member of the infamous "Manson family", she was sentenced to life imprisonment for the attempted assassination and was released on parole on August 14, 2009, after serving 34 years."

After her release from Prison, she had - allegedly at least - gone to live in a town called Marcy in New York State. However, a website called the Federal BOP Inmate locator failed to find her when I tried to look her up, later that evening. She would now be 66, and as far as I can ascertain, nobody knows anything about her activities for the past five years, or if they do, they are not telling. A quick look at Facebook reveals several Lynnette or Squeaky Frommes one of whom claims to live in Marcy and to have studied at Columbia University, but as I know only too well, despite the fact that it is allegedly illegal, it is quite easy to open a Facebook account and call yourself whatever you want.

Personally I thought that it was highly unlikely that this long term disciple of Charlie M had suddenly started a campaign of sending enigmatic and disturbing messages to a disabled part time journalist, who by this time, was driving round and round the outskirts of Norwich trying to battle the one way system and find the main hospital.

There was a loud dinging sound from Corinna's telephone. I grabbed it. Corinna was driving and would want to know what the message was, and if it was some obscure psychobabble from a serial killer whom I felt perfectly deserved to have been locked up in durance vile since 1969, I wanted to make sure that I got to it before she did. But I needn't have worried; it was my elder stepdaughter wanting to know where we were. And it so happened that just as I was punching in her telephone number into the telephone keypad, I saw a signpost pointing to the hospital.

"Next right!" I shouted, just as Shosh picked up the telephone, and then had to explain to her that I hadn't been shouting at her - a complicated explanation which continued as we entered the car part, drove to the disabled parking bay by the front entrance and waved a greeting to her and her husband Gavin who were sitting by a particularly peculiar piece of modern sculpture waiting for us.

Then my iPad 'pinged again'. It was another message from Lynnette.

"Are you ready for the end of the world?"

Deciding not to dignify that question with an answer, because the only possible answers could be YES or NO, and either of them would be bound to open up a level of dialogue with this bloody woman that I, at this time at least, was unwilling to enter, I just switched the iPad off, hugged Shoshannah and went into the hospital foyer to get our bearings.

Thus began - what, if you will excuse me lapsing into cliche, I can only describe as - a long night of the soul; one of the most tortuous and stressful periods of time that I have ever spent. It only lasted about six or seven hours, or at least the first phase did, but it was the longest six or seven hours that I have ever spent.

The first thing that we did was - if you do not mind me reverting to my family background in the military - establish a bridgehead in the hospital canteen. We then sent a text to Olivia's partner Aaron to tell them that we had arrived and sat down to wait for an answer.

It was a long wait.

Eventually we received a brief answer from Aaron acknowledging the message, but not imparting any further information. there is a quote from Robert Heinlein (I think it is in *Farnham's Freehold* [1], but I cannot find my battered and dog-eared copy) saying something to the effect that babies and kittens arrive in the small hours of the morning after a long wait. The Dean of Science Fiction was a much wittier and better author than me, and so my misuse of his bon mot is perforce going to be an anticlimax. But I grasped the essence of it and steeled myself for a long evening. I spent about ten minutes wandering about getting my bearings, but I found the disabled toilets, registered the car as being OK to be in the disabled bay with two jolly nice fellows on the reception desk, and then returned to the others and their base camp in the canteen, and wondered what to do next.

I switched my iPad on again and logged into the hospital wifi network. Opening my email client I found that I had hundreds, which - as it had been something like seven hours since I had last checked my emails - was no real surprise. They were the usual collection of electronic flotsam and jetsam that I tend to get in my inbox, and I was relieved to see that none of them were from Lynnette or anything to do with *Xtul*. I sorted through the motley collection, and deleted all the obvious phishing scams, the people trying to sell me Viagra, the softcore pornography, and the letters from people claiming to be my 'Brother in Christ' and discovered a handful of interesting cryptozoological articles which I reposted on the CFZ blogs, and some emails from friends wishing us all good luck and sending their love to Olivia.

---

1. *Farnham's Freehold* is a science fiction novel by Robert A. Heinlein. A serialised version, edited by Frederik Pohl, appeared in *Worlds of If* magazine (July, August, October 1964). The complete version was published in novel form by G.P. Putnam later in 1964. *Farnham's Freehold* is a post-apocalyptic tale, as the setup for the story is a direct hit by a nuclear weapon, which sends into the future a fallout shelter containing Farnham, his wife, son, daughter, daughter's friend, and black domestic servant. Heinlein drew on his experience in building a fallout shelter under his own house in Colorado Springs, Colorado in the 1960s.

The book is popular with survivalist groups as it combines the civil engineering and physics of fallout shelter survival with the social dynamics of "lifeboat rules," or autocratic authority under extreme conditions, a theme further explored in depth in *The Number of the Beast*. To paraphrase Mr. Farnham, "How do you know who is the officer in the lifeboat? The one with the gun."

I emailed my long term partner in crime, Graham Inglis, back home in Woolsery where he was keeping the home fires burning and looking after the animals. I told him that we had arrived safely, that Olivia was in labour and her waters had broken, and that I would telephone him when I had any further news, and pressed 'Send and Receive'.

The message to Graham went off safely, and there was one new message in its stead.

It was from Danny Miles and read:

> "You probably won't believe me but those messages from Lynnette are nothing to
> do with me. be careful of her .... She is very dangerous. And don't believe all that
> you see. They are messing with your head!"

They certainly were, but as there was nothing I could do about it, and I certainly wouldn't be so cruel as to add to the stress levels that Olivia's mother, sister and brother-in-law were already feeling, I did a Captain Oates [1]. "I'm going out for a cigarette", I said. "I may be some time"....

XV

The next three days were quite possibly the longest, and the most emotionally charged of my adult life. I have no biological children of my own, but after getting together with Corinna in the spring of 2005 I soon began to love her two daughters as if they were my own. By the time that we got married two and a bit years later, I was thinking of them AS my own, and to be honest I don't think that I could love either of them any more than I do, even if they had been my own flesh and blood.

Although I was terribly excited at the prospect of becoming a grandfather for the first time, I was also acutely conscious of the fact that I was the only person in the family who had a qualification in any of the medical sciences, and as my nursing qualification was to look after handicapped people, the only obstetrics that I knew anything about we abnormal ones, and although I tried to continually remind myself that the human race had been successfully giving birth for hundreds of thousands of years with a fair amount of success, I was only too aware of what could go wrong. The text from Aaron which had cheered and encouraged the others, had

---

1. Captain Lawrence Edward Grace "Titus" Oates (17 March 1880 – 16 March 1912) was an English cavalry officer with the 6th (Inniskilling) Dragoons, and later an Antarctic explorer, who died during the Terra Nova Expedition. Oates, afflicted with gangrene and frostbite, walked from his tent into a blizzard. His death is seen as an act of self-sacrifice when, aware that his ill health was compromising his three companions' chances of survival, he chose certain death.

According to Scott's diary, before Oates exited the tent and walked to his death, he uttered the words "I am just going outside and may be some time."

done the complete opposite to me, and I was frankly terrified. However I didn't want anyone else to know that, so I kept my own council, and went outside for as many cigarettes as I truthfully thought that I could get away with.

Just outside the main entrance of the hospital was a huge, stainless steel doughnut shaped sculpture. There was an engraved brass plaque below it explaining what it was meant to symbolise, but it was so encrusted with pigeon shit as to be illegible. I assume that because it was positioned outside the main entrance to that part of the hospital which housed the Maternity Wing, that the huge doughnut was meant to symbolise the female reproductive tract, but even to my mind that seemed a little crass, and laid it open to all sorts of amusing nomenclature, of which the Latin *Cloaca Maxima* was the least offensive.

It was also the place where all the smokers of the hospital patient community congregated. There was a thing that resembled the racks on the bicycle sheds at my old *alma mater* but which held heavy duty wheelchairs, there were a couple of the large freestanding ashtrays like the one that they used to have in the old dole office at Magdalen Road in Exeter back in the days that the powers that be believed that it as more than their lives were worth to deny cigarettes to the great unwashed. The presence of these ashtrays, which were overbrimming with soggy fag ends, was incongruous as there was also a notice proclaiming that Norwich Hospitals were a smoking free zone. And every time that I went out there, even when it was pissing down with rain, there were patients in their dressing gowns, some with fairly major disabilities and some heavily pregnant puffing away on their rollups.~

The constant stream of apocalyptic messages from 'Lynnette' were beginning to wear away at the fragile barriers of my mental health: '*Xtul* Lives *Xtul* Rules', 'No Sense Makes Sense', 'In my mind's eye I see fires in your cities' and 'healter skelter [1] is coming down fast'! The stream of *Xtul* propaganda and misquoted pearls of wisdom from The Gospel according to Charlie kept on coming, and at one point I was having a hard time deleting them off my iPad as fast as they were coming in.

I chainsmoked, and tried to use music to boot out the increasingly tormented and tumultuous sensory input, but as I could only get hold of two albums from my Dropbox account, that weren't actually by Xtul, and they were a collection of Irish rebel songs sung by a tenor in a voice tremulous with emotion, to the accompaniment of an accordion player, a mandolinist, and a bodrhan player who were struggling to stay in time and in tune, and a bootlegged copy of Scott Walker's almost entirely unlistenable *Bish Bosch* album[2], this was not really a successful experiment. Then my headphones packed up, and I found myself watching the hustle and bustle of a busy general hospital at night through a haze of cigarette smoke whilst

---

2. This mis-spelling was certainly intentional. The words HELTER SKELTER had been mis-spelled by Patricia Krenwinkel when they were written in blood at 3301 Waverly Drive Los Angeles

3. *Bish Bosch* is the fourteenth studio album by the American singer Scott Walker. It was released on 3 December 2012 on 4AD. The album has been described by its creator as being "the final installment in a trilogy" that also includes *Tilt* (1995) and *The Drift* (2006). At seventy-three minutes, Bish Bosch is Walker's longest studio album, as well as also containing his longest song, the twenty-one minute forty-one second "SDSS1416+13B (Zercon, A Flagpole Sitter)".

Epizootics blared out as loudly as I dared from the speakers of my little tablet.

This served as a suitably surrealchemical backdrop to my increasingly frantic prayers.

I believe in God, but in a truly pantheistic way. To me, God is the universe and everything in it. "Thou art God" said St Foster to St Michael [1]. But as St Michael replied...who isn't? But the fact remains that I believe in a deity, even though I find it hard to explain my conception of the nature of that deity. But as I very much dislike organised religion, and will describe myself as a Christian Anarchist vaguely after the fashion of St Francis [2], and even then only if pushed, and believe that worship can only be as part of a 1:1 relationship between the supplicant and the deity, I don't really talk about my beliefs in such matters. But I do pray, although I don't think that I have ever prayed as hard in my life as the night that I sat out in mild drizzle beneath the foggy sky asking that my darling stepdaughter and her baby girl would both come through the experience of childbirth unscathed.

The biggest cultural event of late 2014 had been Kate Bush's return to live performance [3], and - totally unwittingly - I found myself mirroring one of her songs [4] and trying to make a deal

1. *Stranger in a Strange Land* is a 1961 science fiction novel by American author Robert A. Heinlein. It tells the story of Valentine Michael Smith, a human who comes to Earth in early adulthood after being born on the planet Mars and raised by Martians. The novel explores his interaction with—and eventual transformation of—terrestrial culture. The title is an allusion to the phrase in Exodus 2:22. According to Heinlein, the novel's working title was *The Heretic*. Several later editions of the book have promoted it as "The most famous Science Fiction Novel ever written".

2. Saint Francis of Assisi (Italian: San Francesco d'Assisi); born Giovanni di Pietro di Bernardone, but nicknamed Francesco; 1181/1182 – October 3, 1226) was an Italian Catholic friar and preacher. He founded the men's Order of Friars Minor, the women's Order of St. Clare, and the Third Order of Saint Francis for men and women not able to live the lives of itinerant preachers, followed by the early members of the Order of Friars Minor, or the monastic lives of the Poor Clares. Francis is one of the most venerated religious figures in history.

3. *Before the Dawn* is a set of concerts performed by British singer Kate Bush in 2014. The residency in the Hammersmith Apollo consisted of 22 dates, and was her first series of live shows since her first tour in 1979. The show was filmed on 16–17 September 2014 presumably for DVD release, though this has not been officially confirmed. On Friday 21 March 2014, Bush announced via her website her plans to perform live. A further seven dates were added to the original fifteen due to the high demand following the pre-sale ticket allocation, which went on sale Wednesday 26 March to fans who had signed up to her website. Tickets went on sale to the general public at 09:30 on Friday 28 March and were sold out within 15 minutes; some reports say 14, some 10, some as little as 7 minutes. Kate Bush was subsequently nominated for two Q Awards in 2014: Best Act in the World Today and Best Live Act but did not win either award. She did win the Editor's Award at the Evening Standard Theatre Awards for taking musical performance to new heights.

4. "Running Up That Hill" is a song by the English singer-songwriter Kate Bush from her 1985 album, Hounds of Love, released in the United Kingdom on 5 August 1985.Originally titled "A Deal with God", representatives at EMI were hesitant to release the song as titled due to possible negative reception due to its use of the term "God". Bush relented and changed the title; however, the album version of the song is listed as "Running Up That Hill (A Deal with God)". Ten years later Bush said: "I was trying to say that, really, a man and a woman, can't understand each other because we are a man and a woman. And if we could actually swap each other's roles, if we could actually be in each other's place for a while, I think we'd both be very surprised! [Laughs] And I think it would lead to a greater understanding. And really the only way I could think it could be done was either... you know, I thought a deal with the devil, you know. And I thought, 'well, no, why not a deal with God!' You know, because in a way it's so much more powerful the whole idea of asking God to make a deal with you. You see, for me it is still called "Deal With God", that was its title.

with God. If Olivia and the baby were OK, I told the Almighty, would h/she please take my life instead of theirs. But once again there was no answer.

Then suddenly I noticed that I was no longer alone. If I was the sort of writer who writes fairy stories, this would be the point that there would be a clatter of little hooves, and little Panne would have trotted out from behind the giant stainless steel vaginal doughnut to tell me that everything was going to be OK. If I was the sort of writer who wrote messianic fantasy stories, this would be the moment that the sky would open, and that a voice of the apocalypse would speak to me out of the riven clouds to tell me something important for good or for ill. But nothing of the sort happened. What did, however happen, was that I heard a squeak of a wheelchair, and looked around to see three extraordinary and apparently ill matched people there besides me.

In the wheelchair was a middle aged man with long, matted hair. He was wearing a long white bloodstained nightshirt which completely failed to hide the fact that he had no legs. And the wheelchair was being pushed by a tiny man with an ancient, wizened face and an enormously fat woman. All three of them were smoking and a halo of tiny insects appeared to be flying around the head of the man in the wheelchair, who was lolled to one side, and was muttering continuously. All throughout the evening the procession of expectant mothers had been punctuated with a few amputees and other people who seemed not to have been dealt a very good hand of cards by a beneficent providence. I assumed that there was some sort of post operative physiotherapy department or something of that sort which shared a hospital entrance with the Maternity Department, and as statistically more people have babies than have limbs surgically removed, it would explain why there were more smokers out there in the drizzle by the enormous steel vulva than there were amputees.

Under other circumstances I would have been intrigued enough to try and find out what these three strange people were doing here, and who they were.

The simple fact that there appeared to be a slowly spreading bloodstain on the front of the wheelchair man's body itself merited investigation, and the fact that more and more tiny insects; mostly diptera[1] and pyralid[2] moths were circling his head should have intrigued me as both a fortean zoologist and an entomologist. But it didn't. I was simply so steeped in terror at not knowing what was happening upstairs in Delivery Suite C12 that I just didn't give a toss about anything else.

---

1. Flies

2, The Pyraloidea (pyraloid moths) are a moth superfamily containing about 16,000 described species worldwide (Munroe & Solis 1998), and probably at least as many more remain to be described. They are generally fairly small moths. Among all Lepidoptera, pyraloids show the most diverse life history adaptations. The larvae of most species feed on living plants either internally or externally as leaf rollers, leaf webbers leaf miners, borers, root feeders, and seed feeders. Some species live parasitically in ant nests (Wurthiinae), predate upon scale insects (certain Phycitinae), or live in the nests of bees (Galleriinae). The larvae of the Acentropinae are adapted to life under water, and certain Phycitinae and Pyralinae are adapted to very dry environments and their larvae feed on stored food products. Others feed on animal detritus such as carrion and faeces.

Then the man in the wheelchair began to speak, and in a cold, lifeless voice as solemn as a marble gravestone and as still as a corpse, he spoke words that I knew very well indeed:

> *"And a message flashed in the sky by the sun,*
> *Be careful this is only a game"* [1]

And the fat woman then leered at me with the sort of smirk that looked just like when a small girl pretends to be an adult, puts on makeup and does what she thinks is a sexy voice, but which just turns out to be mildly disturbing:

"Listen to him, he knows what he is saying"....

Just then my iPad beeped again. I looked down just in case it was a message from Aaron or Corinna about Olivia's progress. But it was another message from Lynette.

Without bothering to read it, I typed an answer: "Fuck off you mad bitch!", wondering why I hadn't thought of doing that before. Then I looked up to speak to my three strange companions. It had only been about thirty seconds, but they were gone, and there was no sign that they had ever been there, except for three half smoked cigarettes on the ground, and a cloud of small insects in the air.

I finished my cigarette and went back inside the hospital and limped down the corridor to the canteen where Corinna, Mother, Shosh and Gavin had set up camp in a small semicircle of comfortable armchairs around a round table. I sat down, joining them, and a few minutes later Corinna received a text from Aaron. Olivia had finally given birth and I was now a grandfather.

Whispering up unspoken prayers of thanksgiving to every deity I could think of, I joined in the general festivities which were still going on twenty minutes or so later when an exhausted looking Aaron turned up to fill us in on what had happened. It turned out that my worst fears had been justified and that it had been a difficult and painful birth, but that both Mother and baby Evelyn were fine and completely out of danger.

The next forty eight hours went by in a blur. We took Aaron back to the house he shared with Olivia, and then went to my brother-in-law's house thirty miles away where we stay d the night on his floor. I am mildly feral, and the idea of sleeping on a floor wrapped in a blanket and using my old leather jacket as a pillow didn't phase me one instant.

After another day at the hospital, during which we went up to see Olivia on the Maternity Ward, and I met my granddaughter for the first time, we went back to my brother-in-law's house where we slept a second night on the floor.

---

1. From *Sling It!* A song on side two of *The Psychomodo* by *Cockney Rebel* released in 1974. My favourite record by my favourite band. Sadly I sullied my relationship with the band by going and working for head honcho Steve Harley in the early 1990s. One should never attempt to meet, and certainly not work for one's heroes.

The next day Olivia and the baby were discharged and we drove her home, and then left them to it, as we drove back to Oakham in Rutland, and then back to Devon. It was half way back to Devon that I realised that since I had written back to Lynnette telling her to fuck off, I had received no further IMs from the *Xtul* camp, not indeed from anyone else who wasn't family or friends congratulating us on having attained grandparenthood.

The journey home was uneventful, and we arrived home to a maelstrom of wagging tails and joyful barks from the dogs. Once we had got all our things in from the car, I was sitting in my study drinking a cup if tea, smoking a meditative cigarette, and reading the last few day's post when my old friend and business partner Graham came into the room.

Graham and I have been friends for a quarter of a century, and have worked together on various projects for nearly as long, and he probably knows me as well as does any other person on this planet with the possible exception of Corinna and my cousin Pené. I asked him whether there was anything that I needed to know about the various animals in the CFZ, or about anything else that might have transpired during our absence.

"Not really", he replied, "but there was one weird thing. This evening at about dusk I was in the garden and what looked like a young girl came up to me. I say looked like, because she was wearing a long black cloak and I could not see her face at all. She gave u a message. She asked me to tell you that she had to go away, but that you need to go to Britannia to ask why. I suppose that is something to do with your mortgage. That's with the Britannia Building Society isn't it?"

I suddenly felt an extreme rush of guilt. I had forgotten all about Panne, and even before I looked in her cupboard I knew that she was gone. But before I could think, or even say anything there was a thunderous knock on the door. I shouted "Come In!" And to my shock there were two uniformed policemen and a sinister looking man wearing a long, dark, overcoat standing on the doorstep....

XVI

I stared at the advancing policemen blankly. It has been over fifteen years since I had the boys in blue visit my house. That was back in 1997 after a young girl[1] was killed in an inexplicable, and still unsolved murder, only a street away from where I had been living for many years, and where - in the aftermath of my own horrific divorce - my friend and

---

1. Schoolgirl Kate Bushell was murdered as she walked a neighbour's dog a short distance from her home in Exwick, on the outskirts of Exeter. Bushell, aged 14, set off from her home in Burrator Drive, at 4.30pm on 15 November 1997. When she failed to come home, her parents called the police. A search located her body in a field next to Exwick Lane at 7.35pm that evening. She had been brutally murdered. Ironically in view of my previous footnotes I misheard the Policeman who first spoke to me and thought he was saying that Kate Bush, who of course had connections with *Cockney Rebel,* had been murdered. The lexilinks continue.

partner in crime Graham Inglis spent much of his time. Being by far the weirdest and most non–conformist people in the little red brick estate, as well as the only single men, we were obviously going to be suspects. We were both quite happy to give DNA samples, having absolutely nothing to hide, but as we were questioned in some considerable detail about our activities that weekend, as said activities had involved Olympic levels of substance abuse, and a mildly debauched party, we were not particularly willing to share too many details with the rozzers.

But we were innocent. We knew that we were innocent, and eventually - despite my suspicions that the Birmingham Six, and the Guildford Four[1] were just about to be joined by The Exwick Two - we were eliminated from the enquiry, and although it took me two years to get back the Gurkha kukri that I had hanging on my wall, we essentially left the affair without a stain on our characters.

But on this occasion what on earth could I have possibly done. I kept the implacable look of injured justice on my face as I struggled to stay calm, wracking my brains to try and think what the hell I could have done wrong! "Yes, Officer. can I help you?" I said in the grimly patrician manner that has saved my bollocks from the fire on many occasions, and which even now seems to alert the plods to the fact that - contrary to appearances - they were not dealing with some crusty traveller, but an old fashioned English Gentleman.

However, on this occasion, the boys in blue looked singularly unimpressed as they surveyed the piles of mildly esoteric bric-à-brac which lay heaped in piles across my tiny study. Their companion in the black overcoat, whom I was rapidly beginning to suspect was more than plain CID, if only because that acronym stands for Criminal Investigation Department, and I honestly couldn't think of anything even vaguely criminal for which I could have been pulled up.

He looked at me with steely grey eyes. "I believe that you know a man called Daniel Miles," he said.

I slumped into my battered office chair. "What the fuck has he done NOW?" I asked.

I could see a flicker of humour pass for a fraction of an instant across his countenance. But it

---

1. The Birmingham Six were six men—Hugh Callaghan, Patrick Joseph Hill, Gerard Hunter, Richard McIlkenny, William Power and John Walker—sentenced to life imprisonment in 1975 in England for the Birmingham pub bombings. Their convictions were declared unsafe and unsatisfactory and quashed by the Court of Appeal on 14 March 1991. The six men were later awarded compensation ranging from £840,000 to £1.2 million.

The Guildford Four and the Maguire Seven were the collective names of two groups of innocent people whose convictions in English courts in 1975 and 1976 for the Guildford pub bombings of 5 October 1974 were eventually quashed after long campaigns for justice. The Guildford Four were convicted of bombings carried out by the Provisional Irish Republican Army (IRA), and the Maguire Seven were convicted of handling explosives found during the investigation into the bombings. Both groups' convictions were eventually declared "incorrect and unsatisfactory" and reversed in 1989 and 1991 respectively after they had served 15–16 years in prison. None of the policemen involved have been convicted of the torture and framing of the Guildford Four and Maguire Seven.

vanished almost immediately. "I don't think that there is any need for language like that, Sir", he replied, but I took a deep breath and said. "This is my house, and I will use any language I see fit here, officer. I will not be antagonistic and aggressive, but I am damned if I will temper my vocabulary to suit the sensibilities of an uninvited visitor. Now either arrest me, or sit down and we will discuss the matter like gentlemen..."

And much to my amazement, my high-handed attitude actually worked, and as he made no move to arrest me, I gestured to him to sit down. "I am afraid that I don't have enough chairs in here for your colleagues...", I started to say, but the ice was broken. He told the two uniformed policemen to go outside and sit in the car, and acquiesced like a lamb when I asked them to park up by the church rather than annoying my neighbours by blocking the lane outside.

They left. Graham was still hovering in the background, and I dispatched him for coffee and whisky. Much to my surprise the plainclothes policeman, who I suspected by now was almost certainly Special Branch, graciously accepted both. I didn't bother to ask him whether he was OK with me smoking, and lit one up anyway.

"You haven't answered my question," I said, sounding far more confident than I was feeling. "What the hell has that idiot Danny Miles done now?"

The policeman made himself comfortable and adjusted himself in his seat. "The trouble is, sir, that we don't know. We were hoping that you would be able to tell us."

I looked at him in silence. I would love to say that at this point I raised one eyebrow quizzically, but although my wife, my adopted nephew Max, and even my mother-in-law, can do this undoubtedly impressive facial contortion, I can do nothing of the sort. So I just scowled at him, and asked another question, although this time I was pretty sure that I knew the answer. "Why me?"

He had the good grace to look mildly embarrassed. "Well, sir, you have helped us with our enquiries on previous occasions..."

I snorted. "And I am sure that your records will have told you that I was found to be entirely blameless on each of those occasions," I barked angrily, because - unlike most citizens of this sceptre'd isle - I have attracted the attention of the security forces on at least three other occasions over the past twenty years.

The first took place during the last year of the John Major administration, when the Conservative Government was reliant on the capricious and stormy political friendship of the Ulster Unionists [1]

---

1. The Ulster Unionist Party (UUP) is one of the two main unionist political parties in Northern Ireland. It governed Northern Ireland between 1921 and 1972 and was supported by most unionist voters throughout the conflict known as the Troubles. The party is led by Mike Nesbitt. Since 1999, the UUP has lost support among Northern Ireland's unionists to the Democratic Unionist Party (DUP) in successive elections at all levels of government. In 2009, the party entered an electoral alliance with the Conservative Party and the two parties fielded joint candidates for elections to the House of Commons and the European Parliament as Ulster Conservatives and Unionists – New Force (UCUNF).

to stay in power, and was getting more and more concerned that anti-government interests from Britain and Ireland would team up to try and bring the government to its knees.

Well it so happened that in the spring of 1995 I had a telephone call from a very drunk ex-Royal Marine sergeant who claimed to have been in charge of one of the detachments of Royal Marines, who, ten years earlier, had been hunting The Beast of Exmoor[1]. He claimed that they had shot a big black cat, but as they had been on private land without permission they had buried the body and vowed to say nothing about it. However, because my informant was down on his luck he was prepared to take me to the body...for a consideration.

I was sceptical, especially when, in an attempt to establish his bona fides, he told me (in confidence) that he had been part of a detachment of Marines acting as bodyguards to the then Princess of Wales as she visited her "Fancy Man" in rural Devon. This was months before the relationship between Princess Diana[2] and James Hewitt[3] became public knowledge. I had discussed the claims about the Beast of Exmoor in writing and on local radio, and because I had vaguely known Hewitt when we were both schoolboys (he was an egregious little shit even then) the increasingly paranoid Conservative administration decided that I was obviously trying to destabilise the royal family, and - according to several sources, especially *On the trail of the saucer spies, UFOs and Government Surveillance* by my friend Nick Redfern - my phone line was tapped for several months.

A couple of years later, the taps were renewed when circumstantial evidence suggested that I was an IRA sympathiser (I wasn't but had friends who were) and even appeared in a drunken

1. The Beast of Exmoor is a cryptozoological felid (see phantom cat) that is reported to roam the fields of Exmoor in Devon and Somerset in the United Kingdom. There have been numerous reports of eyewitness sightings, however the official Exmoor National Park website lists the beast under "Traditions, Folklore, and Legends", and the BBC calls it "the famous-yet-elusive beast of Exmoor." Sightings were first reported in the 1970s, although it became notorious in 1983, when a South Molton farmer claimed to have lost over 100 sheep in the space of three months, all of them apparently killed by violent throat injuries. Descriptions of its coloration range from black to tan or dark grey.

2. Diana, Princess of Wales (Diana Frances;[fn 1] née Spencer; 1 July 1961 – 31 August 1997), was the first wife of Charles, Prince of Wales, who is the eldest child and heir apparent of Queen Elizabeth II. Diana was born into a family of British nobility with royal ancestry as The Honourable Diana Spencer. She was the fourth child and third daughter of John Spencer, 8th Earl Spencer and the Honourable Frances Shand Kydd. She grew up in Park House, which is situated on the Queen's Sandringham estate, and was educated in England and Switzerland. In 1975 she became Lady Diana Spencer, after her father inherited the title of Earl Spencer. Her wedding to the Prince of Wales on 29 July 1981 was held at St Paul's Cathedral and reached a global television audience of over 750 million. While married, Diana bore the titles Princess of Wales, Duchess of Cornwall, Duchess of Rothesay, Countess of Chester and Baroness of Renfrew. The marriage produced two sons, the princes William and Harry, who were then respectively second and third in the line of succession to the British throne. As Princess of Wales, Diana undertook royal duties on behalf of the Queen and represented her at functions overseas. She was celebrated for her charity work and for her support of the International Campaign to Ban Landmines. From 1989, she was the president of Great Ormond Street Hospital for children, in addition to dozens of other charities. Her beauty and charisma ensured that Diana remained the object of worldwide media scrutiny both during and after her marriage, which ended in divorce on 28 August 1996. Her death in a car crash in Paris on 31 August 1997 was followed by intense public mourning.

3. James Lifford Hewitt (born 30 April, 1958) is an English former household cavalry officer in the British Army. He had an affair with Diana, Princess of Wales for five years, receiving extensive media coverage after revealing details of the affair.

photograph taken at a gig by an Irish republican rock band, in *An Phoblacht*. But again, the taps were removed eventually.

Most recently, in 2012, I shot a video for the title track of Merrell Fankhauser's [2] *Area 51 Suite*. I'm rather proud of this. Not only is it the first pop video that I have directed which didn't feature either me, my band, or some mate of mine screaming avant garde nonsense, but I almost got arrested by Special Branch whilst making it. Although Area 51 is in Nevada, it was filmed in North Cornwall outside GCHQ, because of their impressive satellite dishes.

Worryingly for the state of the nation's security, the base security forces noticed the fat hippy with an expensive camera but failed to notice to relatively small teenagers (one dressed in an alien mask) and a large, bumbling dog with impressive jowls. The police were very nice to me when we spoke on the telephone, and I am pretty sure that I have avoided being sent to some secret interrogation facility on Diego Garcia, as they seemed to believe everything I said (which was good, considering that it was the pure and unadulterated truth).

So, I have attracted the nation of Britain's guardians of law and order on at least three occasions, and as I have written and spoken widely about my negative view of both the British and American governments (check out my book *Island of Paradise* for the really damning stuff) I am not at all surprised that I have a file on me, and that it remains open. But Danny? He is just an irritating small town conman, and - if I may steal Tim Good's [4] phrase - of no defence significance whatsoever.

1. *An Phoblacht* is a monthly 32-page newspaper published by Sinn Féin in Ireland. Editorially the paper takes a left wing Irish republican position and is generally supportive of the Northern Ireland peace process. Along with covering Irish political and trade union issues the newspaper also frequently features interviews with celebrities, musicians, artists, intellectuals and international activists. The paper sells an average of up to 15,000 copies every month and was the first Irish paper to provide an edition online and currently having in excess of 100,000 website hits per week. The paper notes each month on its editorial page that while it is published by Sinn Féin, articles in the paper "do not necessarily reflect the views of Sinn Féin".

2. Merrell Wayne Fankhauser (born December 23, 1943, Louisville, Kentucky, United States) is an American singer, songwriter and guitarist, who was most active in the 1960s and 1970s with bands including the *Impacts, Merrell & the Exiles, HMS Bounty, Fankhauser-Cassidy Band*, and *MU*. In addition, 12 songs recorded by *Merrell & the Exiles* were later released under the group name *Fapardokly*, even though that group never actually existed. After moving to San Luis Obispo, California in his teens, he began playing guitar, and got his first break playing in movie theaters and talent shows. In 1960, after one of these shows, he joined a local band The Impacts as lead guitarist. In 1962, they recorded an album which was later released, without the band's knowledge, by Del-Fi Records, and which included a tune "Wipe Out" which Fankhauser suggested later provided the (uncredited) basis of the hit by the Surfaris, although his view is contested.

3. Published in 2007 the blurb reads: "Jon Downes visits the Antillean island of Puerto Rico, to which he has led two expeditions - in 1998 and 2004. Together with noted researcher Nick Redfern he goes in search of the grotesque vampiric chupacabra, believing that it can - finally - be categorised within a zoological frame of reference rather than a purely paranormal one. Along the way he uncovers mystery after mystery, has a run in with terrorists, art historians, and even has his garden buzzed by a UFO. By turns both terrifying and funny, this remarkable book is a real tour de force by one of the world's foremost cryptozoological researchers."

4. Noted UFO author. According to his website: "Worldwide research, interviewing key witnesses and discussing the subject with astronauts, military and intelligence specialists, pilots, politicians and scientists, has established Timothy Good as a leading authority on UFOs and the alien presence - the most highly classified subject on Earth". Hmmm.

I said as much to the man from Special Branch, who was sitting back comfortably sipping my whisky. He looked at me quizzically for a few moments before saying. "But in your writings, Mr Downes, you have intimated that Mr Miles is quite capable of running a cult. Indeed, I believe he did so at one time, and you were a member." He picked up his attaché case and got out a copy of my 2004 biography, in which I described some rather disturbing events during the autumn of 1981, when I was busy opening the doors of perception by the use of psilocybin, and Danny was playing mind games with the more gullible members of the North Devon alternative community. [1]

He turned to the relevant chapter and read out loud:

> I can't remember whose idea it was, but at the end of October someone suggested that we should follow in the footsteps of Carlos Castaneda and indulge in a group psychedelic experience out of doors. The idea was to somehow contact the spirit of the sacred mushroom on the psychic plane, although it has to be admitted that most of those present (including me) thought of it more as a groovy and rather daring Halloween party. I was really looking forward to it until I discovered that in his wisdom Danny had decided to hold this experiment on Abbotsham Cliffs. In many ways this made a lot of sense. If there actually was a sacred mushroom spirit, it stood to reason that he would reside amongst the more tangible proofs of his existence, and as already stated, at the time at least, the best magic mushrooms in the area grew at Abbotsham Cliffs.
>
> I was a little uneasy. Although ten years had passed and I had tried to put the matter out of my mind I had never entirely forgotten the events of June 1972. But, I rationalised wildly displaying a capacity for self-delusion that was remarkable even by my standards. That had been in the woodlands several miles along the cliffs. And it had been in summer. And we had been looking for the werewolf. This time we were engaged on a mystical quest for the spirit of the sacred mushroom. It was obvious that nothing nasty could possibly happen.
>
> On Halloween night, seven or eight of us camped out on the flat land just behind Abbotsham Cliffs. There were three girls and four or five guys, all dressed in the punk styles that were then de rigueur. Cheerfully, we parked our cars in the lay-by, and in the late afternoon sunshine t was a cheerful party that walked the half-mile or so along the footpath to the cliffs. Although it was the end of October it was surprisingly warm, and the two elderly sheep grazing on the scrubland by the cliffs gave the place a delightfully bucolic air.

---

1. The whole chapter has been reproduced as an appendix to this present volume.

We built a large bonfire and as the final rays of the setting sun disappeared into the Bristol Channel, Danny, in his self appointed role of showman and shaman, came around and dispensed what he described as his "funky communion." It was a potent mixture of gin, mushroom tea, peyote and LSD and was the precursor to one of the most horrific nights of my life. It was a night that I shall certainly never forget, and which I seriously suspect will be permanently etched on the psyches of everyone involved.

The evening started pleasantly enough, because although the chemical mixture that we had ingested was incredibly powerful, the mixture of the pleasantly sylvan surroundings, and what we hadn't yet learned to call "chill out" music issuing from what we hadn't yet learned to call a "ghetto blaster" kept everyone in a mellow and happy state of mind.

Danny started to read aloud from The Tibetan Book of the Dead and then began to recite Aleister Crowley's Hymn to Pan. None of us realised at the time, but Danny was (knowingly or unknowingly) manipulating the situation like a master. Although everyone was hallucinating heavily by this time, the three girls in particular seemed heavily affected and, encouraged by Danny, started to behave in a most uncharacteristic manner.

Despite their Mohicans and studiously torn clothes they were actually very reserved young ladies on the whole; but coaxed by Danny they started to become very affectionate and sensual. They danced rhythmically to the music and kissed and stroked each other, the guys in the group (including me) and particularly Danny.

One plump girl called "Sarah" [not her real name because I see her around Exeter sometimes, and she is now an eminently respectable, professional lady] who boasted the particularly unpleasant punk soubriquet of "Scab" even started to undress and dance semi-naked in the firelight.

It would be easy for me to pretend that some sort of totally far out hippy orgy then ensued, but it didn't. Most of the people who were there were too drunk, too stoned, and far too tripped out to perform sexually. I know I was, but again under coaxing from Danny, "Scab" and one of the guys coupled - I won't say `made love` because there was no love, emotion or tenderness - just animal rutting in the firelight as Danny chanted lines from Crowley and the rest of us looked on giggling inanely and waving our hands about to the rhythmic beat of the music.

Eventually everyone passed out, and that was when the fear came.

I have spent more of my life than I like to admit in alternate states of consciousness. Once upon a time I believed it was because I was exploring a genuinely alternative route to spiritual self-empowerment.

Nowadays I believe that all that is rubbish. If there is such a thing as an interventionist God, and for me personally the jury is still out on that one, I am sure that he or she would not wish the objects of his/her creation to perform acts of supplication by poisoning themselves. Although the concept of trying to second guess a deity is a pretty dodgy one, the theories of trying to reach nirvana through substance abuse is a pretty dodgy one. I haven't taken psychedelics since that terrible night in 1981. These days when I go to a different place it is usually with alcohol, or prescribed tranquillisers and occasionally with the fruit of the poppy. And these days, when I take drugs it isn't to reach some magickal and non-existent nirvana - it is purely and simply to blot out the fear.

I am convinced that the fear first came to me on All Hallow's Eve 1981.

The policeman looked at me in silence for a few moments before continuing...

"We have received information that Mr Miles is involved with another cult of young people in North Devon, and this time the casualties are likely to be far more than just three elderly sheep. What do you know about it?"

I replied fairly honestly. I agreed with the policeman that the events taking place in the dank forests on the Cornwall/Devon border were both sinister and worrying. But as far as I could see the police were barking completely up the wring tree.

"Have you heard a song called *Black Flags Rising*?" he asked, taking me completely aback.

I nodded that I had.

"We believe that this is a reference to the black flags flown by Islamist insurgents in the Middle East..." And he looked terribly shocked when I burst out laughing.

"Danny a radical Muslim? Nonsense..." I spluttered, and tried to explain that the black flags in the song were a reference either to Saruman's banners in *Lord of the Rings*, the Anarchist black flag, or to this line from a famous Irish rebel song...

> *"The black flag they hoisted, the cruel deed was over,*
> *Gone was a man who loved Ireland so well,*
> *There was many a sad heart in Dublin that morning,*
> *When they murdered James Connolly, the Irish Rebel"* [1]

85

But this was all obviously too much for my unwelcome visitor, who obviously had no idea what on earth I was talking about.

"So you are saying that they are Irish Muslim anarchists, then sir?"

And I had to spend the next ten minutes trying to explain to the bloody man that I meant nothing of the sort, and that I was a seriously disabled music journalist and zoologist who spent his time breeding tropical fish and raising money for animal welfare projects, and that I was not the new Lord Haw Haw [2] apologist for a band of fundamentalist Irish Muslims, and that I knew next to nothing about what Danny was doing and cared less.

Of course, I wasn't being entirely truthful. I knew more than I was admitting, but the more I thought about it the more I worried about the safety of poor Panne. Truthfully I didn't care what happened to Danny, Mr Loxodonta, Lynnette or any of the others, and suspected that the world would quite possibly be a better place without them.

But I was not prepared to be the agent of their destruction if it also meant the destruction of a sweet little goatgod from the woods who had done nothing more to me than ask for my help and eat my wife's chocolate.

So I obfuscated, bluffed and carried out all the tricks of verbal prestidigitation that I knew how to do. I knew that the policeman knew that I was hiding something, and I knew that he knew that I knew he did. But, thankfully - even in what remains of our crumbling democracy - I knew that I was safe from being arrested on suspicion of treason, just yet, and so I continued to lie, and the policeman continued to probe until we both got tired of the charade and he went home, and I went upstairs to join Corinna and the dogs in bed.

However, unusually for me, I lay awake for hours with a million and one things going round my head. But by the time I finally went to sleep, just as the pale fingers of dawn were tracing filigree patterns across the early morning sky, I knew exactly what to do next.

I would have to do exactly what I had been told back in Norwich. I would have to go and see Britannia.

---

1. James Connolly (Irish: Séamas Ó Conghaile, 5 June 1868 – 12 May 1916) was an Irish republican and socialist leader, aligned to syndicalism and the Industrial Workers of the World. He was born in the Cowgate area of Edinburgh, Scotland, to Irish immigrant parents. He left school for working life at the age of 11, but became one of the leading Marxist theorists of his day. He also took a role in Scottish and American politics. He was executed by a British firing squad because of his leadership role in the Easter Rising of 1916. In 1968, Irish group *The Wolfe Tones* released a single named "James Connolly", which reached number 15 in the Irish charts, It is this song that I quote above.

2. Lord Haw-Haw was a nickname applied to wartime traitor William Joyce, remembered for his propaganda broadcasts that opened with "Jairmany calling, Jairmany calling", spoken in an unintentionally comic upper-class accent. The same nickname was also applied to some other broadcasters of English-language propaganda from Germany, but it is Joyce with whom the name is now overwhelmingly identified. There are various theories about its origin.

XVI

When my family first returned to North Devon in 1971 after an absence of nearly two decades during which my parents fought gallant rearguard actions against the fall of the British Empire in Nigeria and Hong Kong, they quickly made friends with various of the local gentry. In those days there was a remarkable range of minor aristocracy and interesting, though often impoverished, gentlefolk who lived in the area. Woolsery Manor, for example, which in later years was a hotel, then fell into disuse, and now as a derelict building has been bought by the bloke who started Bebo, was inhabited by the Count de St Quentin and his wife, a Swedish princess. They were very kind to me during my first year or two in the village, and encouraged me in my pursuits as an amateur naturalist, and wannabe poet.

They even had a private museum, which inspired me that one day I would have something similar of my own. It housed a remarkably arcane collection of disparate things including the foot of a mummified Egyptian priestess, and Marie Antoinette's [1] christening slippers. I loved visiting them, and was very sad when they left the village for pastures new.

But there were other interesting people as well, so I was not entirely bereft. On an insignificant bend in the road, one of the most obscure lanes between Woolsery and the slightly bigger village of Bradworthy four or five miles away, there was (and is) a cottage even more tumbledown than my own. In it lived an elderly bachelor clergyman and his older spinster sister. The Rev Cymbeline Potts and his sister Britannia were a remarkable couple. Both retired from active duty, (although history didn't really relate whether Miss Britannia had ever had a proper job, or indeed any gainful employment except for looking after her brother) they seemed to do little else apart from frequent junk shops, jumble sales, and auction rooms in search of items to swell their ever growing collection of bric-à-brac.

Their collection encompassed everything from late Victorian militaria to long obsolete items of scientific and quasi-scientific equipment. They even had an epidiascope; a late Victorian equivalent to the overhead projector, which I used to play with for hours, projecting the

---

1. Marie Antoinette (baptised Maria Antonia Josepha Johanna; 2 November 1755 – 16 October 1793), born an Archduchess of Austria, was Dauphine of France from 1770 to 1774 and Queen of France and Navarre from 1774 to 1792. She was the fifteenth and penultimate child of Francis I, Holy Roman Emperor and Empress Maria Theresa. In April 1770, upon her marriage to Louis-Auguste, Dauphin of France, she became Dauphine of France. She assumed the title Queen of France and of Navarre when her husband ascended the throne as Louis XVI upon the death of his grandfather Louis XV on 10 May 1774. After eight years of marriage, she gave birth to a daughter, Marie-Thérèse Charlotte, the first of her four children. During the French Revolution, after the government had placed the royal family under house arrest in the Tuileries Palace in October 1789, several events linked to Marie Antoinette, in particular the June 1791 attempt to flee, and her role in the French Revolutionary War, had disastrous effects on French popular opinion: over a year later, on 10 August 1792, the attack on the Tuileries forced the royal family to take refuge at the Assembly. On 13 August, the family was imprisoned in the Temple. On 21 September 1792, Louis XVI was deposed and the monarchy abolished. After a two-day trial begun on 14 October 1793, Marie Antoinette was convicted by the Revolutionary Tribunal of treason to the principles of the revolution, and executed by guillotine on Place de la Révolution on 16 October 1793.

images of my model aeroplanes onto the wall, and pretending that I was directing a remake of *The Battle of Britain.*

They were, in their own peculiar way, pillars of the local community, and every village fete saw the elderly couple running a tombola, or a stall where they would run a massively eccentric quiz, asking the village children a series of questions about English history that neither the children, or often their parents had even the vaguest idea of what they were talking about. Miss Britannia would always be dressed as her cryptomythological namesake, complete with shield, robe and Graeco-Roman helmet, and their appearance always confused everyone mightily and brought joy to my adolescent heart.

Cunobeline (or Cunobelin, from Latin Cunobelinus, derived from Greek Kynobellinus, Κυνοβελλίνος) was a king in pre-Roman Britain from the late first century BC until the 40s AD. He is mentioned in passing by the classical historians Suetonius and Dio Cassius, and many coins bearing his inscription have been found. He appears to have controlled a substantial portion of south-eastern Britain, and is called "King of the Britons" (Britannorum rex) by Suetonius.

Cunobeline appears in British legend as Cynfelyn (Welsh), Kymbelinus (medieval Latin) or Cymbeline, as in the play by William Shakespeare. His name is a compound made up of cuno- (hound) and Belenos (the god Belenus).

This Cymbeline achieved legendary status in my eyes, but - although he was always very kind to me - he always seemed fonder of my little brother, and my younger, prettier friends. When a rumour went round the village that he was a convicted child molester, they cut him out of our lives completely. Or at least they thought that they did. I was a rebellious enough teenager to take the opposite viewpoint on anything that my parents did, and I had reasons of my own for suspecting that the story was not true....at least not completely so. A year or two later, when I was old enough to own a bicycle, and proficient enough upon the machine to travel around the district unscathed, I started to visit the elderly couple again, and revel in their collection of arcane junk. They always made me welcome, and asked after the rest of my family wistfully.

The Rev. Cymbaline never showed any signs of wanting to seduce me, and the only harm that I ever came to during my visits to their house was indigestion from Miss Britannia's terrible cooking. As I got older, and eventually passed my driving test, my visits to the odd couple became less frequent as I discovered girls and alcohol, and eventually left home, but I would still go and visit them whenever I returned.

In the late 1970s they acquired a maidservant; a taciturn and podgy girl in her late teens, with a hare lip and a serious speech impediment, who they called Lysistrata, although I very much doubt whether that was the name that her parents had given her. Each time I would drive up to visit them, she would answer the door with a grimace and - spraying me with saliva as she did so would announce my arrival, and tell me that "The Master and the Mistress will see you now Sir". For some reason that I could never fathom out, there was something incredibly sexy about this deformed and socially inept young woman, but my knowledge of social convention forbade me from taking the matter any further.

One day, whilst I was sitting with The Rev Cymbaline in the tiny Drawing Room, the subject of my parents came up, and he wistfully told me how much he missed seeing them, and asked me whether there was anything that I could do to repair the rift in their relationship. Sadly, and as tactfully as possible, I told the old man that my parents were disgusted by what they had found out about him, and that they were convinced that if they did so there would have been serious repercussions as far as my brother's safety would have been concerned.

He looked at me with the saddest eyes I have ever seen on any creature except for my dear bulldog cross boxer bitch Prudence, and said: "Things are often more complicated than at first they seem, dear boy. I wish your father would understand that".

I tried to explain that my parents found the complexities of my life too complicated to deal with, and I think he understood. We sat there in silence for about ten minutes, sipping brandy and looking sadly at each other, until Lysistrata shambled in, banged a grubby brass gong and announced that the mistress wished to see us in her parlour.

It was the last time I was alone with him. I returned to Dawlish, my girlfriend, and my own complex sex life, and a few weeks later it turned out that he went into the woods at the back of their cottage, and shot himself with an antique shotgun that he - of course - had never notified the authorities about. My parents went to the funeral, and in the aftermath tried to make friends again with Miss Britannia. But she just sniffed haughtily at them, pulled herself up to her full height of just over five feet and stormed out of the church, clutching her trident and with her rusty helmet plonked back on her head. From then on, as far as I am aware, she never had contact with any of my family again, except on the odd occasions when I would pay a visit to the ever more tumbledown cottage full of junk, where she and Lysistrata eked out a living on State Benefits handed out by an ever more parsimonious government.

Slowly I began to realise that Miss Britannia Potts was a remarkable old lady. Feeling that she and her brother had been well and truly shafted by The Church of England, she turned her back on Mother Church, and began to investigate the old religion of her forefathers. She collected wild herbs which she dug with a silver athame [1] at the full moon and grew them in her little garden, and over the years became a very wise woman, if you know what I mean.

I got married, moved to Exeter and dramatically fell out with my parents, and so for the next twenty years or so my visits back to North Devon were few and far between. However, on the few occasions that I visited my family, I would sneak off for an hour, drive along the network

1. An Athame or Athamé is a ceremonial dagger, with a double-edged blade and usually a black handle. It is the main ritual implement or magical tool among several used in the religion of Wicca, and is also used in various other neopagan witchcraft traditions. A black-handled knife called an arthame appears in certain versions of the Key of Solomon, a grimoireoriginating in the Middle Ages.

The athame is mentioned in the writings of Gerald Gardner in the 1950s, who claimed to have been initiated into a surviving tradition of Witchcraft, the New Forest Coven. The athame was their most important ritual tool, with many uses, but was not to be used for actual physical cutting.

of tiny lanes towards Bradworthy and visit Miss Britannia and Lysistrata. Each time I visited they would look older and more decrepit, but still basically the same.

Ten years ago I returned to Woolsery to look after my dying father, and - against all the odds - the two of us, who had been figuratively at each other's throats for all our lives were reconciled. On his deathbed, a few weeks before the end he said to me that he wondered whether he had been too harsh to the Rev Cymbaline. I answered noncommittally, not wishing to sunder our newfound closeness by admitting that I had continued to visit the old parson and his sister for years, taking them gifts of groceries, and listening to their woes.

In passing, Dad told me that Miss Britannia was still alive, and still living with Lysistrata (the unspoken nuance being that their relationship was somehow unwholesome, whereas I had always considered them two orphans of the storm who had been thrown together by cruel happenstance). Miss Britannia still refused to speak to my Father, but could, he told me, occasionally be seen trudging through the lanes, Lysistrata at her side, still clutching her trident, and always wearing the increasingly rusty Graeco-Roman helmet.

After my Father died I went to visit them again, occasionally. But usually they just would not answer the door. On the odd occasions when they did, Miss Britannia would gaze at me with cloudy eyes over which the fog of Alzheimer's had long since settled, which only occasionally gave any indication that she knew what I was talking about, while Lysistrata, still wearing a tatty and grubby Maid's uniform, crouched by the side of her chair glaring malaevolently at me.

Britannia is an ancient term for Roman Britain and also a female personification of the island. The name is Latin, and derives from the Greek form Prettanike or Brettaniai, which originally designated a collection of islands with individual names, including Albion or Great Britain; however, by the 1st century BC Britannia came to be used for Great Britain specifically. In AD 43 the Roman Empire began its conquest of the island, establishing a province they called Britannia, which came to encompass the parts of the island south of Caledonia (roughly Scotland). The native Celtic inhabitants of the province are known as the Britons. In the 2nd century, Roman Britannia came to be personified as a goddess, armed with a trident and shield and wearing a Corinthian helmet.

The Latin name Britannia long survived the Roman withdrawal from Britain in the 5th century, and yielded the name for the island in most European and various other languages, including the English Britain and the modern Welsh Prydain. After centuries of declining use, the Latin form was revived during the English Renaissance as a rhetorical evocation of a British national identity. Especially following the Acts of Union in 1707, which joined the Kingdoms of England and Scotland, the personification of the martial Britannia was used as an emblem of British imperial power and unity. She was featured on all modern British coinage series until the redesign in 2008, and still appears annually on the gold and silver "Britannia" bullion coin series.

The age of the British Empire, the last few years of which I lived through, was well and truly past. The Empire on which the sun never set was reduced to just over a dozen tiny island possessions of little military or commercial importance. Britannia no longer rules the waves, but I am one of the few people who suspects that she is embodied by a lonely old woman living with a sociopathic maidservant on Disability Living Allowance, in a tumbledown cottage which stank unaccountably of yeast, and because her own world had crumbled around her ears she was stoically waiting for the end of the world for the rest of her species.

My visits there had become less and less frequent, and eventually I stopped going altogether. But I now knew what I had to do next. Despite everything that I felt, it was time for me to go and talk to Britannia.

XVII

I am fundamentally a coward. On a rainy Tuesday morning in early October there were all sorts of things that I would have preferred to do than be negotiating the twisty turny back lames to Bradworthy. Summer had come early this year and even by the end of our annual Weird Weekend on the third weekend of August the leaves were turning brown and beginning to fall. The season of mists and mellow fruitfulness came in with a bang, and by October the winter was very noticeably around the corner. Diabetes, or to be more specific diabetic neuropathy, has played merry havoc on large chunks of my central nervous system, and for several years now I have not been able to feel much beneath my knees.

This makes driving particularly problematical, and I have pretty well stopped driving on long journeys. But I manage to potter around the lanes on occasion, although I never venture further than the supermarket on this side of Bideford. On longer journeys either Graham or Corinna drive me, but on this occasion I had my own reasons not to want company on my journey. The lanes were each decorated by a covering of slimy half decomposed leaves, and the skeletal fingers of the naked bushes on the badly trimmed hedges were silhouetted unpleasantly against the stormy grey sky. I love this part of North Devon, and there are times of the year when I truly believe that it is one of the most beautiful places that I have seen during my travels across the world, but in a grey, wet and inclement October, I will be the first to admit that it can be disturbing and quite unpleasant.

It has been over thirty years since the Rev Cymbeline Potts shot himself in the woods behind the tumbledown cottage that he shared with his sister Britannia and Lysistrata, the peculiar taciturn teenage girl who seemed to have taken up residence with them. What exactly her position was I never did manage to fathom out; whether she was a maidservant, a ward, or something else that I hadn't thought of, I never did know, and as both women became more withdrawn and feral in the years following Cymbeline's death, it was a question that I had eventually decided that I would rather not ask, and to which I probably didn't want to know the answer.

In the intervening thirty years I very much doubt whether the cottage had ever been repaired or painted, and it looked to the casual observer that it had not been cleaned during those years either. The cottage garden which had once been a charming area like a Victorian picture postcard or one of Arthur Rackham's engravings of Kensington Gardens, was now an unschooled wilderness, but one which had somehow retained a wild elegance all of its own. But like the rest of the North Devon countryside, it was hardly at its best at this time of year.

However it was much less prepossessing than normal, as what appeared to be the mauled heads of badgers and foxes were decomposing, impaled upon sticks in the garden, and there was a little heap of what was obviously roadkill (from the tyre tracks upon them) outside the gate.

I parked my battered little Astra outside the cottage gate, which - not at all to my surprise - was hanging half off its hinges - got out, and - leaning heavily on my stick - limped up to the front door. I knocked on the door, and absolutely nothing happened. A minute or so later, I knocked again, and then, a few minutes later, again. On the fifth or sixth occasion, I heard a muffled shout from inside, followed a few moments later by shuffling footsteps.

The door creaked open, and Lysistrata stood slouched on the doormat. "What do you want?" she hissed at me malevolently. I thought to myself that if she was indeed the Potts family's domestic servant, and had been for the past three decades, I truly didn't think that their programme of in service training had been overly effective. I muttered something politely to her, and - a little to my surprise, as I was expecting more difficulties in the matter - she led me into the small parlour where Britannia was sitting, tatting in a rocking chair, and looking vacantly in my direction.

I hobbled over to the least rickety looking chair, and manoeuvred myself into a sitting position. Just for a few moments a thousand years of breeding came to the surface, and this senile old lady with the wild staring eyes, became a *grande dame*. "Bring Master Jonathan a cup of tea, girl", and Lysistrata - who must have been watching a couple of episodes of *Downton Abbey* [1] - curtseyed clumsily and went about her business. I was fifty six last birthday, and I truly don't think that anyone has ever called me 'Master Jonathan' since I was about fourteen. But as I had slowly come to realise over the past few times that I had seen Britannia, that the last few decades might never have happened as far as she was concerned. I was probably preserved in amber as the gangly teenaged boy who had dared to befriend her and her brother against the wishes of his parents, and the prejudices of the populous. Just for a moment I felt a prickle of tears in my eyes, as I realised that she was the only person left in the world who still thought of me as a child.

Lysistrata came in with a cracked, and very dirty mug containing the nastiest cup of tea that I have ever drunk. Then she disappeared into the bowels of the house leaving Britannia and me staring at each other in an uneasy silence.

I hadn't actually thought this through. I knew what I was going to do to a certain extent at least. But I hadn't thought any further than this. How was I going to ask anything, especially something as complex as I needed to ask, to an old woman who gave the impression at least that she didn't know her own name much of the time. In truth, I didn't even know what it was that I wanted to ask her. I mean, I did, but how would I put it all into words that made sense to me, let alone to a senile old biddy who had lived in her own world for decades.

So we sat there in silence, as I desperately tried to marshal my thoughts and work out what the hell I was going to do next. Under normal social circumstances one would have made small talk, but we didn't do anything. Occasionally I muttered the half hearted beginnings of a conversational gambit, but it always petered out after a few words as Britannia Potts stared at me implacably.

Then the last thing that I expected happened. Britannia sat upright, drew herself up to her full five foot nothing, and spoke with the authority and majesty of the social position that she once held at her command. One could surely believe at this moment that her ancestors had been barons who led armies into war and subdued entire colonial nations with a raised eyebrow and a stern look.

"So you want to find the little goat child? I do assure you it is perfectly safe..."

---

1. *Downton Abbey* is a British period drama television series created by Julian, Lord Fellowes and co-produced by Carnival Films and Masterpiece. It first aired on ITV in the United Kingdom on 26 September 2010 and on PBS in the United States on 9 January 2011 as part of the Masterpiece Classic anthology. Five series have been made so far; the fifth airing in the autumn of 2014 in the UK and Ireland, and began airing in the United States on 4 January 2015. A sixth series was commissioned, which, on 26 March 2015, was confirmed to be the final series.

The series, set in the fictional Yorkshire country estate of *Downton Abbey*, depicts the lives of the aristocratic Crawley family and their servants in the post-Edwardian era—with the great events in history having an effect on their lives and on the British social hierarchy.

This totally threw me and I blabbered for a few seconds before marshalling my thoughts to reply...

"Thank you for telling me that, but I would be happier if I could see Panne for myself. Some very disturbing things have been happening lately, and I not only wish to make certain that she is safe, but I want some answers..."

As I spoke, I could hear myself use the sort of formal language that I remembered my father using when, as a boy, a senior grandee of Her Majesty's Overseas Civil Service came to dinner. As I am six foot seven, have unkempt hair half way down my back and a bushy beard, and was wearing an anarchopunk T Shirt and a black leather jacket, this must have sounded more than a little incongruous.

But Britannia Potts was of the generation of doughty ladies, who if they hadn't actually built The British Empire, had presided magisterially over its dissolution, and if she was surprised by this incongruity she didn't say so. With a ladylike smile, that could have been performed at any Government House throughout the Raj, she said:

"One thing at a time, dear boy. If you want the child you must call its Father," and she stood up slowly and gracefully, calling for Lysistrata as she did so. When the grotesque little thing joined us, she beckoned me to stand up and come into the middle of the room. She reached for her trident, which I hadn't noticed before, but which was standing in the corner of the room next to her helmet, and - disturbingly - a meat cleaver. She beckoned to me and Lysistrata, and had as each stand, legs slightly akimbo, and with both hands on the shaft of the trident. Then she began to chant:

"Pan Pan Pan, Io Pan Pan Pan" [1]

And slowly, almost diffidently, Lysistrata and I joined in...

"Pan Pan Pan, Io Pan Pan Pan"

And as other voices joined in from God knows where, the room suddenly changed.

What happened next is almost impossible to describe, although I will try. I am no Thomas de Quincy [2], who wrote:

1. Presumably from Hymn to Pan by Aleister Crowley. The phrase io Saturnalia was the characteristic shout or salutation of the festival, originally commencing after the public banquet on the single day of December 17. The interjection io (Greek ὤ, ἰῶ) is pronounced either with two syllables (a short i and a long o) or as a single syllable (with the i becoming the Latin consonantal j and pronounced yō). It was a strongly emotive ritual exclamation or invocation, used for instance in announcing triumph or celebrating Bacchus, but also to punctuate a joke. So it actually means much the same as Yo does today.

2. Thomas Penson De Quincey (15 August 1785 – 8 December 1859) was an English essayist, best known for his Confessions of an English Opium-Eater (1821). Many scholars suggest that in publishing this work De Quincey inaugurated the tradition of addiction literature in the West.

"Some of these rambles led me to great distances; for an opium-eater is too happy to observe the motions of time. And sometimes in my attempts to steer homewards, upon nautical principles, by fixing my eye on the pole-star, and seeking ambitiously for a north-west passage, instead of circumnavigating all the capes and headlands I had doubled in my outward voyage, I came suddenly upon such knotty problems of alleys, such enigmatical entries, and such sphinx's riddles of streets without thoroughfares, as must, I conceive, baffle the audacity of porters, and confound the intellects of hackney-coachmen."

...and although I have opened the doors of perception on many occasions (admittedly, far less often as I got older) I have never gained any great spiritual insights through having done so, and although I last dipped my toe in the psychedelic ocean over thirty years ago, I remember the chemical dreams came on slowly and gradually replaced, or augmented reality.

Likewise, on the few occasions that I have suffered full blown psychotic attacks, the hallucination sort of flickers in and out of reality, before attaching itself in an insidious way to what is already there.

But on this occasion one reality was immediately replaced by another, almost completely different one. The only thing that was the same was that the three of us were standing, all six of our hands on Britannia's trident, and chanting. But everything else was completely different. We seemed to be out of doors. The sky was blood red, the ground beneath our feet as black as obsidian and as smooth as glass, and.....um....

We were all naked.

This was not the first time I have performed a magickal ritual, or working or whatever you want to call it. It was not even the first time I had done so skyclad. But it was the first time I had been put into the position of doing so without my knowledge. And it was the first time in over a decade I had been naked in front of anyone but my wife or doctor. There didn't seem anything that I could do about it, so I kept on chanting, as did my two companions.

The chants became louder as more and more voices joined in.. Although I couldn't see them I could feel more and more naked bodies joining the throng holding onto the trident. The chanting grew louder and more frenetic.

I could hear drums, and wild music, and my body filled with an unearthly euphoria, something between immense sexual excitement and wanting to throw up.

I started to scream, as did everyone else. And the crimson sky above us parted and an immense sheet of violet lightning crashed through the miasma and came down towards the head of the trident. Everything went black, and I passed out.

XVIII

I woke up with a bloody awful headache. I was lying crumpled on the floor of Britannia's parlour. My mouth was dry, and my temples pounded, and my walking stick was nowhere to be seen. I very much doubt whether anyone reading this would believe me if I claimed to be some sort of total stranger to hangovers. I got my first hangover in 1976, a few days before my seventeenth birthday, and I have been having them with depressing regularity ever since. This felt like a hangover, but on this occasion there was something missing. I hadn't actually had anything to drink.

I don't think that I am an alcoholic, but I will admit that I drink more alcohol than most people deem appropriate in this day and age. One of the more depressing side effects of this is that, quite probably as a side effect of mixing large amounts of brandy with the various psychotropic chemicals which I am prescribed each day, is that sometimes I do get blackouts. There are times that I wake up in the morning, not remembering what I had done the night before, and I have had to learn the discipline of having to reconstruct what happened out of fragmentary memories.

So I tried to do this now. The skill involves gathering all the available evidence, and trying to fill in the gaps. The trouble was that I couldn't remember anything. Also, without my walking stick I was not able to actually get up off the floor. So I crawled across the grubby carpet like an arthritic newt, and then - to my horror - my trousers begun to come off.

I then realised that my clothes were feeling odd...it was as if I hadn't dressed myself properly that morning. It was almost as if someone else had dressed me.

As I crawled, inch by inch, the joints of my legs, and elbows, shooting pain across my body, I caught a glimpse of something moving outside the grubby window. It was Lysistrata, carrying what seemed to be a bundle of roadkill in her dumpy arms, and shuffling across the unkempt lawn. A thought came shooting, unbidden, into my befuddled brain that "I don't recognise you with your clothes on", and - in horror - I remembered some, but not all of what had transpired the previous evening.

Corinna and I have been together for over a decade now, and married for nearly eight years of that time. In that decade I have, and will always be, completely faithful to her, and the only woman apart from her to have seen me even partly *dishabille* was my doctor.

Until last night that is, as the shocking memory of me, Lysistrata, and Britannia Potts, as naked as the day we were born, chanting arcane rhymes, and screaming eldritch fury to the scarlet, lightning-flecked clouds above us as we summoned primal deities from fuck knows where, flooded across my cerebral cortex. I knew that I had done nothing for which I should have reproached myself. But it was a shocking memory, and one, when combined with my burgeoning realisation that it had been one of these two terrifying women who had dressed me after the ritual had concluded, made me feel that what I now realised was not a hangover, was the least of my problems. Eventually I reached one of the armchairs, and levered myself up, and much to my relief I found my walking stick, and after eventually getting my breath back, I staggered to my feet.

The house was as silent as the grave. I looked around, and realised, guiltily, that I actually didn't know what to do next. I had only ever been here in Britannia's parlour, and in her late brother's study, and the drawing room full of junk, and I had no idea how to find my way around the rest of the house. I was in dire need of a pee, but I had no idea how to find a lavatory, and I had grave reservations about exploring the tumbledown cottage unbidden. I also was in a quandry about whether I actually wanted to see either of my hostesses again this soon.

On one side, the rules of gentlemanly behaviour would suggest that it would be massively impolite to just sneak off and pretend the whole thing had never happened, which is what I so badly wanted to do.

On the other hand, for the first time in many years, I found myself in the embarrassing position of having been unexpectedly naked with two women the night before, and the male fight or flight mechanism was kicking in big time, and was telling me to do what human males have always done ever since a Cro Magnon [1] male found himself unexpectedly getting his kit off in the cave of a Cro Magnon female, with whom he was not ready to comingle on a social level; to run like hell.

I felt in my trouser pocket. The car keys were still there. Thank God.

I looked around again. Lysistrata was still waddling about in the garden with two dead and rather mangled badgers under her arm. The only way that I knew out of the house would take me straight past her.

OK I had fancied her when I was about nineteen, but at the age of 55 I think that it was probably her who had dressed me in the wee small hours, and that level of intimacy did not sit comfortably with me. I rationalised to myself that it would probably not sit comfortably with her either, and that - as a gentleman - there was nothing that I could honourably do but sneak out into the back garden, and back to my car. preferably without running into Britannia Potts. And hopefully I would find a

---

1. Cro-Magnon is a common name that has been used to describe the first early modern humans (early *Homo sapiens sapiens*) that lived in the European Upper Paleolithic. Current scientific literature prefers the term European early modern humans (EEMH), to the term 'Cro-Magnon,' which has no formal taxonomic status, as it refers neither to a species or subspecies nor to an archaeological phase or culture. The earliest known remains of Cro-Magnon-like humans are radiocarbon dated to 43-45,000 years before present that have been discovered in Italy and Britain, with the remains found of those that reached the European Russian Arctic 40,000 years ago.

Cro-Magnons were robustly built and powerful. The body was generally heavy and solid with a strong musculature. The forehead was fairly straight rather than sloping like in Neanderthals, and with only slight browridges. The face was short and wide. The chin was prominent. The brain capacity was about 1,600 cubic centimetres (98 cu in), larger than the average for modern humans. However, recent research suggests that the physical dimensions of so-called "Cro-Magnon" are not sufficiently different from modern humans to warrant a separate designation.

lavatory along the way, and if not, there was probably a convenient gooseberry bush in the back garden. But which way was the back garden?

I looked around me again, and realised something strange. Something stranger than normal, I should say. It was a cold and windy day in early October, grey rainclouds scudded across the sky, and the naked branches of the decaying trees silhouetted skeletally against the sky. But somewhere, I was sure that I could hear birdsong.

I looked around once again, and saw a door in the corner of the room. It was slightly ajar, and I remembered that on the occasions I had been to tea with Britannia and Cymbelline over the years, Lysistrata had always made her entry through that door, so it was not an enormous leap of faith to suppose that it led to the kitchen. And where there was a kitchen there might well be a downstairs loo, and - even more importantly - a back door through which I could escape. So I went in, and - to my great relief - found both. After answering my - by this time very urgent - call of nature, I approached the back door. I already knew that the weather outside was particularly grim even by my the standards of North Devon autumn, but I could still hear birdsong, and I could see bright summer sunshine pouring in through the half open back door.

I went outside, and was emerged. The front garden of the cottage was frankly a disturbing mess, which looked as if nobody had lifted a finger to tend it for decades, and the cottage itself was not much better. But this beautifully tended cobbled courtyard garden, was exquisite. It looked for all the world like one of the olde worlde paintings on jigsaw puzzles that my maternal grandmother had enjoyed doing in her dotage, and it was completely at odds with the rest of the place. At the far end of the courtyard was a stile and a path which led into a woodland of such a Disneyesque fairytale quality that I expected to hear high twinkling sounds from a celeste, and some badly animated bluebirds swooping about trilling musically at each other. There was a large, comfortable, stone bench against the cottage wall, looking straight at the stile, and - for the first time that day - I felt one of my most primal urges beginning to well up. I knew that this was one of the urges that I should not even attempt to fight, and so I limped over to the bench, lowered myself down, and reached into my pocket for two of my friends; Mr Benson and Mr Hedges.

Of all the drugs I have taken over the years, the one to which I am most addicted, in fact, the only one to which I have *ever* been truly addicted is cigarettes. I don't think that it is even nicotine or tar to which I am addicted, and am sure in my own heart of hearts, that it is whatever crap that B&H put into the tobacco to keep it burning, make it taste fresh, or whatever, that I am addicted to, because although I have given up smoking for different lengths of time over the years, nearly eight years once, I always come running back to my slavemaster. And if there was ever a day that I sorely needed a cigarette it was today.

So I sat back, luxuriating in the warmth of this unseasonally glorious sunlight and took a deep gasp of my cigarette, as I tried to decide what I was going to do next. But my cogitations hadn't got very far when I could see a small, chestnut brown figure walk slowly out of the woodland, down the path, over the stile and slowly down the cobbled path towards me.

It was Panne.

XIX

T he rest of North Devon was cold, grey and wet, covered with a slimy carpet of decayed leaves. But here, in the back garden of the tumbledown little cottage on one of the less frequented lanes between my village of Woolsery and the little town of Bradworthy, it was a beautiful summer's morning, like something described by the pen of Enid Blyton [1]. It was the sort of summer morning that I knew as a child, and which came less and less often as the innocence of childhood was replaced by the compromises, and moral grey areas of adulthood, and which eventually disappeared for good, round about the time that I realised that my life was never going to work out the way that I had always wanted it to do.

I didn't know whether the place in which I found myself was what the world truly was like beneath all the artifice and shameful compromising of adulthood, or whether it was just the result of some magickal artifice that I didn't (and truly didn't want to) understand. But for the moment, my tired and battered body luxuriated in the glorious golden sunlight as I lazily watched two hummingbird hawk moths [2] feeding from the most luxurious hollyhocks this side of *The Children of Cherry Tree Farm.* [3]

1. Enid Mary Blyton (11 August 1897 – 28 November 1968) was an English children's writer whose books have been among the world's best-sellers since the 1930s, selling more than 600 million copies. Blyton's books are still enormously popular, and have been translated into almost 90 languages; her first book, *Child Whispers*, a 24-page collection of poems, was published in 1922. She wrote on a wide range of topics including education, natural history, fantasy, mystery stories and biblical narratives, and is best remembered today for her Noddy, Famous Five, and Secret Seven series.#

2. The hummingbird hawk-moth (*Macroglossum stellatarum*) is a species of Sphingidae. Its long proboscis and its hovering behaviour, accompanied by an audible humming noise, make it look remarkably like a hummingbird while feeding on flowers. The resemblance to hummingbirds is an example of convergent evolution. It flies during the day, especially in bright sunshine, but also at dusk,dawn, and even in the rain, which is unusual for even diurnal hawkmoths. Its visual abilities have been much studied, and it has been shown to have a relatively good ability to learn colours. The hummingbird hawk-moth is distributed throughout the northern Old World from Portugal to Japan, but is resident only in warmer climates (southern Europe, North Africa, and points east). It is a strong flier, dispersing widely and can be found virtually anywhere in the hemisphere in the summer. However it rarely survives the winter in northern latitudes (e.g. north of the Alps in Europe, north of the Caucasus in Russia).

3, A children's novel by Enid Blyton published in 1940, and a great favourite of mine when I was a child. My Grandmother gave me a copy for my sixth birthday and I treasure it still. The story is about four brothers and sisters (Rory, Sheila, Benjy and Penny), who have been ill, and are sent to live on Cherry Tree Farm while their parents go to America on business. Cherry Tree Farm is owned by their Uncle Tim and Auntie Bess and the children are excited at the thought of being in the countryside, rather than at home in London, for the next few months. The city is associated with all that is dreary and sickly and is described in images of confinement, with the children gazing "out of a window" upon a busy street and "a patch of trees and grass with a tall railing round them." By contrast, the countryside is a place of vibrancy and freedom where the children plan to "go wild." Even the name of the farm — Cherry Tree Farm — conjures up a vision of trees hung with ripe cherries; a picture of health and abundance. In their early days on the farm, the children meet the baby animals and help to feed the lambs and milk the cows. Rory has a close shave with a bull and Penny conquers her fear of the hissing geese. However, it is when Tammylan comes into their lives that the children really get to know the countryside. Tammylan is a hermit or "wild man" who lives alone in a cave (or, in the summer, in a house of willow.) He understands the ways of wild things, helping birds and animals in need and concocting food and medicines from roots and herbs. He is described in animal terms himself, with a hand that "seemed more like a paw, it was so thin and brown," and he relates to animals more easily than to people.

The unseasonable sun beamed gently upon the fairytale garden as Panne walked slowly towards me. If this actually had been a fairy tale, I reflected, there would have been a clearly defined beginning, middle and end to the story. But as I have discovered more and more as I get older, things in life are never clear cut. I suppose that it could be argued that a person's life begins with their birth and ends with their death, but even that isn't really that clearly defined.

If you are writing the biography of someone, you usually talk about their parents and even their grandparents. In one music biography which I had to review about a quarter of a century ago, the first chapter went as far back as the protagonist's antecedents and their activities during The Crusades [1]. And of course the story doesn't end with a person's death either. What happens during a person's life can, and does, reverberate across the centuries that follow. As Ira Howard said: "Life is short, but the years are long. Not while the evil days cometh not."

As Panne walked slowly towards me, I tried to decide what I should do next.

On one level this was already a given; I was going to take her home with me, and then try to explain everything to my dear wife, who was already going to be somewhat perturbed, to say the least, because I had been missing for at least one night - I realised, with a guilty start that I actually had no idea how long I had been away from home, and that I was only *assuming* that it had only been for a single night.

But first, I was only too aware that I knew practically nothing about what was going on, and about the nature of the events into which I had become inadvertently embroiled, and into which it looked like I was just about to involve my beloved family. I had turned my back upon what I very much dislike calling 'psychic questing' the best part of two decades ago. The quest for the Cornish Owlman had not been the only reason that my first marriage had collapsed, far from it, but it had certainly been a causative factor. And although my journeys down the left hand path had continued for a few years, by the end of 2000 I had lost so many people dear to me, and been through so many traumatic experiences to the detriment of my mental and physical health, that I decided - with the help of a long ceremony performed by a witch, an old friend of mine in Leeds [2] - to leave that part of my life behind for good. And since then, I always have.

But now I found myself deep in the middle of something that I truly didn't understand, and for which all my experience - such as it is - had done very little to prepare me. And I knew that, like it or not, I would have to get as many answers as I could.

By now Panne was standing right in front of me, his/her pelt glinting chestnut in the sun. I took his/her hairy little hands in mine and looked straight at her, and was both surprised, shocked, and saddened to see that there were tears rolling slowly down its cheeks, making the fur all matted and dark. I have never hugged a God before, but I put my arms round Panne mulling him/her to me. "I don't know why you ran away", I said in the quietest and calmest voice that I could manage. "I am going to take you home with me, and Corinna and I will look after you. But first you must help

1. A book about Chris de Burgh by Dave Thompson.
2. Joyce Howarth died in 2014 at the age of sixty

me."... It suddenly entered my head, that either due to high magickal protocols, or sheer common sense, I could not try to find out too much at once. I didn't know how much Panne actually knew, but I could see that deity or not, (s)he was a frightened and tired little thing, and I doubted the wisdom of trying to find out too much at once.

"Just tell me one thing," I said calmly, still holding Panne's hands, and looking into his/her (It really doesn't sit right with me to refer to Panne as 'it') tearful eyes, I asked the one question that was foremost in my eyes. "Panne. Who are you?"

Still without saying anything, Panne leaned forward until his/her two little horns were once again touching my forehead. Once again I felt a searing pain across my temples, and an overwhelming wave of nausea, as my world suddenly turned black.

XX

O h for a muse of Fire that would ascend the brightest heaven of invention".

Shakespeare wrote that, and the words are said by the chorus [1] in *Henry V*, the play that I studied for my O Levels back in 1976. I find myself wishing for the same thing because I am not sure how to describe what happened next. Not for the first time in my peculiar life I find myself in the position of trying to describe an experience for which no satisfactory words exist in the English language. This is a challenge which has stumped far greater writers than I, but I shall try and have a go anyway.

It was a bit like being in the audience of a play, except for the fact that my seat (for I remained sitting on the old garden bench throughout what happened) seemed to be on the stage itself. I was apart from the action, in that I was invisible to the actors, but I was right in the thick of the action, only that I was not. I could even pick up a little of the emotions exuded by the protagonists, but whether this was truly the emotions that they were feeling, or whether it was emotions that I was feeling as a reaction to the action I was watching I have no idea. And I don't suppose that it matters very much either.

The pain in the frontal portions of my cerebral cortex was even more debilitating and acute than it had been on the first occasion that Panne had put his/her horns onto my forehead but it allowed me to catch a glimpse of wonderful things that left me with more questions than answers. I was glad that I was sitting when this happened, because I would have surely fallen to the floor in shock and awe if I had been standing. I felt like someone had driven a red hot nail into my forehead and I could feel every one of the ridges of Panne's little horns burning indelibly into my flesh. It truly was, I remain convinced, the worst hurting that I have ever felt.

---

1. A Greek chorus (Greek: χορός, *khoros*) is a homogeneous, non-individualised group of performers in the plays of classical Greece, who comment with a collective voice on the dramatic action. The chorus consisted of between 12 and 50 players, who variously danced, sang or spoke their lines in unison and sometimes wore masks. I feel more like a *khoros* than the protagonist of this book, because for most of the time I was a passive observer of events rather than an active participant.

The only good thing about it was that it didn't last very long, and the wondrous visions that replaced the pain were so extraordinary that the memory of the pain was soon washed away by the Waters of Lethe [1].

I probably shouldn't describe what I saw as 'wondrous visions'. I am afraid that it probably leads the hapless reader into expecting that I am going to describe some sort of glorious vision of Xanadu [2]. Well, I am not. Not unless Kubla Khan's fabled summer palace was actually situated on the outer reaches of a rather rundown trading estate on the outskirts of Barnstaple.

Not for the first time in this story, a location seemed to have been taken straight out of my own memories, and twisted to suit the opportunistic needs of the storyteller whoever he or she was. Because, like Hawkmoor Hospital, this was a place that I knew very well. During spring of 1982 I came to this place on many occasions. Like on so many other occasions in my life it was a mixture of sex, cryptozoology and rock and roll that brought me there.

Let's get the cryptozoology out of the way first. At the end of the last Ice Age when the glaciers retreated, there was only a relatively short time before the land bridges which connected our islands to mainland Europe disappeared, and what are now known as the North Sea, and the English Channel, came into being.

Because there was only a relatively short window of opportunity, only a small number of the reptiles of mainland Europe reached the British Isles, and we resultantly have a very sparse herpetofauna. Two of our rarest reptiles are the smooth snake and the sand lizard, both of which are restricted to relatively small and specialised sandy areas on the south coast of England. However, there have been persistent rumours for years that both species can be found in a number of sites on the north coast of the South West peninsula. There are sand lizards on Braunton Burrows, just a few miles from Barnstaple, and so, when someone (the drummer in a local punk band) told me that they had seen bright green lizards sunning themselves on a sand heap on the outer edges of the aforementioned industrial estate, I wondered whether they could be a hitherto undiscovered colony of *Lacerta agilis*.

I also had more sordid reasons for wanting to be somewhere more secluded, where I could park my car, open the sun roof and bask, lizardlike, in the unseasonably golden sunshine. At

---

1, In Greek mythology, Lethe (Greek: Λήθη), was one of the five rivers of Hades. Also known as the Ameles pota-mos (river of unmindfulness), the Lethe flowed around the cave of Hypnos and through the Underworld, where all those who drank from it experienced complete forgetfulness. Lethe was also the name of the Greek spirit of forgetful-ness and oblivion, with whom the river was often identified. In Classical Greek, the word lethe literally means "oblivion", "forgetfulness", or "concealment". It is related to the Greek word for "truth", aletheia (ἀλήθεια), which through the privative alpha literally means "un-forgetfulness" or "un-concealment".

2. Not that stupid fucking song by Olivia Newton John. Shangdu (also known as Xanadu(, was the capital of Kublai Khan's Yuan dynasty in China, before he decided to move his throne to the Jin dynasty capital of Zhōngdū (Chinese: 中都), which he renamed Khanbaliq, present-day Beijing. Shangdu then became his summer capital. Shangdu (Xanadu) was visited by the Venetian traveller Marco Polo in about 1275, and was destroyed in 1369 by the Ming army under Zhu Yuanzhang. In 1797 historical accounts of the city inspired the famous poem *Kubla Khan* by the English Romantic poet Samuel Taylor Coleridge.

the time I was somewhat involved with a slutty but good natured teenage girl called Samantha, and I had very good reasons for wanting somewhere where I could park my car in peace and quiet, and have an uninterrupted afternoon. So the two of us went to explore the derelict edges of this rather unprepossessing Xanadu, singularly failed to see any lizards whatsoever, although my researches into human biology continued rather successfully.

But none of that is particularly important. It only goes to explain why and how I had quite an intimate (in several senses if the word) experience of the geography of this secret part of Barnstaple that I very much doubt whether one in a thousand of its residents knows exists. We explored, both in the car and on foot, every inch of the run down development, and - thirty three years later - I was seeing it again.

Although, back in 1982 when Samantha and I were exploring, we were the only people there; the owners having gone bankrupt some years before, and nobody caring enough about the place to do anything with it. The place I saw in my dream/vision/trance/psychodrama/ whatever the fuck it was, was very much inhabited. There was a big double garage with the doors half hanging off that I remembered fondly, because it had been outside this unpromising edifice that Samantha and I had finally parked my battered blue Toyota Corona [1] and got down to the non-herpetological business of the afternoon.

The double garage that I was seeing today in my mind's eye was very much inhabited. There was a double mattress on the floor and a couple of old army blankets and an eiderdown on top. Against the wall was a makeshift set of shelves made out of planks and books, and these were crammed with books. There was a Calor Gas stove in the corner, and a box of sundry household impedimenta next to it.

I looked around, and I could see that there were more derelict cars there than there had been upon my visit. And in most of the derelict cars there were blankets or other signs of occupation. And when I looked around at the neighbouring garages which bordered onto the double garage which held such sweet memories for me, I could see that each one had someone living in them, mostly blank eyed women who had the world weary expression worn by people who know that whatever life was going to throw at them, it was never going to get any better or worse for them than it was at this very moment.

The voice of that insufferable ass Loyd Grossman [2] came into my head, as I wondered who

1. The Toyota Corona 1600 Sedan (RT82), which was made in the first half of the 1970s was quite a sexy car.

2. Loyd Daniel Gilman Grossman, CBE, FSA (born 16 September 1950) is an American-Britishtelevision presenter, gastronome and musician who has mainly worked in the United Kingdom. He is currently a judge on ITV Food series *Food Glorious Food*. Grossman has an ongoing career as a singer initially with punk band Jet Bronx And The Forbidden, who reached number 49 in the UK singles chart in December 1977 with "Ain't Doin' Nothing". He returned to playing music in 2008. Following a guest appearance playing "Ain't Doin Nothin" with the Pork Dukes at the Vienna Rebellion punk festival on 27 April 2008, he played with his new band Jet Bronx and the New Forbidden at the 2008 Rebellion Festival in Blackpool and at Glastonbury in 2012 and 2014/ Grossman's television début came in April 1987, as a roving presenter for *Through the Keyhole*, a programme examining the homes of the famous. Before leaving in 2003, Grossman made almost 400 appearances on the programme.

would possibly be living in my (I think I have already explained why I thought of the garage as mine) garage. Then I heard the sound of squeaky wheels and a wheelchair came slowly around the corner.

In the wheelchair was a burly, balding man with the remains of a head of light grey hair, and the ashy skin which comes from terminal cancer, and/or long term opiate abuse, often in conjunction with each other. He wheeled himself along tortuously, and when he pulled up outside the double garage in which I instinctively knew that he was living, he slowed up, dug with some difficulty into one of his jacket pockets and brought out a bottle of Oramorph.

For those of you not in the know, this following passage is taken directly from a NHS website:

Oramorph oral solution is a liquid containing the active ingredient morphine sulfate. Morphine is a type of medicine called an opioid painkiller. Opioids are strong painkillers that work by mimicking the action of naturally occurring pain-reducing chemicals called endorphins. Endorphins are found in the brain and spinal cord and reduce pain by combining with opioid receptors. Morphine mimics the action of endorphins by combining with the opioid receptors in the brain and spinal cord. This blocks the transmission of pain signals sent by the nerves to the brain. Therefore, even though the cause of the pain may remain, less pain is actually felt.

Morphine is, as I am sure that you are aware, used to relieve severe pain.

What that rather clinical little paragraph, and yes, the pun is intentional, doesn't say is that it is also a drug easily open to abuse. I know this from personal experience, having abused it myself on a number of occasions over the years.

It is a volatile and peculiar drug, and whilst it does indeed lull the inexperienced user into a place where he or she feels like they have just had a hot bath, a good meal and great sex, and are now wrapped in a swaddling shroud of warm pink cotton wool, some people also experience the most traumatic and severe hallucinations and delusions.

My father, for example, who was prescribed quite high doses of the drug during his final illness, went through a whole panoply of terrible hallucinations; he thought my mother was in the room with him, that the gardener was climbing in through the window to kill him, and that he was covered with scorpions who were about to rip off his genitals. Compared with that, my experiences were minor, but it remains a drug that I would not recommend to anyone, and one which should only be taken under strict medical supervision. Looking over the shoulder of the occupant of the wheelchair - someone whom I instinctively knew was called 'Eliphas' - as he unpacked a bag of medicine with the logo of the pharmacist at the local General Hospital, NDG, known colloquially as 'The Pilton Hilton', because of the district of the town in which it is situated, I could see that he had three types of cancer medicine. I recognised them from the days when I was a nurse.

I also saw that the bag held a Beretta 84F, an automatic handgun first manufactured in Italy in 1976, and commonly known as 'The Cheetah'. I would rather not say from which part of my peculiarly mis-spent life I recognised that.

XXI

I don't know how many of you reading this ever had a copy of *Doom* on their computer back in the late 1990s [1]. I know that I did. And my compadres and I spent many happy hours shooting at monsters, and once we worked out how to network our PCs, each other. It kept us happy for years. But one thing that I always liked to do, especially when stoned, was to use the 'No Clipping Mode' cheat IDSPISPOPD, and wander about 'behind the scenes', walking through walls impervious to attack and exploring the surprisingly complex landscape.

This was how I felt now. There was no doubt that I was inside the landscape that Panne had 'transported me to', for want of a better word (if I find one I shall let you know), but I was not part of it. I could explore it to a certain extent, but I could have no effect on what was happening in it. It was as if I was a player in Panne's personal video game, and someone had entered a 'no clipping' cheat for me, so that I could see everything that was going on, but not actually join in any of the gameplay.

I also appeared to have limited empathic powers. I could look at the characters and discover a certain amount about them, a bit like hovering your mouse above a character in one of the aforementioned video games, and being rewarded by a dialogue box which explained some vital facet of their character for the benefit of the player.

Looking at the fat man in the wheelchair, I somehow knew his name was Eliphas, and that he was very angry. Looking at his medication I could surmise that he was being treated for a particularly aggressive form of cancer, and the fact that he was in possession of a small, serviceable, and totally illegal handgun, made me surmise that his outlook on life was not necessarily that of a straightforward and law abiding citizen.

As soon as I discovered that I could move around the room, I made a bee line for his bookshelf, because in life I have always found that you can tell a lot about people from the contents of their bookshelves.

I could certainly tell a lot about Eliphas, because although there were only about forty books there, apart from a couple of technical books about chemistry, all the books were ones that could be found

1. Doom (typeset as DOOM in official documents) is a 1993 science fiction horror-themed first-person shooter (FPS) video game by id Software. It is considered one of the most significant and influential titles in the video game industry, for having ushered in the popularity of the first-person shooter genre. The original game is divided into three nine-level episodes and distributed viashareware and mail order. The Ultimate Doom, an updated release of the original game featuring a fourth episode, was released in 1995 and sold at retail.

In Doom, players assume the role of an unnamed space marine, who became popularly known as "Doomguy", fighting his way through hordes of invading demons from Hell. With one third of the game, nine levels, distributed as shareware, Doom was played by an estimated 10 million people within two years of its release, popularizing the mode of gameplay and spawning a gaming subculture. In addition to popularizing the FPS genre, it pioneered immerin certain parts of my ever expanding and rather peculiar library. The trouble is that whilst I will admit to owning books by the Marquis de Sade [1], Adolph Hitler [2], Aleister Crowley and Gerry Adams [3], I also own a lot more books by a lot of other people, which means what I think of as my "nasty shelf" is massively diluted. All that Eliphas had was my 'nasty shelf' writ large, with nothing to dilute it whatsoever.

There were books on the nastier end of ritual magick, the more violent end of politics, and the more apocalyptic bits of religious theory. Feeling disturbed by this I went through the wall into the next lock up garage and found nothing but some litre bottles of ammonia, and a box which said 'medical supplies'.

Deciding that I couldn't get any more information out of these two lockups, I drifted outside, and almost immediately bumped into Panne. Or rather into the human adolescent who I sensed would eventually metamorphose into the little goatfooted Godling, of whom I was getting so fond. The last time I had seen her she had been a little girl playing with her tricycle at some analogue of Hawkmoor Hospital, sometime during the 1970s. Now she looked as if she was eleven or twelve, but she had a feral glint in her eye that had been completely absent as a little girl.

---

1. Donatien Alphonse François, Marquis de Sade (2 June 1740 – 2 December 1814) was a
French aristocrat, revolutionary politician, philosopher and writer, famous for his libertine sexuality. His works include novels, short stories, plays, dialogues and political tracts; in his lifetime some were published under his own name, while others appeared anonymously and Sade denied being their author.

He is best known for his erotic works, which combined philosophical discourse with pornography, depicting sexual fantasies with an emphasis on violence, criminality and blasphemy against the Catholic Church. He was a proponent of extremefreedom, unrestrained by morality, religion or law. The words sadism and sadist are derived from his name.

2. Adolf Hitler (20 April 1889 – 30 April 1945) was an Austrian-born German politician who was the leader of the Nazi Party (German: Nationalsozialistische Deutsche Arbeiterpartei (NSDAP); National Socialist German Workers Party). He was Chancellor of Germany from 1933 to 1945 and Führer("leader") of Nazi Germany from 1934 to 1945. As effective dictator of Nazi Germany, Hitler was at the centre of World War II in Europe and the Holocaust.

3. Gerard Adams (Irish: Gearóid Mac Ádhaimh; born 6 October 1948) is an Irish republican politician, president of the Sinn Féin political party, and a Teachta Dála (Member of Parliament) forLouth since the 2011 general election. From 1983 to 1992 and from 1997 to 2011, he was an abstentionist Westminster Member of Parliament (MP) for Belfast West. He has been the president of Sinn Féin since 1983.

Since that time the party has become the fourth-largest party in the Republic of Ireland, the second-largest political party in Northern Ireland and the largest Irish nationalist party in that region. In 1984, Adams was seriously wounded in an assassination attempt by several gunmen from the Ulster Defence Association (UDA) includingJohn Gregg. From the late 1980s onwards, Adams was an important figure in the Northern Ireland peace process, initially following contact by the then-Social Democratic and Labour Party(SDLP) leader John Hume and then subsequently with the Irish and British governments. In 2005, the Provisional Irish Republican Army (IRA) indicated that its armed campaign was over and that it was exclusively committed to democratic politics.

Under Adams, Sinn Féin changed its traditional policy of abstentionism towards the Oireachtas, the Parliament of the Republic of Ireland, in 1986 and later took seats in the power-sharing Northern Ireland Assembly.

She was small for her age, and had a slim, boyish body, and untidy shoulder length hair. But her eyes were frightening. They burned with a fierceness, which hinted at experiences that a preteen girl should never have had to go through in order to gain eyes like that. I followed her for a while, as she slunk around the small compound looking more like a half starved feral cat than a human, and I was following her when she eventually went to ground in a makeshift 'nest' made out of cardboard and cotton waste. There were several scrapped cars, mostly wheel-less scattered around the yard, and Panne had decided to make her nest in the back of a wrecked minivan.

I continued to look around, and I discovered that although I still didn't understand the 'controls' that allowed me to traverse around the yard, I became better at using them. In a burst of uncharacteristic lasciviousness, I went back (forward?) to the place on the outskirts of the yard where Samantha and I had spent our illicit afternoon in 1982. I suddenly realised with horror that I had no idea what year it was, so there was every possibility that the metallic blue Toyota with the two naked bodies in it might still be there. To my great relief neither the car or the occupants were to be seen. I really don't think that it would do much good to the mental health of the 55 year old me to be confronted by the reverberations of the self-centred womanising of his 22 year old predecessor.

Just for old times sake, I even spent about half an hour looking to see if I could find any sand lizards, but just as in 1982 my search was fruitless. Then I realised that there was a way that I could find out what year it was, or at least what year it was after, and I made my way back to the main yard to check on the dates of the cars as extrapolated from the number plates.

I always remembered that in 1982 there was a band in Teignmouth called *Y Reg* symbolising that they were brand spanking new and up to the minute. So from that I should have no real difficulty in trying to extrapolate the dates of the wrecked cars in the yard.

I was right, it was a doddle. They ranged in date or about a decade from 1975, so the events I was observing could not have happened before the mid-1980s, and I suspected probably not before at least the beginning of the next decade. That made sense, and I had a self-congratulatory glow of satisfaction in what would have been my chest if I had actually had any corporeal substance in this brave new world.

But then I did some mental arithmetic.

If the girl who would become Panne had been five or six when I first saw her in about 1975, she should have been in her early twenties by the time that the early years of the 1990s crawled around. But she wasn't. Fifteen years or so had elapsed but she was still to enter puberty. Something odd - in fact I think I should say that something even odder than that which was already happening - was beginning to happen.

Believe it or not, I had actually forgotten the fear and unease that I had first experienced when I entered the derelict yard, and was even beginning to enjoy myself. But now, the realisation that I couldn't even trust the space-time continuum, was brought back to me with a thump, and I felt more uneasy than ever.

XXII

here being no real point in worrying, I continued to explore, and I found - to my surprise - that there appeared to be an entire community of people living in this derelict builder's yard. They were the deadbeats, the rejects of society, the homeless, the scorned and the unwanted, but rather to my surprise, they were all living together seemingly happily. The yard was clean and tidy, and even though the homes for some of these people were rusted out cars, there were pots of flowers dotted around the place, and no sign of the squalour or depravity that one might imagine that such a community might engender.

Now, I am getting tired of typing that I cannot explain how and why I was able to move around this area, how I was able to see and observe everything that was going on, but still remain separate from it all, and how even time itself didn't seem to work in the way that it should be expected to do. Let's just take it as read. I have no way of explaining it all, so I will just tell you what happened, and - quite truly - if you don't believe me, or if you think I am lying, mad or on drugs then I don't really care. I am writing this down to get the sequence of events right in my head, for my own satisfaction, and I don't really give a hoot what anyone else thinks of the matter.

So I won't attempt to explain how it was all a bit like a computer game; how when I had discovered enough to satisfy me in one situation, I would move on somewhere else as if my magic. Well actually it *was* by magic, and I would discover another missing bit of the puzzle.

It appeared that Eliphas was like the unelected, self-appointed leader of the group. He was a peacemaker who adjudicated any squabbles between residents, dispensed justice occasionally, and generally acted as a cross between kindly village schoolmaster and Mafia Don. I also discovered that he wasn't called Eliphas, which didn't surprise me, and that he had adopted the name (at that stage I hadn't found out what he was really called) what he was really called) after Eliphas Levi [1], a French occult author and ceremonial magician [2]. And a quick perusal of the internet whilst I was

1. Levi was the son of a shoemaker in Paris; he attended the seminary of Saint Sulpice and began to study to enter the Roman Catholicpriesthood. However, while at the seminary he fell in love, and left without being ordained. He wrote a number of minor religious works: *Des Moeurs et des Doctrines du Rationalisme en France* ("Of the Moral Customs and Doctrines of Rationalism in France," 1839) was a tract within the cultural stream of the Counter-Enlightenment. *La Mère de Dieu* ("The Mother of God," 1844) followed and, after leaving the seminary, two radical tracts, L'Evangile du Peuple ("The Gospel of the People," 1840), and *Le Testament de la Liberté* ("The Testament of Liberty"), published in the year of revolutions, 1848, led to two brief prison sentences. In 1852 Levi met Józef Maria Hoene-Wroński.

2. Lévi's version of magic became a great success, especially after his death. That Spiritualism was popular on both sides of the Atlantic from the 1850s contributed to this success. His magical teachings were free from obvious fanaticisms, even if they remained rather murky; he had nothing to sell, and did not pretend to be the inititate of some ancient or fictitious secret society. He incorporated the Tarot cards into his magical system, and as a result the Tarot has been an important part of the paraphernalia of Western magicians. He had a deep impact on the magic of theHermetic Order of the Golden Dawn and later on the ex-Golden Dawn member Aleister Crowley. He was also the first to declare that a pentagramor five-pointed star with one point down and two points up represents evil, while a pentagram with one point up and two points down represents good. It was largely through the occultists inspired by him that Lévi is remembered as one of the key founders of the 20th century revival of magic.

writing this told me, much to my surprise, that it wasn't his name either. "Eliphas Levi," the name under which he published his books, was his attempt to translate or transliterate his given names "Alphonse Louis" into the Hebrew language.

Eliphas (the one in a wheelchair on the outskirts of Barnstaple) had become interested in Levi's three principles of magic, after being diagnosed with terminal, and very aggressive, cancer. Steve Jones, a witch from Yorkshire who holds the distinction of having become a Justice of the Peace, and therefore Britain's first pagan magistrate, told me once that the were three main reasons that people did magick; to get laid, get rich, or get even. But Eliphas was doing it for a fourth reason. He didn't care about dying. he had been in pain for years, but he had become very fond of his homeless parishioners (as he thought of them, hearkening back to the days when the Church of England guaranteed a scholar and a gentleman in every parish, rather than half a dozen ugly lesbians scattered throughout a team ministry) as well as feeling completely responsible for them. And he knew that without him the little community would sooner rather than later fall apart, and he didn't want that to happen. So turning his back on the book learning and scholarship which had sustained him throughout his life, he began to investigate alternatives.

Eliphas Levi was in many ways one of the founders of modern magickal theory, and although I have always suspected that he was really rather a charlatan on the quiet, much of his codification of the secret arts, followed in the lines that I think myself.

That the material universe is only a small part of total reality, which includes many other planes and modes of consciousness. Full knowledge and full power in the universe are only attainable through awareness of these other aspects of reality. One of the most important of these levels or aspects of reality is the "astral light," a cosmic fluid which may be moulded by will into physical forms.

- "One can only define the unknown by its supposed and supposable relations with the known."
- "The divine ideal of the ancient world made the civilization which came to an end, and one must not despair of seeing the god of our barbarous fathers become the devil of our more enlightened children."
- That human willpower is a real force, capable of achieving absolutely anything, from the mundane to the miraculous.
- AXIOM 1: "Nothing can resist the will of man when he knows what is true and wills what is good."
- AXIOM 9: "The will of a just man is the Will of God Himself and the Law of Nature."
- AXIOM 20: "A chain of iron is less difficult to break than a chain of flowers."
- AXIOM 21: "Succeed in not fearing the lion, and the lion will fear YOU. Say to suffering, 'I will that you shall become a pleasure,' and it will prove to be such - and even more than a pleasure, it will be a blessing."

That the human being is a microcosm, a miniature of the macrocosmic universe, and the two are fundamentally linked. Causes set in motion on one level may equally have effects on another.

"Man is the God of the world, and God is the man of Heaven."

As I have already explained, I seemed to be able to go pretty much anywhere I wanted in the dilapidated builder's yard. But there was one place I could not go. There was one little locked room at the back of Eliphas' lock up that was denied to me, and it was here I instinctively knew that Eliphas believed that he was going to uncover the secret that would give him a degree enough of immortality to be able to stay and look after his 'children' for as long as he was needed. But what it was.....I had no idea.

So I followed the lives of this merry band of outcasts; two teenage girl runaways, and a venerable old meths [1] drinker with a long grey beard that made him look like Merlin (perhaps he *was* Merlin, nothing would surprise me much anymore, except that I suspected that I had already met Merlin on a number of occasions over the years, and that although looking superficially similar, they were completely different people). There were two middle aged tramps with wild staring eyes who never spoke to anyone except for each other, and who when they did mostly seemed to converse in a strange idiolect that nobody else could understand, or bothered to try. There was a slight boy with Down's syndrome. he was called Michael, and I realised with a shock that he had been a patient of mine back when. Had been a Nursing Assistant at a small hospital for what were then called Mentally Handicapped young adults in North Devon, thirty five years ago on my personal timeline.

There was an elderly woman with an even more aristocratic accent than my late mother (and that is saying something) and - in her little den in the back of the old minivan was Panne, or at least the girl who would one day become Panne.

I followed their everyday lives, went with the two teenage girls and Michael as they went garbage raiding, taking all the barely spoiled food which was thrown away each day into dumpsters at the back of supermarkets, to be thrown away or salvaged by this disparate little band who were so far below being an underclass that they didn't even have a name.

A song came into my head, sung to the tune (vaguely) of *The Red Flag.* [2]

---

1. Denatured alcohol, also called methylated spirits, is ethanol that has additives to make it poisonous, extremely bad tasting, foul smelling or nauseating, to discourage recreational consumption. In some cases it is also dyed. Denatured alcohol is used as a solvent and as fuel for alcohol burners and camping stoves. Because of the diversity of industrial uses for denatured alcohol, hundreds of additives and denaturing methods have been used. The main additive has traditionally been 10% methanol, giving rise to the term "methylated spirits". Other typical additives include isopropyl alcohol, acetone, methyl ethyl ketone, methyl isobutyl ketone, and denatonium. Denaturing alcohol does not chemically alter the ethanol molecule. Rather, the ethanol is mixed with other chemicals to form an undrinkable solution.

2. "The Red Flag" is a song associated with left-wing politics, in particular with socialism. It is the semi-official anthem of the British Labour Party, and the official anthem of the Northern Irish Social Democratic and Labour Party and Irish Labour Party. The song is traditionally sung at the close of each party's national conference. There are six stanzas, each followed by the chorus. It is normally sung to the tune of "Lauriger Horatius", better known as the German carol "O Tannenbaum" ("O Christmas Tree").

Oh garbage dump oh garbage dump
Why are you called a garbage dump
Oh garbage dump oh garbage dump
Why are you called a garbage dump

You could feed the world with my garbage dump
You could feed the world with my garbage dump
You could feed the world with my garbage dump
That sums it up in one big lump

When you're livin' on the road
And you think sometimes you're starvin'
Get on off that trip my friend
Just get in them cans and start carvin'

I realised with a shock that the song had been written by none other than Charlie Manson. Why did that murderous lunatic keep coming into my head? I asked myself, but could receive no discernible answer.

I went to Barnstaple library with Eliphas one day. He was in extraordinary pain but just wanted to read a short story by Doesteyeovsky [1], so wearing his best jacket, shirt and tie, he wheeled himself up the long road to the Central Library. He settled himself in comfort, and settled down to read the events that befall one Ivan Matveich when he, his wife Elena Ivanovna, and the narrator visit the Arcade to see a crocodile that has been put on display by a German entrepreneur.

After teasing the crocodile, Ivan Matveich is swallowed alive. He finds the inside of the crocodile to be quite comfortable, and the animal's owner refuses to allow it to be cut open, in spite of the pleas from Elena Ivanovna. Ivan Matveich urges the narrator to arrange for the crocodile to be purchased and cut open, but the owner asks so much for it that nothing is done. As the story ends Elena Ivanovna is contemplating divorce and Ivan Matveich resolves to carry on his work as a civil servant as best he can from inside the crocodile.

Laughing out loud, and taking surreptitious sips at a bottle of whisky to dull the pain, he was the happiest I have ever seen him, but as soon as the library staff discovered what was happening he was summarily ejected, and my heart bled for him as, with tears of rage, embarrassment and humiliation rolling down his cheek, he made his tortuous way back to the lock up and the only

---

1. Fyodor Mikhailovich Dostoyevsky Фёдор Михайлович Достоевский; (11 November 1821 – 9 February 1881), sometimes transliterated Dostoevsky, was a Russian novelist, short story writer, essayist, journalist and philosopher. Dostoyevsky's literary works explore human psychology in the troubled political, social, and spiritual atmosphere of 19th-century Russia. Many of his works are marked by a preoccupation with Christianity, explored through the prism of the individual confronted with life's hardships and beauty. He began writing in his 20s, and his first novel, *Poor Folk*, was published in 1846 when he was 25. His major works include *Crime and Punishment* (1866), *The Idiot* (1869), *Demons* (1872) and *The Brothers Karamazov* (1880). His output consists of eleven novels, three novellas, seventeen short novels and numerous other works. Many literary critics rate him as one of the greatest psychologists in world literature. His novella *Notes From Underground* is considered to be one of the first works of existentialist literature. The story that Eliphas was reading is called *The Crocodile*.

family that he had.

That night there was a violent thunderstorm, and the inhabitants of the little family all huddled in their own shelters like frightened woodland creatures. As the rain beat down upon the corrugated iron roof of the lock up where Eliphas lay, drunk to hell, on a grubby mattress, screaming taunts and insults at an unfeeling, uncaring and completely oblivious universe, I sensed that something was different. Something drastic had changed and it was never going to be the same again.

XXIII

With hindsight I know that I cannot have been sitting on the bench in Britannia's garden for more than about ten minutes, but it seemed to me as though whole weeks elapsed, while I floated in limbo above the derelict builder's yard watching the lives of the people who lived there. The nearest analogy that I can give (and it is a very imperfect one) is something I do every day, as I sit in my comfortable old armchair typing away on my iPad and listening to whatever happens to be on my playlist on that particular day.

Opposite me is a 40inch fishtank, quite heavily planted, in which I have a selection of fish that would not have been out of place in one of the mountain ponds I used to explore when I was a child in Hong Kong. It contains a breeding colony of Chinese white cloud mountain minnows, some danios and a large black goggle-eyed goldfish called Chester. To my right, on top of the 1920s glass cabinet that Corinna brought with her when she moved in to live with me all those years ago, is my hifi, and next to it a two foot tank containing a small colony of Japanese fire bellied newts. Quite often during the day when I am meant to be writing deathless prose, I find myself staring at the tanks following the intricate day to day lives of the little creatures who live there. And so it was as I sat hunched on the bench in Britannia's garden, Panne's cute little horns pressed hard against my forehead. I don't know what state of consciousness I was in. I suspect that it wasn't a coma, a dream, or a hallucination, rather some thaumaturgically hypnogogic state for which there is no proper word in the English language. Certainly I am not going to try and invent one because there is no need. I have experienced it, and I seriously doubt whether I shall ever meet anyone else who has been through the same set of experiences, so apart from doing what I am doing now - writing my story down for my own satisfaction as much as anything - I will probably never have to describe what happened again.

I followed the day to day dramas of the little colony, shared their joys and sorrows in an abstract kind of way, but as the days progressed felt more and more disturbed by the change that I could see in Eliphas. His anger and bitterness were palpable, and I watched - helplessly - as a thoroughly decent man was overcome by pain, horror and bitterness and became a monster. As the cancer ate away at him he spent more time hidden away in the back room of his lock up; the one place that I could not follow him. And I became consumed with curiosity to see what on earth he could be doing out there.

I slowly began to realise that the different people living there had their own social roles. The two runaway teenaged girls, quite logically as they were the ones who appeared to be least alienated from the rest of the world, were the ones who went begging, shoplifting or garbage diving in search of food, whilst the older and more taciturn residents were the ones who scavenged across the scrubland and the little wood that lay on the opposite side of the fields behind the yard. There they would gather firewood, snare rabbits, and pick blackberries and hazelnuts. Following a couple of them one day I found that they even had a little kitchen garden, where they grew carrots, potatoes and cannabis, deep in the woods. This wouldn't have happened in my younger days, I thought to myself. As a boy my friends and I roamed all across the woodlands, but with an increasingly sedentary and urbanised population who are becoming ever more divorced from the reality of the natural world, the woods were becoming the demesne of the wild animals, and feral people like my new friends from the derelict builder's yard, and they were able to tend their little crops in peace.

I was, of course, most interested in the little girl who would eventually become Panne. But in this phase of her existence she seemed to spend most of her time with Eliphas, who seemed to be as fond of her as I was of her later caprine incarnation. She would follow him around, even accompanying him up the long hard hill to the Pilton Hilton on the odd occasions that he would go there to receive treatment and more medication. He would slowly and tortuously wheel himself up and down the long hill to the hospital while Panne trotted happily alongside him like a little dog. As far as I could ascertain neither of them said anything to each other. In fact, as far as I could ascertain she never said anything to anyone, but they seemed content enough in their own peculiar existence.

As I followed various members of the strange little commune around, I realised that I could pick up some of their thoughts and feelings, in dribs and drabs at least. However, because I am basically a coward, I did my best not to do this because the stories I learned from each of them were so unutterably sad. The middle aged men had, like Eliphas, once had families and homes, but had lost them through a mixture of poor decision making, bad luck, and - in most cases - the cruelty and duplicity of other people. The teenaged girls had been abused, bullied and humiliated to a horrific degree usually by the very people whom one would have hoped would have been there to help and protect them. The catalogue of depravity and abuse that would enter my head every time I so much as let my psychic guard slip for a moment or two was unbelievable, and will - I am sure - stay with me for the rest of my life. One of the girls had essentially been whored out by her stepfather from about the age of eight in order to pay for his own chemical predilections, and had turned to her stepfather's chemicals in order to numb the pain and terror of being raped and used by an endless parade of total strangers, and - worse - family friends, every night for years upon years. When she had finally summoned up the strength to tell the police her family was torn asunder by the shock, and her mother blamed her for it all and threw her out of the house. I couldn't bear to learn any more, so never did find out how she ended up under Eliphas's protection in the derelict yard on the edge of town.

The two characters who interested me most were - of course - Eliphas and Panne, but I could get nothing at all from Panne, and all the rest of Eliphas' thoughts were so cloaked in a miasma of hatred, anger and bitterness, that I knew I couldn't connect with his mind for very long and retain what was left of my own sanity. So I left well alone.

However, on one of his regular trips to the hospital, with little Panne trotting faithfully by his side, I was serendipitously there when he made a discovery that would change everything.

XXIV

I t was a balmy summer day of the sort that we supposedly fought two world wars to protect and that Alfred Bestall[1] painted and Roy Harper[2] sang about in *One of those Days in England*. She who would become Panne and Eliphas were in Barnstaple High Street, and they were as happy as a terminally ill paraplegic and a little girl traumatised into permanent silence by a catalogue of abuse could possibly be. Eliphas was propelling himself along, his squeaky wheelchair taking all his strength to move, and by his side the little girl skipped along as if she didn't have a care in the world.

But there was something wrong with that world. Although I recognised Barnstaple High Street from the days when I used to hang out there with the local punk contingent, there were a number of differences which finally brought me to the conclusion that I had been heading towards for some time; that the Barnstaple which exists some eighteen miles from my front doorstep, and which I

---

1. Alfred Edmeades "Fred" Bestall, MBE (Mandalay, Burma, 14 December 1892 – 15 January 1986 in Porthmadog, Wales), wrote and illustrated Rupert Bear for the London Daily Express, from 1935 to 1965. In 1935, Bestall was selected to take over the Daily Express's Rupert Bear stories from Mary Tourtel. Bestall improved the stories and plots of Rupert, but more importantly, he created the most beautifully crafted illustrations in the Rupert Bear Annual publications. Much of the landscape in Rupert is inspired by the Snowdonia landscape of North Wales, notably around Beddgelert. He had first visited Beddgelert whilst holidaying with his parents at Trefriw in the Conwy valley in 1912 and 1913, where their holiday home was called 'Penlan'. Bestall produced his last Rupert story on 22 July 1965. He retired from the Daily Express in July 1965, but continued creating Annual publication covers until 1973.

2. Roy Harper (born 12 June 1941) is an English folk rock singer, songwriter and guitarist who has been a professional musician since 1964. Harper has released 22 studio albums and 10 live albums across his 50-year career. Harper's earliest musical influences were American blues musician Lead Belly and folk singer Woody Guthrie and, in his teens, jazz musician Miles Davis. Harper was also exposed to classical music in his childhood and has pointed to the influence of Jean Sibelius's Karelia Suite. Lyrical influences include the 19th century Romantics, especially Shelley, and Keats's poem "Endymion". Harper has also cited the Beat poets as being highly influential, particularly Jack Kerouac. As a musician, Harper is known for his distinctive fingerstyle playing and lengthy, lyrical, complex compositions, a result of his love of jazz and Keats.

His influence upon other musicians has been acknowledged by Jimmy Page, Robert Plant, Pete Townshend, Kate Bush, Pink Floyd, and Ian Anderson of Jethro Tull, who said Harper was his "...primary influence as an acoustic guitarist and songwriter." Neil McCormick of The Daily Telegraph described him as "one of Britain's most complex and eloquent lyricists and genuinely original songwriters." His influence reached across the Atlantic where he was acknowledged by Seattle-based acoustic band Fleet Foxes, American musician and producer Jonathan Wilson and Californian harpist Joanna Newsom with whom he has also toured. In 2005, Harper was awarded the MOJO Hero Award, and in 2013 a Lifetime Achievement Award at the BBC Radio 2 Folk Awards. In 2011, to celebrate his 70th birthday, he performed a celebratory concert at London's Royal Festival Hall. His most recent album, Man and Myth, was released in 2013.

visit when I absolutely have to, and the town which I had been floating through for the past God knows how long - Minutes? Hours? Days Weeks? ; time really had no meaning in my current dreamlike state - were not the same place. At least they, appeared to be the same, but they weren't. It was a different reality.

I would be seriously surprised if there is anyone reading this who doesn't have some conception of the idea of parallel universes which differ on a quantum level. In lay terms, the hypothesis states there is a very large—perhaps infinite —number of universes, and everything that could possibly have happened in our past, but did not, has occurred in the past of some other universe or universes, and that every event that happens has an infinite number of outcomes, and each of these outcomes becomes a whole new universe. The idea was, amusingly, first postulated by the father of the lead singer of the band *Eels* [1], who - not so amusingly then topped himself. I will be the first to admit that I find all this mildly disturbing, and I don't understand the physics behind all this theoretical balderdash, and I truthfully don't really care.

But there were enough differences between the Barnstaple which I have known at various times since the early 1970s and the Barnstaple in which I found myself now, for me to begin to suspect that Dr Everett wasn't just blowing smoke up his own arse, and had a much more switched on view of the mechanics behind the multiverse than I did. But, remember please, that I failed my Maths O level repeatedly, and still count on my fingers, and despite forty years of people trying to tell me still don't understand the difference between mass and weight, or between AC and DC current.

Back in the day, Barnstaple was rather a nice, arty place, where DIY record companies, fanzines, and mildly innovative rock groups flourished. I was disappointed to see when I returned in 2005 after a gap of over twenty years that it seemed far more downmarket than I had remembered. *The Royal Norfolk*, the bar where the rock and roll intelligentsia once hung out was now the *Funky Monkey* party bar, and the indie record and bookshops had largely disappeared.

But THIS Barnstaple was far worse. There were armed police on every street corner. OK I had seen armed police in the United States, and in Mexico they had even had submachine guns, but to see them on patrol outside the Queen's Theatre, armed to the teeth, and to see an armoured car rolling down Boutport Street was a sobering and not a very pleasant experience. One thing that did seem to be a constant, however, between this brave new world and our shabby old one was the popular obsession with Celebrity Culture. The newsagents here, as they are in the analogue of Barnstaple which I visit on the few occasions that I really have to be dragged kicking and screaming out of my house, were chock full of glossy magazines expounding at length upon the latest gallivantings of stars of stage, screen, and reality TV show, but in this horrible fascistic analogue of the old market town of which I was still

1. Eels (often typeset as eels or EELS) is an American alternative rock band, formed in California in 1995 by singer/ songwriter and multi-instrumentalist Mark Oliver Everett, known by the stage name "E." Band members have changed across the years, both in the studio and on stage, making Everett the only official member for most of the band's work. Often filled with themes about family, death and lost love, Eels' music straddles a wide range of genres, which is evidenced by the distinct musical style of every album. Since 1996, Eels has released eleven studio albums, seven of which charted in the Billboard 200. Their most recent The Cautionary Tales of Mark Oliver Everett (2014) was followed by a live album in 2015.

vaguely fond, the pursuit of ennui through pointless and talentless fame had reached even more ludicrous heights than it had in my own country.

For example, no less a personage than the British Prime Minister was touted as the celebrity judge on the latest round of regional heats of some stupid talent show called *Britain's a Talented Place*, and a gaudy coloured poster featuring the grinning mugshot of a smarmy looking person with the sort of face that appealed to focus groups (think Tony Blair if he had been one of the stars of *Neighbours*) advertised the fact that the North Devon heat of this massively banal and totally pointless exercise in providing audiovisual bread and circuses for the marching moron consumers was coming to Barnstaple in a couple of weeks.

While she who would be Panne skipped around enjoying the sunshine, Eliphas sat in his chair in front of this poster in the big glass display case outside the Queen's Theatre. It was as if he was transfixed; for hour after hour he just sat there staring at the poster, and there were tears rolling down his cheeks.

XXV

Now we come to the bit that I have been dreading. I have seen my share of death; I saw my first corpse when I was about nine years old. It was the summer when Chairman Mao's Cultural Revolution[1] had reached a particularly bloody and unpleasant phase, and gangs of Red Guards were kidnapping, torturing and killing people suspected of being bourgeoisie or intellectuals or both. My family were living in Hong Kong at the time, and every weekend we put to sea in our boat the *MV Ailsa*.

One weekend, we were chuntering along happily on the way to one of our regular picnic spots on a beach on one of the outlying islands when we encountered three mutilated, naked human bodies, surrounded by fish and seabirds floating down the current of the Pearl River which flowed from the hinterland out into the South China Sea. I was in my customary position in

---

1. The Cultural Revolution, formally the Great Proletarian Cultural Revolution, was a social-political movement that took place in the People's Republic of China from 1966 until 1976. Set into motion by Mao Zedong, then Chairman of the Communist Party of China, its stated goal was to preserve 'true' Communist ideology in the country by purging remnants of capitalist and traditional elements from Chinese society, and to re-impose Maoist thought as the dominant ideology within the Party. The Revolution marked the return of Mao Zedong to a position of power after the Great Leap Forward. The movement paralyzed China politically and significantly affected the country economically and socially.

The Revolution was launched in May 1966, after Mao alleged that bourgeois elements had infiltrated the government and society at large, aiming to restore capitalism. He insisted that these "revisionists" be removed through violent class struggle. China's youth responded to Mao's appeal by forming Red Guard groups around the country. The movement spread into the military, urban workers, and the Communist Party leadership itself. It resulted in widespread factional struggles in all walks of life. In the top leadership, it led to a mass purge of senior officials, most notably Liu Shaoqi and Deng Xiaoping. During the same period Mao's personality cult grew to immense proportions.

the bow of the boat, looking out for interesting sea creatures or the occasional white tailed sea eagle or frigatebirds in the sky above.

So it was me who saw the hideously disfigured and mangled bodies, the flesh coming off in strips, several minutes before my Father who was at the helm. We were technically outside HK Territorial Waters, so even if we had been in possession of a short wave radio set (something that was rigidly controlled by law at the time) he would not have been able to report the find to the Marine Police, so he steered away as fast as he could in a vain attempt to stop my Mother or little brother seeing them.

As a nurse, nearly twenty years later I saw corpses on a number of occasions, and twice in my life (the second and most recent occasion being my Father) I have sat by someone's bedside, holding their hand as they passed from this world into the next. I have been the first qualified person on the scene at a number of accidents, and have twice given resuscitation to someone who has died whilst I was doing it. Over the years I have seen more than my fair share of death, horror and destruction, but nothing prepared me for what happened next.

I had basically been observing Eliphas, the girl who would become Panne, and the rest of the disparate band of outcasts who lived in the disused builder's yard on the outskirts of the trading estate in something approaching real time, but now all that changed. In some ways it was like observing events in slow motion, in other ways it was like seeing a carefully edited *film noir* version of events, but mostly (and I don't know whether this will be more frustrating for the reader, or for me - someone who actually prides himself on being able to write a coherent narrative) but I have found it hard enough to describe what has happened so far. The rest of the story basically defies description in any rational manner, and as I want to present you, the reader, with some sort of story that makes sense, rather than a venture into the wilder echelons of *avant garde* literature, I am going to try and novelise the rest of the tale. I will be the first to admit that this is at least partly laziness on my behalf, but I will also be the first to admit that my skills as a writer has probably reached its apogee, and even if they haven't they are not going to improve in time for me to finish this story, because we are very near the end, and I am beginning to have had enough of telling it.

I watched Eliphas sitting in his wheelchair and staring at the poster in the big glass display case outside the Queen's Theatre for what seemed like hours, and then followed him as he and Panne made their way up the High Street, to continue their chores. Their first stop was a chemist. This mildly surprised me, because by this time I was reasonably *au fait* with Eliphas' routine, and ever since I had been watching him and his friends, he had been collecting his cancer medication which were, by the way, mostly palliative, and mostly heavy duty analgesics, on Tuesday afternoons from the pharmacy at the District Hospital, and I had assumed that he would have made any other purchases that he needed at the same time. So I followed them in. The little girl who would become Panne (I have always felt guilty that I have not known her true name) made a bee line for the free samples of smelly things of the sort that girls of her age have made a beeline for ever since there have been girls and smelly things, whilst Eliphas went to the counter and purchased three large bottles of iodine.

He put them carefully in the pannier baskets of his wheelchair, and the unlikely pair made their way out into Barnstaple High Street. They made their way up the road a decent way until they found another chemist, and did exactly the same thing, and after visiting a third and a fourth chemist they made their weary way back to the builder's yard, but not before stopping off at a hardware shop where they bought a two pint bottle of ammonia.

Then I had an epiphany, and - for the first time - understood to my horror, exactly what Eliphas was planning. And with this new realisation, areas in his psyche that had originally been blocked off to me were finally 'visible' (to use an entirely inadequate word) and, furthermore, I could finally 'enter', albeit in the aether, the locked back room of Eliphas' lock up which had previously been blocked to me. Not at all to my surprise I found it was actually as big in area as the area in which he lived. It contained a workbench upon which was a small laboratory containing various items of chemical equipment that I vaguely recognised from the days when I had studied for my GCE O Level in Chemistry at Bideford Grammar School in the mid-1970s. And, not at all to my surprise, I saw that stacked up against the other wall were floor to ceiling Dexion shelves containing hundreds of bottles of iodine and ammonia.

I think that it was a novel by Robert Heinlein that first introduced me to the concept of nitrogen triiodide. If my memory serves me well, the main protagonist in the book claims that it had been nicknamed 'Proletarian Dynamite' by none-other than Che Guevara. But as my library is at this point in my life acting as home to a slightly dotty but very loveable eighty-six year old lady, and a temporary shelter for a crushingly neurotic rescue medium of uncertain years, my copy of Che Guevara's *Radical Writings on Guerrilla Warfare, Politics and Revolution,* (Filiquarian Publishing, 2006, ISBN 1-59986-999-3) is presently beyond use, as is my copy of *Farnham's Freehold* by Robert Heinlein.

Nitrogen triiodide is the inorganic compound with the formula $NI3$. It is an extremely sensitive contact explosive: small quantities explode with a loud, sharp snap when touched even lightly, releasing a purple cloud of iodine vapour; it can even be detonated by alpha radiation. $NI3$ has a complex structural chemistry that is difficult to study because of the instability of the derivatives. *The Anarchist Cookbook,* [1] another book which is hidden in the interstices of my library, goes even further. However, here I am trying to explain a complicated and rather unsettling narrative rather than teaching the mischievous reader how to blow things up, so I won't go into any more detail here. Sufficient to say that it is a grey sludge which is a precipitate formed when one mixes iodine and ammonia. It is perfectly harmless until it is dry, but as soon as it is dry it is a volatile, and fairly violent explosive whose main characteristic is that the explosion apparently does not produce heat, but does produce large amounts of iodine gas which both chokes and stains.

Over the next few days I watched as Eliphas made enormous amounts of this stuff, and packed it into the frame of his spare wheelchair.

---

1. *The Anarchist Cookbook*, first published in 1971, is a book that contains instructions for the manufacture of explosives, rudimentary telecommunications phreaking devices, and other items. The book also includes instructions for home manufacturing of illicit drugs, including LSD. It was written by William Powell at the apex of the counterculture era in order to protest against United States involvement in the Vietnam War.

All day and much of each night he worked away, his only companion being the little mute girl whose name I never did find out. As he withdrew further and further away from the affairs of the rest of his tribe, the little girl whom I would eventually know as Panne, grew closer to him. She moved out of her little nest in the back of the minivan, and ate and slept alongside the middle-aged man. Tuesday came and went, and for the first time Eliphas failed to go for his medication, and took regular swigs from a bottle of Oramorph as he worked away at his deadly task.

The Anarchist's Cookbook suggests that NI3 is too volatile to be a tool in the armoury of the serious urban terrorist, but as I was rapidly beginning to realise, it was perfect for what Eliphas had in mind. "What happens when a bomb is dedicated in close containment, by a cripple dressed in an elephant suit? That's what I call entertainment" ran the lyrics of one of *Xtul's* most disturbing yet catchy songs, and for the first time I understood what it meant.

XXVI

I didn't know everything by a long chalk, but I suddenly though imperceptibly found myself deep inside the psyche of this complex, angry and deeply unhappy man, and without realising it I found myself understanding a hell of a lot more than I had before.

Once upon a time there was a mild mannered school teacher called David Prentiss. He had a liking for 19th Century light opera and cheap whisky, and - in the normal scheme of things - would not have really done much to impact upon the world stage. I say 'mild mannered' deliberately, because not only does the description fit, but it is the one which always seems to be given to everyone from Clark Kent to the inoffensive bloke who lives on the corner who turned out to be a serial killer, that reveals shocking hidden depths in an unexpected manner.

David lived in Barnstaple with his neurotic and mildly annoying wife and his spoiled and massively over indulged teenage daughter Sabrina, known to everyone, for reasons I could never fathom, as 'Tabby'. It was the middle of the first decade of the 21st Century, or about a decade ago on my own personal timeline. He was not unlike many of the people I have met over the years. He had married the girl he met at University, only to find that twenty years later they had very little in common anymore. Both David and his wife were rigidly conventional, and neither of them would never have considered leaving the other, so they plodded on in an increasingly unhappy suburban nightmare, taking out their angst on each other in the petty little ways that only an unhappily married couple can do, so wrapped up in their own mutual misery that they totally failed to see what their daughter was becoming.

Tabby was initially no worse and no better than any other girl in her mid-teens, but with two parents who gave her money rather than attention, and who were too wrapped up in their own problems, at work and with each other to pay heed to her wants and needs. Here my late mother would have said something about The Devil and "idle hands", which for once would not have been purely irrelevant.

She was cursed with shoulder length blonde hair, a curvy figure, and that look of bovine vacuousness that has appealed to teenaged boys and less scrupulous adults since the world began, and it was not long before Tabby, sometime in her thirteenth year, found out how to make these attributes work for her, and from then on her family were doomed. A world where everyone from the age of seven up has a mobile phone and an account on at least one piece of social media has many advantages, but allowing teenagers who are already riddled with angst and hormones in equal quantities to have these makes peculiar social problems of its own.

In 2005 (I believe) a teenage girl who may or may not have been called Olivia Fields, posted photographs of herself wearing what appeared to be a Pierrot costume, cat ears and with what was claimed to be menstrual blood smeared on her cheeks. The pictures appeared on the notorious 4Chan image board, the denizens of which, deciding that she looked like she had been smoking crack, named her 'Cracky Chan', and a whole subculture of internet life was born.

Some of the photographs in later photo sessions were explicit enough to be classed child pornography, and although she soon disappeared from the internet leaving thousands of baying fans behind her, a whole generation of replacements arrived, demanding compliments and later gifts paid for through semi-anonymous Amazon.com wishlists, and the phenomenon of camwhoring was born. Tabby was one of these girls.

Each night, while her mother went to evening classes, social groups, book clubs and everything else that she could think of to fill her useless and uninspiring life with reason, and her father sat downstairs with his headphones on, and drinking endless glasses of whisky and coke as he listened to *Les pêcheurs de perles* by Bizet [1] over and over again, she would cavort and display herself on camera for the legions of young (and not so young) men who showered her with increasingly expensive gifts for a series if increasingly explicit photographs.

It is to her parents eternal shame that neither of them noticed the change in their little girl. Neither of them noticed that she was wearing a seemingly endless procession of new outfits, very few of which (had either of them been paying attention) they would have considered suitable for their thirteen year old daughter.

Tabby was a vain and self-cantered girl, but she wasn't stupid. She was neither academically successful nor popular at school, and she soon came to realise that if she behaved in real life the same way that she behaved online that she should be able to replicate her social success. So that is exactly what she did, and at first it worked perfectly for her. But her new found popularity went to her head, but she had not realised that the IRL analogue of being a

---

1. *Les pêcheurs de perles* (*The Pearl Fishers*) is an opera in three acts by the French composerGeorges Bizet, to a libretto by Eugène Cormon and Michel Carré. It was first performed on 30 September 1863 at the Théâtre Lyrique in Paris, and was given 18 performances in its initial run. Set in ancient times on the island of Ceylon, the opera tells the story of how two men's vow of eternal friendship is threatened by their love for the same woman, whose own dilemma is the conflict between secular love and her sacred oath as a priestess. The friendship duet "Au fond du temple saint", generally known as "The Pearl Fishers Duet", is one of the best-known numbers in Western opera.

---

camwhore was something that she really didn't want to be, nor that the exciting young men with hoodies and cigarettes with whom she had surrounded herself were not likely to take no for an answer.

Even now, her parents would probably have been able to sort matters out had they been paying even the slightest bit of attention to her, but they weren't and they didn't. They didn't notice that their daughter's friends seemed to be all loutish teenage boys who seemed to be always hanging around the place. They didn't notice that her bedroom started smelling of cigarettes, and the only reason either of them knew that she had started drinking was when David noticed that one of his bottles of gin had disappeared.

This was where in any properly ordered family something would have happened.

But David was too ashamed of having bought an extra bottle of gin without his wife's knowledge, his wife was too deep in a morass of self pity to care, and by this time it didn't matter, because Tabby had run away to escape from her lecherous schoolboy tormentors into what she hoped was the safety of the arms of some middle-aged bloke of uncertain provenance that she had met on Facebook. Tabby was the last thing keeping David and his wife (whose name I never did learn) together, and one night soon after she didn't return home either.

This is where David stopped going to work, and began drinking seriously. He lost the house in the inevitable divorce, and after a few months living in his car, ended up in the derelict builder's yard. By this time he was Eliphas. David Prentiss was long gone, and you know what? Nobody actually cared.

XXVI

I t is quite frightening how quickly a person can become a non-person. It can happen very easily, and it is far more difficult to reverse the process. It has happened to friends of mine, and on one occasion it nearly happened to me. And it happened to David Prentiss. Within weeks of him stopping going to work, he had drifted off the radar of society.

When he found out that his house was going to be repossessed, and that - divorced, jobless and homeless - he was forever alienated from the life that he had led before, and which he had never actually liked much, he set to work. It is a myth that people suffering from deep depression are incapable of action. On the contrary, some people, when they are at the bottom of what I believe Bunyan called the Slough of Despond, achieve a strange plateau of calm and lucidity and are able to make quite complex plans, which is why - I believe - so many suicides are so well planned and executed. Prentiss reached this state quite easily. As the saying goes, you don't know what you've got until you lose it, but although that is usually taken to mean one specific set of circumstance, some people don't know how unhappy they have been until they are forced to confront the issue. And so it was for David Prentiss. As he trudged from one grubby bedsit to another looking for the cheapest, he realised how much he had hated his wife, and how even the loss of his daughter (whom until a few months before, he would have said was the light if his life) was really something of a relief.

So he was surprisingly cheerful when he moved into a grubby little bedsit at the top of Sticklepath, and took stock of his position. Over a period of about a week he sold all of his possessions. He sold all the furniture in his house, he took the doors and windows out of their frames, and even unscrewed the surprisingly expensive shower unit, and sold the whole lot for cash. He realised in a moment of lucidity that his expensive hifi and collection of valuable opera and jazz records were the trappings of his old life, and had little to do with his new one so he sold them all. He cashed in his pension from the National Union of Teachers, and keeping only his books and his clothes he settled down to his new life.

Back in the mid-1980s David had fancied himself a poet, and had become mildly successful, actually managing to sell a few poems here and there to arty magazines. He was also an enormous fan of David Bowie, and he spent the money he had inherited from his Aunt Doris on his twenty first birthday going to New York to see his hero on stage in the leading role of *The Elephant Man*. That evening transformed him and he became completely obsessed with the life of Joseph Carey Merrick, (1862-1890).

As Wikipedia explains:

> "Merrick, was an English man with severe deformities who was exhibited as a human curiosity named the Elephant Man. He became well known in London society after he went to live at the London Hospital. Merrick was born in Leicester, Leicestershire and began to develop abnormally during the first few years of his life. His skin appeared thick and lumpy, he developed enlarged lips, and a bony lump grew on his forehead. One of his arms and both of his feet became enlarged and at some point during his childhood he fell and damaged his hip, resulting in permanent lameness. When he was 10, his mother died, and his father soon remarried. Merrick left school at the age of 13 and had difficulty finding employment. Rejected by his father and stepmother, he left home. In late 1879, Merrick, aged 17, entered the Leicester Union Workhouse.
>
> In 1884, after four years in the workhouse, Merrick contacted a showman named Sam Torr and proposed that Torr should exhibit him. Torr agreed and arranged for a group of men to manage Merrick, whom they named the Elephant Man. After touring the East Midlands, Merrick travelled to London to be exhibited in a penny gaff shop on Whitechapel Road which was rented by showman Tom Norman. Norman's shop, directly across the street from the London Hospital, was visited by a surgeon named Frederick Treves, who invited Merrick to be examined and photographed. Soon after Merrick's visits to the hospital, Tom Norman's shop was closed by the police, and Merrick's

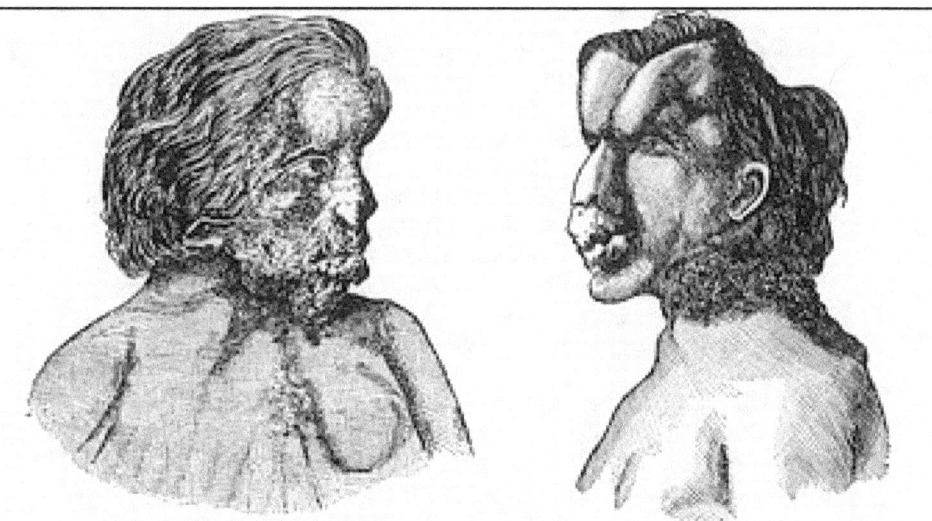

Fig. 287.—Head of the " Elephant-man."

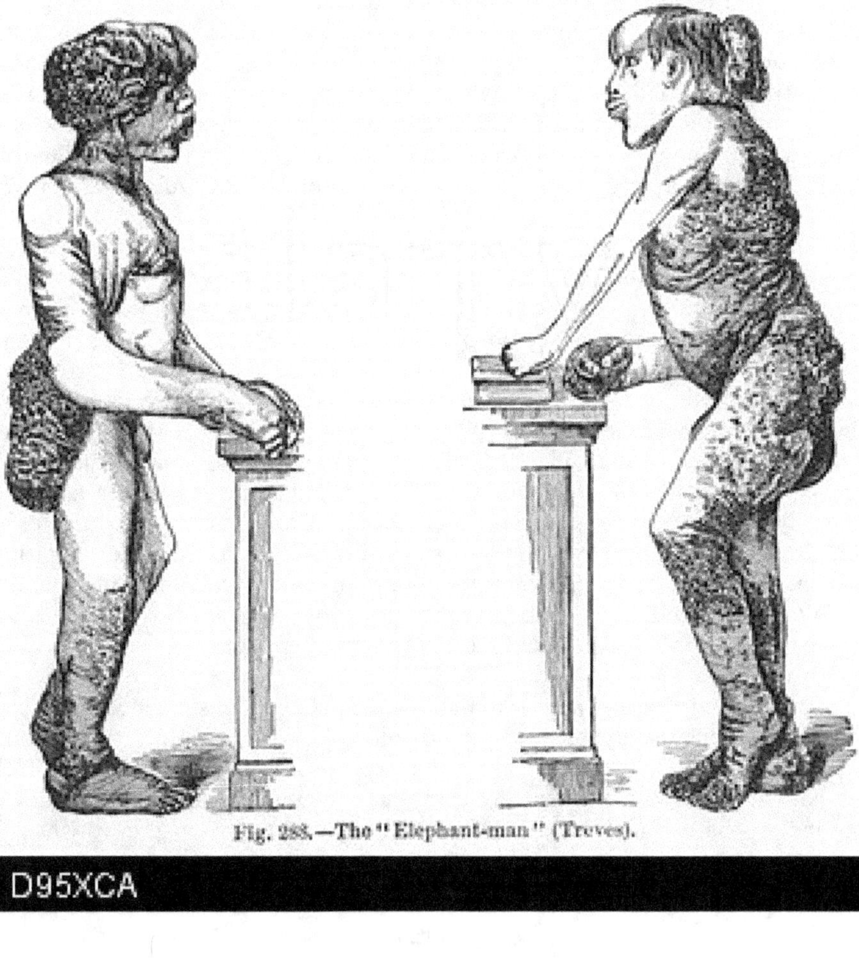

Fig. 288.—The " Elephant-man " (Treves).

managers sent him to tour in Europe.

In Belgium, Merrick was robbed by his road manager and abandoned in Brussels. He eventually made his way back to London; unable to communicate, he was found by the police to have Dr. Treves's card on him. Treves came and took Merrick back to the London Hospital. Although his condition was incurable, Merrick was allowed to stay at the hospital for the remainder of his life. Treves visited him daily, and the pair developed quite a close friendship. Merrick also received visits from the wealthy ladies and gentlemen of London society, including Alexandra, Princess of Wales.

Aged 27, Merrick died on 11 April 1890. The official cause of death was asphyxia, although Treves, who dissected the body, said that Merrick had died of a dislocated neck. He believed that Merrick—who had to sleep sitting up because of the weight of his head—had been attempting to sleep lying down, to "be like other people"."

In the current vernacular, people with gender dysphoria "identify" as being a different gender to that as which they came into the world. The people who believe that they are emotionally or psychologically of a different race than that which they appear to be are said to 'identify' with being black, or white, or Jewish, or whatever. If the expression had been in the cant phraseology of the time, there is no doubt that David Prentiss, a young white man with a tendency to podgyness and a slightly receding hairline, identified with The Elephant Man, to such an extent that he even adopted a pachydermous *nom de plume*.

Although David found the story of Joseph Merrick fascinating for what he believed it told him about the human condition, and about our species' attitudes to disability, he also became obsessed with elephant men as a whole, from Merrick to Ganesha. There are three species of elephant currently accepted by science, in two genera: the Asian elephants in the genus *Elephas* and the two African species in the genus *Loxodonta*. The opening scenes of David Lynch's film *The Elephant Man* refer to the old Victorian superstition that birth deformities are caused by pregnant mothers being frightened by something which is so terrifying that the psychic shock undergone can actually effect the development of the foetus in the womb. It depicts Merrick's mother as having been frightened by an escaped circus elephant. Although David knew that this was nonsense (opinion is divided whether poor Merrick suffered from a rare condition called neurofibromatosis type 1, or an even rarer condition called Proteus Syndrome, or even an incalculably rare combination of the two) the idea took root in his head, and he adopted the *nom de guerre* of Mr Loxodonta, in order to write his poems.

This had a mildly irritating and completely unexpected consequence; he occasionally received cheques made payable to 'Mr Loxodonta' and those jolly nice people at the national Westminster Bank would completely refuse to let him pay them into his bank account. back in the 1980s, things were completely different than they are today on either our timeline, or the one upon which David had been born. In those days when 'The War on Terror' was thirty years in the future, it was reasonably easy to open Post Office savings accounts, and even Building Society accounts under false names. Even I had one, for much the same reason as Mr Loxodonta. All you needed was a friendly neighbourhood postmaster, and a papertrail to provide verismilitude to your claims, and Bob was your Uncle. It wasn't long before David had a Post Office savings book in the name of his pachydermous alter ego. Although his days as a poet were not going to last, he kept the account open over the years, and when all the Post Office savings accounts were migrated to the National Girobank sometime in the 1990s, David made sure that he filled in the requisite paperwork, (I didn't bother, and have been kicking myself ever since) and so he had a pretty fireproof bank account in a false name that was almost completely untraceable to him. There was only about fifty quid in the account, but by the time he had made a series of deposits with the proceeds of selling everything that he owned which could be converted to ready cash, and even some of the goods and chattels which the courts had said were now the lawful property of his ex-wife, there was a healthy balance in there of nearly twenty thousand pounds; more than enough to keep him going as he carried out his only remaining lifetime's ambition, that of drinking himself into an early grave, and reading as much as he could in order to improve his mind as he did so.

They say that all men need a garden shed. I have several, but my museum and my conservatory are so chock full of assorted impedimenta that they are not fit for purpose, but I suppose that my converted potato shed where I work every day probably fills that social role for me. But David didn't have that luxury, and soon tired of commuting each day to the off license and the library and bringing back the fruits of his labours to a dingy bedsit to read and get drunk. So he went in search of a manshed, and after several weeks of driving around the less well trodden highways and byways of the borough of Barnstaple, he found the derelict lock ups on the edge of the industrial estate, which I, and anyone else who has been following this convoluted narrative know very well by now.

He found, to his mild amusement, that the properties were so undervalued that he was not allowed to rent them individually, but that he could rent the whole yard for thirty quid a week. So he did, and slowly began the mildly Herculean task of turning a couple of the lock ups into a place where he could spend his days drinking and reading and waiting to die. Much to his pleasure he found that those in charge had been so disinterested in the whole area, that they had forgotten to turn off the electricity supply, so his favourite lock up even had heat and light. He even found that a short walk from the main entrance to the industrial estate there was a pleasantly louche pub called *The Beagle*, and he found himself spending more and more of his time there of an evening, and as it was a mildly pleasant summer, and he was still conscientious enough not to really approve of drink driving (unless he really *had* to), he quite often staggered back to his lock up, now furnished with a comfortable mattress, to drink and read through the night.

And so it was late one night after a lock in at *The Beagle* when he was staggering home without a care in the world that he staggered into the path of an oncoming lorry, and the resulting accident lost him the use of his legs forever.

XXVII

He was so drunk that he literally didn't feel a thing. he was rushed to hospital, and his right leg was amputated below the knee before he had a chance to sober up. Bizarrely, the loss of his leg hardly effected his life at all. He was fast tracked to an ill-fitting prosthetic limb which never worked properly, a small but useful stipend from an uncaring society who pretended that the welfare of its unfortunates was of at least some interest, and a wheelchair. Best of all, as far as he was concerned, he got an apparently endless supply of mind expanding narcotics.

Life was good.

Needless to say his little bedsit had no disabled access whatsoever, but as he had been spending less and less time there it didn't really matter. He visited about once a week to see if there was any post with which he had to deal (which really meant, missives from the DWP which might effect his seventy five quid a week disability money), but as this only meant unlocking the front door and sifting through the post on the table just inside the door to see if there was any post, which there hardly ever was, it didn't impinge on his average weekly routine overmuch.

And what was that routine? Most of the time it involved reading, drinking, and dreaming his life away with bitter dreams about how he was going to get his own back on society. He had always wanted the time to read as much as he wanted, and now he had the chance. The mixture of his expanded literacy and his expanded synapses produced a bizarre and convoluted series of labyrinthine wish fulfilment fantasies. I know exactly what he was going through, because on a much smaller level I had been through much the same experience.

He read widely on esoteric matters, Crowley, Mathers[1] and Levi. He read about Christian Rosenkreuz[2] and managed to fool himself that he might even have existed. He read Marx[3], and Hitler, and everything in between. He read the great anarchist philosophers, and he read about Charles Manson whose incarcerated dreams of dune buggies pouring down the mountain[4]

1. Samuel Liddell (or Liddel) MacGregor Mathers (8 or 11 January 1854 – 5 or 20 November 1918), born Samuel Liddell Mathers, was a British occultist. He is primarily known as one of the founders of the Hermetic Order of the Golden Dawn, a ceremonial magic order of which offshoots still exist today.

2. According to legend, Christian Rosenkreuz was a doctor who discovered and learned esoteric wisdom on a pilgrimage to the Middle East among Turkish, Arab and Persian sages, possibly Sufi or Zoroastrian masters, supposedly in the early 15th century; returned and founded the "Fraternity of the Rose Cross" with himself (Frater C.R.C.) as Head of the Order. Under his direction a Temple, called Sanctus Spiritus, or "The House of the Holy Spirit", was built.

3. Karl Marx (5 May 1818 – 14 March 1883) was a philosopher, economist, sociologist, journalist, and revolutionary socialist. Born in Germany, he later became stateless and spent much of his life in London in the United Kingdom. Marx's work in economics laid the basis for much of the current understanding of labour and its relation to capital, and subsequent economic thought. He published numerous books during his lifetime, the most notable being *The Communist Manifesto* (1848) and *Das Kapital* (1867–1894).

4. *Revolution Blues* by Neil Young from the album 'On the Beach' (1974) "I got the revolution blues, I see bloody fountains, And ten million dune buggies comin' down the mountains."

resonated pleasantly with his own power fantasies. He read classic literature and ephemeral pulp scifi, children's books and reference books, and followed his own peculiar vision of Calliope wherever she led him.

When I was a boy in Hong Kong, one of my favourite books on nature study described an experiment that I tried out with glee. According to the book, if you put a basin of water out in your garden, even in the most urban of environments, within weeks it would become colonised by water creatures. I tried the experiment out, and even in our concreted courtyard at Mount Austin Mansions it worked as if by magick. Within weeks there were copepods, mosquito larvae, and even a water snail living there, from whence they had come I have no idea. I have tried this experiment out over again, most recently this summer as I write, and it is as if water, that most magickal of compounds, somehow imbues the landscape with some sort of alchemical magnetism which attracts life where once there was none.

I have seen this alchemical miracle happen elsewhere in nature. the monarch butterfly, *Danaus plexippus* is native to North America where its marathon migrations between southern Canada and Mexico have become legendary. In 1979 I saw the migration leave, and I very much doubt if I have seen any greater numbers of any species, than these untold millions of squirming butterflies which enveloped entire trees. Individually they are very beautiful butterflies, but en masse they were a nameless and indescribable obscenity. But that is a story for another day.

Over the years they have colonised many parts of the globe, most recently Madeira and parts of southern Spain and Portugal. It seems that wherever people introduce their foodplant, the milkweed, the butterfly will soon colonise. It is an undoubted fact that vagrants turn up all over the world, even the UK, but one day I want to try out an experiment. I want to rent a field and sow it with *Asclepias* because I would hazard quite a large bet that within ten years there would be monarchs breeding there.

But so it seems to be with people, because within weeks of Eliphas (as he now decided to call himself, both as a homage to his magickal mentor, and as a pun on his old poetical *nom de guerre* - Loxodonta is one genus of elephants, Elephas is the other) had started living in the corner of the once deserted but still pretty much derelict builder's yard but various timid examples of human flotsam and jetsam drifted there, and encountering no opposition from the landlord, settled there semi-permanently.

In one of the Narnia books by C S Lewis [1], a character asks Aslan the divine Lion for some information about another character. Aslan replies "Child, I am telling you your story, not hers. No one is told any story but their own." My position is a parallel one. Somehow I found myself with a psychic link to this complex, tortured, and highly intelligent man, and so I could see what had happened through his eyes and his eyes alone. In fact I couldn't, but there are no words within the English language which can possibly explain the peculiar psychic symbiosis

---

1. *The Horse and His Boy* is a novel for children by C. S. Lewis, published by Geoffrey Bles in 1954. It was the fifth published of seven novels in *The Chronicles of Narnia* (1950–1956) and one of four that Lewis finished writing before the first book was out. It is volume three in recent editions, which are sequenced according to Narnia history. Like the others it was illustrated by Pauline Baynes and her work has been retained in many later editions.

in which I found myself, and so I won't even try. Although I was intrigued by the backstories of these poor battered people, I soon came to discover that Eliphas wasn't, and so what he didn't care about, I could never know.

But these people arrived over the next few months, and some of them stayed, and Eliphas in his own peculiar way began to feel responsible for them in a way he had never really been able to for his own long gone wife and child. First to arrive was Michael, the man with Down's Syndrome, for whom I had cared lightyears away in a different universe when I had been a Nursing Assistant in Bideford in the early 1980s, then two elderly drunks and the teenage girls, and finally the little mute girl who would somehow and someday become Panne.

On the whole the odd little community knocked on together as I have already described. They shared the tasks, dived into supermarket skips for food, shoplifted, and begged for food. One night there was unpleasantness when a newly arrived youth tried to force his attentions on one of the teenage girls. She screamed, and Michael leapt on him, biting at his throat. The rest of the colony of the damned ran to her assistance and drove the assailant away. As he left, he was still snarling incoherent threats over his shoulder at them.

It was soon after this that Eliphas managed to buy a gun from one of the less salubrious men that he met one Friday night at *The Beagle*.

With the newfound responsibility of being *de facto* Generalissimo of a ragtag band of outlaws, Eliphas' opium dreams became more and more messianic.

Although there are several plausible hypotheses to explain the Manson Family's 1969 killing spree, many people believe that the one under which he was convicted is actually the least likely hypothesis. Some people maintain that the killings at Cielo Drive were purely because Doris Day's son Terry Melcher who owned the house had "snubbed" Manson during his attempts to land a record contract, and that the killings were his rebuttal. Others believe that the motive was even more simple; an attempt to free gaoled family member Bobby Beausoleil by committing copy cat murders to the one for which he had been imprisoned in order to cast doubt upon the case against him.

But even though Manson's doctrine of Helter Skelter may not have been the true motivation for the killings, there is no doubt that Manson believed that a global race war which he named after the *Beatles* song on their eponymous 1968 double album, was imminent. The case that prosecutor Vincent Bugliosi, who died as I was writing this narrative, convicted Manson and his co-defendants upon, was that The Manson Family had been trying to kickstart Helter Skelter with a series of grotesque and bloody murders which he thought would be blamed upon black activists, thus provoking the conflict that Manson was dreaming of.

Manson believed that the Book of Revelation predicted that when the peoples of the world fought each other to destruction at Armageddon, 122,000 people hiding in a "bottomless pit" would eventually emerge, and become rulers of the world. Charlie, of course, wanted to be the leader. [1]

But Eliphas didn't want to be a leader.

In recent years Manson was instrumental in starting. Movement called ATWA.

From their Facebook page: "ATWA stands for Air, Trees, Water and Animals and obviously no one owns it because the Earth belongs to itself, it belongs to you and you belong to it - a system of sustainability and reverence. We use the term 'official' after our name here on FB only to allow ourselves to be found by those seeking us. We are but one of the voices of ATWA, and ATWA is the voice of all life. There are other ATWA representatives all around the world that are true to the concept and being of ATWA, and defend this planet in the same honor and love as us. You are ATWA."

The non hierarchical nature of ATWA appealed to Eliphas, and he read as much about it as possible. Like all of us, he knew perfectly well at the back of his mind that mankind was destroying the planet that gave us birth as surely and certainly as if it was being done on purpose. But like most if us, he kept that knowledge at the back of his head and ignored it as much as he could. But now, with his slowly growing band of feral outlaws as his self-imposed responsibility, he started to take far more interest in the world about him than he ever did before. And what he saw appalled him.

As Roger Waters once sang, we are a species who is rapidly amusing ourselves to death [2], but more importantly we are breeding ourselves to death, and heading towards a Malthusian [3] death crisis with Gadarene certainty. But if the leaders of our various nations could not agree

---

1. Rev.14
[1] And I looked, and, lo, a Lamb stood on the mount Sion, and with him an hundred forty and four thousand, having his Father's name written in their foreheads.
[2] And I heard a voice from heaven, as the voice of many waters, and as the voice of a great thunder: and I heard the voice of harpers harping with their harps:
[3] And they sung as it were a new song before the throne, and before the four beasts, and the elders: and no man could learn that song but the hundred and forty and four thousand, which were redeemed from the earth.

2. *Amused to Death* is a concept album, and the third studio album by former Pink Floyd bassist and songwriter Roger Waters. It was released in 1992.

3. Malthusianism is a school of ideas derived from the political/economic thought of the Reverend Thomas Robert Malthus, as laid out in his 1798 writings, An Essay on the Principle of Population, which describes how unchecked population growth is exponential while the growth of the food supply was expected to be arithmetical. Malthus believed there were two types of "checks" that could then reduce the population, returning it to a more sustainable level. He believed there were "preventive checks" such as moral restraints (abstinence, delayed marriage until finances become balanced), and restricting marriage against persons suffering poverty and/or defects. Malthus believed in "positive checks", which lead to 'premature' death: disease, starvation, war, resulting in what is called a Malthusian catastrophe. The catastrophe would return population to a lower, more "sustainable", level. The term has been applied in different ways over the last two hundred years, and has been linked to a variety of other political and social movements, but almost always refers to advocates of population control.

on a strategy to save the planet, and most people didn't even care, what could an insane, opiate and brandy addled cripple living in a derelict builder's yard with a plethora of tramps and runaway children even dream of doing? Nothing was the sad truth, so Eliphas carried on dreaming.

In the still of the night when the nightjars churred in the wood on the other side of the river, and his innocent little tribe slept the sleep of the just, Eliphas fantasised about a world where he would be able to kickstart his own particular version of Helter Skelter into action. After all, he rationalised, ever since the 1960s, despite the efforts of more liberal administrations, conflicts between people of different races and religions were getting worse all over the world, and it was only a matter of time before one of these sparks set the whole world alight. And when it did millions, if not billions, of people were going to die, and Manson's interpretation of the eschatological [1] predictions of St John the Divine might actually come to pass.

Only Eliphas was not going to lead his children into any bottomless pit, if only because there almost certainly was no bottomless pit, and even if there was, he - Eliphas - wouldn't know where to start looking. No, he thought to himself. If anyone was going to survive such a conflict it would be the ones who were already living outside society. Not only would nobody bother killing them, because they were not of any spiritual, racial, cultural or military significance whatsoever, but they were already learning quite quickly how to live away from society's wholly inadequate safety nets.

"That'll learn 'em" he chortled to himself as he drifted off to sleep. The important thing would be that if a significant proportion of the human race were to destroy themselves in meaningless squabbles over dogma, industrial activity, factory farming and everything else which was destroying what was left of the environment would grind to a halt, and life on the poor beleaguered planet might actually have a chance to repair itself. And the comings and goings of a tiny band of post apocalyptic hunter gatherers in North Devon wouldn't matter a jot or tittle to anyone, and his dreams were filled with imaginative ideas about how the slaughter could be maximised.

But he knew that these were nothing more than dreams and that a one-legged cripple in a lock up would never be in the position to influence events on the world stage one iota.

Then one day, at one of his routine appointments at Barnstaple Hospital, a blood test looking for something else entirely, showed that he had a particularly aggressive type of cancer. It was inoperable, and Eliphas only had a few more months to live.

This was the day that everything changed forever.

---

1. Eschatology is a part of theology concerned with the final events of history, or the ultimate destiny of humanity. This concept is commonly referred to as the "end of the world" or "end time".

The word arises from the Greek ἔσχατος eschatos meaning "last" and -logy meaning "the study of", first used in English around 1550. The Oxford English Dictionary defines eschatology as "The department of theological science concerned with 'the four last things: death, judgment, heaven and hell'." In the context of mysticism, the phrase refers metaphorically to the end of ordinary reality and reunion with the Divine. In many religions it is taught as an existing future event prophesied in sacred texts or folklore. More broadly, eschatology may encompass related concepts such as the Messiah or Messianic Age, the end time, and the end of days.

XVIII

nd that just about takes us up to date, or at least to the point that Mr Loxodonta and Panne were when I psychically eavesdropped upon them while they were on the pavement outside the Queen's Theatre. The spectre of his imminent demise had forced Mr Loxodonta to put things into proper perspective for once. Like all of us, he had always secretly considered that although he would not actually live forever, that he would have unlimited swathes of time stretching out before him in order to put his dreams, plans and ideologies into practise.

But now all that had been taken away from him. He had six months or so left of his life, and into that six months he had to cram whatever he wanted to achieve in the time that he had left. If he was honest with himself, he knew that his fantasies about saving the planet through mass genocide, and leading his raggle taggle band of children to some mythical New Jerusalem, were just that ... fantasies. His life had never turned out the way that he had wanted, and he realised now that the abject failure of his marriage, his profession as a teacher, his family and his career as a poet, had left him completely full of hatred for the rest of his species, and that only his recently found custodianship as Lord Protector of a disparate band of outlaws, all even more socially inept than he, came close to giving him any chance of redemption.

But now it was nearly over. And he had two problems left to deal with. The mechanics of dying, he realised much to his surprise, didn't actually worry him at all. But he wanted his death to actually achieve something. And what the hell was he going to do with the people that he realised with a start that he was beginning to think of as his real family? The sad truth was that there was very little that he *could* do, but he emptied his building society account, realised as many of his possessions as he could for cash, and paid the rent on the yard for another ten years in advance, which - he figured to himself - meant (if nothing else) that his little tribe would be safe for the foreseeable future, which was more than could have been said for them before they had drifted into being under his protection.

But he was left with one great ambition. In fact, I think that 'ambition' is far too small a word. Let us say 'determination' instead. He was determined to make his death *mean* something.

One thing that you may or may not know about long term opiate users, whether they do it for recreational reasons, for medical reasons, or for some complex mixture of the two. They are almost always very paranoid people. There is something in the complex alkaloids which come from the juice of the opium poppy, which enhances the paranoia inherent within the human race. And Loxodonta was no exception. His orgy of reading and drug taking which had taken place over the two or three years that he had been living either mostly or entirely at the builder's yard had left him to believe in a whole range of conspiracy theories including two or three that he had cooked up for himself.

He had become completely convinced that not only was the whole planet going to hell in the proverbial handcart, but that those who had been put in charge of us by a not so benevolent providence were not only perfectly aware of this but complicit in its destruction. Forget about such tangential truths as the connection between George Bush's family oil company and Bin Laden Oil. These other connections were there for all to see and were unarguable. Practically everyone in public office in the industrialised western world had business interests which were entirely at odds with the future of the planet, and nobody cared. Even on a local level, district councillors across Loxodonta's native North Devon were complicit in the tearing up of woodland and hedgerow to make sops for the tourist industry, and there was only one possible motivation: money!

In Matthew 6:24 Jesus was quoted as saying: "No one can serve two masters. Either you will hate the one and love the other, or you will be devoted to the one and despise the other. You cannot serve both God and money."

"Fuckin' right Matthew" thought Loxodonta to himself. As he got older he was becoming more and more of a pantheist believing that the Universe (or Nature as the totality of everything) is identical with divinity, and or that everything composes an all-encompassing, immanent God. And following on from this eminently sensible belief (which he had got from Spinoza via P.G.Wodehouse) then every attack on the imperium of Mother Nature is nothing short of active blasphemy.

One of the other things that he believed was that those in power were actively fostering a cultural state of affairs whereby an increasingly urbanised and sedentary population were becoming ever more divorced from the reality of the natural world. One night when the pain had been too much even for his increasingly complex cocktail of analgesics, recreational pharmaceuticals and alcohol to deal with he had reached one of those precious moments of lucidity - a calm eye in the midst of a shitstorm of agony. And he believed that he understood exactly what the motivation of successive British political administrations had been. That the standards of the educational system, publicly sponsored entertainment, and pop culture had been deliberately dumbed down because it is far more easy to control people who cannot think than those who reason for themselves. And that if society in general is not interested in the world about us, it is far more easy to exploit it to destruction. And that in an aggressively capitalistic society like the ones across most of the western world, people are only useful if they are consumers. if they stop consuming then they are no longer any use to grease the cogwheels of society.

And he wrote:

> "Money is the reason.
>
> Money is the reason that people no longer care about the environment, at least not in a 'hands on' manner. Even Government legislation which *appeared* to be pro conservation was actually nothing of the sort. In a country where children cannot catch tadpoles or caterpillars, play conkers, or even collect dead leaves in

a National Forest, how the hell are they ever going to develop an empathy with nature? Not by playing *Animal Crossing* that's for sure.

Money is the reason that the television channels are full of facile talent shows while funding for art and music lessons in school has fallen to unheard of lows. And it is the reason that no-one writes protest songs any more, and why schoolkids and university students no longer protest against what they think is unfair in the land. They are too busy learning to be the next generation of consumers.

Money is the reason that the Welfare State, arguably the most noble British innovation of all time, is being systematically dismantled whilst visible taxation levels plummet (invisible ones are a completely different matter) whilst Bankers, Politicians and the like have ever more generous pay packets and bonuses despite the undeniable fuck up that they are making of the world under their care. It is nothing short of ethnic cleansing against an unprofitable underclass."

Mister Loxodonta had become somewhat of a devotee of Ted Kaczynski, otherwise known as The Unabomber known for his wide-ranging social critiques, which opposed industrialisation and modern technology while advancing a nature-centred form of anarchism. However, he wasn't just a political theorist. Between 1978 and 1995, Kaczynski engaged in a nationwide bombing campaign against people involved with modern technology, planting or mailing numerous homemade bombs, ultimately killing a total of three people and injuring 23 others.

However Loxodonta didn't have that much time left. He only had a few months before the pain that was consuming him more and more each day got too much to bear, and he would either have to seek full time medical help, or take matters into his own hands. He had already made up his mind to do the latter. His little Beretta which he had bought in order to protect his burgeoning flock, was still hidden in his lock up, unused. It would give him the best way of avoiding the inevitable, if his other broader plan hadn't come to fruition first.

In 1995, Kaczynski had mailed several letters, including some to his victims and others to major media outlets, outlining his goals and demanding that his 50-plus page, 35,000-word essay *Industrial Society and Its Future*, abbreviated to "Unabomber Manifesto" by the FBI, be printed verbatim by a major newspaper or journal. He stated that if this demand were met, he would then end his bombing campaign. The document was a densely written manifesto that called for a worldwide revolution against the effects of modern society's "industrial-technological system"

It is very densely written and almost impossible to read unless one tried very hard.

I have read it, and agree with much of it. Loxodonta read it and it was as if he was St Paul on the road to Damascus. He didn't have time to write a 35,000 word essay. But he didn't need to. All that he needed to say was compacted together into the three paragraphs and one line that are reproduced above. The only thing left was to work out how to disseminate this to the widest possible audience.

And slowly he put his plan together. He wrote letters to the editors of all the daily newspapers, and the most important of the regional ones. He even wrote to the editors of the best known international papers such as *The New York Times, Pravda, Bild* and the *Washington Post*. But he didn't post them. He needed to find one, decisive and cataclysmic way that he could put himself, momentarily, in the public eye long enough to persuade these people, who were probably just as much part of the conspiracy as the politicians, that it was in their short term interests (they would make a lot of money through extra sales) to print it.

And then, that summer afternoon when he and Panne had been dawdling outside the Queen's Theatre, he found exactly what he was looking for: The British Prime Minister, First Lord of the Treasury and Minister for the Civil Service, Head of Her Majesty's Government, Privy Counsellor, and keeper of the Queen's Peace, was going to be in the Queen's Theatre in a few days time as guest judge in the sort of facile talent show that Loxodonta hated so much. It would be emotionally satisfying as well as politically expedient to make him, in particular, the target of his final burst of spite.

XXIX

So I think you can all probably guess what happened next.

Loxodonta, with the mute little girl, she-who-would-become-Panne by his side, started to stockpile his supplies of Nitrogen tri-iodide in earnest, and packed them into the panniers that had been added to his wheelchair by the jolly kind people at a local charity for the disabled. He also packed the highly volatile paste into the frame of his chair, and added a cunningly fashioned detonator that he made out of a spring loaded toy pistol to the arm rest.

Day after day and night after night he worked, producing the deadly paste and packing it in while it was still wet, and therefore safe. And each night when he was too exhausted to work any further he would fall asleep, fully dressed, on his grubby mattress with the faithful little girl curled up like a puppy at his feet.

When the day of his destiny finally dawned it was oddly anticlimactic. It was close, humid and claustrophobic as he roused himself from what he promised would have been his final night's sleep upon this earth (and as he didn't believe in a life after death, his final night's sleep anywhere, if you want to nit pick). He was in particularly bad pain that morning, and he had nothing to do than propel himself the half mile or so into town where he could join the excited crowds waiting to see the Prime Minister pass judgement on a homogenous selection of over made up teenaged girls gyrating anorexically in their skivvies while chirping songs with titles like *Ooh my Boyfriend sexes me up* and *Ooh sexy boyfriend* not to mention *Sexy Boyfriend oooh yeah* and........ well, you get the picture. So he decided to forgo breakfast, and poured himself a pint glass of the sort of cheap liquor that-one can buy at supermarkets, which - for legal reasons - cannot be called 'brandy' and has to be known as '36 percent proof Brandy Flavoured Spirit', with a chaser of oramorph.

He lit a cigarette and slowly wheeled himself to the shed which contained the surprisingly expensive chemical toilet that he had bought from the camping shop. Hoisting himself onto the chemical loo was an uncomfortable, slightly precarious and oddly degrading task, and he felt a mild buzz of pleasure that this would be the last time he would ever have to attempt it. When he had finished, he locked the shed door upon leaving. He had agonised long and hard over whether he should leave his private lavatory for the use of his ramshackle little tribe after his spectacular exit from reality, but he came to the conclusion that - unfortunately - there was no way that they would manage to change the chemicals or keep the place in an even vaguely sanitary condition, so he decided not to even risk letting them use it.

When he returned to his lock up, he reached for a long cardboard box in the corner, and opened it. As I had already found out, he had become massively obsessed with the mythos surrounding 'The Elephant Man', and was particularly intrigued by the references to him in Alan Moore's retelling of the Jack the Ripper legend [1]. So, he had decided that whilst making his final statement, his big 'Fuck You' to the society that he hated so badly, that he would have to do so in character, and carefully he donned the wrinkled grey tunic and the huge rubber head complete with trunk and tusks.

All too soon it was time to go. He knew that the police would find it easy to trace him, so he left three carefully addressed envelopes on his unmade bed. One was a legal document passing over his lease to the members of his little tribe that he would leave behind. He had vested these rights in Michael, the fellow with Down's Syndrome that I had recognised from my days as a nurse in a time stream either so far away or so close on a quantum level as to make any attempts to measure the distance meaningless.

The second envelope contained a copy of his one page manifesto, with a concisely written letter explaining what he had done, what he was intending to do, and why he was doing it. And the third envelope contained a rhyming couplet that had amused him, and that he hoped would tickle the fancy of the more discerning tabloid editors, and maybe even make the front pages:

> *"What happens when a bomb's detonated in close containment,*
> *By a cripple in an elephant suit, that's what I call entertainment!"*

---

1. *From Hell* is a graphic novel by writer Alan Moore and artist Eddie Campbell, originally published in serial form from 1989 to 1996 and collected in 1999, speculating upon the identity and motives of Jack the Ripper. The title is taken from the first words of the "From Hell" letter, which some authorities believe was an authentic message sent from the killer in 1888. The collected edition is 572 pages long. The 2000 and later editions are the most common prints. The comic was loosely adapted into a film of the same title, released in 2001.

And, of course, he had already mailed copies of all three documents to the news editors of every national, important provincial, and North Devon newspaper, sending them second class, so they would arrive the day after he, and the Prime Minister, had left the Queen's Theatre in a miasma of iodine, ammonia, flesh and bone. He felt like Archbishop Latimer [1], lighting one small candle to illuminate a world in which he felt that all the lights had gone out.

Then it was time.

He hadn't told any of his little tribe what he had intended to do, and he had no intention of saying messy goodbyes. It was time for the self proclaimed modern day elephant man, to take his chariot of destruction and leave without a word. So that's exactly what he did.

As he left the derelict builder's yard, and started upon his own personal *Via Dolorosa* [2] there was a clap of thunder, and the summer storm which had been threatening to erupt for hours if not days finally let loose its entire fury upon the world of men. It seemed oddly appropriate, and Loxodonta had a broad grin on his face as he took a hefty swig from the hip flask of alcohol and oramorph, and started his last journey with the rain pouring down his face.

The summer storm raged overhead, and the lightning split the sky in great electric forks of fury. Loxodonta wheeled himself away from the builder's yard where, he now realised, he had actually been happier than at any other period during his tormented but oddly banal life. The rain poured down with an intensity seldom found outside the tropics, and was soon overflowing the blocked and badly maintained gutters, and soon began to go over the pavements themselves, and by the time that he was trying to negotiate Boutpourt Street, it felt like he was trying to paddle upstream in a canoe.

There is something strange about the British mindset. We pride ourselves on the 'Spirit of the Blitz' but as soon as there is more than a couple of inches of snow or rain, we begin to panic and the powers that be treat it as an emergency.

"Hey you in the wheelchair!" screamed the voice of flustered authority. It was a thuggish looking policeman brandishing a baton as if it was a Uzi. "You are blocking the flow of traffic and causing chaos..."

---

1. Hugh Latimer (c.1487 – 16 October 1555) was a Fellow of Clare College, Cambridge, and Bishop of Worcester before the Reformation, and later Church of England chaplain to King Edward VI. In 1555 under Queen Mary he was burned at the stake, becoming one of the three Oxford Martyrs of Anglicanism. Latimer was burned at the stake with Nicholas Ridley. He is quoted as having said to Ridley: "Play the man, Master Ridley; we shall this day light such a candle, by God's grace, in England, as I trust shall never be put out."

2.   The *Via Dolorosa* (Latin,"Way of Grief", "Way of Sorrows", "Way of Suffering" or simply "Painful Way") (Arabic: (طريق الآلام: is a street, in two parts, within the Old City of Jerusalem, held to be the path thatJesus walked, carrying his cross, on the way to his crucifixion, and ultimately, his bodily resurrection from the dead three days later. The winding route from the Antonia Fortress west to the Church of the Holy Sepulchre—a distance of about 600 metres (2,000 feet)—is a celebrated place of Christian pilgrimage. The current route has been established since the 18th century, replacing various earlier versions. It is today marked by nine Stations of the Cross; there have been fourteen stations since the late 15th century, with the remaining five stations being inside the Church of the Holy Sepulchre.

He didn't seem to have noticed that Loxodonta was dressed as an elephant. The cripple in the wheelchair just ignored him and went on his slow and tortuous final journey. He didn't regret not having said goodbye to his adopted family, but he did wish that he could have said goodbye to the little mute girl that he was so fond of.

And then, almost before he realised it he was there at the theatre, and much to his horror his journey through the storm must have taken him longer than he had expected, because there was already an expensively dressed compere with an epileptic grin on stage, and the Prime Minister and his retinue of greening, fawning, expensively educated simpletons we already sat in the orchestra pit, ready to make or break (at least for fifteen minutes) the reputations and hearts of a motley collection of talentless wannabees. Being in a chair he was confined to the lower level, but this suited Loxodonta fine. He could get to within feet of the Prime Minister and the other judges, and remain a relatively safe distance from the rest of the audience, and although he was resigned to the fact that there was likely to be collateral damage, but they would mostly be chinless old Etonians so they wouldn't really be missed.

He was the only person in the disabled section, which is exactly what he had thought would happen. By this point in time the disabled, the sick and the infirm had become so marginalised from society, and had been so demonised as 'workshy scroungers' by the fatuous twat that he had come to see and his colleagues that they all stayed at home, afraid to come out into the daylight where they would merely be an embarrassment to good honest consumers and taxpayers. The security at the theatre hadn't batted an eyelid when Loxodonta, still dripping wet, wheeled himself through the Disabled Entrance. They had taken one look at his grotesque costume and decided that he had to be some sort of comedy act, and just let him in without even the most cursory of searches.

This had almost certainly saved their lives, because Loxodonta was so determined to make his political point that he had vowed that if detained by security men, he would have detonated his chairbomb there and then, rather than return crestfallen to his lockup.

He wheeled himself as close as he could to the crash barrier which separated him from the judges.

"Mr Prime Minister", he called, reaching into his pocket for the small but deadly Beretta. His target, the man that had become - in Loxodonta's eyes at least - a figurehead for the social changes that he despised so much, turned and found himself facing the barrel of the gun which would kill him.

The moment that Loxodonta had been working for all these weeks had finally arrived. He spoke coldly, calmly and with psychotic menace:

"You really are a nasty little shit, Mr Prime Minister" he said, and squeezed the trigger, shooting him in the face with a single bullet.

Knowing that he only had seconds before he was overpowered by the PM's bodyguards, who had proved singularly unhelpful so far, and were presently clustered around the fallen body of their client, who was making feeble gasping and gurgling sounds he reached to the makeshift detonation switch that he had attached to the arm rest of the wheelchair. But then something jogged his elbow, and he looked around. It was the silent little girl from the lockup; the one that he had always thought was deaf mute, the one whom he had become so fond of.

He gasped in horror. He had intended to kill the Prime Minister, and it looked as if he had achieved his aim. He had then intended to kill himself, and make his death one which would reverberate around the whole world. And he didn't give a damn if he took some of the fawning morons who surrounded both the PM and the other judges of this fatuous and ridiculously expensive farce. But the last person that he had ever intended to hurt was this strange little girl who had cuddled up to him during his long dark nights of the soul, and whose name he still didn't know.

It is true, he thought. Each man does kill the thing he loves.

But he couldn't bring himself to do it. Even though it would totally negate all his plans, he could not kill this innocent child who personified everything that he felt was being destroyed by the system he hated so much.

He hesitated, and slowly brought his hand back from the switch. He was about to put his hands up in the universally recognised gesture of surrender when the girl opened her mouth and, for the first time since he had known her, spoke.

"My name's Panne", she said, and grabbed his hand and forced it down onto the detonator switch.

XXX

Although I was not there, the shock of the explosion was palpable. I winced instinctively and pulled my head backwards, and an earth-shattering swathe of pain went through me as my own personal reality came rushing forward to meet me. I was back in Britannia's garden in a peculiarly storybook setting. Everywhere else in North Devon was undergoing a typical late autumnal day of sleet grey skies and rotten leaves, but here - as a result of whatever magick surrounded us - we were on a glorious summer day.

It is amazing how, even in the most shocking situations, it is the banal that makes its impact on one's mind. Out of the corner of my eye I noticed two things which - for me - enhanced the surreality and weirdness of my position far more than mere summer's sun where there shouldn't have been.

My late Father used to enjoy watching WW2 movies on the television and then complaining all the way through them that the character was driving a car of the wrong year, or that the version of Spitfire featured in one of the action scenes did not come into service until mid-1944 when the movie was set in 1941. This used to immensely irritate me when I was a child,

but as I grew older I began to empathise with him.

My Father's biggest beef with the movie of *Mary Poppins* [1] was, like so many other people's, Dick Van Dyke's peculiar cockney accent, but mine was always that in a scene where the eponymous heroine was in an English country garden she was singing a song to an American robin, which is a bird the size of a thrush which is completely unlike the well known European bird that one can see each year on Christmas cards, and which sums up the ethos of the present day Festive Season perfectly by being a vicious and territorial killer.

American movies, especially those of Disney and his ilk fall into this type of trap all the time, portraying England as if - zoogeographically - it was a suburb of some city in the Mid West, and so I was not particularly surprised to see - in this fairy tale garden, where all the colours looked like they had been inexpertly applied in Adobe AfterEffects [TM], to spectacularly garish effect, to see that the butterflies hovering around the over lush and luminously coloured hollyhocks were American species like monarchs and giant swallowtails, and that there was a flying squirrel climbing up one of the trees, and two woodchucks gambolling on the lawn in the middle distance.

But none of this mattered. In front of me, kneeling before me, propping up her (I know that I really should refer to Panne as 'it' but that just doesn't sit well with me) injured body with difficulty, was a battered little figure, moaning in pain and trying to speak. Panne's face looked as if someone had kicked it, and there was blood dribbling from its eyes, nostrils and the corner of her mouth. I reached to comfort her, but she pushed me away.

"You must understand it all," she gasped, as if speaking in a human tongue was an impossible effort. More blood spurted out of her nose slits as she reached up for my head and pulled me forward so that her little horns were pushed hard into my forehead. There was another flash of searing pain and everything went black.

I suppose that I had been expecting to find myself in the middle of the theatre in the aftermath of a horrific explosion which would - no doubt - have killed the elephant man responsible, as well as the British Prime Minister, most of his entourage and Christ only knows who else.

But I wasn't.

I was in the last place that I would have expected to be, but unlike the oddly anodyne and slightly sickening fairy tale garden behind Britannia's tumbledown cottage, I was somewhere that made perfect sense. More peculiarly, I was in a place that I knew well, although I had not been there for many years.

---

1. Mary Poppins is a 1964 American musical fantasy film directed by Robert Stevenson and produced by Walt Disney, with songs written and composed by the Sherman Brothers. The screenplay is by Bill Walsh and Don DaGradi, loosely based on P. L. Travers' book series of the same name. The film, which combines live-action and animation, stars Julie Andrews in the titular role of a magical nanny who visits a dysfunctional family in London and employs her unique brand of lifestyle to improve the family's dynamic. Dick Van Dyke, David Tomlinson, and Glynis Johns are featured in supporting roles. The film was shot entirely at the Walt Disney Studios in Burbank, California.

I was in the middle of a woodland in North Devon. I was no longer seeing things through the eyes of Mr Loxodonta, or - for that matter - anyone's eyes but my own. I was looking down upon a little woodland glade that I knew very well, where I had picnicked, fished and camped as a boy, and that I had not seen in over forty years.

During the 1970s and 1980s my father ran a Management Consultancy for some of the local farmers and agricultural contractors, and one of his clients was a farmer near Hartland who owned lots of wilderness as well as the area that he farmed, and like many of the local farmers used to allow my friends and I to wander reasonably at will across his property looking for fish and butterflies and whatever else took our fancy. He also had a remarkably pretty daughter with whom I occasionally went swimming *au naturel* in the very same trout pool that I was now looking at, but that - I think, but as with everything else to do with this peculiar story, I cannot be sure - is another story entirely, and has nothing to do with this present narrative.

I had a perfect film director's vantage point from which to view the events that were unfolding before me. It was as if I was suspended from an enormous cherry picker above the scene which was perfectly lit for my delectation. And it was just like I was looking at a stage set below me.

However, before I describe what I saw, and - most importantly - what happened next, let me point out something very important. The first part of what happened only took a few seconds, and will certainly take longer to read about than it actually took to happen, and even longer for me to put into words.

At first the glade was completely empty, and the midnight silence was broken only by the distant sound of a dog (presumably from the farm that I knew was about half a mile to the east on the other side of the dense hazel woodland) howling at the full moon, the sound of the gently trickling stream gurgling into what used to be our secret swimming place, and the little snuffling, whispering sounds of an English sylvan summer's night.

Then, after only a few seconds there was a tear in the fabric of reality, and two figures were there; Loxodonta, slumped forward in his chair, alive or dead I didn't know, and Panne, her clothes and her hair on fire, screaming in terror. Loxodonta sat upwards with a start, and tried to reach out to help her, but it was as if he was fused to his seat. Panne, screaming the most anguished and terrified sounds that I had ever heard, leapt into our old swimming pool, and there was a sizzling sound as the cool water extinguished her flames.

Loxodonta was still struggling in his chair. I though that he was still wearing his costume, but I could see that something completely inexplicable had happened. he had indeed become fused to his wheelchair, but he had also become fused to his costume, and instead of there being a man in an elephant costume in a wheelchair, the three aspects had become one; the man was gone and something that looked vaguely the same but who was completely different was there in his stead.

Then I heard a sound from the river, and for the first time since I was fifteen I saw a naked female figure emerging from the deceptively deep waters. Except this time she was covered in wet hair, and had little curved horns on her forehead. It was Panne as I knew 'her', and the little mute girl from the lock up had vanished forever.

The two figures stared at each other for several seconds; each seemed to accept the radical sea change of the other without question. Panne stood in front of Mr Loxodonta. I thought they were going to speak but they stood in silence. Then Panne went around the chair and took the handlebars of the wheelchair in her hands, and with Panne pushing Loxodonta's chair the unlikely couple walked off into the darkness. Soon the sound of the squeaky wheel faded into the sounds of a Devon night, the dog on the farm howled again, and it was as if the little drama had never happened.

XXXI

The previous time that I had pulled my forehead away from Panne's, causing a rift in the psychic connection between us, reality (or what passed for reality in the completely unreal environs of Britannia Potts' garden) had snapped back in jaggedly like lightning rents in the fabric of my mind, but now 'reality' slowly appeared like an expensive crossfade in one of the bigger budget Hollywood movies, that a smalltime film maker like me can only dream of.

The crossfade seemed to take forever, and as it is something out of the ordinary reality of space and time, I am not even going to attempt to tell you what actually happened and how long it actually took. But soon enough I was sitting back on the bench, reaching into my pockets for cigarettes, and trying to work out what to do next.

I looked down at Panne who was kneeling slumped in front of me with 'her' head in my lap. Panne appeared to be unconscious, or at least asleep, but 'she' was definitely alive, and peculiarly, she was no longer covered in blood. Gently I lifted up the head of the little goatling, and noted with pleasure that 'her' face was no longer covered with blood, and the bruising appeared to have gone.

Lighting a cigarette with one hand, I took deep breaths of the pale blue-grey smoke as I decided what to do next. I obviously couldn't stay here, and neither could I leave Panne. So I levered myself to my feet with my stick and pulled the little creature to some semblance of an upright position, and using a move that I had been taught back in the says when I was a nurse, well over thirty years before, I started to hobble towards my car.

I don't want to bellyache about my aches and pains, because this is neither the time nor the place, but this is vaguely germane to the story. Although I have never exactly been a man of action, eighteen years ago I climbed hillsides and explored cave systems in Puerto Rico, and even ten years ago I was relatively mobile.

Now, I am almost entirely crippled, and in constant pain. I am only banging on about this to make the point that I am not claiming to be any hairy chested man of action. Even within my cryptozoological toilings, I am these days a theorist rather than a fieldworker, and when I *do* go into the field, as I did for example in my expeditions to Texas in search of the grotesque and rather baffling blue dogs, I tend to do all my travelling by car and truck rather than on foot. So manhandling a semi-comatose hairy godling under one arm, even the fifty odd yards that it took to get back to my car was no easy undertaking.

No sooner than the path turned the corner of the tumbledown cottage (which made the tumbledown cottage in which my family and ai live seem like a well tended mansion) everything changed. The warm summer's day, and the fairytale garden with brightly coloured flowers and American butterflies flitting from hollyhock to hollyhock were suddenly replaced with the cold grey drizzly reality of North Devon at the beginning of winter.

A murmuration of starlings swirled in the slate grey sky above us and an unpleasant mixture of drizzle and light sleet meandered down drunkenly. Then, and I really don't know from whence they came, Britannia Potts, Lysistrata and two hooded figures were standing in front of us, with their hands held up in front of the, like traffic policemen.

I will not pretend that I have ever had the sunniest of dispositions. And these days, as a result of my various ailments and my increasing age, I am (according to my wife, whom I live very much) a grumpy old sod. But after having spent an uncomfortable night off my tits on the floor of a cottage that I realised now that I shouldn't have visited in the first place, and after having experienced at second hand Loxodonta's and Panne's apotheosis [1], and now with the dead weight of a little goatfooted woodland godling half under my arm, and half over my shoulder, (I can't explain any better than that, and won't try) I was in an even worse mood than usual.

"What the fuck do you want?" I snarled.

The four of them just stood and stared at me in silence.

"What the fuck do you want?" I repeated.

Now, while trying to recount this narrative in some semblance of order I have got tired of resorting to the literary artifice of saying that there were no words in the English language to adequately explain what happened next, but - once again - there aren't.

A message flashed in the sky by the sun, "be careful this is only a game..." But by this time I

---

1. Apotheosis (from Greek ἀποθέωσις from ἀποθεοῦν, apotheoun "to deify"; in Latin deificatio "making divine"; also called divinization anddeification) is the glorification of a subject to divine level. The term has meanings in theology, where it refers to a belief, and in art, where it refers to a genre.

In theology, apotheosis refers to the idea that an individual has been raised to godlike stature. In art, the term refers to the treatment of any subject (a figure, group, locale, motif, convention or melody) in a particularly grand or exalted manner.

had really had enough of all this shit. My blood sugar was dipping, and I was beginning to feel violent. "I have had enough of all this!" I shouted. "Get out of my fucking way!" And I tried to push past them. And then some half remembered words that I had got from a book that I didn't really believe flashed into my mind, and I shouted:

"Κύριε ο Θεός ημών, ο Βασιλεύς των αιώνων, ο παντοκράτωρ και παντοδύναμος, ο ποιών πάντα και μετασκευάζων μόνω τω βούλεσθαι."

And as I did so I thrashed out with my stick, desperately trying not to loose my balance. I don't know whether it was the stick or the ancient Greek exorcism which I didn't believe in and only half remembered, but the two hooded figures disappeared and Panne and I were left staring at the two mad women that I had known for so long.

"Just get out of my fucking way" I croaked wearily, and much to my surprise they did. I bundled Panne unceremoniously in the back seat of the Astra, squeezed myself into the driver seat, and drove the two miles back to Woolsery.

Epilogue

And, believe it or not, there really isn't much left to tell. During the short drive home, I was doing my best to marshall my thoughts and work out how to tell my long suffering wife what had happened. I was sure that she would have been very worried that I had not returned home the previous evening, if indeed it *had* been the previous evening. I was so disorientated by having travelled forwards and backwards through time with Panne and Loxodonta that I truly didn't know *what* day it was.

But it turned out that I had only been gone for less than twenty four hours, and that Britannia had telephoned Corinna the night before, and in her best *Grande Damme* voice had introduced herself as a friend of my late father, told her that I would be spending the night away, and even warned her that I would be accompanied by a poorly youngster who would need looking after.

How she knew all this before it had even happened, and how she had managed to lull my dear wife into a false sense of calmness I am not sure, but when I got home Corinna greeted me as if nothing had happened.

She didn't even bat much of an eyelid at Panne.

I had wondered vaguely how I was going to explain the advent into our household of a naked hairy creature with the horns and hooves of a goat and the physique of a young teenage girl, but in the event Corinna was much less shocked than I had been when I had first met Panne. She is a mother and a grandmother after all, and her maternal instincts kicked in the moment she saw her.

Together we manhandled Panne up the stairs and into a makeshift bed that Corinna had made up in what used to be my Father's Dressing Room. There Panne slept for the next couple of days before eventually beginning to venture out and play with the dogs.

Nine months later, I am sitting in my favourite armchair trying to type deathless prose on my iPad, and finish this narrative before my diabetes becomes too much for me and I need to rush upstairs for a pee. Panne is still here, and shows no signs of any godlike powers of any kind. After the events surrounding the *Xtul* winter song I have heard nothing from Danny or anyone to do with the band but something mildly unsettling *did* happen in the early spring.

It is a matter of record that one of my hard drives died on me, and I had to pay over seven hundred quid to recover the data on it, which included all of the music and sound files I had from *Xtul*. Whilst I was waiting for the replacement drive to come back with the recovered data, I went down to my office one morning to find that a portable hard drive marked "MUSIC" was missing, and there were telltale signs that someone or something had been into my office overnight. Two days later the drive (which had contained nothing more interesting than a whole pile of *Led Zeppelin* bootlegs) was returned in the post.

When I got the recovered data back I made sure that I sent backups of all the data to several friends, as well as lodging a copy with my bank, and uploading it to a cloud drive. I have no idea what I am going to do with it, but *Xtul* are too good a band for me to let slip completely through my fingers.

Panne hasn't spoken a word since moving in to the old Dressing Room where we plonked 'her' eight months ago. But 'she' seems to be a happy little thing, and the two dogs, and four cats gaze adoringly at 'her' whenever she flits past them. Sometimes they all curl up together in a hairy pile in the corner of the room, and as spring turned into summer one could sometimes see Panne skipping through the beech trees on the east side of the garden where we have the Bealtiane fire each year, Prudence (as senior dog) waddling earnestly by her side, and Archie and a procession of cats and a kitten trotting behind.

And what do Mother and Graham who live here, and the motley collection of scientists, musicians and social malcontents who visit here think about having a godling in their midst?

Truthfully, I don't think that any of them have noticed.

FIN

Backing the Wrong Horse

I met Hiro Onada [1] Once
a steely little man with fire in his eyes
he looked at me I was beneath contempt
cos I never died for my Emperor

I really don't know if I'd been like him
thirty years later undefeated
when the world around had forgotten what he stood for
ever got the feeling you've been cheated

You ask why I'm so bitter and twisted
you're not gonna like it but you insisted
I'm the way I am because of people like you
and the stupid things that you people do
the way you ignore everything Id been taught
the way you refuse me when I've asked for support
your culture, your religion
its a third rate sham
but you dare to question me about what I am
fuck it, I had enough long ago
but didn't have the courage to fight back or let go
and its only now at the end of my days
that I have started to fight my way out of the maze

it is either fight back or drink myself into oblivion
or put money in the pockets of some faceless Bolivian [2]
but if I turned my body to a walking pharmacy

I wouldn't be a threat and I would die quite harmlessly,
and I'd rather use my talents and the time I've got left
to fight back against a system which has left me bereft
Once I had a family and prospects and a home
but now I am a nobody they'd rather leave alone
an ugly inconvenience that doesn't tick the boxes
they can't get away with culling me like
pheasants, deer or foxes
and no matter how they try they are never gonna quench
the spirit of an elephant thats's out for revenge

For once in my life I'm going to die for a cause
taking arms for something to set me free
a guerilla fighter up against a world that doesn't care
but with the ghosts of countless million men behind me
And the cemeteries and hospitals are full of the men
and the women that societies mistreated
and every day people we voted for do it again
ever get the feeling you've been cheated [3]

The day I left the cancer ward nobody took me home
I could see from their expressions
that none of them really care
they left me in the doorway then went back to their lives
as I shuffled down the long hill in my wheel chair
to a trading estate lock up costing thirty quid a week
where the winos and the idiots
live their lives out unmolested
it is not a bad place to end up if you're a homeless freak
cos at least your never gonna get arrested
with a bottle of cheap sherry from a discount supermarket
you sit and make communion with the sky
lying on your mattress and your scrap of stolen carpet
knowing no-ones going to miss you when you die

But over the years I have amassed a few belongings
which will help me in my grand retaliation
I think I'll be the first freak since Marinus Van der Lubbe [4]
who's death will shape the fate of a whole nation
I'm doing this for me, and not for dogma or for paradise
or because a priest or officer told me to [5]
I'm doing this because I truly think that it is right
and this is something that truly I have to do
I'm not afraid of death cos I've been afraid all my life

and this end I've chosen really seems too easy
and this thing I'm going to do
will not just set my children free
but in the end I know its also going to free me

But sometimes it only ever takes one man
to play a game with people's destiny
and when I carry out my solemn sacred plan
I know its gonna work out best for me
those who sit in judgement over us are guilty as sin
then a jurisprudence lesson's sorely needed
and I'm the man whose going to make the judgement begin
because I've always had the feeling we've been cheated

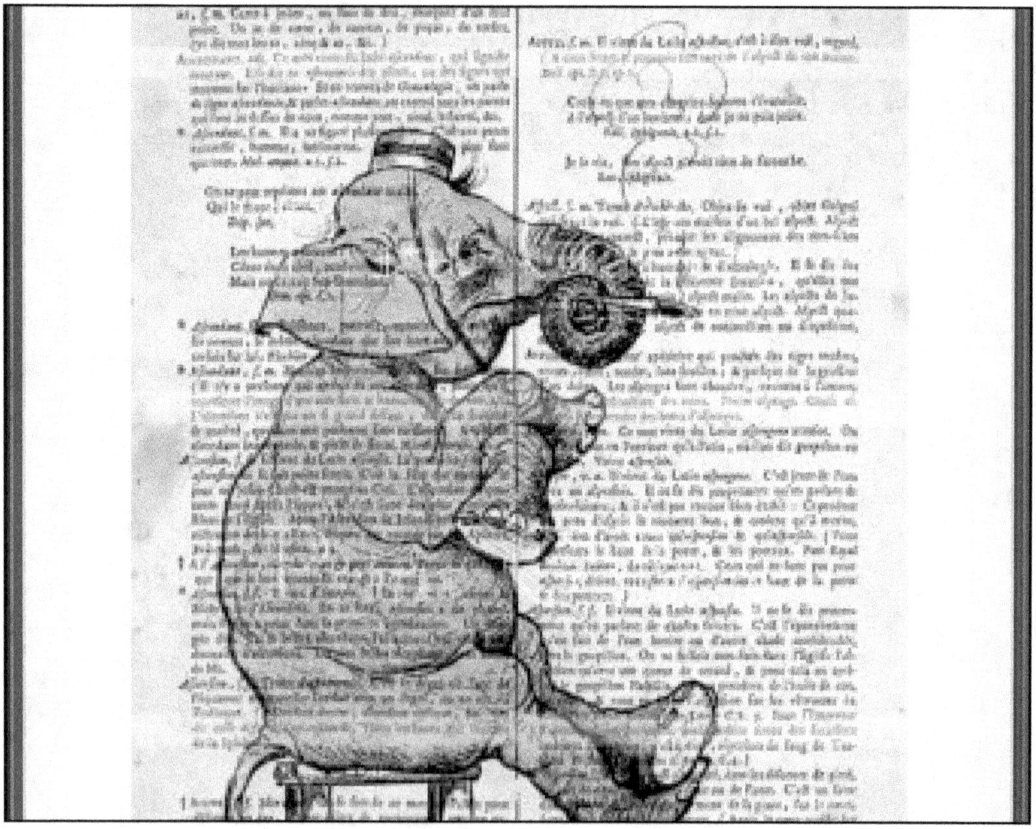

Three Girls

There's a run down trading estate on the outskirts of town
with a builders yard with the buildings half fallen down
and a bank of lock ups for a knockdown rent
and a pile of old cars scrapped and battered and bent
and there's people who live in this derelict mess
men who believe they are monsters at best
there are winos and folk running from community care
but there's three girls I know who are also living there

One girl climbs a stairway to the stars
and spends each night asleep in the back of cars
she told me once to get away from stuff
she was being like this and living rough
but when you're hiding from your captors and times are tough
it doesn't really matter that you've had enough

Most people live there cos there's no other option
cos their victims of abuse or cos they're simply forgotten
I live there cos its quiet and I quite like the company
of a disparate band of outcasts who all despise society
I live there because I'm just that kind of man
and its the only place that I can safely get on with my plan
its the only place I know where no-one questions the motives
of a psychotic dying cripple
who knows how to make explosives

Another girl is a demon with a knife
I know she walks the streets most every night
she's even kind of cute you know,
I know that cos she tells me so every morning
I know that cos she screams it out as a warning

Its quite beautiful out here when you're the only one
The yellow of the ragwort [6]
in the last rays of the setting sun
Sitting in silence away from those that hate ya
watching the brownstone [7] revert to mother nature
and you realise the human race is curiously insignificant
and the people who live here with me
are oddly sweet and innocent
and its solely up to me to try and ensure their rebirth
and make sure that the meek and mild do inherit the earth

The third girl only smiles and cannot speak
anywhere else they would treat her like a freak
but here instead this girl has grown
into a creature of her own
but late at night you hear her moan
at the field of hate that fear has sown

So when I heard her crying I knew exactly what to do
how I could strike back and destroy everything we knew
how to send a message down into the heart of the machine
that had turned a thing of beauty into
something quite obscene
and my own life might mean something if I ended it this way
and show the pigs in power that we had something to say
and that they couldn't keep the enslaved masses
quiet any more
and they couldn't rule the country
in the way they had before

And slowly but not as slowly as it seemed
I collected all the chemicals I'd dreamed
I took them back gently to the place I could hide
and made fifty pounds of Nitrogen Triiodide [8]
I opened up my wheelchair and put it inside
and each night I lay dreaming of my final ride

A dream of the Crocodile in a Thunderstorm

I was thrown out of the library
just because I brought some whisky
to numb my pain as I sat there
quietly reading Dostoyevsky [9]
a cripple in a wheelchair
is not supposed to be literate
but just like me they wanted to
sit in judgement on the idiot [10]

I felt just like the protagonist
in the crocodile [11]
who sits and carries out his tasks
wrapped in another body
so grotesque as to make the people cry
or maybe smile
as I sit back numbed by whisky
and the sweet fruit of the poppy [12]

Somewhere deep inside the aether
when any child is born
three old women weave a tapestry [13]
until the threads are torn
I don't believe in providence,
but I believe in fate,
and I'll do my best to change the world
before it gets too late

"ANOTHER SUCH VICTORY, AND I AM UNDONE."—Pyrrhus.

Fires in your Cities

Finally my day has come, explosives in my chair
and the whisky and the morphine mean
that I don't really care
Boutpourt Street in the pouring rain's my Via Dolorosa [14]
and I know that what I plan to do
couldn't really be much grosser
"You there in the wheelchair", the policeman shouts across
"You're blocking the flow of traffic
and your just causing chaos"
a cripple in an elephant suit is the thing they least expect
but if you think I'm causing chaos man,
just watch what I do next

There'll be fires in your cities if they ever let me free
there'll be slaughter on the highway there'll be carnage on TV
when I was young I was too ugly to be loved
now I'm far too beautiful to be set free [15]

A diet of bread and circuses [16] always kept the masses quiet
let the consumers just consume and make sure they don't riot
serve up a ritual victim [17] as a target for contempt
they call it reality TV [18] but I know just what it meant
give one a pointless title, and another ridicule
treat another like a hero for a day and another like a fool
and if a few people's lives do get ruined along the way
its collateral damage [19] or friendly fire [20]
that's what the army say

And now they show these programmes live

and so it seems to me
if I turn the tables on these scum, live carnage on TV
what happens when a bomb's detonated in close containment
by a cripple in an elephant suit,
that's what I call entertainment
but is there a good reason why all these people are gonna die?
yes, it might send a message to the people who ask why
these morons are paid billions,
but close the schools and clinics down
and let a living nightmare replace what was once my town

An evil bitch [21] once claimed there was no thing as society
and she spent the rest of her wretched life
trying to make that come to be
and she's pretty well succeeded because all that we have left
is a government of criminals paying their way by theft
is enough people made a stand against
the shallowness they spout
then I'd like to think that soon
the truth would begin to come out
and I'd like to think that one day people might see
just what was meant
by a suicide bomber in a wheelchair dressed as an elephant

I always thought when it was time to die
you'd be overwhelmed with emotion
but as it was I just felt numb and it all went in slow motion
I looked around and all I could see was hysterical ugly faces
full of avarice and spite and greed
and wanting to change places
with the grinning morons on the stage I knew would soon be dead
and I had a moment of doubt and fear
and wished I was somewhere else instead
and then I felt a movement and felt somebody hold my hand
it was the silent girl from the lock up she smiled at me and
she said 'My Name's Panne' and...

Elephants

The next thing I knew we were out in the darkness
In a forest somewhere by a stream
Panne's clothes were burning,
The poor girl was screaming
And I felt stuck in a bad dream
She jumped in the water,
I wanted to help her,
But I couldn't move in the dark
Then the moon came out from behind big banks of clouds
And I heard a dog start to bark

How my plan had failed I had no idea
But I knew that we both should be dead
But somehow we weren't; beyond my comprehension,
We were here in the forest instead
I stared at the water, but the child had banished,
And then by the light of the moon
Something was emerging from out of the darkness
I knew it would be with me soon

Then I saw who it was as she stood there,
the moonlight reflecting from off her wet skin
No longer a child, something else entirely
A changeling [22] but still painfully thin
She was covered in hair, she had horns on her forehead

And hooves where she'd only had feet
Panne screamed in triumph (the dog had stopped barking)
And I knew her change was complete

Panne is a Goddess, but I'm still a cripple
imprisoned inside this damn chair
But I realise how now I am feeling quite different
Still scared but now somehow aware
The elephant suit was no longer a costume
The mask was welded to my face,
So the two of us just set off into the darkness
And bade farewell to the human race

Mr Loxodonta

My name is Mr Loxodonta [23]
And when your mind begins to wander
Into places that you know
You really shouldn't let it go
In the gaps between your dreams
Where you hear the idiots scream
That's basically where I am found
Playing games with light and sound

My name is Mr Loxodonta
I'll find you when you don't want to
Explore realms of world as myth
And pantheistic multiperson
Solipsism 101, [24]
The games of chance have just begun
I'm dying but it doesn't matter
My alter-ego just gets fatter

My name is Mr Loxodonta
I won't be around much longer
because I'm twisted, cold and brash
and all over you like a rash
I'm the stuff of febrile dreams
where nothing's ever what it seems
and if you think that sounds unreal
you know precisely how I feel

My name is Mr Loxodonta
a conundrum for you to ponder
what's behind my ears and trunk?
do I live just like a monk?
in many ways I'm your worst nightmare
but out of mind is out of sight, yeah
and I slink like fungus out of wood
and what I have to say's not good

My name is Mr Loxodonta
you tell me just what you want, sir
but I'll just tell you what you'll get
and your nightmare isn't over yet
there's something you should know my friend
the world you know's about to end
and no-one's going to forgive
and there's nothing left for them to give

My name is Mr Loxodonta
And when your mind begins to wander
Into places that you know
You really shouldn't let it go
In the gaps between your dreams
Where you hear the idiots scream
That's basically where I am found
Playing games with light and sound

Endnotes

AUTHOR'S NOTE: Some of these will have been covered elsewhere in the book in the form of footnotes but as Andy Warhol proved repetition can be art

1. Hirō Onoda (小野田 寛郎 *Onoda Hirō*, March 19, 1922 – January 16, 2014) was an Imperial Japanese Army intelligence officer who fought in World War II and a Japanese holdout who did not surrender in 1945. In 1974, his former commander travelled from Japan to personally issue orders relieving him from duty. Onoda had spent almost 30 years holding out in the Philippines. He held the rank of Second Lieutenant in the Imperial Japanese Army.

2. Playing along with the cultural shibboleth that suggests that all folk from Bolivia are involved in the cocaine industry, which is obviously untrue.

3. "Ever get the feeling you've been cheated?" asked a weary Johnny Rotten at the conclusion of the Sex Pistols' first (and last) U.S. tour. The show took place at the one-time hippie haven of the Winterland in San Francisco on Jan. 14, 1978 and would be the band's final performance — at least until their 1996 reunion. By then, however, Sid Vicious was long dead.

4. Marinus (Rinus) van der Lubbe (13 January 1909 – 10 January 1934) was a Dutch council communist convicted of, and executed for, setting fire to the German Reichstag building on 27 February 1933, an event known as the Reichstag fire.

5. Superior orders, often known as the Nuremberg defence, lawful orders or by the German phrase Befehl ist Befehl ("only following orders", literally "an order is an order"), is a plea in a court of law that a person, whether a member of the armed forces or a civilian, not be held guilty for actions which were ordered by a superior officer or a public official.

6. *Jacobaea vulgaris*, syn. *Senecio jacobaea* is a very common wild flower in the family Asteraceaethat is native to northern Eurasia, usually in dry, open places, and has also been widely distributed as a weed elsewhere. Common names include ragwort, common ragwort, tansy ragwort, benweed, St. James-wort, ragweed, stinking nanny/ninny/willy, staggerwort, dog standard, cankerwort, stammerwort, mare's fart and cushag. In the western US it is generally known as tansy ragwort, or tansy, though its resemblance to the true tansy is superficial. It is also one of the recurrent motifs in the writing of Bill Drummond who is a hero to us all.

7. Probably Brownfield rather than brownstone. Brownfield is a term used in urban planning to describe land previously used for industrialpurposes or some commercial uses. Such land may have been contaminated with hazardous waste or pollution or is feared to be so whereas Brownstone is a brown Triassic-Jurassic sandstone which was once a popular building material. The term is also used in the United States to refer to a townhouse clad in this material.

8. Nitrogen triiodide is the inorganic compound with the formula NI_3. It is an extremely sensitivecontact explosive: small quantities explode with a loud, sharp snap when touched even lightly, releasing a purple cloud of iodine vapor; it can even be detonated by alpha radiation. NI_3 has a complex structural chemistry that is difficult to study because of the instability of the derivatives.

9. Fyodor Mikhailovich Dostoyevsky Russian: Фёдор Михайлович Достоевский; (11 November 1821 – 9

159

February 1881), sometimes transliterated Dostoevsky, was a Russian novelist, short story writer, essayist, journalist and philosopher. Dostoyevsky's literary works explore human psychology in the troubled political, social, and spiritual atmosphere of 19th-century Russia. Many of his works are marked by a preoccupation with Christianity, explored through the prism of the individual confronted with life's hardships and beauty.

10. *The Idiot* (Russian: Идиот, *Idiot*) is a novel written by the 19th-century Russian author Fyodor Dostoyevsky. It was first published serially in *The Russian Messenger* between 1868 and 1869. *The Idiot*, alongside some of Dostoyevsky's other works, is often considered one of the most brilliant literary achievements of the "Golden Age" of Russian literature.

11. "The Crocodile" (Russian: Крокодил, *Krokodil*) is a short story by Fyodor Dostoyevsky that was first published in 1865 in his magazine *Epoch*. The story relates the events that befall one Ivan Matveich when he, his wife Elena Ivanovna, and the narrator visit the Arcade to see a crocodile that has been put on display by a German entrepreneur. After teasing the crocodile, Ivan Matveich is swallowed alive. He finds the inside of the crocodile to be quite comfortable, and the animal's owner refuses to allow it to be cut open, in spite of the pleas from Elena Ivanovna. Ivan Matveich urges the narrator to arrange for the crocodile to be purchased and cut open, but the owner asks so much for it that nothing is done. As the story ends Elena Ivanovna is contemplating divorce and Ivan Matveich resolves to carry on his work as a civil servant as best he can from inside the crocodile.

12. Opiates are analgesic alkaloid compounds found naturally in the opium poppy plant *Papaver somniferum*. The psychoactive compounds found in the opium plant include morphine, codeine, andthebaine. The term *opiate* should be differentiated from the broader term *opioid*, which includes all drugs with opium-like effects, including opiates, semi-synthetic opioids derived from morphine (such asheroin, hydrocodone, hydromorphone, oxycodone, and oxymorphone), and synthetic opioids which are not derived from morphine (such as fentanyl, buprenorphine, and methadone). All opioids, including the opiates, are considered drugs of high abuse potential and are classified as Schedule I drugs.

13. In Greek mythology, the Moirai (Ancient Greek: Μοῖραι, "apportioners", Latinized as Moerae)—often known in English as the Fates—were the white-robed incarnations of destiny (Romanequivalent: Parcae, euphemistically the "sparing ones", or Fata; also analogous to the GermanicNorns). Their number became fixed at three: Clotho (spinner), Lachesis (allotter) and Atropos(unturnable). They controlled the mother thread of lifestyle of every mortal from birth to death. They were independent, at the helm of necessity, directed fate, and watched that the fate assigned to every being by eternal laws might take its course without obstruction.

14. The *Via Dolorosa* (Latin: "Way of Grief," "Way of Sorrows," "Way of Suffering" or simply "Painful Way";Arabic: طريق الآلام)is a street within the Old City of Jerusalem, held to be the path that Jesus walked on the way to his crucifixion. The winding route from the Antonia Fortress west to the Church of the Holy Sepulchre—a distance of about 600 metres (2,000 feet)—is a celebrated place of Christian pilgrimage. The current route has been established since the 18th century, replacing various earlier versions. It is today marked by nine Stations of the Cross; there have been fourteen stations since the late 15th century, with the remaining five stations being inside the Church of the Holy Sepulchre.

15. This chorus is a melange of quotes and misquotes from serial killer and cultist Charles Manson. " In my mind's eye my thoughts light *fires in your cities.*" and "When I was a child I was an orphan and *too ugly to be* adopted. Now I am too *beautiful* to *be* set free." Both of these taken from the book *Helter Skelter* by Vincent Bugliosi and Curt Gentry (1974)

16. "Bread and circuses" (or bread and games; from Latin: *panem et circenses*) is metonymic for a superficial means of appeasement. In the case of politics, the phrase is used to describe the generation of public approval, not through exemplary or excellent public service or public policy, but through diversion; distraction; or the mere satisfaction of the immediate, shallow requirements of a populace, as an offered "palliative." Its originator, Juvenal, used the phrase to decry the selfishness of common people and their neglect of wider concerns. The phrase also implies the erosion or ignorance of civic duty amongst the concerns of the commoner.

17. Sparagmos (Ancient Greek: σπαραγμός, from σπαράσσω sparasso, "tear, rend, pull to pieces") is an act of rending, tearing apart, or mangling, usually in a Dionysian context. In Dionysian rite as represented in myth and literature, a living animal, or sometimes even a human being, is sacrificed by being dismembered.

18. Reality television is a genre of television programming that documents unscripted real-life situations, and often features an otherwise unknown cast. It differs from documentary television in that the focus tends to be on drama and personal conflict, rather than simply educating viewers. Reality TV programs also often bring participants into situations and environments that they would otherwise never be a part of. The genre has

160

various standard tropes, including "confessionals" used by cast members to express their thoughts, which often double as the shows' narration. In competition-based reality shows, a notable subset, there are other common elements such as one participant being eliminated per episode, a panel of judges, and the concept of immunity from elimination.

19. Collateral damage is a term in general for unintentional death, injury, or damage inflicted incidentally to the intended target. In military terminology, it is frequently used where non-combatants are unintentionally killed or wounded and/or non-combatant property damaged as result of the attack on legitimate military targets. The unintentional destruction of friendly targets is called friendly fire. Critics of the term see it as a euphemism that dehumanizes non-combatants killed or injured during military operations, used to reduce the perception of culpability of military leadership in failing to prevent non-combatant casualties

20. Friendly fire is an attack by a military force on friendly forces while attempting to attack the enemy, either by misidentifying the target as hostile, or due to errors or inaccuracy. Fire not intended to attack the enemy, such as negligent discharge and deliberate firing on one's own troops for disciplinary reasons, is not called friendly fire. Nor is unintentional harm to non-combatants or structures, which is sometimes referred to as *collateral damage*. Use of the term "friendly" in a military context for allied personnel or materiel dates from the First World War, often for shells falling short. The term *friendly fire* was originally adopted by the United States military. Many North Atlantic Treaty Organization (NATO) militaries refer to these incidents as blue on blue, which derives from military exercises where NATO forces were identified by blue pennants and units representing Warsaw Pact forces by orange pennants.

21. Margaret Hilda Thatcher, Baroness Thatcher, LG, OM, PC, FRS (née Roberts, 13 October 1925 – 8 April 2013) was the Prime Minister of the United Kingdom from 1979 to 1990 and the Leader of the Conservative Party from 1975 to 1990. She was the longest-serving British Prime Minister of the 20th century and is the only woman to have held the office. A Soviet journalist called her the "Iron Lady", a nickname that became associated with her uncompromising politics and leadership style. As Prime Minister, she implemented policies that have come to be known as Thatcherism. She is quoted as saying: "*I think we've been through a period where too many people have been given to understand that if they have a problem, it's the government's job to cope with it: 'I have a problem, I'll get a grant.' 'I'm homeless, the government must house me.' They're casting their problem on society. And, you know, there is no such thing as society.*" Many of us believe that it is the only real job of a government to look after the weakest in society, and if it does not do so there is no point in having a government.

22. A changeling is typically described as being the offspring of a fairy, troll, elf or other legendary creature that has been secretly left in the place of a human child. Sometimes the term is also used to refer to the child who was taken. The apparent changeling could also be a stock or fetch, an enchanted piece of wood that would soon appear to grow sick and die. The theme of the swapped child is common among medieval literature and reflects concern over infants thought to be afflicted with unexplained diseases, disorders, or developmental disabilities.

23. African elephants are elephants of the genus *Loxodonta* (from the Greek words *loxo* (oblique sided) and *donta* (tooth)). The genus consists of two extant species: the African bush elephant and the smaller African forest elephant. *Loxodonta* is one of two existing genera of the family, Elephantidae. Fossil remains of *Loxodonta* have been found only in Africa, in strata as old as the middle Pliocene.

24. See *The Number of the Beast* by Robert Anson Heinlein (1980)

APPENDIX

An excerpt from my book *Monster Hunter* (2004)

A t that time I lived in a tiny village called Woolfardisworthy, which was about nine miles from Bideford. However, reasonably regularly I visited my friend Jim for the weekend and on one June weekend Jim and I conspired together to go werewolf hunting.

We left Jim`s house soon after breakfast and cheerfully walked along Abbotsham Road, past our school gates towards the village where the werewolf was supposed to have his haunt. We walked along the very same lanes that *Stalky and Co.* had explored a century or so before, and although they are very different now, thirty years ago, only the thinnest veneer of tarmacadam made any difference at all to the landscape explored by Kipling and his tear-away friends in the 1880s.

The hedgerows were alight with Mayflowers and honeysuckle, but as we approached the village of Abbotsham, and the coast path that led towards Abbotsham Cliffs these were replaced by gorse and furze, and the silver washed fritillaries which hawked up and down the hedgerows like stealth bombers over Iraq, were replaced by the ethereal fluttering Holly Blues, and the exotic and slightly sinister beauty of the day flying burnet moths.

Climbing over a field gate at a predetermined point, our expedition became an illegal one as we shamelessly trespassed across farmer's fields towards our destination. About a mile and a half from the road that we had left was the beginnings of a wood. This was, allegedly at least, the beginning of our destination, and we started to feel a little uneasy.

Sheepishly we entered the wood. Neither of us were boy scouts so our woodcraft was not of the kind of which Baden-Powell would have approved; but we had both read *Swallows and Amazons* so we felt that we vaguely knew what we were doing. In all my life of wandering through woods, forests, thickets, jungles and rain forests across the world I have never come across one that was completely silent. Except for this one.

Here and there one could see the mangled and dilapidated remains of a rhododendron bush, indicating that this had once been a carefully managed piece of woodland. Now it was just abandoned wilderness. It felt to us like we were the only visitors here for decades - if not longer. There was absolutely no sound except for the crunching noise of twigs and dead leaves scrunching beneath our feet. No bird song, no buzzing insects, no tiny scurrying animals.

Then we noticed something else strange. Apart from the occasional dirty grey-green of the sickly rhododendron leaves, there was practically no colour. Although it was midsummer, all the trees and bushes at eye level anyway appeared to be dead. If you looked up, you could see the outline of the leafy canopy silhouetted against the blue sky, but down here in the wood itself it was as dead as a morgue.

We carried on in silence. We were both uncomfortable but neither of us wanted to be the first to suggest that discretion should be the better part of valour and that we should get the hell out of there as quickly as possible. So we carried on. After what seemed like a lifetime (but was probably only about half an hour) the undergrowth began to thin out and before us we could see a rusty, three-strand barbed wire fence. Being the intrepid souls that we were, we didn't hesitate to clamber over. I tore the seat of my jeans to blazes and was soundly scolded by my Mother when I got home but that is another, and completely irrelevant story.

We carried on through the wood, and it wasn't long before we realised that we were approaching the edge of what appeared to be a large and completely overgrown garden, which was nearly as badly tended as the wood had been. However, at least here there were signs of life; and the terrible feeling of black oppression that had been the *genius loci* of the wood behind us was gone.

Realising that whereas before we were trespassing and we could probably have got away with it, there was now no doubt that we were perpetrating a criminal act, and furthermore, perpetrating a criminal act on the property of a rich and influential local landowner who may or may not have been a governor of our school we became very stealthy indeed. If such a thing as a time machine existed, it would, I am sure, surprise the heck out of any of my friends and colleagues (who have only known me as an overweight, and clumsy middle aged man who often walks with a stick), to have seen me thirty years ago as a very stealthy thirteen year old who had read enough books about Red Indians to know how to glide from bush to bush in a relatively inconspicuous manner.

As we progressed around the perimeter of the dilapidated old garden, we suddenly saw the most wonderful sight of our young lives. The 1960s may have made sexual liberation *de rigueur* amongst certain sections of society, but back in 1972 the thirteen year old Jonathan Downes had only the vaguest idea of what a naked woman actually looked like.

By modern standards the girlie magazines of the era were pretty prudish and I had only ever seen a few of them, and the anything-goes culture of the internet where every conceivable sexual taste can be viewed at the click of a mouse button was a generation in front of us. I had no sisters or any close female relatives, and although I was painfully aware of the theoretical differences between boys and girls, I was far too shy to have ever had a girlfriend. Although Jim had a rather cute sister a year younger than him, they came from a strict Methodist family and I am certain that he was as innocent as me, and was as amazed and overjoyed as I was, when we crept Red Indian style around the bushes on the edge of a clearing and saw, there, lying on a blanket in the middle of the small patch of grass a naked girl of about our age.

She was obviously sunbathing and was lying on her tummy, blissfully unaware that only a dozen yards or so away two aghast teenaged boys were crouching in the long grass staring at her. She was perfect, like a wood nymph. Even now, three decades later, the memory of her long, muscular legs, dirty blonde shoulder length hair, straight back, and rounded, almost boyish buttocks conjures up the classic image of femininity for me. Jim and I crouched in the long grass for at least ten minutes watching her and drinking in every possible aspect to savour in our minds over the years ahead.

Believe it or not, this wasn't a sexually voyeuristic thing. It was more an almost religious experience when for the first time we understood what the immortal and non-existent Lazarus Long had meant when he said "what a wonderful world it is that has girls in it."

Then, joy of joys, she turned over, and for a few brief minutes, as she lay on her back with her eyes shut we grokked in their fullness every detail of her breasts, her belly, and that mysterious dark triangle between her thighs. Then she sat up and opened her eyes.

The spell was broken. We knew that she hadn't seen us, but the probable repercussions if we had been caught not only trespassing in the private garden of one of our school governors; but, spying on someone who was most probably his naked daughter, were too grim to contemplate. Taking one last look at the naked wood nymph, who had managed to destroy her image of Elysian loveliness by hauling on a Donny Osmond T shirt and lighting a cigarette, we decided that discretion was the better part of valour and crept back towards the deserted wood.

By this time we had forgotten that our original quest had been for a werewolf. I don't think either of us had actually fully believed in the legend, and, to be quite honest, we weren't even sure if the garden in which we had spies upon the naked girl, was the one that belonged to the house that reputedly harboured the werewolf. Anyway, we were hungry, there were fifty pence pieces burning figurative holes in our pockets and there was a little shop back on the outskirts of Northam that sold the most delicious pasties known to man. We decided to take what we believed was the most direct path through the wood to get to Northam where we could eat pasties, drink pop and relive our adventure of the morning.

We set off in what we fondly believed was the right direction for Northam. Although we were undoubtedly intrepid, direction finding was not our strong suit and we soon became hopelessly lost. As we went deeper and deeper into the wood the atmosphere became more and more unpleasant.

The wood was still oppressively silent, but now, it seemed to us, that it was not just the absence of birdsong or insects - but the absence of *anything*. The nearest analogy that I can come to this happened to me about seven years later when I was visiting Toronto. I was visiting The Natural Science Museum to see the impressive, though horrific, exhibition of mounted Passenger Pigeons, when I was sidetracked into a gallery where elementary physics experiments were being demonstrated to High School children. Well, although I wasn't a High School pupil, I wasn't much older, and found the displays both interesting and informative. However, one, in particular, freaked me out completely. It was a room that had been lined with some sort of total sound insulating board so that when you entered it you could hear nothing at all except for the sounds of your own body. Even your footsteps on the ground were silent. The *only* sounds that you could hear were those of your bodily functions and any sounds you happened to utter.

This exhibit freaked me out mightily because, just for a second I was back in the middle of that evil wood in North Devon, and this time I didn't even have my mate, Jim, there to keep me company.

Back in 1972, we were moving as fast as we could. By this time we had completely lost interest in the Northam bun shop. We just wanted to get the hell out of this accursed wood. Then it hit us. A stench such as I have never encountered before or since rolled up towards us through the shrivelled, blighted, stunted trees. Now, I have examined dead animals in the tropics where corpses are reduced to a putrefying mess within hours. I have observed a human autopsy and have conducted dissections of creatures ranging from a woodlouse to a bottlenosed dolphin. I have seen quite a few dead humans, some in particularly unpleasant conditions. On one occasion I even ended up giving attempted mouth-to-mouth resuscitation to a corpse that had drowned on its own vomit. I am not a squeamish man, and I was an even less squeamish youth, but this smell was the most disgusting that I have ever encountered.

We proceeded gingerly. If it hadn't been that we were acutely aware that it would have been appallingly unmanly, I'm sure that we would have held each other's hands for comfort. In fact, if I'm going to be honest, with the hindsight of thirty years, I'm not certain that we didn't. The stench was all pervading, and although we did our best to avoid whatever its source was, it felt like we were being inexorably drawn towards the epicentre of the phenomenon.

Then suddenly there it was: A dead roebuck. Its head caught in a barbed -wire fence and its tortured body splayed out behind it, bloated with putrefaction. Its intestines were spread out besides it. Three decades later I was to encounter a similar phenomenon. As I wrote in my 1999 book, *The Rising of the Moon*, a similar occurrence took place during the summer of 1997:

"A mutilated roebuck was found at a nature reserve on Woodbury Common during the height of the UFO activity in August. Interestingly, although the animal was too decomposed for any thorough examination of its wounds, it had been dismembered and both its legs and head were detached from its body. There were, however, no teeth marks as one would expect from predation by `normal` carnivores, nor were there the marks of knives, which would have been found on the bones if the animal had been butchered by a human. Again, although the evidence is not conclusive, and indeed the investigation has not yet been concluded, it appears that this unfortunate beast may have been a genuine UFO related animal mutilation!"

I have no idea whether there had been any strange lights seen in the sky over the Torridge Estuary at the time that the poor unfortunate beast we found in 1972 had died; and to be quite honest I don't really care, because to this day I am convinced that I know what killed it. In the half-light we could see an amorphous shadow of what appeared to be an enormous black predatory creature crouching over the carcass of the roebuck. If you looked at it directly there was nothing to see, but out of the corners of our eyes it was clearly visible. That was just too much for our last vestiges of intrepidness and the two of us, explorers no longer but frightened children, ran like hell until we finally found ourselves on the cliff path which traverses the long journey between Abbotsham and Westward Ho!

We were back in the sunshine. We were safe. And we never spoke about what had happened again. Soon afterwards our friendship disintegrated in the way that adolescent friendships often do. We never fell out but simply grew apart. It was as if the burden of our shared experience that day was too much for two adolescents to be able to bear and still remain friends.

To this day I am convinced that not only did we see our first naked female body that day, but that we also encountered the Abbotsham werewolf. With the benefit of hindsight I'm not too sure that the two events weren't somehow interlinked.

The years passed. An elderly relative died and left enough money to send my brother and me to a minor public school on the edges of Exmoor. It was a particularly horrid time in my life. There, I found it even more difficult to avoid the twin spectres of "School Spirit" and compulsory-sports. I lasted two and a half terms before being expelled. I left home to work in Exeter, and later moved to Bracknell in Berkshire. After a few misadventures I moved to Canada in the summer of 1979, but after a few months I came back again. I was rootless, shiftless and miserable. I got a job in Bideford as a nurse for the Mentally Handicapped, I managed a local punk band for a while, and I took a lot of drugs.

Nearly a decade after Jim's and my adventure I was back on Abbotsham Cliffs. It was the autumn of 1981 and I was a young, arty punk rocker with an obsessive interest in exploring alternative realities as a tool to achieving a path of spiritual development. This path, for me and my cronies, at least, took the form of ingesting large amounts of psilocybin mushrooms (often washed down with neat gin), listening to *Metal Box* by *Public Image Limited* and waiting for a spiritual revelation which never arrived. It so happened that the best magic mushrooms in the area grew on Abbotsham Cliffs.

Looking back, I am fairly certain that the mental health problems which have plagued me intermittently ever since started during the beautiful Indian Summer of 1981, when fuelled by Timothy Leary, Carlos Castaneda and other gurus of brain damage, I joined in a series of psychic experiments that certainly precipitated my first, temporary, descent into madness and terror. I am also pretty sure that in some strange way the horrific experiences that I am about to describe are linked, surely and inextricably with Jim's and my innocent hunt for a werewolf during the summer of 1972.

Our psychic drug experiments started innocently enough. Initially we just wanted to see what all the fuss was about. My first magic mushroom trip took place under the vague supervision of a fey young man called Danny Miles. Years later he turned up again, and the resulting mayhem is described in my book *The Blackdown Mystery*. In that book I describe how we first met, and I make no apologies for repeating the passage here:

"I first met Danny Miles at an obscure North Devon rock festival during the late summer of 1981. In those days I was an innocent and not very streetwise fellow in my early twenties, and I still believed that world peace could be achieved by the ingestion of various noxious substances whilst sitting in muddy fields listening to musical ensembles make whooshing noises on (what seem to me now) to be very primitive synthesisers.

I was, I believe, watching Hawkwind playing a spectacularly inept version of `Master of the Universe`, and like most of the rest of the audience, who were cold, muddy and uncomfortable, pretending that I was enjoying myself whilst in reality I was in dire need of both a lavatory and a nice cup of tea and totally unwilling to avail myself of the horribly rudimentary versions of either facility that had been laid on for our "comfort" by the euphemistically named "organisers" of the event. About a hundred yards to my right were the serried ranks of the local Hells Angel fraternity who were encamped en masse like an iron-clad phalanx of doom. It was only twelve years after Altamont, and even in the bucolic wastelands of rural Devon, they felt that they had something to live up to. Unfortunately, for me at least, they had decided to set up camp immediately between the area where I had set up my tiny tent and parked my car and the main exit, and several of the nastiest and meanest looking of them were patrolling the area armed with pool cues and what I think were hollowed out pickaxe handles that had been filled with molten lead. I was therefore somewhat marooned, and feeling uncomfortable, isolated, alone and more than a little frightened.

Suddenly, in the middle of what appeared to me to be a sea of greasy black leather jackets, emerged a delicate, fey looking figure, wearing an extraordinary array of satins and silks in a variety of peacock colours. It looked for all the world as if one of the gaily coloured inhabitants of one of Arthur Rackham`s fairy paintings had suddenly been transported into the middle of a field of leather-clad Neanderthals. The figure tripped gaily towards me, and appeared to my addled brain to be floating like a surreal, and rainbow-hued butterfly above the sea of mud and motorbikes. As it got closer I could see that it was a youth, hardly old enough to shave with an angelic halo of light brown hair surrounding a face that was covered with intricate paintings of butterflies and lotus flowers. He came and sat next to me and my companions.

Much to my amazement everyone else who was with me seemed to take this apparition in their stride. "`Lo Danny", one of them grunted cheerfully, "`ow are y`doing?". Another friend asked him what the hell he had been doing wandering blithely through the middle of the taciturn, unfriendly and potentially dangerous crowd of bikers. "Ahhhhh they`re harmless." he said, in an Irish accent that he seemed to be *able to turn on and off at will, "and anyway they wouldn't hurt me...I am legion, I am many".*

His name was Danny Miles, and for reasons known best to himself he had recently adopted the nom-de-guerre of `Legion the Cosmic Dancer`. I got to know him reasonably well over the next few years, and he would occasionally drift into my life, causing chaos for a few weeks and then disappear as simply as he had arrived. During the years when fashions were led by Culture Club and the New Romantics, Danny was in his element. He paraded his omni-sexuality for all to see like some magnificent, (if slightly deranged) bird of paradise and flirted outrageously with boys and girls alike. As the decade of Thatcherism advanced and my life became more normal, and I drifted into my disastrous marriage and the twin pitfalls of a job and a mortgage I saw less of him, but he would still turn up once in a while, and we would sit up long into the night drinking wine, gazing at the stars and talking about nothing in particular as I dreamed dreams of my lost youth. Danny never seemed to either grow any older or to settle down.

It was Danny, who, one night in late August arrived unannounced on the doorstep of my flat in Northam with a little plastic bag full of dried and shrivelled fungi which he then proceeded to make into the most disgusting "tea" that I have ever tasted. He persuaded me to drink the revolting stuff with him, and sitting side by side we sat back on my sofa, listening to loud rock music and waiting for something to happen.

Nothing did.

Then, there was a knock on the door. It was my new next-door neighbours coming to pay a courtesy call and introduce themselves. I have always noticed in life that the sort of person who has a notice on her office wall saying: "You don`t have to be crazy to work here but it helps," is usually the most annoying, pointless and conformist person in the building. If you can imagine a family of people like that you can imagine my new next-door neighbours. They were pleasant, well meaning people, but I think that they were rather taken aback when they found that they were now living next door to a wild eyed man with spikey hair and a wispy beard and his outrageously camp friend. The fact that we were both beginning what was my first, but by no means my last, experiment with psychedelic drugs was also a definite negative point.

We invited them in, but the thick smell of incense and the strains of *The Grateful Dead* intoning *Anthem of the Sun* out of my hi-fi speakers seemed to phase them somewhat. We gave them cold beers from the fridge, but when I noticed my guest's face beginning to look like he was wearing clown makeup it was definitely time for us to get rid of them. I can't remember how we managed it, but we hustled them out of the door without causing major offence, and I then settled back to experience my first "trip."

It was like nothing I had experienced before: My body felt like it was being bombarded by tiny bubbles and I found myself swimming in a sea of shifting images and glorious glowing colours. Occasionally I would find myself drifting into an ugly or disturbing place where I really didn't want to be, but Danny - to my eternal gratitude - would coax me out of it, and I would continue with the positive, joyous aspects of the experience.

After about five hours I began to come down, and I realised that this alternate reality was something that I wanted to explore further, and so I began a pattern that would last pretty well solidly for the rest of that year.

If I had known that, twenty years later, I would be diagnosed with a serious psychotic disorder, and that during my bad periods I would have similar experiences *every* night, but without the aid of stimulants and more importantly without the aid of someone to talk me out of it, I don't think I would have touched magic mushrooms (or peyote which I tried soon after) with the proverbial bargepole, but I did, and there is nothing I can do to change it. As my grandmother once said to me when I was a very small boy "if ifs and ands were pots and pans we'd all be travelling tinkers" and this is something I have believed solidly ever since. Once something is done, its done and there ain't nothing you can do about it!

Over the next few days Danny introduced me to such books as *The Doors of Perception* by Aldous Huxley and various writings by Timothy Leary. By this time, our nightly trips were taken *en masse* with a group of friends, and after a week or so Danny evolved the ritual of guiding us through the trip by reading excerpts from the *Tibetan Book of the Dead* and other esoteric scriptures.

I can't remember whose idea it was, but at the end of October someone suggested that we should follow in the footsteps of Carlos Castaneda and indulge in a group psychedelic experience out of doors. The idea was to somehow contact the spirit of the sacred mushroom on the psychic plane, although it has to be admitted that most of those present (including me) thought of it more as a groovy and rather daring Halloween party. I was really looking forward to it until I discovered that in his wisdom Danny had decided to hold this experiment on Abbotsham Cliffs. In many ways this made a lot of sense. If there actually *was* a sacred mushroom spirit, it stood to reason that he would reside amongst the more tangible proofs of his existence, and as already stated, at the time at least, the best magic mushrooms in the area grew at Abbotsham Cliffs.

I was a little uneasy. Although nine years had passed and I had tried to put the matter out of my mind I had never entirely forgotten the events of June 1972. But, I rationalised wildly displaying a capacity for self-delusion that was remarkable even by my standards. *That* had been in the woodlands several miles along the cliffs. *And* it had been in summer. *And* we had been looking for the werewolf. This time we were engaged on a mystical quest for the spirit of the sacred mushroom. It was *obvious* that nothing nasty could possibly happen.

On Halloween night, seven or eight of us camped out on the flat land just behind Abbotsham Cliffs. There were three girls and four or five guys, all dressed in the punk styles that were then *de rigueur*. Cheerfully, we parked our cars in the lay-by, and in the late afternoon sunshine t was a cheerful party that walked the half-mile or so along the footpath to the cliffs. Although it was the end of October it was surprisingly warm, and the two elderly sheep grazing on the scrubland by the cliffs gave the place a delightfully bucolic air.

We built a large bonfire and as the final rays of the setting sun disappeared into the Bristol Channel, Danny, in his self appointed role of showman and shaman came around and dispensed what he described as his "funky communion." It was a potent mixture of gin, mushroom tea, peyote and LSD and was the precursor to one of the most horrific nights of my life. It was a night that I shall certainly never forget, and which I seriously suspect will be permanently etched on the psyches of everyone involved.

The evening started pleasantly enough, because although the chemical mixture that we had ingested was incredibly powerful, the mixture of the pleasantly sylvan surroundings, and what we hadn't yet learned to call "chill out" music issuing from what we hadn't yet learned to call a "ghetto blaster" kept everyone in a mellow and happy state of mind.

Danny started to read aloud from *The Tibetan Book of the Dead* and then began to recite Aleister Crowley's *Hymn to Pan*. None of us realised at the time, but Danny was (knowingly or unknowingly) manipulating the situation like a master. Although everyone was hallucinating heavily by this time, the three girls in particular seemed heavily affected and, encouraged by Danny, started to behave in a most uncharacteristic manner. Despite their Mohicans and studiously torn clothes they were actually very reserved young ladies on the whole; but coaxed by Danny they started to become very affectionate and sensual. They danced rhythmically to the music and kissed and stroked each other, the guys in the group (including me) and particularly Danny.

One plump girl called "Sarah" [not her real name because I see her around Exeter sometimes, and she is now an eminently respectable, professional lady] who boasted the particularly unpleasant punk soubriquet of "Scab" even started to undress and dance semi naked in the firelight.

It would be easy for me to pretend that some sort of totally far out hippy orgy then ensued, but it didn't. Most of the people who were there were too drunk, too stoned, and far too tripped out to perform sexually. I know I was, but again under coaxing from Danny, "Scab" and one of the guys coupled - I won't say `made love` because there was no love, emotion or tenderness - just animal rutting in the firelight as Danny chanted lines from Crowley and the rest of us looked on giggling inanely and waving our hands about to the rhythmic beat of the music.

Eventually everyone passed out, and that was when the fear came.

I have spent more of my life than I like to admit in alternate states of consciousness. Once upon a time I believed it was because I was exploring a genuinely alternative route to spiritual self-empowerment. Nowadays I believe that all that is rubbish. If there is such a thing as an interventionist God, and for me personally the jury is still out on that one, I am sure that he or she would not wish the objects of his/her creation to perform acts of supplication by poisoning themselves. Although the concept of trying to second guess a deity is a pretty dodgy one, the theories of trying to reach nirvana through substance abuse is a pretty dodgy one. I haven't taken psychedelics since that terrible night in 1981. These days when I go to a different place it is usually with alcohol, or prescribed tranquillisers and occasionally with the fruit of the poppy. AND these days, when I take drugs it isn't to reach some magickal and non-existent nirvana - it is purely and simply to blot out the fear.

I am convinced that the fear first came to me on All Hallow's Eve 1981.

I don't know how long we had been lying on the bare cold ground. The fire had all but gone out and all that was left were some feebly glowing embers. I don't know what it was that made me wake up because all was still. The only sound was the sea breaking on the rocky shore a hundred yards or so away. Then, on the other side of the campfire someone or something began to moan. I thought at first that it was one of my companions, suffering a bad dream or a worse trip, but the noise was too steady, too rhythmical and too unearthly to be human.

Unlike some people, I had always known which parts of the psychedelic experience were real, and which were chemically induced hallucinations. However it has to be said, in my defence, that I had never before or since imbibed such a potentially lethal cocktail of psychoactive drugs. At the time I felt that I was entirely awake, completely straight and that whatever it was that was happening to me was part of my own objective reality. However I may have been wrong. I may have been dreaming, I may have been hallucinating, or it may have been the first glimmerings of the madness that was to plague me in later life. Maybe it was a bit of all three - or maybe not.

The dull, thrumming moan continued, and was joined by another and another in a weird unearthly harmony such as I have never heard since. As a musician and composer I have sometimes, in idle moments, tried to recapture the sound using computer generated sound programmes, or old analogue synthesisers which I have lying about the house, but I have never come close. It was like nothing else I have ever experienced, and, I hope against all hope, that it is something that I will never experience again.

Then the sky began to change colour. The deep midnight blue was subtly changed into something else. Something was not quite right. H.P.Lovecraft wrote of a place where *The Angles are Wrong*, but that night Abbotsham Cliffs became a place where the colours were wrong. The only time I have ever experienced anything even approximating what I saw that night was during the total solar eclipse of August 1999.

At the time I was working as editor of a magazine called *Quest* that was published by a rampant crook called Roy Bird who ran a company called Top Events Ltd. They had an appalling reputation for not paying their debts, honouring their subscriptions, or parting with any money whatsoever. Bird was always investing cash in hare-brained schemed and promotions which were usually cancelled before they actually happened, with Bird pocketing whatever money had been sent in advance ticket sales.

One promotion of his that actually *did* come to pass was a cross channel cruise to coincide with the solar eclipse. The ferry was to sail along the line of totality so we on board could get the best possible view of what was, at least in the UK, a once in a lifetime experience.

As the disc of the sun slowly disappeared I began to feel a very primal panic. I ceased to be an intelligent and reasonably cultured middle-aged writer and surprisingly quickly reverted to being a primal savage. I clutched my girlfriend's hand, and much to my surprise I found that tears were rolling down my cheeks. I looked around, embarrassed. Even more to my surprise I realised that most of the people I could see were crying. This was just something so completely alien to any of our shared life experiences. From our earliest days, daytime meant the sun, even if it was hidden behind clouds, and for the first time in any of our lives - and there were about 1500 people on the ferry - the sun had disappeared. The rational part of my brain *knew* perfectly well that this was only an uncommon astronomical phenomenon. The sun (like it says in the song) had been "eclipsed by the moon" and I knew perfectly well that, in a few minutes, everything would be back to normal in the UK for the next seventy-four years.

However, emotionally I knew no such thing. I was like an ancient savage who believed that the celestial sphere had been devoured by the inexorable force of the daemonic serpent-dragon and in my heart of hearts I was convinced that the sun had gone for good, and that within the blink of a cosmic eye, I, together with all life on earth would shrivel and die away forever.

The worst thing about this sunless world was the strange, colourless, half-light. Everything was tinged with a murky and unpleasant shade of puce. It was as if the creator had finally tired of the antics of his unruly and ungrateful servants and vomited back all the collected prayers, hopes and fears of mankind throughout the ages all over the pantheon of his creation. The entire world was the colour of vomit, and for what seemed like a lifetime, although I was in the middle of a crowd of 1500 people together with my then lover and many of my closest friends, I felt utterly desolate in a world which God - or at least the oldest God known to mankind - had deserted.

As I lay on the cold turfs of Abbotsham Cliffs I was filled with the same feeling of isolation. The sky, and indeed the rest of the landscape, didn't have the puce vomit stains of the world in the middle of the Eclipse, but was just as wrong. The colours just didn't make sense. Two decades later I am no nearer to describing the colours I was viewing than I was then. However, the colours were so different from anything I had ever experienced that, although I was still lying on the edge of Abbotsham Cliffs, I was actually in a world completely alien - not only to me but to the rest of the human race.

I felt that this was a world that had never known humans, and where humans were not welcome. The strange moaning continued, and it seemed to blend in inextricably with the sound of the surf breaking on the rocks below. Years later I was to discover that only twenty or so miles along the coast to the east, well within living memory, the people of Lynton believed that they could hear the song of the sea - or perhaps it was the merfolk who live in the sea. And although the song was beautiful, it was also deadly: whenever anyone heard it a sudden and usually bloodthirsty death was sure to follow.

The sound wasn't music; at least not in the way that either you or I understand the term music. Like the landscape it was completely alien and part of a world where human beings were simply not welcome. By this time the sky was surprisingly light, but the full moon, which beamed mercilessly down upon us, is impossible to describe. If you can imagine the dying glimmer in your pet dog's eyes as the lethal injection takes effect, or the sickly glimmer of a streetlight engulfed in the smoke from a house-fire then you might have the beginnings of an idea of the horrible, deathly light which threw the landscape into sharp, two dimensional relief.

I sat up, and looked around me. I could see my companions sitting up also. All except for "Scab" who was lying, still naked, spread-eagled as if crucified on the smooth turf.

We were all silent and completely motionless. The horrid moaning harmonies became louder and louder and as we looked on horrified we could see that we weren't alone. I am using the plural rather than the singular because I assume - indeed I *have* to assume, that the other people there saw the same thing that I did.

We weren't alone: there was a total stranger in our midst. A naked female silhouette, that of a girl and much younger than us, was standing over "Scab's" supine body. She stood erect with her arms outstretched above her and her legs akimbo, perfectly mirroring the pose of the naked, plump punk girl lying at her feet.

The moaning noise continued, and it seemed to me that it was coming from the open mouth of this mysterious stranger. The noise got louder, and more rhythmical. It began to pulse like an African War Drum or an electronic oscillator. I don't know what happened next. It would be easy to say that this strange unearthly girl began to make love to "Scab" but this would be simplistic. They didn't even touch, but somehow in a strange and indescribable way they became one.

I suddenly felt paralysed and could see someone standing over me. It was the same girl, and as far as I could see, not only was she still standing over "Scab," but she was standing, completely naked, over everyone else in our party. Somehow she was everywhere and nowhere, something and everything and in at least eight places at once.

I looked up at her and felt a slight twinge of recognition. Could this be the same girl that Jim and I had spied upon eight years before? One thing was certain: the sound, which was getting painfully loud in my ears, was coming from her. It was her song but although, like her, it was beautiful in a strange way it was a terrible song that no human being was every meant to hear.

Then she entered me. Without touching me she entered my body and my soul and took me to a level of sexual ecstasy that was quite beyond my comprehension. As we became one under the pale death-coloured moon, her song built up to a disgusting crescendo like a thousand rabid dogs howling and screaming at each other.

I passed out. When I woke up I was lying in a pool of my own vomit, and although the familiar scenery of Abbotsham Cliffs were back to normal I knew that I would never be the same again. I looked around at my companions of the night before. Everyone was dazed. One of the girls had covered "Scab" up with her overcoat and was trying to rouse her. The whole place smelt of death and decay, and at that moment I decided that I would never take psychedelic drugs again. And I never have.

On the way back to our cars we passed the stretch of pasture where, only the evening before, the two elderly sheep had been grazing. They were still there, but they were both dead. Although none of us investigated any closer, one appeared to have been ripped completely to pieces and the other had its throat torn out.

The only thing that any of the rest of us had in common was that we were friends of Danny's, so when I stopped taking psychedelic drugs, I stopped seeing the others. "Scab" works in an office in Exeter; and one day, whilst I was waiting for my psychotherapy appointment at Wonford House Psychiatric Hospital in Exeter during the early spring of 1998, I saw one of the other members of our jolly band. Now twenty years older, he had the sunken eyes and sallow skin of someone whose liver is beginning to fail after decades of substance abuse. Our eyes met for a moment. We recognised each other, but after all this time there was really nothing to say so we passed each other in silence.

ANIMALS & MEN ISSUES 16-20
THE JOURNAL OF THE CENTRE FOR FORTEAN ZOOLOGY
NEW HORIZONS
Edited by Jon Downes

BIG CATS LOOSE IN BRITAIN

PREDATOR DEATHMATCH
NICK MOLLOY
WITH ILLUSTRATIONS BY ANTHONY WALLIS

THE WORLD'S WEIRDEST PUBLISHING COMPANY

PHENOMENA
Edited by Jonathan Downes and Richard Freeman
FOREWORD BY Dr. KARL SHUKER

A DAINTREE DIARY
Tales from Travels in the Daintree
tropical North Queensland, Australia
CARL PORTMAN

THE COLLECTED POEMS
Dr Karl P. N. Shuker

STRANGELYSTRANGE
but oddly normal
an anthology of writings by
ANDY ROBERTS

HOW TO START A PUBLISHING EMPIRE

Unlike most mainstream publishers, we have a non-commercial remit, and our mission statement claims that "we publish books because they deserve to be published, not because we think that we can make money out of them". Our motto is the Latin Tag *Pro bona causa facimus* (we do it for good reason), a slogan taken from a children's book *The Case of the Silver Egg* by the late Desmond Skirrow.

WIKIPEDIA: "The first book published was in 1988. *Take this Brother may it Serve you Well* was a guide to Beatles bootlegs by Jonathan Downes. It sold quite well, but was hampered by very poor production values, being photocopied, and held together by a plastic clip binder. In 1988 A5 clip binders were hard to get hold of, so the publishers took A4 binders and cut them in half with a hacksaw. It now reaches surprisingly high prices second hand.

The production quality improved slightly over the years, and after 1999 all the books produced were ringbound with laminated colour covers. In 2004, however, they signed an agreement with Lightning Source, and all books are now produced perfect bound, with full colour covers."

Until 2010 all our books, the majority of which are/were on the subject of mystery animals and allied disciplines, were published by `CFZ Press`, the publishing arm of the Centre for Fortean Zoology (CFZ), and we urged our readers and followers to draw a discreet veil over the books that we published that were completely off topic to the CFZ.

However, in 2010 we decided that enough was enough and launched a second imprint, `Fortean Words` which aims to cover a wide range of non animal-related esoteric subjects. Other imprints will be launched as and when we feel like it, however the basic ethos of the company remains the same: Our job is to publish books and magazines that we feel are worth publishing, whether or not they are going to sell. Money is, after all - as my dear old Mama once told me - a rather vulgar subject, and she would be rolling in her grave if she thought that her eldest son was somehow in `trade`.

Luckily, so far our tastes have turned out not to be that rarified after all, and we have sold far more books than anyone ever thought that we would, so there is a moral in there somewhere...

Jon Downes,
Woolsery, North Devon
July 2010

CFZ PRESS

Other Books in Print

Wildman! by Redfern, Nick
Globsters by Newton, Michael
Cats of Magic, Mythology and Mystery Shuker, by Karl P. N
Those Amazing Newfoundland Dogs by Bondeson, Jan
The Mystery Animals of Pennsylvania by Gable, Andrew
Sea Serpent Carcasses - Scotland from the Stronsa Monster to Loch Ness by Glen Vaudrey
The CFZ Yearbook 2012 edited by Jonathan and Corinna Downes
ORANG PENDEK: Sumatra's Forgotten Ape by Richard Freeman
THE MYSTERY ANIMALS OF THE BRITISH ISLES: London by Neil Arnold
CFZ EXPEDITION REPORT: India 2010 by Richard Freeman *et al*
The Cryptid Creatures of Florida by Scott Marlow
Dead of Night by Lee Walker
The Mystery Animals of the British Isles: The Northern Isles by Glen Vaudrey
THE MYSTERY ANIMALS OF THE BRTISH ISLES: Gloucestershire and Worcestershire by Paul Williams
When Bigfoot Attacks by Michael Newton
Weird Waters – The Mystery Animals of Scandinavia: Lake and Sea Monsters by Lars Thomas
The Inhumanoids by Barton Nunnelly
Monstrum! A Wizard's Tale by Tony "Doc" Shiels
CFZ Yearbook 2011 edited by Jonathan Downes
Karl Shuker's Alien Zoo by Shuker, Dr Karl P.N
Tetrapod Zoology Book One by Naish, Dr Darren
The Mystery Animals of Ireland by Gary Cunningham and Ronan Coghlan
Monsters of Texas by Gerhard, Ken
The Great Yokai Encyclopaedia by Freeman, Richard
NEW HORIZONS: Animals & Men issues 16-20 Collected Editions Vol. 4 by Downes, Jonathan
A Daintree Diary -
Tales from Travels to the Daintree Rainforest in tropical north Queensland, Australia by Portman, Carl
Strangely Strange but Oddly Normal by Roberts, Andy

Centre for Fortean Zoology Yearbook 2010 by Downes, Jonathan
Predator Deathmatch by Molloy, Nick
Star Steeds and other Dreams by Shuker, Karl
CHINA: A Yellow Peril? by Muirhead, Richard
Mystery Animals of the British Isles: The Western Isles by Vaudrey, Glen
Giant Snakes - Unravelling the coils of mystery by Newton, Michael
Mystery Animals of the British Isles: Kent by Arnold, Neil
Centre for Fortean Zoology Yearbook 2009 by Downes, Jonathan
CFZ EXPEDITION REPORT: Russia 2008 by Richard Freeman *et al*, Shuker, Karl (fwd)
Dinosaurs and other Prehistoric Animals on Stamps - A Worldwide catalogue
by Shuker, Karl P. N
Dr Shuker's Casebook by Shuker, Karl P.N
The Island of Paradise - chupacabra UFO crash retrievals,
and accelerated evolution on the island of Puerto Rico by Downes, Jonathan
The Mystery Animals of the British Isles: Northumberland and Tyneside by Hallowell, Michael J
Centre for Fortean Zoology Yearbook 1997 by Downes, Jonathan (Ed)
Centre for Fortean Zoology Yearbook 2002 by Downes, Jonathan (Ed)
Centre for Fortean Zoology Yearbook 2000/1 by Downes, Jonathan (Ed)
Centre for Fortean Zoology Yearbook 1998 by Downes, Jonathan (Ed)
Centre for Fortean Zoology Yearbook 2003 by Downes, Jonathan (Ed)
In the wake of Bernard Heuvelmans by Woodley, Michael A
CFZ EXPEDITION REPORT: Guyana 2007 by Richard Freeman *et al*, Shuker, Karl (fwd)
Centre for Fortean Zoology Yearbook 1999 by Downes, Jonathan (Ed)
Big Cats in Britain Yearbook 2008 by Fraser, Mark (Ed)
Centre for Fortean Zoology Yearbook 1996 by Downes, Jonathan (Ed)
THE CALL OF THE WILD - Animals & Men issues 11-15
Collected Editions Vol. 3 by Downes, Jonathan (ed)
Ethna's Journal by Downes, C N
Centre for Fortean Zoology Yearbook 2008 by Downes, J (Ed)
DARK DORSET -Calendar Custome by Newland, Robert J
Extraordinary Animals Revisited by Shuker, Karl
MAN-MONKEY - In Search of the British Bigfoot by Redfern, Nick
Dark Dorset Tales of Mystery, Wonder and Terror by Newland, Robert J and Mark North
Big Cats Loose in Britain by Matthews, Marcus
MONSTER! - The A-Z of Zooform Phenomena by Arnold, Neil
The Centre for Fortean Zoology 2004 Yearbook by Downes, Jonathan (Ed)
The Centre for Fortean Zoology 2007 Yearbook by Downes, Jonathan (Ed)
CAT FLAPS! Northern Mystery Cats by Roberts, Andy
Big Cats in Britain Yearbook 2007 by Fraser, Mark (Ed)
BIG BIRD! - Modern sightings of Flying Monsters by Gerhard, Ken
THE NUMBER OF THE BEAST - Animals & Men issues 6-10
Collected Editions Vol. 1 by Downes, Jonathan (Ed)
IN THE BEGINNING - Animals & Men issues 1-5 Collected Editions Vol. 1 by Downes, Jonathan
STRENGTH THROUGH KOI - They saved Hitler's Koi and other stories

by Downes, Jonathan
The Smaller Mystery Carnivores of the Westcountry by Downes, Jonathan
CFZ EXPEDITION REPORT: Gambia 2006 by Richard Freeman *et al*, Shuker, Karl (fwd)
The Owlman and Others by Jonathan Downes
The Blackdown Mystery by Downes, Jonathan
Big Cats in Britain Yearbook 2006 by Fraser, Mark (Ed)
Fragrant Harbours - Distant Rivers by Downes, John T
Only Fools and Goatsuckers by Downes, Jonathan
Monster of the Mere by Jonathan Downes
Dragons:More than a Myth by Freeman, Richard Alan
Granfer's Bible Stories by Downes, John Tweddell
Monster Hunter by Downes, Jonathan

CFZ Classics is a new venture for us. There are many seminal works that are either unavailable today, or not available with the production values which we would like to see. So, following the old adage that if you want to get something done do it yourself, this is exactly what we have done.

Desiderius Erasmus Roterodamus (b. October 18th 1466, d. July 2nd 1536) said: "When I have a little money, I buy books; and if I have any left, I buy food and clothes," and we are much the same. Only, we are in the lucky position of being able to share our books with the wider world. CFZ Classics is a conduit through which we cannot just re-issue titles which we feel still have much to offer the cryptozoological and Fortean research communities of the 21st Century, but we are adding footnotes, supplementary essays, and other material where we deem it appropriate.

Headhunters of The Amazon by Fritz W Up de Graff (1902)

Fortean Words

The Centre for Fortean Zoology has for several years led the field in Fortean publishing. CFZ Press is the only publishing company specialising in books on monsters and mystery animals. CFZ Press has published more books on this subject than any other company in history and has attracted such well known authors as Andy Roberts, Nick Redfern, Michael Newton, Dr Karl Shuker, Neil Arnold, Dr Darren Naish, Jon Downes, Ken Gerhard and Richard Freeman.

Now CFZ Press are launching a new imprint. Fortean Words is a new line of books dealing with Fortean subjects other than cryptozoology, which is - after all - the subject the CFZ are best known for. Books include a look at the Berwyn Mountains UFO case by renowned Fortean Andy Roberts and a series of forthcoming books by transatlantic researcher Nick Redfern. CFZ Press are dedicated to maintaining the fine quality of their works with Fortean Words. New authors tackling new subjects will always be encouraged, and we hope that our books will continue to be as ground-breaking and popular as ever.

Haunted Skies Volume One 1940-1959 by John Hanson and Dawn Holloway
Haunted Skies Volume Two 1960-1965 by John Hanson and Dawn Holloway
Haunted Skies Volume Three 1965-1967 by John Hanson and Dawn Holloway
Haunted Skies Volume Four 1968-1971 by John Hanson and Dawn Holloway
Haunted Skies Volume Five 1972-1974 by John Hanson and Dawn Holloway
Haunted Skies Volume Six 1975-1977 by John Hanson and Dawn Holloway
Grave Concerns by Kai Roberts

Police and the Paranormal by Andy Owens
Dead of Night by Lee Walker
Space Girl Dead on Spaghetti Junction - an anthology by Nick Redfern
I Fort the Lore - an anthology by Paul Screeton
UFO Down - the Berwyn Mountains UFO Crash by Andy Roberts
The Grail by Ronan Coghlan
UFO Warminster - Cradle of Contract by Kevin Goodman
Quest for the Hexham Heads by Paul Screeton

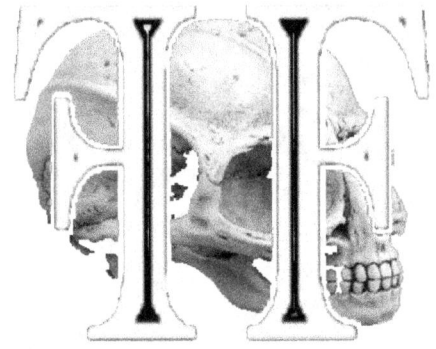

Fortean Fiction

J ust before Christmas 2011, we launched our third imprint, this time dedicated to - let's see if you guessed it from the title - fictional books with a Fortean or cryptozoological theme. We have published a few fictional books in the past, but now think that because of our rising reputation as publishers of quality Forteana, that a dedicated fiction imprint was the order of the day.

We launched with four titles:

Green Unpleasant Land by Richard Freeman
Left Behind by Harriet Wadham
Dark Ness by Tabitca Cope
Snap! By Steven Bredice
Death on Dartmoor by Di Francis
Dark Wear by Tabitca Cope
Hyakymonogatari Book 1 by Richard Freeman

"ANOTHER SUCH VICTORY, AND I AM UNDONE."—PYRRHUS.